Zara Cox wri... She lives in th... with her hubby ... ... kids. She loves to read and travel. In 2017 she managed to visit her number one bucket list destination—Hawaii—and is now actively pleading with her husband to live there! She loves to hear from her readers and you can get in touch with her via Twitter (@zcoxbooks), on Instagram (zaracoxwriter) or Facebook (zaracoxwriter).

Avril Tremayne is an award-winning author of sexy, modern, urban romances, featuring heroes strong enough to make any woman swoon and stronger heroines who nevertheless refuse to do so. She took a circuitous route to becoming a writer, via careers in nursing, teaching, public relations and corporate affairs—most recently in global aviation, which gave her a voracious appetite for travel. She currently lives in Sydney, Australia, but is feverishly plotting to move her family to Italy for half of every year. When she's not reading or writing Avril can be found dining to excess, drinking lots of wine and obsessing over shoes. Find her at avriltremayne.com, on Facebook at avril.tremayne, on Twitter, @AvrilTremayne, or on Instagram, @avril_tremayne.

If you liked *Close to the Edge* and *Getting Lucky*, why not try

Beddable Billionaire by Alexx Andria
Forbidden Pleasure by Taryn Leigh Taylor

Discover more at millsandboon.co.uk

CLOSE TO THE EDGE

ZARA COX

GETTING LUCKY

AVRIL TREMAYNE

MILLS & BOON

All rights reserved including the right of reproduction
in whole or in part in any form. This edition is published
by arrangement with Harlequin Books S.A.

This is a work of fiction. Names, characters, places, locations
and incidents are purely fictional and bear no relationship to
any real life individuals, living or dead, or to any actual places,
business establishments, locations, events or incidents.
Any resemblance is entirely coincidental.

This book is sold subject to the condition that it shall not,
by way of trade or otherwise, be lent, resold, hired out
or otherwise circulated without the prior consent of the publisher
in any form of binding or cover other than that in which it is published
and without a similar condition including this condition
being imposed on the subsequent purchaser.

® and TM are trademarks owned and used by the trademark owner
and/or its licensee. Trademarks marked with ® are registered with the
United Kingdom Patent Office and/or the Office for Harmonisation
in the Internal Market and in other countries.

First Published in Great Britain 2018
by Mills & Boon, an imprint of HarperCollins*Publishers*
1 London Bridge Street, London, SE1 9GF

Close to the Edge © 2018 Zara Cox

Getting Lucky © 2018 Belinda de Rome

ISBN: 978-0-263-26649-8

MIX
Paper from
responsible sources
FSC˜ C007454

This book is produced from independently certified FSC™ paper
to ensure responsible forest management.
For more information visit www.harpercollins.co.uk/green.

Printed and bound in Spain
by CPI, Barcelona

CLOSE TO THE EDGE

ZARA COX

MILLS & BOON

To Grace Thiele,
for being the physical manifestation of Lily Gracen.

CHAPTER ONE

Caleb

THE QUICK GLANCE at my wrist was a bad idea. I knew the moment my gaze dropped to the black-and-azure face of my watch that I'd added another half hour to this circus.

Shit.

"Oh, am I wasting your time? Do you have somewhere *important* to be?" the whiny voice demanded.

I sighed.

The ability to turn circumstances, good or bad, to my advantage was what had earned me my renowned status. But no one starts life thinking they were going to do what I do, be what I am.

A fixer.

I wasn't complaining, though. I was great at my job. Sometimes I wish I wasn't *this* damned good... Oh, who the hell was I kidding? Most days I loved my job. Tonight, not so much. The 2 a.m. calls were the worst. Especially when they interrupted a very promising pre-fuck blowjob.

But hey, what was a small case of blue balls when

the siren song of work beckoned? As evading tactics went, it was an effective way to hold the demons at bay.

I shoved my hands into my pockets and glared at the glassy-eyed man-child straddling the banister in front of me. "Yes, actually. I do have somewhere else to be. So if you're going to jump, get it over with so I can get on with my night."

Christ, you've surpassed yourself this time, Steele.

My client's slack-faced shock confirmed my thought. "Are you fucking serious?"

"As Zachary Quinto's eyebrows. This is the fourth time I've had to deal with your…unhappiness this month alone. Normally, I would've washed my hands of you or dragged you to rehab. But I promised your father I'd look out for you. The only thing you're addicted to is laziness—"

"You don't know what you're talking about. The band kicked me out!"

"Because you set your GPS to Cabo instead of your studio in Culver City. Last month it was Vegas. The month before it was Atlantic City, right?"

"I can't just turn up and sing! I need inspiration," Ross Jonas sulked.

"And you think you're going to find that by jumping off this balcony tonight?" I shrugged. "Go ahead, then. I can have you in a nice corner slab in the morgue by sunrise."

His jaw dropped again. "Holy fuck, you're something else."

I closed my eyes and wished those words were coming from a different mouth, preferably the scarlet-painted female one I'd left in my bed. When I opened them again, Ross was still there. Shame.

I wasn't twisted enough to wish my client dead but I wanted this over and done with.

He wasn't going to jump.

We'd been through this dance enough times. He chose this suite because there was a deep pool conveniently situated six floors below. And if by some exceptionally bad luck he didn't make it, I had four guys on the ground floor of the Beverly Hills Hotel ready with a giant inflatable to catch his sorry ass because sadly, this wasn't my first rodeo with a pseudo-suicidal client.

I would've dropped him as a client a long time ago, for his selfish antics for starters, and because I never took on suicidal clients, not even ones who were faking it. I wasn't ashamed to admit suicide was a red-hot button for me. But Ross's father was my first client, the guy who'd given me a break in a cutthroat place like LA, then gone out of his way to recommend my services to others. And when Victor Jonas had all but begged me to look out for his son, I'd agreed unconditionally.

The worst Ross, only child of rich, overindulgent parents, would suffer tonight if he did jump, was having the wind knocked out of him.

Whereas I was destined to suffer a stronger resurgence of the nightmares I fought each night, not to mention the cold shoulder of a pouty redhead if I didn't wrap this up fast. "Yes, I *am* something else. And *you* have ten seconds to shit or get off the pot."

I straightened from my leaning position against the French doors and moved toward him. He glanced furtively behind him and paled. "Fuck," he muttered.

Two feet away I stopped and crossed my arms. "Listen to me. You keep flirting with death like this and one day you'll succeed. Do me a favor, Ross. Put a little bit of the effort you use to jerk me around into doing some *actual* work. You might be surprised at how good it feels to reap the results of your hard work."

The belligerence drained from his face. "But I'm out of the band."

"Call your guys in the morning. Beg if you need to. Humility goes a long way if you truly mean it," I said. I had no clue whether that was true or not. Humility wasn't exactly a strong suit of mine. "And while you're at it, try showing up when you say you will. Deal?"

When he nodded I stepped back, staying alert as he slowly climbed down. Relieved, I followed him back into the suite he'd checked into for the purpose of pulling this shitty, dangerous stunt.

I breathed through the fury and resisted the urge to tear another strip off him. "One of my guys is going to stick around, make sure you get to Culver City nice and early in the morning. Sound good?"

I slapped him on the shoulder and headed for the door. With any luck, my date would still be warming my bed.

"Hey, Caleb."

I turned around. "Yeah?"

"Would you...really have watched me jump?"

My face tightened. "If you wanted to, I couldn't have stopped you." I paused a beat. "Did you?"

He shook his head sheepishly. "No."

My anger spiked another notch. "Pull a stunt like this again and I'll push you myself."

I left him standing in the middle of the living room, shoulders hunched, pondering that.

My jaw tightened as the elevator rushed me to the

ground floor. Unfortunately, the memories Ross had triggered weren't as easy to leave behind as I exited the five-star hotel.

For my mother it'd been third time lucky. Or *unlucky*, depending on which side of the fence you stood on. My steps faltered as the acid-sharp pain that always accompanied the memory of her death plowed through me.

Damn Ross Jonas.

With a deep breath I walked out, handed a twenty to the valet attendant holding out the keys to my Bugatti and slid behind the wheel.

Before I could pull away, my phone beeped. Tugging it out of my pocket, I found a centerfold-worthy picture gracing my screen. The accompanying message flashed seconds later.

This is what you could've had tonight. Call me never!

I was torn between a smile and a scowl. A smile because if I chose to call her right then, she would've answered. A scowl because the redhead was the first to tweak my interest in a while, and I'd hoped she would end this uninvited dry spell that had taken over my sex life. But despite my earlier anticipation, the desire to get her back in my bed was dwindling fast. I stared at the picture again and stroked my dying wood a second before I hit the Delete button, erasing her from my contacts altogether.

I gunned the engine onto the Pacific Coast Highway, pointing my car toward Downtown LA. With my bedroom plans now shot to shit, and in no mood to return to an empty bed and dreams filled with memories I didn't cherish, work was the next best option.

Nevertheless, I cursed when my phone rang. "Dammit, doesn't anyone sleep anymore?" I griped.

Maggie, my assistant, answered, "You don't pay me to sleep. You specifically stated during my interview that I wasn't allowed to sleep."

"*You* don't get to sleep. That doesn't mean you can interrupt mine. I'm shocked I need to explain that to you."

"Tell me you're not heading to Fixer HQ right now and I'll hang up."

I didn't bother because she had a GPS tracker on my car. Once or twice that tracker had saved my skin and extricated me from some unsavory situations.

"What do you want, Maggie?" I switched lanes, enjoying the sweet purr of the engine.

"Wow, someone's grumpy," she muttered under her breath, then said briskly, "We have an urgent situation."

I tapped my finger against the wheel. "Aren't they all?"

"This one is less sex, drugs and rock and roll, more... something else."

I suppressed a growl. "By all means, hold the dramatics."

My sarcasm bounced right off her thick skin. It was one of the many reasons she was invaluable. "I'm sending you the address her people sent me. You can be there in fifteen minutes."

The joy in my ride gone, I cursed. "Her *people*? Did you not explain to them that I don't deal with *people*? That it's one-on-one or not at all?"

Maggie sighed. "I know how to do my job, Caleb. Trust me, please, just a little?"

I frowned. I didn't trust blindly because I didn't trust anyone. Maggie knew this. Why she was choosing to tap into a resource not readily available to me wasn't improving my mood. The sizeable monthly paycheck I signed bought me her hard work and loyalty. I didn't expect anything else, and certainly not her request for me to trust her.

My phone buzzed with the incoming address. "I'll be in touch." I hung up, pulled off the road long enough to check out the Mulholland Drive address before I executed a slick U-turn.

High walls and electronic gates greeted me when I reached the property. Everything about this smelled like trust-fund princess with her panties in a twist about her latest flame. Or a chihuahua kidnapping that wasn't worth my time.

Only the assurance that Maggie excelled at her job made me roll down my window and press the intercom.

The cast-iron gate slid back, and I drove up the cobbled driveway of a large stone mansion. In typical Hollywood style, the original property had been remodeled into a grotesque status symbol, with little care for artistic design.

I hid my lip curl as I stepped out and spotted the rent-a-cops stationed on either side of the house.

The front door swung open to reveal a young, sharply dressed man on the threshold. He seemed out of place in this setting but I wasn't here to judge. "Good evening, Mr. Steele. If you'll come with me?" He didn't offer his name and I didn't ask for it. This was LA, where even D-list celebrities were paranoid about revealing their identities to the wrong person.

The inside of the mansion was as gaudy as the outside, the designer having gone to town with an explosion of golds and leafy greens splashed across every surface.

Suppressing a shudder, I went down a hallway into a large living room, growing impatient when a look around didn't produce the *her* Maggie had mentioned.

"Wait here, please."

He left. I paced, silently hoping this trip would be worth my while. I had a dossier full of needy clients but their demands were nothing I couldn't handle in my sleep. Thoughts of sleep, or the woeful lack of it lately, ramped up the disquiet inside me.

I was busy smashing it down when the double doors opened in front of me.

At the first sight of her, my gut clenched tight and my lungs flattened with expelled air I wasn't interested in replenishing.

I wasn't sure whether it was the shock of her roughly chopped white-blond hair that gripped my attention or the wide, full red lips currently getting sucked between her teeth. Maybe it was the bright, oval-shaped green eyes staring directly at me. Or the lush petiteness of the body draped from head to toe in black leather and lace.

Leather and lace.

The combination was lethal enough without the silver-studded leather cuffs encircling both wrists and her slim throat.

Jesus.

She was a cross between a wannabe punk rock star and a BDSM enthusiast's wet dream.

She stared at me, our height disparity forcing her to angle her head and expose her delicate neck to me. Edgy hunger burned through me as I tracked her alabaster-pale face, the lightest flutter of her nostrils, the velvet smoothness of her mouth. The racing pulse beneath her choker.

She inhaled and exhaled slowly. "I hear you're a fixer."

"You heard correctly." I wasn't in the phone book. Referrals were strictly by word of mouth. I sent silent thanks to whichever client had sent her my way.

She gave a brisk nod. "Before we start, we need to discuss an NDA," she said in a sexy voice I wanted in surround sound in my head.

I was used to nondisclosure agreements. No one worth a damn did business these days without first whipping out an NDA. But whether it was the time of night or my general mood lately, I shook my head.

"Before we discuss NDAs I need the broad strokes of the job first." Who was I kidding? This woman, whoever she was, intrigued me. I was fairly sure I was going to take the job.

Her mouth firmed. "Fair enough. I've picked up a stalker," she said matter-of-factly. "It started off as cyberstalking but in the past three weeks it's escalated to physical stalking."

The bolt of unexpected protectiveness shot through me, unsettling me enough to make me cross my arms. "And you haven't called the cops because…?"

"Because it could be linked with the work I'm doing."

"What work?"

"Extremely sensitive work that I can't discuss without you signing the NDA." She held out the document.

My intrigue spiked. "Okay, let's see it."

It was seven pages long, far more detailed than the standard three-page NDA, with her name left blank. I noticed her studying me from the corner of my eye as I read it a second time. When I was done, I shifted my gaze to her, my interest mounting when she met my eye boldly. "It looks good. Pen?"

As if on cue, the door opened, and the young guy who opened the front door walked in. I watched him, then her, looking for signs of a relationship. She nodded her thanks when he produced a pen, but there was nothing else in her gaze that tweaked my senses.

I grimaced at the relief that shot through me, and signed.

She took the pen and inserted her name.

Lily Angela Gracen.

I stared at the name, searched the corners of my mind and came up empty as the guy witnessed the document.

As she walked him to the door I allowed myself a second, more intimate look.

Hell, she was *stunning*.

No one deserved to be stalked, online or in real life, but *fuck*, looking at her, I understood why she could become an object of some psycho's obsession.

The moment the thought crossed my mind, I froze, rejecting the idea of her being in danger, even while my cock stirred to life, excited by the magnificent vision crossing the room toward me.

She moved with understated but sexy awareness, a woman who acknowledged her considerable attributes but didn't need to flaunt them. A woman who knew the power of those curvy hips, her plump lips and generous breasts.

Despite her combat boots adding a couple of inches to her height, she barely came up to my chest. Petite, perfectly proportioned, she was the epitome of a filthy, decadent Pocket Venus.

She probably weighed no more than a hundred and ten pounds. On a good day I bench-pressed twice her weight. My mind reeled with images of how she would feel in my arms.

Easily pinned against a wall, her naked, delicious weight trapped between my greedy hands.

Easily tied down to a bed with silk ropes if that was her thing, her skin flushed pink as she straddled the fine line between preorgasmic tension and a screaming climax.

Easily subdued and tossed into the back of a van by some unhinged asshole with entitlement issues.

I yanked myself away from lurid sexual scenarios and adjusted my stance to ease the constriction in my pants as the most gorgeous creature I'd seen in a long time stopped before me.

"Who was he?" I nodded at the door.

"He came with the house rental. I asked him to stick around to witness the document."

"Okay, now that I've signed your document, let's start again. I'm Caleb Steele. Fixer."

She stared at the hand I held out. "Lily Gracen, chief coder for Sierra Donovan Media."

Despite what was happening to her, she had more than a little sass. And if she was a coder, she had brains, too. A lethal combination on any given day.

Packaged in that body, I got the strongest suspicion I was in for an exhilarating ride.

After several moments she took my hand.

The second I felt the warm sizzle of her flesh, experienced an extra shot of testosterone through my system and watched her eyes widen in mutual acknowledgment of the rush, I accepted my reality. Signed NDA or not, the unholy fire spreading through my bloodstream had only one destination.

I was going to cross a helluva lot of lines, all of which started and ended with one fact.

I was going to fuck Lily Angela Gracen.

CHAPTER TWO

Caleb

WHOA. TAKE IT down a notch or six, cowboy.

Getting involved with Lily Gracen while she was my client had *bad idea* written all over it. I'd learned that lesson the hard way.

Which was why I broke my rules for no one.

A fixer's first and last defense against failure was his neutrality. Starting out I'd disregarded that by getting involved with Kirsten. A young actress on the precarious rise, her cultivated vulnerability had slipped beneath my guard, triggered emotions she'd expertly manipulated to suit her purposes. Emotions that had turned me into a laughingstock and nearly tanked my reputation.

Never again were two words I abided by.

Already, my sexual attraction to Lily Gracen was getting in the way of that neutrality. And that bite of protectiveness the moment I saw her? That needed to go, as well. My task was to find her stalker without messy emotions getting in the way.

But…once that was done, there would be nothing stopping me from rewarding myself with a taste of her.

Yeah, I wasn't perfect. At no point in my life did I try to be. You can't go countless rounds in the boxing ring of life without emerging with a few scars both inside and out.

I'd dragged myself from the rougher parts of South Central LA and into the twenty-thousand square feet of a Malibu mansion via some seriously rocky terrain, experiencing every imaginable facet of human nature along the way.

It was the reason I now lived by three simple rules:

Protect the innocent and vulnerable at all cost. Always.

No sleeping with clients, no matter how tempting.

No sleeping with the fucking clients, no matter how fucking *tempting.*

The foundation of rule one would never waver. I feared for the foundation of rules two and three as I held on to Lily's hand, drifted my thumb across one satin-smooth knuckle. She gratified my touch with a sharp catch of her breath.

God, I wanted to hear that sound louder, preferably preceding a scream as I buried my cock inside her sweet little pussy.

But first, I needed to get down to business.

She beat me to it by tugging her hand out of mine. "Shall we discuss the details?"

As she walked away, I caught the scent of her perfume—earthy, evocative of rain-soaked heather, the kind that invited you to roll around in when the sun came out. I wanted to follow that scent with my nose. And then with my hands and my mouth.

Down boy, I cautioned my cock when it jumped in agreement.

"Sure."

She sat down at one end of the sofa, crossed her legs and waved me to the seat next to her. "Sit down, Mr. Steele."

The take-charge attitude from such a diminutive person was an unexpected turn-on. I let her have the leeway. For now.

I sat, dragging my gaze from her shapely calves and thighs. "One thing you should know—I won't be managed. If you want me to catch this…person, you'll let me do my job."

She stared at me for a moment, then shrugged. "We'll get to that in a moment."

Again, I tried not to react like a horny teenager to the sound of her voice, but God, it was something else. Hell, from the top of those roughly chopped locks to the tips of her boots, she was something else.

"Is Steele really your last name?" she asked abruptly, her slender arms folded.

I raised an eyebrow. "Do you always go out dressed like that?" Okay, not how I'd wanted to start, but it was a pertinent question. I didn't have a problem with the way any woman dressed, but some guys out there were sick enough to form vile opinions about women based on the way they dressed.

Her pointy little chin rose. "What's wrong with the way I dress?"

I laughed, absently noting how the sound scraped my throat. "Nothing to me. But everything to the wrong person."

She inhaled sharply. "What does that mean?"

"That I hope your stalker is the type who's just obsessed with your outer appearance. Those are the easiest to catch because they can't help themselves. They'll slip up and attempt to make physical contact with you sooner rather than later."

A tiny shiver went through her but her gaze didn't waver. "Why are you assuming the stalker's interest is sexual?"

"Because I have eyes. You're a fucking knockout. But if you say it's not, I'm willing to delay a final verdict on the bastard until I hear all the facts."

A light blush bloomed into her cheeks. From the way her lips pressed together I could tell she hated that little evidence of her emotions. I enjoyed it a little too much. "Are you always this blunt?" she asked.

I folded my arms to prevent them from doing something stupid. Like tracing that blush down to her throat. "Always. That going to be problem?"

Her small fingers gripped her biceps. "Only if you don't like having it reciprocated."

"I'm good with blunt. I prefer it, even. And yes, Steele is really my name."

It was one of the few facts my mother blessed me with in the midst of her dark despair; and one of the first things I did when I established solid, reliable contacts through my work was to find the man whose blood coursed through my veins. Turned out I came from a long line of mostly no-good Steeles. A shocking percentage had been criminals. Of those that were alive, including my father, I wanted nothing to do with in this lifetime.

I refocused on her as she recrossed her legs, and I couldn't stop myself from staring. The hem of her black leather skirt had ridden up to midthigh, and she was making no move to pull it down. That tiny bit of exhibitionism ramped up my temperature another hundred notches. My tongue grew thicker and I watched her foot bounce for several seconds before I realized she was waiting for me to speak.

I cleared my throat and forced my brain back on the right track. "You think your stalker isn't interested in you personally. So it's work related?"

"I think so."

"Okay. Tell me about the project you're working on."

She hesitated.

"I need to know where to start looking. Who to rule out," I pushed.

She toyed with the tiny spikes on her wrist cuff as she weighed her words. "It's an algorithm that significantly comprises data. On a small scale it can store almost fifteen times as much data as on the ordinary thirty-two-gigabyte chip you use on your phone."

Okay, that blew my mind a little. But I suspected my mind was about to be blown even further. "And on a larger scale?"

"If our planned launch is successful next month, it can render almost all the current data storage algorithms obsolete in under a year." She spoke with quiet but fierce pride.

I gave a low whistle. "And you wrote the code? All of it?"

There was no false modesty. Just a firm nod. "Yes. It's all mine."

"That's impressive."

Her gaze rose from her wrist to mine. The determined fire and pride that burned in her eyes said she knew what she was capable of, and was hell-bent on going after it. I could see how that would piss a few male egos off.

"Thank you," she responded in a low, husky voice.

Impossibly, the evidence of power she held in her small body and that huge brain of hers turned me on even more. I was a greedy enough asshole to admit that I wanted to experience what that power blazing through her felt like. I wanted to see her drunk on it, if only for a moment, so I could feel the intoxicating afterburn of it.

But that urge would have to be curtailed for a while because, unfortunately, her revelation had thrown open several avenues where the threat could be coming from.

I rose, thankful that with the much bigger problem on my mind, my body was calming down a little from its sexual frenzy. Although I still needed to turn away to hide the semi-erection throbbing behind my fly. I was crossing the room when I heard her question.

"Is something wrong?"

I glanced at her over my shoulder. "That depends on how wide your circle of trust is. And how wide *their* circles are. I suggest we get things moving sooner rather than later." I pulled out my phone and was about to hit the first number on my speed dial when it blared to life.

Maggie's uncanny timing was impressive. But not if she was calling with anything that might distract me from Lily Gracen.

"Yes?" My voice was terser than I intended, but what the hell. The night was turning out to be interesting in some ways and extremely frustrating in others.

"Just checking in. On the off chance I blew it, I wanted to know if I should tender my resignation now or get some sleep and do it in the morning," Maggie said with a pinch of sarcasm that straddled the fine line between amusing and insubordinate.

But despite my irritation, I toyed with giving her a bonus for landing me this job.

"We have a new client."

"Yes! Great job, Maggie. I've no idea what I'd do without you, Maggie. I'll even consider giving you that pay raise you've been hinting at for the last six months, Maggie."

"Keep talking about yourself in the third person and your boss will think you're a lunatic and fire your ass."

"I don't want that. At all. What do you need me to do?" she asked, back in my preferred super-efficient mode.

I strolled to the farthest window while I updated Maggie on the assignment. "My first thought was to keep her completely off the radar while I hunted down this creep, but I've changed my mind."

"O…kay."

"I need you to prepare a couple of safe houses. Have the jet on standby, too. We might need to change location quickly."

"Yes, boss. Right away, boss."

"Don't be a smart-ass, Maggie."

"Absolutely not. Safe houses. Private jet. Check."

"Good girl. And if you insist on it, you can go get some sleep after that. But I need you bright and early in the morning. Got it?"

"Of course. I'll text you once it's done."

I hung up, satisfied with taking the direct approach to Lily's problem.

I turned around. She'd stopped messing with her cuff, but her fingers were linked over one knee, and the look in her eyes was mildly censorious.

"You have something to say?"

"Do you treat all your employees like that?"

I pocketed my phone. "Like what?"

"Like they're one level up from chattels."

I retraced my steps back to her. "I don't have a problem cracking the whip, if that's what you mean. I find it works best if it's established clearly who's boss." I didn't add that Maggie often rolled her eyes when I used my dominant voice. Which was pretty much all the time.

"So that's your thing? You like to lord it over people?"

I shoved my hands in my pockets as I stood over her. This time the disparity was even more acute, and her upturned face was even more exposed. Fuck, she was so small, such a delicious morsel wrapped in a bundle of sharp brains and fierce beauty. That feral urge to possess her stormed through me, firing up every cell in my body.

Still, I should probably have curbed the words that slid to the tip of my tongue. But hell, I was never one to back down from speaking my mind. I'd learned the hard way how high the cost of holding my tongue could be.

"Would you like me to lord it over you, sweetheart?"

Her eyes widened into alluring green pools. Her nostrils pinched delicately as she inhaled too quickly. "Excuse me?"

"I will, Lily Gracen, but only if you ask me very, very nicely."

Lily

There were so many things wrong with his statement that I didn't know where to start. I wasn't even sure where shock ended and annoyance started. Which was surprising since for the past three years I'd lived in an environment dominated by the worst type of male ego—one with a half-decent brain and a bottomless bank account.

Silicon Valley wasn't the place for shrinking violets, and while my start at SDM may not have been conventional, I soon learned to find my voice or be flattened by pompous assholes.

That voice was now trapped somewhere between my throat and my tongue as I stared up at the seriously gorgeous man planted before me, watching me with eyes that started saucy little fires in my body.

I cleared my throat. "You're forgetting who hired whom, Mr. Steele. Technically, I'm your boss. If anyone will be *lording* anything, it'll be me."

For some reason that made his piercing blue eyes gleam. "I don't have a problem with a woman calling the shots. Within reason, of course."

Between his eyes and his deep, sexy, gravel-rough voice, I forgot, for a moment, the sinister threats hanging over my head, jeopardizing everything I'd worked hard for. I was so close to living my life on my terms. To being free of the devil's bargain my stepfather had struck with my employer to keep me shackled.

But staring at Caleb Steele, the deep unease I'd been bottling down since my stalker's first contact faded a little, enough for me to experience new, equally unsettling sensations.

The thinly disguised sexual interest in his eyes had lit a fire beneath my skin from the moment our eyes met. I knew the way I chose to dress, the individual statement I made with my hair and clothes, meant I attracted looks that my younger, teenage self would've shied away from. But that was before I was forced to grow a hard shell. Before it became clear that no matter what I did, all I would ever be was a monthly check to my stepfather for the meager attention grudgingly tossed my way through years of bitter, enforced parenting, and a means of harnessing my talent from Chance Donovan, the man I worked for.

But freedom was within my grasp.

Once I got rid of my stalker problem.

Somewhere in a place I refused to visit very often, the sting of rejection resided. But that pain had diminished significantly over time. In fact, I discovered the neat little trick that the more I worked the less I thought about my dismal past.

Except that work was now in jeopardy. The jagged circle of thought brought me back to my solution— Caleb Steele.

The man who stood before me was a tower of raw masculinity and unapologetic dominance.

His dark blue eyes were commanding to the point of hypnotic, and he dripped the kind of sexual assurance that very few men could carry off.

As for the impressive bulge I glimpsed as he strolled across the room a few minutes ago…?

I pressed my suddenly hot thighs together, struggled not to drop my gaze to the part of his anatomy that was unnervingly close to my face and cursed the blush creeping my neck.

You have a stalker, *Lily Angela Gracen. The last thing you should be thinking about is how incredible it would be to give your first blowjob to this drop-dead gorgeous man who's staring at you as if he wants to take a very big, very greedy, bite out of you.*

I stepped back from the edge of insanity as he leaned down, bringing his impressive height and stunning physique closer.

"Lily... Can I call you Lily?" he asked in that insanely sexy voice.

Enough already. My control may be slipping from me in other areas of my life. I wasn't going to let it slip here. "No. You can't. You haven't earned that right."

He raised one sleek, dark eyebrow, and hell, even that small action was crazy-hot. And when he smiled, his eyes gleamed with a new, carnal light that threatened to set me on fire all over again. "I don't usually go in for the brownie points system but if that's what turns you on..." He shrugged.

I frowned. "You misunderstand. Deliberately, I suspect. We're not discussing what turns me on. Or...having you lord...whatever over me." *Thanks, brain, for choosing today to deliver my speech in stupid ellipses!* "That's not going to happen, either, by the way, just so we're clear. *I'm* all about having this problem handled, ASAP, so I can get on with my life. Plus, I'm friendly with people I trust, and I don't trust you." There. Direct and to the point.

"You don't trust me...yet. That's okay. I'm skeptical, too. For instance, I'm not totally convinced that a bodyguard or a private investigator can't handle this job. So, Lily...how are *you* going to convince *me* to get off the fence?"

I hated the ground-shifting sensation that came with the idea that he could walk away. My research had indicated he was the man for the job. I didn't have time to find another. "You want me to pay you double? Is that it?"

The snap of irritation in his eyes indicated I'd caused offense. My stomach knotted harder.

"I turn away three out of five clients. Money isn't an issue for me. If you want me, do better."

"Fine. I was told you're the best of the best. I need the best."

He didn't answer for several drawn-out seconds. His hands returned to his pockets, and he rocked on his feet before he nodded. "Great. You've got me."

Convinced the loaded words were just in my mind, I ignored the heat pooling in my pelvis and pressed on. "It's almost two in the morning. Every second that passes is a second I'm being kept from doing my job. So can we proceed, Mr. Steele?"

"Does anyone else know you're being stalked?"

"Not yet, but if the threats continue I'll have to inform Chance Donovan. He's my boss and CEO of SDM."

Thoughts of Chance cooled my churning jets. As the moneyman behind my project, he was under pressure from his board of directors to deliver the code on time. Over the past month, that pressure had been redirected my way, with hints of the unpleasant consequences should I fail to meet my deadline.

"I'm hoping you'll fix my problem before that becomes necessary."

Caleb nodded, and I caught a different gleam in his eyes. Respect. Maybe a little admiration. For some absurd reason, pleasure fizzed through me.

"I was going to suggest a safe house but I'm guessing you'll draw attention to your absence if you don't show up at work?"

"Yes. Usually, I can come and go as I please, but I have a team working with me."

His eyes narrowed. "A team?"

"The algorithm I'm building is huge. I have three teams of three working independently on different aspects of the code to minimize leaking of confidential information. They all report to me."

"So they don't know exactly what you're working on?" he fired at me.

"No." That had been Chance's idea. One I disagreed with but had no choice but to accept.

My expression must have given me away because Caleb frowned. "What aren't you telling me?"

My gut told me Caleb was the kind of guy who needed full disclosure or he might walk. "Chance and I have a history."

"What kind?"

"I was fourteen when I...came to his attention."

His gaze stayed fixed on me. "Let me guess. You hacked him. He caught you and convinced you to work for him instead."

A cute anecdote except for the part where I became tied to my so-called savior via a thousand wires made of veiled threats. I tightened the knots of pain and bitterness threatening to unravel. "Something like that," I replied. "Anyway, I can't be away from Sunnyvale for long. Which is why I'm going back tonight. What I want to know is will you be coming with me?"

A hard glint entered his eyes. "I will. On one condition. If we're going into your stalker's territory, you'll agree to do things my way, including letting me step into a situation if I think it's for your own good."

"But—"

"No buts. It says so in the small print of my retainer."

We faced off, a vortex of thunder and lightning swirling around us, eddying us dangerously closer. "It said I had to relinquish reasonable power to you. Not *all* power."

"'*There will be times when the fixer may have to take an* act-first-explain-later *approach to a situation. The client agrees to comply if such a situation arises.*' Did you make a note of that line?" His voice was low but deadly soft.

"Sure, I read that part. And you're probably used to having your every mandate agreed to immediately. Unfortunately, you and I will have a big problem if you insist on being...rigid."

"I can be as flexible as any situation demands. But not in this case. You forget. You *need* me."

I hated my words being thrown back in my face. Almost as much as I'd hated the thought of hiring a bodyguard and waiting the stalker out.

I was weeks from being free of Chance and my stepfather. The thought of adding even an extra hour's delay to that liberating moment was unacceptable. Still, relinquishing control was hard. "Do you find a client taking charge of their own safety a deal breaker for you?"

My question seemed to throw him off. A tiny frown pleated his brow, and then his striking blue gaze left mine to scour my body before returning to my face. As I watched, he reeled himself in. Like the man, his expression was fascinating to watch. It was as if he'd been in danger of overstepping a line and had coldly and ruthlessly corrected his course.

"No, but if you want an obedient thug, feel free to pick one of those rent-a-cops outside."

"All right. If you're up to something more challenging, then I agree to your terms."

The direct taunt to his supposedly flawless record—and yes, to his ego—was one I made with my breath held tight. For reasons I couldn't fathom, I hated the thought of him walking away even more.

With a single step, he closed the gap between us and lowered his lips to my ear. "Be very careful where you throw your little gauntlets, Lily Gracen. One might come back to bite you in your delectable ass."

It was impossible to stop the hot little shiver that raced through me. He saw it, and a bright blue flame lit his eyes.

"Well, be warned. I bite back."

"This is going to be very interesting," he mused. Then without taking his eyes from mine, he reached for his phone. I heard faint ringing in the background before it was answered.

"Maggie, is the primary crew in place?"

"Yes, they'll land in Palo Alto in thirty minutes. They can be at Miss Gracen's house in an hour. Do we have a green light?"

He lowered the phone. "Do I have the green light, Lily?"

"Your team is already in San Francisco. So you intended to take my case all along?"

He shrugged. "I needed to make sure you were fully committed but I saw no reason not to start the ball rolling."

I took a steadying breath. "I don't appreciate being toyed with, Mr. Steele."

All traces of humor left his face. "Then we're in total agreement because this is no fucking joke."

His harsh reply tightened the skin on my nape, warned me there was something else going on here.

"My guys are waiting," he pressed. "All they'll be doing tonight is setting up a few cameras outside the property and scoping out the area. They're experts, trustworthy, handpicked by me. They won't rifle through your underwear drawer or whatever naughty things you keep in your closet if that's what you're worried about. So, do I have the green light, Lily?" That last bit was muttered with a hot little taunt as his gaze raked my face.

I fought to hold on to my irritation and dismiss the tiny lick of embarrassment.

So okay, I wasn't the tidiest person at the best of times. And being neck-deep in my project, I'd let my standards slip a little further and canceled my cleaning service because I hated the disruption. Which meant any number of personal items, including the ones I used to de-stress after a hard day's coding, could be scattered anywhere in my house.

The joy of living alone meant I could pleasure myself anywhere from my bathroom floor to the movie room lounger where I usually crashed when I couldn't be bothered to drag myself to my bed. The thought of Caleb Steele's men reporting my habits back to him made my palms burn with humiliation.

Which was absurd.

I was a grown woman, for heaven's sake. One with healthy needs I wasn't ashamed of satisfying in defiance of the restrictions Chance Donovan had tried to place on me.

Nope, I wasn't going to think about Chance or how he tried to control me through Scott, my ex-boyfriend.

Very soon they'd both be so far in my rearview I'd need a telescope to see them.

"You have the green light," I said, blanking my mind to the possibility of my sex toys being discovered. "You'll need a code to get into the house."

The small cocky smile that curved his lips suggested that he really didn't, but he chose not to vocalize the fact. "Shoot."

I rattled out a long alphanumeric code. He impressed me by not asking me to repeat it and recited it to Maggie without hesitation.

About to hang up, he paused when Maggie called his name. "Yes?"

"The pilot is still on standby. I'm assuming you and the client are returning to Palo Alto, too?"

"Yes, we'll be at the airport in half an hour." He hung up, the blue of his eyes drenching me with the sensation of being swallowed whole. "Come on. Let's go get this bastard out of your life."

I grabbed my things and followed Caleb Steele outside with the distinct feeling he'd left out a vital part of his statement. Something along the lines of...*and then we can get onto more important things*.

Or maybe that was all in *my* dirty imagination.

CHAPTER THREE

Lily

IT WASN'T THE first time I'd ridden in a Bugatti—Silicon Valley was crawling with billionaire tech geeks who collected supercars like they were baseball cards.

But it was the first time I'd ridden in a supercar driven by a man like Caleb Steele. And this, too, was turning out to be a sex-steeped experience.

The man drove his car like he was making love to it. Scratch that. He drove like he was fucking it. Smooth. Sexy. Relentless. Each flick of the gear and flex of his thigh as he switched from gas to brake was a hypnotic symphony. One so absorbing I couldn't look away.

I realized my lip was caught between my teeth, and my fingers were digging into the soft leather, and forced myself to release both. To take a breath unfortunately filled with sandalwood and prime male, in order to get my brain on track.

Caleb Steele was the type of guy who would see my discomfort as a weakness and use it to his advantage.

"Where are we flying from?" He'd been mostly silent since we left the mansion. Admittedly, I found it a little disconcerting, especially since I'd anticipated being peppered with questions.

He changed lanes again before he answered, sending me a sidelong glance that left me with that faint impression of what being electrocuted by a low current would feel like. Even after he looked away, I experienced aftershocks.

"Van Nuys Airport. Don't worry, petal. I'll have you home in no time."

"I don't like pet names, Mr. Steele."

"You don't like pet names and you don't want me to use your first name. The only way I'm calling you *Miss Gracen* is if we're role-playing naughty teacher/ stern principal."

I was gripping the seat again. *Dammit.* I forced myself to uncurl my fingers before I damaged them because I needed them to write code. "Maybe this wasn't such a great idea, after all."

Watchful blue eyes gleamed wickedly in the lights from the dashboard. "Sorry, baby, it's too late to change your mind. You're stuck with me."

Baby. Sweetheart. Petal. He probably had an endless list of pet names he tossed at women.

Short of lowering myself to his level and calling him Big Guy or Sexy Ass or Hot Rod, I had to concede this round. "Fine, you can call me Lily. Because, heaven forbid, you run out of pet names and start calling me *honey cheeks.*"

"Thank you, Lily," he said in a low, deep voice that rumbled over me like delicious hot fudge over a sundae. "And by the way, I would never peg you as honey cheeks. Not with that flawless pale skin." That slow-building, insanely sexy smile returned. "Is it deliberate?"

"Is what deliberate?"

"Your paleness. It works well with the Goth vibe but it must be hell to avoid the sun when you live in California."

"What does the paleness of my skin have to do with the case?" *Or anything else that doesn't make me think of sex?*

"Zilch. This is insatiable curiosity on my part. So?"

"So, you'll just have to accept that it won't be satisfied this time."

"Shame," he murmured. "I'll just have to use my imagination."

I averted my gaze, but I was still thinking about that smile, the effortless sensuality he wove into the most innocuous words, when he swung the powerful sports car onto the exit ramp leading to the airport.

After passing through security, Caleb drove into a brightly lit hangar and parked next to a gleaming white jet. Its steps were lowered, the engine humming. The pilot and copilot were talking to two airport officials as we alighted but my attention was drawn to the woman standing at the bottom of the steps.

Her short, sequined silver tube dress, long silver necklaces and rows of hooped earrings ruled her out as an attendant. She was shrugging into a bomber jacket when Caleb stepped out and came around to open my door.

"Do we need to discuss appropriate work attire again?" His tone was bone-dry as he addressed her.

She reached up to free her bun, then gave a resigned grimace. "Not that you'll care but I interrupted my date to return to the office for this assignment."

"A *date*? With an actual guy?" Heavy skepticism laced his voice as he retrieved my overnight bag.

The woman rolled her eyes and turned to me. After a quick once-over, she held out her hand and smiled. "I'm Maggie, Mr. Steele's long-suffering assistant. You must be Lily Gracen?"

At my nod, her face turned serious. "We'll catch the A-hole who's doing this to you. Don't tell my boss I said so, but he's ace at what he does. Our success record is pretty impressive. You're in good hands."

Caleb slammed the door. "Cut the corporate spiel, Maggie. Lily already knows she can trust me."

I ignored him, and smiled at Maggie. "Thanks."

"Did you bring what I needed?" he asked his assistant.

Maggie nodded. "Everything is already on board."

"Are we cleared to fly?" he pressed impatiently.

"Almost." She pointed to where the copilot was talking to the ground crew. "They're not happy that you're flying outside curfew—"

"You told them it was an emergency, right?"

"Yes, boss. They still need to tick their boxes. Give them a minute."

"I don't have a minute," he snapped, turning toward the group.

"Seriously, they're almost done—" Maggie started, but he was already walking away. She stopped talking, looking a little perplexed.

I frowned. "Is he always—?"

"The definition of a bull in a china shop? Surprisingly, no," Maggie answered her own question, her voice contemplative. "Sure, he's impatient and he wants everything done yesterday, but it takes a lot to ruffle his feathers. Although..."

"Although?" I prompted after a throb of silence, telling myself it was just mild curiosity that triggered the desire to know what made the enigmatic fixer tick. What made him give a damn and what bounced off those impressive shoulders?

Maggie's sharp, gray-eyed gaze snapped to me. I suspected the evasive answer before she opened her mouth. "A testy client earlier tonight before he came to see you. That's all."

I suppressed surprisingly sharp disappointment and glanced over to where the man I'd appointed as my fixer was gesturing impatiently to the men. He stood over a head taller, easily the most striking, and the low timbre of his voice rumbled through the large space, sending a decadent shiver to my lady parts.

After a minute the officials handed over papers to the copilot.

Caleb returned and picked up the overnight bag he'd set down next to the car. "We're clear to fly. Shall we?"

I sidestepped him when he reached for my arm, prompting another raised eyebrow I ignored. The lingering tingle between my thighs insisted touching him was a bad idea.

"Great to meet you, Maggie," I said.

The assistant smiled. "Likewise."

I walked up the stairs to the plane, aware that he trailed behind me. Drawn by an undeniable need, I looked over my shoulder. He'd paused with one foot on the bottom step; his eyes were fixed on me. Or rather on my ass. That insane tingle intensified between my legs.

I barely had time to step back before he was towering over me. For a handful of seconds, he stared down at me. Then his gaze flitted past me to the small cabin.

"Go grab a seat, Lily. We need to be wheels up before the stiffs out there find another reason to delay us."

The interior of the plane was as pristine and classy as the outside. Fitted in mahogany and cream tones, the club seats were grouped into two sections, one side with a shiny table separating the seats and the other without.

I chose the seat with a table. Anything for a buffer between Caleb and myself.

He watched me slide into the window seat. He didn't immediately sit down, even though the jet was rolling out of the hangar. Instead, he took his time to shrug off his lightweight jacket. The midnight blue shirt underneath was fitted, lovingly following a streamlined torso.

When he pivoted to hang up his jacket, the muscles in his back rippled with a sleek, edgy synergy that triggered a need to see him minus that shirt. Unlike me, he was perfectly tanned, the Californian sun having found the ideal specimen to blaze upon. Without a doubt, he would be firmly toned all over.

The urge to glide my fingers over those muscles intensified the incessant throb in my pussy.

I inhaled unsteadily, shifted my gaze and focused on securing my belt as he slid onto the seat opposite me. A moment later one arm extended toward me.

Annoyingly agitated with my skittish emotions, my head jerked up. He was unbuttoning his cuffs, casually folding back his sleeves, exposing thick, brawny arms overlaid with silky wisps of hair.

The innate grace flowing through the moment was almost hypnotic.

God. Enough.

The man was mouthwateringly attractive, granted. But I'd never lost my head or hormones like this, not even during the brief months I thought I was in love with Scott Wyatt, the man Chance planted in my life to manipulate me. Even before I found out his true motivations, Scott didn't set me on fire with a mere look.

After he was done with his hot little arm-porn display, Caleb rested his arms on the table. "Do you want a drink?"

"I'm good, thanks."

He nodded and glanced at his watch. "It is three in the morning, and we land in about forty-five minutes. We can use the time to discuss the case, or you can get some sleep?"

"You're giving me a choice?"

He smiled. "I'm not a complete ogre, Lily, regardless of whatever impression Maggie gave you."

It unsettled me that he'd read me so accurately. But wasn't that why I chose him? He'd risen to the top of my list almost immediately when I searched on the dark web because he was a maverick to the core. Totally unscrupulous when he went after something he truly wanted.

And the way he was staring back at me strongly suggested I was somewhere on his *want* list.

Maybe that was the reason I should've been bone-tired but felt oddly invigorated despite being awake for twenty hours straight. If I'd been coding, I'd be getting ready to crash hard by now.

My stalker's latest "gift" arriving in my mail this morning had wiped rest from my mind.

That unwelcome reminder refocused me. "I'm fine to answer your questions."

His brisk nod signified the switch back to fixer mode. "We'll get to the background stuff when you've had some sleep. For now, tell me when you first realized you'd attracted someone's attention?"

I didn't need to think hard. The memory was etched in my mind. "About seven weeks ago I received a piece of what looked like my code in an email. It was a very rough copy but it got my attention. And no, I wasn't able to find out who sent it."

"So we could be dealing with corporate sabotage."

The possibility shocked me. "You think one of SDM's competitors could be behind this?"

The underhanded tactics that went on in Silicon Valley weren't a secret, but usually they involved throwing enough money at an acquisition to secure it or throwing even more money at a problem to make it go away.

His mouth twisted. "You'd be surprised at the lengths companies would go to get an edge on the market. If your code is as revolutionary as you say it is—"

"It is," I confirmed. The possibilities of my algorithm scared me a little but I was extremely proud of what I'd achieved. The thought of someone stealing it filled me with equal parts fury and fear.

Caleb leaned back but it didn't release me from the raw force field of his personality. I was convinced he'd need to be in another state for that to happen.

"Then I suggest we make a list of the top twenty companies you think might benefit from this code."

I shook my head. "That'll be nearly impossible to investigate before the deadline."

A fierce light blazed in his eyes. "Make the list, Lily. I'll take care of it."

I got the unassailable impression that he would. The depth of that belief scared me a little. But it excited me even more. Which was ludicrous and a lot disturbing considering I detested being taken care of.

Not true. You hate that no one's cared enough without having an ulterior motive. Just like you hate that soft place inside you that wants to be taken care of.

I tightened my gut against the abrading truth. But it was no use. Lately, I hadn't been able to suppress thoughts of my stepfather as easily as I used to. Truth was, my stalker had amplified the yawning cavern of my life. He, or *they*, had exposed vulnerabilities that made me feel raw and fearful and *alone*. It was that last sensation I especially despised. I wanted that aloneness gone, and if I had to endure Caleb Steele for a while to achieve a return to normal, then so be it.

"Okay, I'll have it ready for you in the morning."

"Good. Tell me when you first noticed this wasn't just an online thing?" he whipped back, sharp eyes narrowed.

A swell of fear met quiet fury at the recollection of that first violation. "Two weeks ago I got another piece of code in the mail. It's a long way from the one I was working on, but someone out there is taunting me with knowledge of what I'm working on."

A muscle rippled in his jaw. "Did they make demands? Ask for money?"

"No."

"They're trying to scare you into changing your routine. Trip you up in some way. When was the next time?"

"He left me another code on top of my bike outside a coffee shop four blocks from my house."

His mouth thinned. "So he knows where you work and live."

I fought the shudder that rolled up my body. "Looks like it."

His hands curled into loose fists but his breathing didn't change. He carried on staring at me with a level look, then nodded for me to go on.

"The last time was yesterday morning. I received another code, but with a picture of me attached."

"A picture?" Caleb asked.

I nodded, a sheet of ice unravelling through me at the recollection. "It was taken two days ago. I was shopping."

"Fuck." Caleb's jaw rippled with tension before he leaned forward, bristling with quiet fury. "What happened to the package?"

"I have it at home."

His expression tight, he reached for his phone and had another conversation with the unflappable Maggie, issuing terse instructions about retrieving the package and having a discreet service dust it for prints. Just as briskly, he hung up and dropped the phone on the table between us.

"Tell me about your online activities, outside of the work you do for SDM."

"That's a very broad question." The plane dipped, taking a little bit of my stomach with it. "You want to know if I messed up somewhere?"

"I'm sure you didn't but something you did triggered this."

The logic was too sound to dismiss. I tried to suppress it but my unease grew. "You don't think I covered my tracks?"

A smile twitched his lips. "You're a coder. I'm sure you can clear your caches in your sleep. And I'm not talking about porn. Although I'd love to know which sites you prefer."

A flush heated my chest and spread lower to my abdomen. "Mr. Steele—"

"Lily?" he responded with a heavy dose of snark.

I took a calming breath. "I don't leave a trail of where I buy my lingerie or post minute-by-minute details of where I'm going to be at any given time of day. I know how to protect myself."

"And yet he found you," he stated with bracing finality.

After a moment, I looked at him. "What do you want to know specifically?"

"Coders make decent hackers. If you hacked your way into a job with SDM, you must be great. What's your hacker handle?"

All of a sudden the name that sent shivers down the spines of faceless dark web hackers felt pretentious. "Cipher Q."

His brows slowly rose. "You're Cipher Q?"

Another emotion swept in to mingle with the cocktail swirling inside me. This time it was most definitely not *unpleasant*. "You know about me?"

He shrugged. "Cyber crimes are a problem for a few of my clients. Maggie and a few people on my payroll keep an eye on things like that for me. A few months back she wouldn't shut up about some big-deal hacker contest going on. You won, if I remember correctly?"

The kick of pride warred with the need to set him straight. "Yes, but it was all aboveboard. No cyber crimes involved."

"Who came second?"

"Nordic Razor."

"What do you know about him? How did he take coming second?"

"You think he's doing this?"

His shoulders rippled beneath his shirt as he shrugged again. "Not everyone likes losing to a woman."

I shook my head. "It's not him."

"I'll be the judge of that. I need the names of everyone who took part in the contest, too."

"At this rate I'll be spending all my time compiling lists for you. I won't have time to work."

He shot forward and the force of his dominant personality hit me like a tidal wave. "You won't be working at all if this situation escalates. Did you forget already that I'm in control here?"

I'm in control.

Words I'd heard far too many times in my life. Words that had imprisoned me for far too long. My teeth met in a grinding clench. "I don't like being ordered around, Mr. Steele."

"Too bad. Until this bastard is in custody, you'll not only do as you're told, you'll also learn to love it."

Maybe it was something in his voice. Or the words he used with me. But my fury faded, along with that carnally needy, traitorous voice that wanted to say, *Yes, Caleb. I'll learn to love it.* That tingle between my thighs still throbbed, but it was with a different sort of need.

A burning need to, for once in my life, grab and keep the upper hand. To put this man in his place once and for all.

Because, fuck that noise. My days of pretzeling myself to please others were nearly behind me.

I unclipped my seat belt and was out of my seat before I fully processed my actions.

Being pint-size had its advantages. It made crawling on top of the table a piece of cake.

I relished Caleb's unguarded intake of breath as I leaned forward and shoved my face in his. With a couple of inches separating us, I caught every fleck of surprise in his eyes as he watched me.

"You really think you're in control here?" I murmured softly.

A slow, assured smile widened his sexy mouth. "I know it," he rasped.

"I see." I scooted another inch closer, glided my tongue over my bottom lip. His demeanor changed. His ravenous gaze dropped to my mouth and his next breath wasn't quite so steady. "You didn't ask me how I found you to handle my problem, Mr. Steele."

His eyes grew wary. Good. "Maggie handles background stuff."

I nodded. "Hmm. She did ask me the right questions. But I'm afraid I told a little white lie. I don't personally know the client I named as my reference. I found him, and your whole client list, some other way."

A muscle ticked in his jaw. "You hacked me."

I allowed myself a little smile. "No, I *skimmed* you. But you know what I could've done if I wanted to?"

His eyes narrowed. "What?"

"Uncovered every…single…detail about you."

Silence throbbed. The muscle jumped faster. "What's to stop me from bending you over this table right now, giving you the spanking you richly deserve before I dump you in Palo Alto and walk away?" he breathed through gritted teeth.

The erotic image of his palm turning my ass pink threatened to wipe off my smile. I ignored the balloon of heat dampening my panties and traced my fingers over his jaw, suppressing a gasp at how warm and vibrant he felt.

His sharply exhaled breath washed over my face.

"Because I took a little peek at your active cases. I wanted to make sure I'd be your number one priority. Your most exciting case finished two weeks ago. You're a man of action, and you're bored, Mr. Steele. Right now mine is the juiciest case to drop into your lap."

My thumb skated dangerously close to his lips. He bared his teeth, and another image flashed into my mind—how those perfect whites would feel grazing my clit.

"I could always take the vacation I've been promising myself for a while now," he rasped.

"You won't. Because I also saw the way you looked at me when I walked into the room tonight. The way you're looking at me right now."

My fingers drifted down his solid neck to his collarbone, then over his hard chest to rest on his belt. Without breaking eye contact, I closed the gap between us and brushed my lips, whisper-light, over his, reveling in the instant clutch of lust that darkened his eyes.

"I know you're rock-hard for me, that you've imagined a dozen different positions in which to fuck me."

I drew back and pried my gaze from his to the fists clenched with white-knuckled control on the table on either side of my body. "But you won't touch me, not until you catch my stalker. Because you don't mix business with pleasure. I know that about you, too."

My hand dropped to its final destination, gliding over the stiff, mouthwateringly impressive bulge behind his fly from root to tip. A strangled growl left his throat.

"So, you think you're in charge, Mr. Steele? Dream the fuck on."

CHAPTER FOUR

Caleb

JESUS FUCKING CHRIST.

I stared at her, torn straight down the middle between fury and pleading. Between shoving her ass out of my plane and begging her to stroke my cock again. Harder. Between admitting that yes, she and her case intrigued me, and the urge to say *to hell with it*.

Back in her seat, she stared at me, a saucy smile lifting her delicious mouth. A smile I promised to wipe clean the first opportunity I got.

Shit.

Women with mouths like hers shouldn't be allowed to swear unless there was immediate, no-holds-barred fucking involved. Because between that, the almost-kiss and tortuous stroking of my dick, I was now guaranteed to walk around with a hard-on strong enough to shatter glass.

Even my fury at her invading my privacy wasn't enough to calm the fire raging in my crotch. The knowledge burned, though, along with a need to know what else she found when she went... What did she call it? *Skimming?*

Did she know about my mother's suicide? About the desperate but ultimately fruitless measures I'd used to try to save her? About that one session with the child psychologist after my meltdown? Thankfully, the nightmares that had dogged me since her death weren't on record anywhere.

Still...she'd crossed the line.

Why?

"That was a dangerous little play you staged there, Lily. Is control really that important to you?"

The answer blazed in her eyes before she lowered them. "Isn't it to everybody?" she fired back.

Okay. Control, or giving it up, was an issue for her. I tucked away that piece of info.

But despite her spine of steel, I didn't need to look hard to spot her apprehension. Plus, she was on edge. Clients in that state tended to knee-jerk the hell out of situations.

I took a breath as the plane taxied to the hangar. "You went to a lot of trouble to hire me. Don't fuck it up by digging into my life again. Trust me, I'll know. And I won't give you a pass next time. In return, I'll loop you in as much as I can. Deal?"

She stared at me, the fire raging in her eyes for another second before she offered a curt nod. "Deal."

I rose from my seat, uncaring that my erection still throbbed stiff and eager in my pants.

She'd stoked the fire. She deserved to burn a little. And from the pink staining her cheeks as her beautiful eyes dropped to my crotch, she was burning all right. Still twisting with fury and lust, I leaned down and whispered, "As for your assessment about how many ways I want to fuck you, try a few dozen times north of your calculation. And, guess what?"

Defiant eyes met mine. "What?"

"I know you want me, too, so I guess I won't be the only one suffering, huh?"

She didn't answer, not that I was expecting one.

We both retreated into our thoughts as we exited the plane.

The ride Maggie had organized was a sturdy SUV with darkened windows, which I appreciated. Sadly, there were a million ways for stalkers to spy on their victim these days, and a million ways for victims to respond if they felt powerless.

The thought triggered a question that helped to drag my attention off Lily's small but perfect body and thoughts of what I wanted to do to her. "Do you own a gun?" I asked after stashing our bag and hopping into the driver's seat.

Her eyes widened as she shut her door. "A gun? Why would I own a gun?"

"Don't look so surprised. You'd be shocked by how many people exercise their right to carry a firearm. I don't want to be surprised down the road." I rolled my shoulder as unwelcome thoughts of Kirsten, my ex, and phantom pain from my bullet wound registered.

Lily caught the movement, questions filling her eyes as she replied, "No, I don't own a gun. And I don't intend to arm myself, regardless of this situation."

"Good."

She kept quiet, until curiosity got the better of her. "Were you—?"

"You've pried enough for one night, Lily. Let's focus

on why I'm here, okay?" The snap in my voice made her flinch, but I didn't regret it.

I stuck to a quieter, longer route from the airport to Lily's address in Menlo Park. She started to fidget when we turned into the tree-lined road that housed a row of impressive mansions.

"Will your guys still be there?"

I checked the time on the dashboard. "No. Maggie texted me when they left. They'll come back tomorrow to take care of the security inside the house."

Surprise widened her eyes. "Oh. Thanks."

I glanced over to see her worrying the inside of her lip again. "You're welcome. Wanna tell me why having them inside the house makes you so nervous?"

She averted her gaze. "I'm not comfortable with strangers invading my space," she muttered.

I sensed she wasn't being entirely truthful but let the matter drop. "Okay."

She looked relieved as I checked out our surroundings.

Half of the properties were displayed in all their sprawling glory, but the other half were hidden behind palm and fir trees. Many places for a stalker to hide.

Lily pulled out her phone and hit a button on the screen, nodding at the property coming into view. "It opens the gates."

The electronic gates were swinging open much too slowly. "They need to open faster. You don't want to be a sitting duck out here while the gate takes its sweet time to let you in. I'll get it fixed."

She nodded. "Okay."

When the gap widened, I drove through. Compared to the other houses on the street, hers was on a smaller scale but still impressive enough to blend comfortably into the neighborhood.

Built on two levels with a tapered roof, the tiered white European-style mansion took up several thousand square feet, with tall rectangular paned windows that drew an inward grimace. All her stalker needed was a decent set of binoculars and he could follow her every move when she was home. And that second floor tier was also a problem especially if my suspicion that one or all of the bedrooms came with a terrace overlooking the backyard was confirmed.

The front door looked solid enough, though. I couldn't do anything about the Roman pillars framing the front porch, but the seven-foot potted plants on either side of the door needed to be relocated.

She opened her door and jumped out. I stopped myself from growling my annoyance and got out, reaching her just as she climbed the last step onto the stone-laid porch.

I touched her upper arm. "Wait."

Apprehension flickered across her face. "Your security people were just here. Surely you—?"

"Can't be too careful. Keys?"

She dug through her satchel and handed the keys over. I unlocked the door and saw a large foyer.

"There's a light switch on your left," she said.

I flicked it on, bathing the large space in a warm golden glow. An alarm beeped from a panel next to the switch. I entered the code.

Silence settled in as I took in the layout of the first floor. Two short corridors forked from the entrance foyer on either side of a grand staircase made of wood and trellised iron. At the end of the left hallway, I saw shadowy frames of sofas and a coffee table, which meant the right hallway probably led to the kitchen.

I motioned her inside and turned the dead bolt on the door. "Stay here. I'll check out the other rooms," I murmured. The gun I'd tucked in my back before we left the airport rested reassuringly against my skin.

She sucked in a slow breath before her gaze met mine. "I prefer to come with you," she whispered firmly.

The statement wasn't made out of fear of being on her own. No, Lily was nervous.

The possible reason why hit me with a punch. "Do you live here alone?" I demanded.

"What if I do?" Her chin rose, daring me to have a problem with it.

"Hey, I'm not judging." The size of the house didn't warrant the question. "I'd rather not surprise anyone at four in the morning."

Her gaze swept away. "Oh, right. No, there's no one else here," she murmured.

"Okay, you can come. Just stay behind me, got it?"

She jerked out a nod, albeit a distracted one.

There were no surprises in the kitchen or the pantry, same for the sizeable laundry room. I double-checked the outer doors to make sure they were locked before inspecting the other rooms on my way into the living room.

I guessed the reason for her uneasiness a few minutes later.

The two living rooms connected by a long entryway with a door leading to a study weren't exactly untidy, but they weren't pristine, either.

A discarded throw on one side of the sofa, an empty

glass on the table, cushions on the floor in front of a marble fireplace. Over one arm of another sofa, a tank top draped precariously with a black lace bra tucked into the sleeves. Besides the superficial untidiness, all the surfaces were clean, and the decor was tasteful enough to show someone cared enough to make the house a home.

However, when I glanced over, her cheeks were pink, adorable shades of strawberry over the cream.

"So I'm not the tidiest person in the world," she said defensively. "When I'm buried in work I forget to pick up after myself. And I gave my housekeeper time off, so…" She shrugged, then skirted the sofa, her gaze darting furtively around the room.

"You like to be comfortable in your own space. Nothing wrong with that." Except the sight of those plump cushions in front of the pale marble fireplace was restoking the fire she started on the plane.

She snatched the tank and bra off the sofa and dropped them into a cabinet drawer.

I dragged my gaze from her to properly study the room. Two sets of doors led outside. Lots of windows covered by expensive-looking drapes. All to be secured tomorrow.

As if drawn by magnets, my eyes returned to the cushions, to the hint of bright pink poking out from between two cushions. Before I could confirm what it was, Lily moved to block my view of it.

I raised an eyebrow and her color deepened.

"Shall we move on?" she blurted.

I ate the grin threatening, welcoming the chance to cool my raging libido. "By all means."

We retraced our steps to the foyer and headed downstairs to the basement.

A flick of a switch illuminated the corners of the impressive movie theater, equipped with everything a movie buff needed, including luxury loungers and an extensive 1950s-style snack and drinks bar at the far side of the room. I checked out the bar, the small pantry and the bathroom before motioning for her to enter.

She made a beeline for the front row and the object lying out in the open.

The bright pink object was the same as the one I saw upstairs, but this vibrator clearly stood out against the black sheepskin throw discarded on the middle seat facing the giant screen.

My breath locked in my lungs as an image of her spread out on the lounger with her favorite gadget between her legs sideswiped me. Before I could recover from it, another image punched through. This time I was the one positioned between her legs, seeing to her pleasure as whatever chick flick she preferred played in the background.

Only she wouldn't be able to concentrate on a single thing on the screen. Hell, no.

She would be half out of her mind, grabbing my hair and arching her back as she begged me to *please, please, please* get her off.

My pulse kicked into uncomfortable levels as I watched her grip close over the sex toy.

"Can I make a suggestion?" My tongue felt as thick as the hard-on pressing against my fly.

Her fingers clenched around the pink object. "No."

I adjusted myself before moving toward her. "If

you're that embarrassed by having anyone see your naughty toys, maybe don't leave them lying around?"

"A gentleman wouldn't mention this," she snapped.

"And a lady wouldn't have crawled onto the table on my plane, teased me with her body and stroked my cock without at least buying me a drink first, but here we are."

"I didn't stroke you…it," she replied hotly. "I just…" Her blush deepened.

I laughed, enjoying her discomfort a little too much. Not so much as the memory of her hands on me because it triggered a craving for more of the same.

"Lily, I don't really care what toys you play with so there's no need to feel bad about it. I am curious about what else you have stashed around the place, though. Personally, I like cold beers in coolers handy around my place but I guess with you it's sex toys? Is it super-efficiency or do you just get crazy impatient when the mood grabs you?"

Sharp, irritated green eyes aimed lasers at me. "I'm going to bed, Mr. Steele. Please take that as a sign that I won't be answering your inappropriate questions." She shot for the door, moving quicker than I anticipated.

I intercepted her before she reached the foyer. "I haven't checked upstairs yet."

"Then I suggest you get on with it." She headed for the stairs.

"Stop." There was more grit in my tone, more pressure in my grip.

"Don't talk to me like I'm Maggie, Mr. Steele," she bit out.

My thumb slid over her skin before I could stop myself. "I would never mistake you for Maggie. You're in

a class of your own, sweetheart. And call me Caleb."
The gruffness in my voice was a direct testament to
what touching her was doing to me.

It had some effect on her, too, if her parted lips and
the small gust of breath that escaped was evidence
enough. I was completely stumped by the effect of that
tiny sound on my dick.

The undercurrents that had swirled around us since
we first set eyes on each other strengthened by the
minute.

Shit, I needed to cool off before I did something
crazy, like drag her close and taste her sinful mouth
properly.

"Let's get this over with. Same rule applies: you
stay behind me."

After confirming everything was good, I grabbed
the bags from the car, fighting the temptation to pour
myself a drink. Much as I wasn't looking forward to
sleeping under a strange roof, I couldn't compound my
rest with alcohol. The nightmares always found a way
to filter through anyway.

Teeth clenched, I headed back upstairs.

Maybe choosing the bedroom next to Lily's wasn't
the brightest idea. Most nights the nightmares only
triggered cold sweats. But there were times when that
last image of my mother ripped...*sounds* from me.

I eyed Lily's door. She'd shut it firmly in my face
after a curt good-night.

A tight smile tugged at my mouth. She wouldn't
appreciate being called a spitfire but that was exactly
what she was. Despite the dark clothes and alabaster
skin, she blazed red-hot underneath, a fuse ready to
explode.

My grip tightened on the doorknob. Was she using her little pink toy right now to take the edge off her irritation with me? To bring much-needed relief from the shadows lurking in the dark?

Fuck, I was in danger of dying from blue balls if I didn't get myself under control.

CHAPTER FIVE

Caleb

IT WAS BARELY daylight when the ashen image of my mother's lifeless face jerked me from sleep to the pinging of the alarm. I ignored my racing heart as I sprinted for the door and yanked it open, relieved that it wasn't the continual blare announcing a possible intruder. Until I remembered that I was dealing with a tech-savvy stalker.

Downstairs, I took a moment to listen. Only the muted chorus of birdsong broke the silence.

Followed a second later by the faint splash of water. The gun I grabbed from the nightstand before leaving my room bumped against my thigh as I moved toward the open living room door and stepped through it.

Thirty feet away from the back patio, the pristine lawn gave way to stone tiles and a larger-than-average pool.

And right there, swimming without a care in the world, was Lily.

Irritation and disbelief drove me past the large ivy-twined oak pergola with the center fire pit and the loungers that stood to one side of the swimming pool.

My gaze was fixed on the figure weaving through the water, completely oblivious to my presence.

I watched her swim one lap. Then another. I breathed in and out. Slow, deep to get myself under control.

No joy.

"Lily." My voice pulsed with the quiet fury running through my veins.

She didn't stop. Her strokes were flawless and efficient, her strong kicks propelling her swiftly away from me toward the far end of the pool. I trailed after her, watched her execute a neat underwater flip, turn and launch herself into another lap. The move was smooth enough for me to see the wireless swimming earbuds plugged into her ears. My pissed-off barometer ticked up another notch.

I tugged my T-shirt over my head and stepped out of my sweatpants before diving into the pool. Two hard kicks later, she was in front of me. Alarm flared in her eyes as my hands closed on her arms. She fought back, clawing and thrashing the water before she realized who she was fighting.

In that time an unhealthy number of what-if scenarios whizzed through my head, darkening my already foul mood.

"Are you out of your mind?" I made no effort to keep my temper from showing.

She sluiced water out of her eyes with one hand and attempted to push me away with the other. The hell I was budging. "Can you not yell at me, please?"

"I asked you a question."

"Well, you're not going to get an answer if you don't let go of me. Or lower your voice by a couple of thousand decibels."

Fine, so my voice was a little loud. It was barely daylight and I'd slept like shit. "I said—"

"I heard you the first time. I'm pretty sure the neighbors heard you, too." She attempted to break free. I held her tighter, propelling her from the center to the side of the pool.

The water wasn't deep but with her small stature, her feet dangled above the bottom. When she tried to move again, I trapped her with one leg.

She wriggled, braced one hand on my shoulder. The small charge that detonated inside me at her touch was perfectly echoed in her expression. A tiny hitch in her breathing, and then her hand disappeared into the water. "What are you doing?" Her voice squeaked but that fire that was never far from the surface blazed pure challenge with her glare.

I shoved away the effect of her hand on me and glared right back. "I think that's my question. What the hell were you thinking, coming out here on your own?" I demanded.

The first rays of the sun chose that moment to emerge and bathe her face in golden light, illuminating the pearls of moisture dotting her pale, beautiful skin. I couldn't take my eyes off the three fat drops clinging to her top lip. Or the pure temptation of her full lower lip.

"I couldn't sleep. Swimming relaxes me—wait, why am I explaining myself to you?" She shifted impatiently, her toes brushing my bare calf.

I clenched my teeth and tried not to let the heat stabbing my groin distract me. Now that I had her attention, it was probably wise to let her go.

Not until I made my point.

"Do I really need to spell it out to you? And these things in your ears?" I tugged the earbuds out and tossed them onto the tiles. "How the hell do you expect to hear anything with them plugged in?"

"I always swim with my earbuds in. And no, I can do without that narrow-eyed judgment. This is my home. My life. I can do whatever I want."

"You have a thing for control. Trust me, I get it. But you don't know when this creep will step things up another level. Why the hell didn't you wake me if you wanted to swim so badly?"

She blinked. "I swim every morning, and I don't need your permission to do it."

"For fuck's sake. That's what I'm here for—"

"I'm not going to live in fear and let some random stranger pull my strings!"

The forceful words hit the tranquility of the cool morning. Echoed all around us before settling like a boulder between us. Lily froze as if her outburst had electrified her into silence. The stunned look on her face confirmed she hadn't meant to voice them.

When she went a little pale, I frowned my concern. "Lily—"

"Let me go!"

Her hands rose in the water. One braced on my stomach, the other brushed my upper thigh, then my bare hip. Her green eyes went wide. A moment later her gaze dropped down my chest, and then lower. She gasped. "Are you...*naked*?"

Despite my disgruntlement, I smiled. "I don't get my favorite sweatpants wet for just anyone, sweetheart."

Delicious heat poured into her cheeks as her hands jerked away from my body. "Oh, my God!"

"Why the outrage? Just a few hours ago you were stroking—"

"Shut up!"

I followed the blush, unable to take my eyes off the alluring sight of it. God, I wanted to taste that blush, trail it with my tongue up and down her body.

"My, what a hot little temper you have. I could—"

The words choked off as the hands that pushed me away a minute ago clutched my head and yanked me down to meet her waiting lips.

She kissed me. Then bit me. Hard. Then swallowed my stunned groan into her open mouth as she swiped her tongue over the sting. Once, twice, then with slow, dragging licks that rained fire through my body.

Jesus.

I parted my lips to better taste her. She immediately slid her tongue into my mouth, pressing her velvety lips harder against mine as she licked her way inside the way I wanted to lick her pussy—bold and relentlessly. She nipped the tip of my tongue. I groaned again at the taste of her. She was just like I imagined she would be.

Heaven and hell.

Sin and absolution.

Pleasure and—

She pushed me away as quickly as she'd pulled me close. My stunned brain was still absorbing her spectacular taste when she whirled away, planted her hands on the edge and launched herself out of the pool.

"What the fuck—?" The rush of saliva in my mouth as I watched the water glide off her body was disgraceful enough to make me grimace. Jesus, she was breathtaking.

Her glare didn't hold much power, diluted as it was by her arousal. "That was to shut you up. Nothing more."

My eager gaze raked her incredible body, took in her erect nipples, the pulse racing at her throat. "You sure about that?"

She looked off to the side. After a minute she balled her hands. "Swimming alone is off the table for now. I'll agree to that."

"Let's make a list so there's no confusion. Five minutes in the kitchen okay with you?"

Her eyes still refused to meet mine. "Fine."

Beneath the water, my cock pumped to full, eager life as the sun rose higher, giving me an even better view of her.

The black one-piece was skimpier than most two-piece suits purely because it was held together by a crisscross of ties designed to draw attention to her impressive curves. I stared my fill while telling myself if my gawking made her uncomfortable then it would be a little payback for what she'd just put me through. But I accepted that my reasons were far baser.

She looked even smaller in her bare feet. God, handling her during sex would be infinitely delightful. She turned away and my gaze dropped to her heart-shaped ass, her shapely legs and the cutest ankles I'd ever seen.

I bit back a groan as my groin kicked hard.

Hell, at this rate, I'd need a cold shower before I could conduct a coherent conversation.

When she reached the lounger and grabbed a towel, I struck out for the far side where I'd dropped my clothes.

I hauled myself out, hoping the cool air would do what the tepid water hadn't been able to achieve, and calm my excitement.

Her sharp intake of breath reached me as I bent to pick up my pants.

Don't turn around. Don't—

I turned and surprised her gaze on my ass. On any given day, I would've tossed out a cocky remark, encouraged her to look her fill if she promised to let me do the same. But we were already in uncharted territory and it'd barely been twelve hours since we met.

Not to mention, there were cameras out here, set up by my team, recording every second of our little show. Set-jawed, I pulled on my pants. First priority after our talk would be to access the security feed and delete that stretch of footage.

She'd disappeared by the time I locked the doors and went into the kitchen. Her coffee machine looked as if it hadn't been touched since it came out of the box. After setting it up, I grabbed two mugs and waited for the machine to do its thing.

She walked in just as the first cup filled. The thin, long-sleeved sweater wasn't temperature-raising in and of itself except it was cropped, exposing a good three inches of her midriff. Paired with black leggings hugging every glorious inch of hip, thigh and legs, it was incredibly potent. I swallowed a groan and busied myself making the second cup. Which took all of ten seconds.

"How do you take your coffee?"

She looked surprised at the offer. "Umm...cream with two sugars and a splash of vanilla."

I found the ingredients, stirred them into her cup and handed it over. "If it sucks, keep it to yourself."

She accepted the coffee, took a careful sip, then blinked. "It's good. Thanks."

I got mine and joined her at the kitchen island. "Why buy a coffee machine if you don't intend to use it?" I asked just for something to do other than stare at the mouth whose taste was now stuck in my head.

"I didn't buy it. It was here when I moved in, along with most of the furniture." Her reply was the stiff, don't-go-there kind.

I ignored the alarm bells. "How long have you lived here?"

Her face tightened. "Three years."

"And you've only worked for SDM?"

She nodded and leaned her hip against the counter. I forcefully redirected my gaze up to her damp hair, anything not to stare at the silky stretch of bare midriff skin or the luscious curve of her hip.

"So why not a condo nearer to SDM's offices in Sunnyvale?" This part of Silicon Valley was CEO territory, usually favored by those with families.

Her long, sooty lashes swept down. "Accommodation came as part of my signing package and this one was available. It was supposed to be temporary until I found my own place but…it grew on me. When the opportunity came up for me to buy it, I did." She shrugged. "Also saved me time on house-hunting."

The well-rehearsed answer heightened my suspicion that something else was going on here. I left it alone for the moment.

"Besides swimming, what else takes you outside on a day-to-day basis?"

"Nothing I can't live without for the time being."

"Great. So we're agreed that you'll give me a heads-up before you head outside?"

Rebellious green eyes met mine across the granite

top. "If it'll stop you from diving naked into my pool, then yes." Impatiently, she set her half-finished coffee on the counter with a snap. "By trapping me in my own home, isn't he winning?"

"You're not trapped. You just won't be doing stuff by yourself for a while. Besides, if he thinks you've got someone else in your life he might show his hand sooner."

She frowned. "Someone in my life?"

I shrugged. "He doesn't know who I am. That'll make him nervous. Enough to show his hand, I'm hoping."

She absorbed the words for several beats. "And if it doesn't?"

I felt my face harden. "Then we'll step up the game, take the fight to him."

My days of sitting around, waiting for things to happen were long behind me. Trusting other people to do the right thing for my mother had cost her the ultimate price. She'd suffered for years until she'd taken the only option she felt available to her, leaving me to deal with the aftermath.

The bitter pill I've swallowed all these years rose to the back of my throat again. Ruthlessly I pushed it back down.

Her gaze dropped for a moment. "The other reason I hired you was because your success rate is one hundred percent. I guess you're good at what you do," she murmured as she toyed with the handle of the mug.

I silenced the cocky bastard inside that wanted to strut at the hidden meaning in her words as she tugged one corner of her lower lip between her teeth. "I have a lot riding on finishing my algorithm," she added.

The admission wasn't an easy one and I admired her a hell of a lot for voicing it. It was probably why I skirted the counter to stand in front of her. Why I tucked my finger under her chin and raised her gaze to mine. "We'll catch the bastard. I promise," I said.

Her nostrils quivered delicately as she took a breath. This close, I could see the faint shadows and fear she was fighting lurking in her eyes. She'd been brave up to this point but the edges of her composure were beginning to unravel. I opened my mouth, to promise fuck knows what, but she stepped back.

"Um, about that kiss…"

The memory of it blazed a path through me. "Yeah?"

"It was out of line. I'm sorry."

"I'm…not."

She stiffened. "What?"

I tossed out an offhand shrug, despite the wide pit of *what-the-fuck-are-you-doing* yawning before me. "Technically, I didn't break my rules. *You* got me hard as fuck on the plane. *You* kissed me in the pool."

Her eyes widened. "And that makes it okay?"

"That makes me…okay with not losing any sleep over it." In fact, the more I thought about it the more I grew okay with it.

"Is that how you usually give yourself a pass?" she asked, her face tightening.

"Since you're the only client I've allowed to…handle me like that, I'll say no."

Lily's mouth dropped open.

My answering smile felt tense as thoughts of Kirsten flared up. With her, I did all the chasing, right into the trap she set for me. Since her, my personal encounters had been kept strictly sexual, with a time limit of no more than two months. I'd discovered that was when nesting behavior began cropping up.

One or two women had called me a cold bastard. I'd learned to live with it. I could probably live with Lily's brand of shutting me up, too, although I was a little unnerved that I was inviting her to smudge the lines. "So if the urge takes you, feel free to go with it."

She gasped. "Are you serious?"

I shrugged.

"Well, it won't," she said briskly. "Are we done here?"

Disappointment cut sharp but I brushed it off. "For now. My team will be here at nine to finish setting up inside. What are your plans for today?"

"I'm going to the office in a couple of hours. It's quieter on the weekend. I get a lot more done there."

"We'll go together."

She nodded and walked over to the sink with her cup. After rinsing it, she bent over to place it in the dishwasher. I ogled her heart-shaped ass for a cock-hardening few seconds before redirecting my gaze.

"I'll have the list ready for you in half an hour," she said as she walked out.

I leaned against the counter after she was gone, willing my hard-on to subside even as I tossed around the rationale I'd given her for bypassing my rules.

Would she take it? Did I really want her to?

Hell, yes!

The powerful need behind the thought propelled me from the kitchen in search of something else to occupy my mind.

For the next hour I explored the two acres attached

to the house, assessing possible weak points and compiling a list for the security team to tackle.

In the garage I found a gleaming black single-rider motorcycle with chrome detailing next to a compact Mini. Both were characteristically diverse, but somehow encompassed Lily Gracen's personality perfectly.

Smiling, I finished the check and returned to the house. I set myself up in the dining room and sent emails to Maggie and the security team. Then I logged on to the security feed, played it through until I reached the moments from the pool.

The cameras displayed shots from different angles, but the one placed in the pergola perfectly captured the moment I reached Lily. It showed the tight expression in both our faces as we talked. Her shock at finding me naked. The moment she pulled my head down for that memorable kiss. The perfect arch of her spine and ass as she rose from the water two feet from me, and my blatant hunger as I stared.

I selected the seven-minute frame and moved my finger to the delete button. Only to pause at the point when she glanced over at me after I came out of the pool. Her gaze didn't linger for more than a few seconds, but the effect of watching her watch me pull on my pants was an extreme turn-on. Like a testosterone-filled sucker, I hit Rewind. Watched the kiss. And again. Until my balls screamed under the pressure I was putting on them. Until my dick roared with the need to fuck.

Hard and fast and rough.

Damn. I wish I hadn't watched it. Lily was an extremely attractive female with a delectable exterior wrapped around a core of steel. Not to mention a healthy sex drive she wasn't shy about satisfying with sex toys.

But despite my weakness for strong, intelligent women, rules were rules. They'd kept me at the top of my game for the best part of a decade.

I shut the laptop and shoved away from the table. My hand slipped beneath the waistband of my sweatpants and I gave myself a quick, jaw-clenching few strokes before standing up.

I wouldn't touch her while she was my client. But there was nothing stopping me from ensuring the ball was kept front and center in her court.

CHAPTER SIX

Lily

HIS SECURITY TEAM arrived right on schedule.

Three men carrying six large black cases grunted various forms of hello before they went to work.

Ninety minutes later they were done and gone. The setup was state-of-the-art and discreet enough to almost blend into the decor but their presence still felt intrusive.

"How soon do you want to head to the office?" Caleb asked after running me through the security procedures.

I paused halfway up the stairs and turned to face him. He was right behind me, so close I could smell traces of chlorine mingling with his natural body scent, which didn't help my desperate need to forget what happened at the pool.

God, he'd tasted incredible—erotic, intoxicating and potentially addictive. Everything I imagined a real man tasted like. And that was with a kiss I'd surprised him with.

Like on the plane last night, taking control had felt... wonderful. Liberating. I went to sleep craving more of it. I woke to the memory of my hand stroking his thick, hard cock. It was what drove me to the pool to cool off.

Except I'd left it craving more of Caleb.

He was waiting for an answer. And I was staring at his mouth like a horny idiot.

I turned away sharply before that left brow completed its mocking ascent. "I just need to transfer data from my laptop to my office work station. So ten minutes?" I needed to be free of his distracting presence for a few hours. The man brought new meaning to the term *larger than life*.

"Sounds good."

Five minutes later I was standing in my closet, assessing my clothes with a critical eye. The notion that I was taking extra time to dress because of *him* intensified my churning emotions. But the powerful thrill that came from knowing Caleb Steele was attracted to me was unstoppable. It was the kind of power that could go to a woman's head.

But power was corruptible. I should know. Between Chance and my stepfather, they'd used their power over me to control my every move.

It wouldn't be like that between Caleb and me, though. He'd given me the green light. Hell, he'd *urged* me to use my power.

And I'd be lying if I didn't admit I was sorely tempted.

God, you're losing it.

I tugged off my leggings and replaced them with black leather pants. I kept my sweater and usual accessories of leather wrist cuffs and choker but I hesitated before reaching for my favorite red lipstick. It drew attention to my mouth, and made me feel sexy but after this morning, did I want to encourage that around Caleb?

Yes, you do. Maybe, even a little too much...

Frowning, I impatiently reached for the peach lip balm.

The earlier I got to the office, the quicker I could disappear into my work and forget my stalker, and Caleb, existed.

He was waiting at the bottom of the stairs, eyes on his phone when I reached the landing. I hated myself for half hoping he wouldn't look up while my stomach churned in hope that he would. Both wishes were answered when halfway down the stairs his head slowly lifted. His gaze collided with mine before those unnervingly hot eyes swept down my body, all the way to the tips of my heeled boots before conducting a slower return journey.

Hell, he wasn't even hiding the fact that he wanted me anymore. Now he'd told me to come for him, he was granting me unfettered access.

By the time I reached the last step, the simmering heat that hadn't quite dissipated since our pool encounter was stoked into foot-high flames, licking their way up to my nipples and turning them into traitorous points of need that stood out against my thin sweater.

As if he could read my thoughts as easily as he could read my body, his gaze dropped to linger on my breasts, then rose to my face again as his breathing altered.

I'm not sure how long we stood staring at one another.

His phone beeped with an incoming message. His gaze dropped for a second, and then he stared back at me.

"Are you ready?" His voice was gruff.

My head bobbed a nod.

As he turned to open the door, I noticed he'd changed into dark jeans, a black T-shirt and a dark brown leather jacket. "We'll take the SUV."

I stopped. "I usually go to work by bike but I understand that it's no longer a viable option. So we'll take my car."

"No disrespect to your car, but I prefer not to arrive with leg cramps. And before you say it, no, I won't follow while you drive your car."

"But—"

"Sorry, this is one of those nonnegotiable scenarios we talked about. The safe house is also still an option."

I stalked to the SUV and yanked open the door, worryingly aware this man had the ability to unbalance me with very little effort.

I studied his profile as he started the engine and rolled the large vehicle toward the gates. After he drove through, he flashed me a smile, intensifying the heat blazing through me.

God, had I not stood my ground last night, I would currently be ensconced in a cabin in the middle of nowhere with him.

Mr. if-the-urge-takes-you-feel-free-to-go-with-it.

Erotic thoughts and images bombarded me, enough to keep me silent as he drove toward SDM's Sunnyvale offices.

At the checkpoint, I showed my ID, confirmed that Caleb was with me and directed him to my parking spot.

A curl of pride drifted through me as I saw him read the sign attached to my name—*Junior Vice Pres-*

ident—Programming & Coding. Despite the yoke around my neck in the form of my debt to Chance and my stepfather, I knew I'd earned this position. That I was capable of conquering even bigger mountains. It was what I intended to do the moment I was free of my twin oppressors.

Caleb's glance showed cool respect.

A knot loosened in my chest. Which in turn made me madder that I'd wanted to see that respect in his eyes. Wanted him to see me through another set of lenses than those of a powerless victim needing help from a fixer.

Throwing the door open, I jumped out.

"Lily, wait—"

I was half a dozen cars away when he caught up with me. "What?"

"You don't rush off and leave me behind. Understood?" he gritted out. He was annoyed, too, but trying to hide it with a fake smile. His fingers slipped around my wrist, his gaze scanning the parking lot before returning to mine. "He could be anywhere, including right here in this parking lot, waiting for an opportunity to strike."

I felt the blood leave my face. His hold tightened momentarily, a gesture of comfort despite his annoyance. "I know it's a pain in the ass but it will become much easier if you accept a few temporary changes."

"Like agreeing for you to become my shadow?"

Annoyance receded to leave a smile that looked more genuine. "I was thinking more like your second skin but I'll settle for shadow."

I tried not to recall the feel of his golden skin against mine and failed miserably. "Okay, can we go now?"

"Sure."

And just like that, he'd gotten his way again. Deciding that keeping score would only mess with my sanity, I headed for my place of work.

SDM's San Francisco offices were shaped like two bananas facing each other, connected by glass and steel walkways on every floor. The hardware development and tech team took up one building, and the software, programming and coding team took up the other.

I entered the left building and smiled at the guard behind the security desk. "Morning, Charlie."

The stout, middle-aged man smiled back. "Morning, Miss Gracen."

"This is Mr. Steele. He's a...consultant visiting from LA for...a while. Can you sort out a security pass for him?"

Charlie's gaze swung to Caleb before he nodded. "Sure thing."

Caleb handed over his ID for verification, took the pass handed over and studied it with a frown as we headed for the elevator.

"What?"

He leveled his blue-eyed gaze at me. "You're a lousy liar."

Heat rushed into my face and I redirected my attention to the LED floor counter. "I'll take that as a compliment."

From the corner of my eye, I caught his deepening scowl.

"Something else bothering you, Mr. Steele?"

"Charlie suspected I wasn't a consultant, and yet he gave me a security pass anyway. I wasn't searched.

Like those rent-a-cops in LA, he would've been use-less if I truly wished you harm," he snapped.

I hit the emergency stop button on the elevator, my temper once again bubbling to the surface. "First of all, Charlie is good at his job. The normal procedure for bringing a guest into the building is way more stringent than that. He let a few things slide because *he knows me*. Second, you assume that if you'd been holding a weapon on me I would've folded like a cheap noodle. I can take care of myself. If you don't believe me, try me."

The words were hardly out of my mouth before he lunged for me. Strong hands gripped my waist, lifted me high and pinned me against the wall.

"What the hell?" My voice was a husky mess.

"Okay. Challenge accepted."

I tried to snatch the breath he'd knocked out of me with his action and proximity. All I got was a knee-weakening hit of his intoxicating scent. That and in-tense deep-blue eyes.

His gaze dropped to my lips. He exhaled, long and deep, still staring at my mouth for breath-stealing sec-onds. His grip tightened around my waist, imprinting heat from his touch directly onto my skin. A low, in-sistent throb started between my legs.

I dropped my satchel and brought one knee up, only to have him block me with a smooth deflection a few inches before it made contact between his legs. His low laugh made me see red. I slammed both wrists against his neck. The gleam in his eyes mocked me and I knew he could've evaded me if he'd wanted to. But with the semi-blunt spikes from my cuffs digging into his ca-rotid, he was going nowhere.

His thumbs pressed into my hipbones, his body pinning me harder into the wall. "And here I thought those cuffs were just to drive up a man's blood pressure," he breathed against my lips.

The ends of his hair teased my fingers, sparking a need to twist them into his hair. "You can't really be talking since I've just virtually ripped your throat out," I murmured.

He gave another laugh. "True. Score one to you."

"Great. You can...let me go now." Why did the second part of that sentence stick in my throat?

He shook his head. "Not until you agree to stop calling me Mr. Steele."

"And if I don't?" I challenged.

"Technically, I'm dying. I deserve a last wish, don't you think?"

"And your last wish is for me to say your name?"

His gaze dropped to devour my mouth. "Yeah. But I wouldn't mind another taste of you, too. Or those hot little hands on my cock again. Hell, I'll take whatever you give."

"You... I..."

"Ball's in your court, baby," he encouraged thickly, then flexed his hips, offering the vivid imprint of his cock between my thighs as he gave a strained laugh. "Literally."

Dear God. He was thick. And long.

The ache between my legs intensified a thousand times, plumping my clit as my pussy clenched hungrily. I tunneled my fingers through his hair, then grabbed a handful, exerting a little force as I hooked my legs around his waist.

His chest vibrated with a smothered growl as he

planted himself more firmly between my thighs. The layers of clothing between us were all but nonexistent as he pressed the solid rod of his cock against my sex.

"Fuck," he groaned. "Your hot little pussy feels so good against my cock."

I lowered my head until our lips were millimeters apart. Then I slowly undulated my hips, deepening the friction.

"Shit," he growled, his gaze darting between my mouth and where we were pressed together below the waist.

"You like that...Mr. Steele?" I drew my hips back up, nice and slow.

His jaw clenched tight and a shudder powered through him. "You teasing little witch. You'd like nothing better than to see me come right here, wouldn't you?" he muttered.

I wanted him to lose a little control, but not with the bothersome layers of clothes between us. I wasn't going to tell him that, though. "Would you die happy, then?"

"Not even close," he hissed. "Not when I'd rather have you, hot and wet and tight around my—"

"Hello? Is everything okay in there?" A disembodied voice asked from the panel on the elevator wall.

Caleb's jaw flexed, and he swore under his breath. "We're fine," he growled without taking his eyes off me.

"You sure? We have a technician here if you need help?" the helpful voice offered.

"Let me go," I muttered against his lips.

For a charged moment he resisted. Then his grip loosened and he allowed me to slide down the wall. With every inch, the heat of his erection singed me, announced its potency in a way that made my nipples sting and my pussy wetter.

It was ten kinds of inappropriate but for the life of me, I couldn't summon an ounce of regret. All I could think about was what it would feel like to have that thickness *inside* me.

"To be continued, I hope," he murmured against my cheek as my feet met the floor.

He took a step back. Then another. Reluctantly, his hands dropped. Then, without taking his eyes off me, he stabbed the button that released the elevator.

The small rattle before the carriage continued its journey restored some sanity. But even then a large part of me was suspended in disbelief at what I'd done.

Sex with Scott—before I found out that Chance had planted him in my life to control and spy on me—had been lukewarm at best.

What happened to my body when it was within touching distance of Caleb was nothing short of stupefying.

I avoided looking at him as I led us through the open plan space that led to my corner office. Like most tech companies in Silicon Valley, the space was designed to invite easy lounging with the aim of sparking ideas through socializing.

I entered my office, set my satchel down and fired up my three monitors. From the corner of my eye, I saw Caleb checking out the area before refocusing on me.

When he started walking toward me, I reached into my satchel. "Here's the list you asked for."

His hot gaze lingered on my face and mouth for a few ferocious moments before he took the piece of paper. "Thanks."

"If you need somewhere to work, there's a spare desk and computer next door."

He reached into his jacket and I forced myself not to ogle the way his T-shirt stretched across his torso. "No, thanks. This is all I need." He waved his phone at me.

He walked across the room, dropped onto the sectional sofa next to the wall and propped one foot on the coffee table. A minute later his fingers were flying over the keyboard.

I greatly resented the fifteen teeth-grinding minutes it took for me to focus, but eventually I was back in the groove. I spent the next few hours going over the tweaks I'd made that morning.

The snags my coding had hit were frustrating, but I couldn't rush this or SDM would miss the first major beta-testing deadline.

Not gonna happen.

My burning need to be done with Chance depended on everything going smoothly.

There were times I wished I hadn't hacked him. Times I wished I'd called his bluff when he'd turned up at my house with a patrol car and threatened me with jail unless I did what he—and my opportunity-grabbing stepfather—wanted.

Thoughts of how easily Stephen Gracen had thrown his own stepdaughter under the bus slashed painfully through me.

I was stealthily breathing my way through it when Miranda, my assistant, entered.

Her gaze swung to Caleb. And stayed.

His head snapped up, but the laser-eyed scrutiny he'd given my other employees was nowhere in sight.

Instead, a slow smile broke over his face as he stared at my tall, attractive assistant.

"Hi," he drawled, slowly rising to his feet.

Miranda's toothpaste-white smile lit up her face. "Hi, I'm Miranda." She strode to him, her hand outstretched. "And you are?"

He took her hand. "Caleb."

"Caleb. Hi," she repeated. Then just stood staring up at him.

I slowly disengaged my clenched jaw. Cleared my throat. They both looked at me.

I opened my mouth to explain Caleb's presence, then remembered his gibe about me being a lousy liar. When his eyebrow started to creep up, I redirected my attention to Miranda. "I wasn't expecting you in today."

She reluctantly dropped Caleb's hand, but I noticed a pronounced sway in her hips as she crossed to my desk. "It was either go off-road biking with the guys from design or finish the assignment you gave me on Wednesday."

"It could've waited till Monday," I replied. Her work had nothing to do with my secret project but she had an aptitude for programming that I utilized when necessary.

She shrugged. "Programming beats the risk of a broken arm, no matter how exhilarating the boys claim biking can be." She glided a hand over her sweater dress and glanced at Caleb. "I prefer a different type of excitement."

He slid his phone into his back pocket and crossed his arms, and I swore Miranda groaned under her breath.

"I'll let you get on with it, then." I couldn't help the irritation filtering through my voice.

She nodded, then flicked Caleb one last glance. "See you around?"

Caleb smiled. "I'm sure you will."

To his credit, or more likely because he knew he could have her if he wanted, he didn't watch her sashay to the door. Instead, he turned his blue gaze on me.

Oh, hell no. I wasn't about to answer questions about Miranda.

The tall brunette could double as a supermodel any day of the week, and was constantly hit on outside the office.

And technically, she didn't fall under Caleb's no-dating-clients rule.

I fixed my gaze on my screen and continued working.

He got the message and returned to the sofa.

An hour later his shadow fell across my desk.

The breath I sucked in didn't quite catch. Irritated by my body's continued betrayal, I raised my head. "Can I help you?"

His mouth twisted in a parody of a smile. "You seem different. Much less…tense." He snapped his fingers. "That's it. You look relaxed."

I cursed the flush that crawled up my neck. "I don't know what you're talking about."

"Sure you do. You're in your element."

"Is this conversation going anywhere? I have a ton of work—"

My breath rushed out when he leaned across the desk and drifted a finger down my cheek. "You really don't need to be so jumpy around me. You especially don't need to get defensive every time I give you a compliment."

"I wasn't—"

"You want to pretend you're offended because I said you're more at home here with your computers than in that gilded cage you call a home. But you don't have to be."

The accuracy of his words made me jerk away from his touch.

My house was luxurious on many levels. But there was more to what I'd told Caleb last night. Truth was, it was also my cage. Chance had stashed me there when I'd first arrived in San Francisco because he'd wanted me isolated. *Still* wanted me isolated. For now it was a place to eat and sleep but it would never be my home.

Caleb was watching me closely, reading my every expression.

My gaze dropped to his throat as I cleared mine. "I'm not. You're mistaken."

He sighed. "What's your favorite restaurant?"

I blinked. "What?"

"Food. Lunch. Where?"

"Why?"

"Jesus. You love making me sweat, don't you, Lily?"

My fingers curled around the edge of my desk, unable to stop myself from replaying those moments in the elevator. The feel of his cock between my legs, his strained voice as he whispered his wishes to me.

All that power and glory under my control…

He leaned closer, sunlight glinting off his dark, mahogany-tipped hair. "What's going through that mind of yours, I wonder?"

I dragged my gaze from his body and named the

Japanese restaurant I liked. He tapped it into his phone and I heard a whoosh of a text.

"Why do we need to go out at all? This place has a takeout service. We could just order in."

He shook his head. "Like I said, it's time to change things up a little. Your stalker knows your routines so let's introduce a new element into the equation."

"Let me guess? You?"

"Yep. We're putting ourselves out there. Besides, I have questions about the people on the list you gave me. I prefer we do it somewhere we won't be interrupted." He jerked his head to where a couple of analysts conversed outside my office. One of them looked up and started to wave.

Caleb's glower froze it dead. They quickly dispersed.

"Wow, you must be very proud of yourself," I said.

He turned back. "Last night you told me what you're working on is top secret."

"It is."

He indicated the clear glass windows. "I would've thought you'd be locked away in a basement somewhere in one of those Faraday Cages."

I opened my mouth, closed it again and tapped a command to shut down my laptop.

"Come on. I'll show you how it works. Then maybe you'll stop glaring at everyone who comes into my office."

He smirked. "I can't make that promise. And I didn't glare at *everyone*."

No. Miranda got the full effect of his megawatt smile. I didn't want to examine why that bothered me so much.

In the elevator, I made sure to keep a distance between us although I didn't escape the sizzling heat of his gaze as he lounged against the opposite wall.

Damn, I'd probably never ride an elevator again without thinking about Caleb Steele.

The code I inputted dropped us down to Basement Level 3. The guard outside the elevator took Caleb's electronic gadgets. We walked down a corridor to a silver metallic door.

"To answer your question, both buildings are equipped with specialist reflective glass that makes it hard to spy on monitors from outside. And then there's this." I led him into a warehouse-size room completely empty except for the large meshed structure in its center with a desk and one chair.

"The Faraday Cage," Caleb muttered.

I nodded.

"What's that?" He nodded to the pedestal set up against the left wall with a small laptop built into it.

"Every keystroke I make on my laptop or work station upstairs is immediately saved into that laptop. Every twenty-four hours, I transfer data from the laptop to the supercomputer in the cage. Hacking it isn't impossible, but it'll be very difficult. And I didn't come down here to work because as you can see there's only room for one down here." I didn't want him prowling outside the cage, like a predator wolf, disturbing me with his presence.

Caleb walked around the cage, examined every inch of the space before returning to where I stood.

"You designed all this?"

I licked my top lip. "Yes."

His gaze heated up, his eyes telling me he wanted to touch me and do other intensely filthy things to me. Things forbidden by his rule. "All that beauty and brains in this killer little package."

That darned swell of pride rose again, mingling with the sizzling fires his eyes evoked in me. "Is that your way of saying you're impressed?"

"It's my way of saying I'm *very* impressed."

Before I could stop myself, I was smiling, shamelessly basking in his praise.

His eyes dropped to linger on my mouth, and his nostrils pinched a little as he inhaled. "You have a beautiful smile, Lily. You should use it more often."

I knew Caleb was attracted to me, but the look in his eyes as he called me *beautiful* shook loose something mildly disquieting inside me.

Just shut up and enjoy the moment.

Except I was enjoying too much of it altogether.

I was paying him to be here. Once his job was done, this would be a distant memory.

Unless you make it infinitely memorable?

I turned away sharply, the potency of that temptation taking me by surprise. Under the guise of taking the laptop to the Faraday Cage to transfer my latest work, I couldn't stop thinking about the possibilities.

Caleb and me.

Doing the dirty.

Last night he'd given me the green light. This morning in the elevator, he'd all but begged me to third-base him.

What was stopping me?

The discovery that Scott was just a pawn strategically placed in my life and not just a guy I'd met at a party and subsequently dated had left a huge deficit in my trust bank, not to mention a gaping vacancy in my sex life. This might be my chance to balance the sex part without the messiness of wondering about authentic emotions.

Plus, if our three brief encounters were an indication, the sex would be off the charts.

"Lily."

God, that voice. Would he sound like that when he was deep inside me, pounding my brains out?

"Lily?"

I snatched in a breath, schooled my expression and turned. "Yes?"

"You done?" he asked with a raised eyebrow.

"Uh-huh."

"Good. Time for lunch."

As we entered the elevator, I remembered other fragments of our conversation upstairs. "You said you had questions."

He was watching me with hooded eyes as if he knew the thoughts running through my head. "Yeah," he replied absently.

"What kinds of questions?" I asked.

He slid his hands into his back pockets. "Different kinds. Personal and professional. Wanna start with the personal?"

My breath caught. "I—"

"Great. When was the last time you had sex?"

CHAPTER SEVEN

Caleb

"YOU'RE GOING TO have to answer me sometime."

After a sharp intake of breath and a furious blush, which took all my severely tested control not to trace with my fingers, she'd clammed up.

To be fair, having a couple of SDM employees join us in the elevator had put the brakes on that conversation.

But she'd maintained silence in the SUV and all the way to the restaurant.

I parked in front of the Japanese restaurant, ignoring the valet waiting for us to exit the vehicle.

"I'm happy to repeat the question if you want? Sex, Lily. When—?"

"I heard you the first time," she snapped, puffing out an annoyed breath as she reached for the door.

I stepped out, a little annoyed with myself, too. Truth be told, I didn't intend to ask her that. Not immediately.

But as suspected, with every revelation of her brilliance, I grew more attracted to Lily Gracen. I'd come within a whisker of calling bullshit on my own rules and kissing her in the Faraday Cage room. After that little cock-teasing incident in the elevator, who the hell would've blamed me? Shit, I was getting hard just thinking about the way she'd worked me between her legs.

And yes, I was a little peeved that she managed to get herself under control before I did. All the same, this was a subject that needed addressing, so why the hell not?

I made eye contact with the two-man security team I had Maggie send ahead, and escorted Lily into the restaurant. The waiter showed us to the private booth I requested.

"Lily." Maggie called this my rumbling volcano voice. "This will go a lot faster if you didn't stop to dissect every question or take offense at it."

She barely blinked at my don't-fuck-with-me tone, studied the menu for a minute before she closed it with a snap. "What has sex got to do with anything?" she hissed.

I shrugged. "Maybe nothing. Maybe everything. I thought you were in a hurry for this to be over?"

"I am, but—"

"How old are you?" It was another pertinent question I hadn't yet asked. She was over the age of consent but the flashes of innocence I spotted every now and then demanded investigation.

"Twenty-four," she answered with a frown. "How old are *you*?" she tossed back.

If she didn't know then she'd told the truth about skimming my past. That put a plus tick in her favor.

"I'm asking the questions here, but if it'll make you

cooperate, I'm twenty-nine. I'm six-foot-four. I have all my own hair and teeth. Oh, and I'm single."

A hungry little expression flitted across her face but she hid it well. "How long have you been a fixer?" she returned.

"You must have missed what I just said about questions."

"I'm supposed to trust you with my safety. I deserve to know a little bit about you, don't you think?"

Fair point. In her shoes, I would have a few hundred questions, too. She wasn't a blind follower. Another turn-on. Still… "You get three questions. *After* you answer all of mine."

That earned me a sarcastically raised eyebrow that somehow managed to connect straight to my cock. Fuck.

"What's your deal with SDM? You said you had history," I said.

Her face immediately shuttered. "They put me through college and hired me straight after."

Interesting. "And college was?"

"MIT."

"You're from the East originally?"

The waiter arrived at our table. Lily ordered a soda and six bite-size platters of assorted dishes without consulting the menu.

"I'll have what she's having but with a beer," I said.

The waiter nodded and hurried away.

"Why does it matter whether I'm from the East or not?" she asked warily.

"Is that one of your questions for me?"

"It's a query generated by the fact that I think you're wasting time on pointless questions."

She was unsettled by my line of questioning. Which triggered a need to know more. "You're being stalked, Lily. You don't think details of your background will inform me as to who is after you?"

Her shoulders slumped a little but in direct contrast, her chin angled up. "Fine, I grew up in Maine, but we moved to Boston when I was ten."

"We?"

"My stepdad and I. And before you ask, neither of my biological parents are in the picture. They haven't been for a very long time."

I crunched on that piece of information for a minute. I wanted details but sensed it wasn't an easy subject, so I dropped it. I had ways to find that out on my own anyway.

"You have a boyfriend?" Living alone didn't mean she wasn't seeing anyone.

Her mouth—her very fuckable mouth—compressed but I spotted the flicker of anguished fury in her eyes. The kind that came from a nasty betrayal. "No. I don't have a boyfriend. If I did, I wouldn't—" She stopped short.

"What? Have sex toys?" I shrugged. "That could indicate a voracious appetite, not the absence of a sex life. Although I'm guessing you're not the kind of girl to wrap your legs around a man's waist and rub your pussy so beautifully against his cock if you belonged to another?"

"God, you're unbelievable," she said under her breath.

"I'm plain-speaking. There's a difference, sweetheart." Mixed signals led to complications. After Kirsten, I wasn't prepared to take that risk.

"When was your last relationship, casual or otherwise?" I pressed. It was obvious I would need to pry every piece of info from her.

Her gaze dropped, and she toyed with the tableware. "Eight months ago."

"How long were you together?" *Where did you meet? I hope he was a lousy kisser and even worse in bed.*

Jesus, Caleb. Get a fucking grip.

"Six months."

Not long by any stretch, but long enough for me to be mildly jealous at the thought of some guy having a claim on her.

The waiter's arrival gave me a moment to examine that jealousy, grimace with disgust at myself for sticking steadfastly to my second and third rules.

I watched her pick up a roll of sushi with her chopsticks and dip it in teriyaki sauce. I did the same and we ate in silence for a while.

"Who ended the relationship?"

She froze. I couldn't stop myself from staring at her glistening mouth, wondering how it would feel when I slid my cock between her lips.

I looked up. She was staring at me. Her cheeks heated up as she accurately read my thoughts.

"Answer the question, Lily."

She dropped her chopsticks, her face tightening again. "I did. And you're wasting your time with this. Scott isn't the one doing this."

"I'll be the judge of that—"

"No! I know what I'm talking about so please drop it," she hissed.

"Not until you tell me why any guy whose veins

aren't filled with ice water would quietly walk away from you?"

Her lashes swept down for a moment, then rose again, a challenging fire in her eyes. "Not every guy I come into contact with is a potential stalker."

"Scott wasn't just any guy, though, was he? What aren't you telling me, Lily?"

She remained silent for a long stretch. And I waited her out, biting down my impatience.

"Because Scott wasn't just a guy I met at a party. Chance paid him to seek me out."

Shock bolted up my spine. "What? Why?"

She swallowed and her hands balled into small fists. When she lifted her gaze her beautiful green eyes were far too haunted. "Because he wanted...*wants* to control me."

Jesus. "Again, why?"

"What does it matter?" she snapped. "All you need to know is SDM and Chance need this algorithm. It'd be absurd for him to jeopardize it by having someone stalk me, so just...just take my word for it that it's not Scott, okay?"

I didn't voice the world's worst cliché right then because I didn't want to piss her off even more, or sound like a hormone-addled teenager but, fuck me, she was so incredibly gorgeous when she was mad I lost the ability to think clearly for a minute.

I let her take the deep breaths she needed to calm down.

"You slip into Bostonian when you're agitated, you know that? It's cute."

She looked adorably nonplussed before she shook her head. "Nothing about any of this is *cute*, Mr. Steele."

"I disagree. I wonder, do you sound like that during sex, too?"

Green eyes snapped fire at me. "You'll *never* find out."

I couldn't help myself. I had to touch her again. I reached out and traced the curve of her lower lip with my finger. Soft. Firm. Satin-smooth. "Are you sure about that, Lily?"

She inhaled sharply and her eyes turned a shade darker. "Can we not turn everything into a sexual tennis match? It's really exhausting."

Reluctantly, I retreated. "Has there been anyone else since Scott?"

She picked up her chopsticks again. "Someone briefly. Nothing serious."

"Who, and for how long?"

She sighed. "Mark Callen. For two months. He bought me a coffee at where I get my breakfast. I… I wanted to make sure Chance wasn't still interfering in my life."

My jaw gritted. "Was he?"

She shook her head.

I relaxed a little. "Did you sleep with him?"

Her glare burned me but I didn't let up.

"No," she answered eventually.

I was swimming in relief when she took a sip of her soda. I watched her throat move, wondering why the hell I found that so sexy.

Hell, was anything about her not sexy?

Yeah, the way she kept snippets of information from me. That didn't turn me on even a little.

That Chance thing really pissed me off, though. I made a note to have the asshole checked out.

As for Lily, I wanted to know everything about her. Lily Gracen fascinated me the way no other woman had.

"So you went out with him for two months but didn't sleep with him. What the hell did you do? Hold hands and read each other poetry by candlelight?" I asked.

"So what if we did?" she lobbed straight back.

"Then I'd say it's great you dumped the dickless wonder. You deserve way better than that."

"God, you really are a Neanderthal, aren't you?" she snapped before pushing her plate away. Apparently, we were done eating.

"No, I'm a man with basic but fundamental needs. If I have to endure the R word, then I sure as hell expect some regular fucking as part of the bargain. Otherwise, what's the point?"

"So sex has to be a guarantee in a *relationship* or you're out?"

I took in her white-blond hair and the choker around her neck that howled at me like a damn siren call. The semi-erection that flared to life if she so much as breathed in my direction thickened behind my fly. "I like sex. It's the single decent thing the good Lord granted humanity. I feel zero guilt for loving it. So yes, sex is a hell of a priority for me."

Fresh heat flared in her cheeks, but she still delivered the most dick-torturing smile I'd ever seen. "Except when it comes to your clients, though, right, Mr. Steele?"

Dammit. She was too fucking much. I breached the gap between us, spiked my fingers into her hair and tightened my fist.

She glared at me but didn't struggle to get away.

"I'm beginning to think you enjoy taunting me by refusing to use my name," I breathed.

"I don't have a problem with saying your name."

I tugged her even closer. "Then do it."

She looked me straight in the eyes, her tongue darting out to moisten her lips. "Caleb."

I tilted her head until she had no choice but to raise that gorgeous face, offer up those luscious lips to me. "Again."

She glared fiercer at my instruction, then parted her lips. "Caleb."

The soft, whispered delivery was deliberately provocative. I knew it. But it still chopped me off at the knees. "Fuck." With a groan, I lowered my head, but stopped a breath from her lips. "Kiss me, Lily."

"Why?" she breathed defiantly even as her eyes devoured my mouth.

"Because you're *dying* to. Take it, baby. Take what you want."

Her ragged moan was music to my ears but hell for my cock. All the same, I let go of her, put the power in her hands and nearly roared with triumph as she leaped on me.

And goddamn it all to hell if she didn't taste twice as heady, twice as decadent, as before.

It started with one hot little sound under her breath as my teeth grazed her bottom lip. A cross between a whimper and a sigh, it snaked down my groin, curled itself around my cock and stroked me into rigid life. And that was before I'd even tasted her properly. I nipped her again, resisting the urge to take a deeper, more satisfying bite.

The promise of more lay within, but I was more than

content, for now, to just sample her plush lips. Over and over. To hear the tiny sounds turn into moans, to feel her strain toward me as her own hunger clawed at her.

Her hands delved beneath my jacket, clawed at my T-shirt before she slipped them underneath.

In that moment I stopped caring that we were in a public place.

A breath I didn't remember holding expelled from me as her small nails dug into my skin. I suppressed a growl and fought the need to ravage, reminding myself that besides every shitty thing happening in her life, she hadn't had sex in a while. Exhibiting even a fraction of the wild craving whipping through me might send her into retreat mode, and fuck if I was going to allow that to happen.

But God, she was exquisite. The way her lips clung to mine was driving me insane.

"Jesus, you taste amazing." I couldn't help the words from spilling out when we broke apart to get a hit of oxygen.

She tensed. I sucked her bottom lip into my mouth and trailed my tongue over her velvety skin. A sigh and a moan rewarded my effort.

I'll stop in a minute.

We hadn't finished our talk. Plus, we needed to put on the brakes before we were thrown out for public indecency.

Besides, I couldn't sustain this much longer. Not without throwing my rules out the window, flattening her to the booth seat and delivering on every single promise and filthy fantasy I'd harbored since she walked into my life.

But I *could* drag her a touch closer. I *could* slide one

hand down her back and mould it around her pert little
ass, reconfirm that her flesh was as tight and supple
as I imagined.

I would stop. Right after she gave me another of
those exceptionally indecent moans.

CHAPTER EIGHT

Lily

HOLY. SHIT.

What the hell was happening to me? Why did Caleb only need to crook his finger before I threw common sense out the window and jumped him?

And these sounds I was making? Yeah, I *really* needed to stop moaning like a whore in church. But up until a minute ago, he'd let me take the lead in our little make-out session.

Then something flipped.

Now, the way he was using his mouth, his tongue, heck, his teeth? In the few times I let him kiss me, Mark's teeth always managed to collide with mine, generating an unpleasant nails-on-a-chalkboard sensation.

Caleb knew how to use his. Little nips at the corner of my mouth that shot fire straight between my legs, even bites on the very tip of my tongue where I had no clue I was so sensitive.

Our previous encounters, I'd felt like I'd plugged into a steady current. *This* was probably what it felt like to bungee jump off a helicopter over a live volcano after being injected with pure adrenaline.

Three numbskulls from the research department confessed to doing that once for the intense rush. I still believed they were completely insane, but if what they experienced was remotely close to what I was feeling now, then…yeah…I got why they would chase such a thrill.

Caleb's tongue swiped between my lips, instantly igniting a yearning to feel it swiping between my legs on its way to concentrate on my clit, now throbbing insistently.

And God, his hand was kneading my ass in that superhot way again.

His hand slipped lower to the curve of my butt and nudged me closer until somehow, I was in his lap. Was that the slow grind of the thick erection against my thigh? Holy…God. He felt even bigger than this morning in the elevator.

The thought of all that power and girth inside me freaked me out a little. Okay, a *lot*.

Until I reminded myself that I had the power. I could stop anytime I wanted. By simply pulling back. Letting go.

Let go!

I dragged my hand down from where it'd ended up on his ripped chest. Down to his waist, to the solid square of his belt buckle. Any lower and I would touch his cock again. I moaned at the intense urge to do just that.

Then I heard the faint clink of cutlery.

We were in a restaurant. In a private booth, yes, but still a public place. And for the third time since I woke up, I was sucking face with the man I'd hired to find my stalker.

Oh, God.

Maybe that adrenaline kick I imagined had really been a hormone shot? Because the sensations racing through my body all craved one thing—Caleb's cock inside me.

I scurried backward from the hot body and the erection digging into my thigh. One hand was still buried in my hair, imprisoning me as he stared down at me with fiery eyes that promised as much filthy fucking as his lips had pledged.

"Lily." His voice was thick. He cleared his throat and swallowed.

Those few precious seconds helped me put more daylight between us. I grabbed his wrists and tugged his hands from my body. He dropped them but not his searing gaze.

I busied myself by picking up my glass of soda and taking a sip I prayed wouldn't choke me. Thankfully, it went down smoothly, cool enough to restore a tiny bit of sanity. "So, you think this little display helped?"

His eyes narrowed. "What?" He shifted away and dropped one hand into his lap. I forced myself not to watch him adjust the bulge behind his fly.

"My stalker. If he's watching. You think it helped or was it all a waste of time?" I forced out as I smoothed my hands over my hair. My scalp still tingled deliciously from when he'd grabbed and pulled my hair. Did he do that during sex, too? I slammed my thighs together before the image of him doing that added to the fire scorching my pussy.

He exhaled sharply. "That wasn't why you kissed me and you know it."

"Do I?" I challenged because, *dammit*, I was out of sorts in more ways than one, and this seesawing from being in total control to losing it around him was driving me nuts.

His eyes gentled. "You don't need to panic, Lily. I'm not going to use this against you. That's what you're afraid of, isn't it?"

My breath shuddered out as panic flared. "Stop talking as if you know me. You don't!"

"I know that control is important to you. Is it because of what your asshole boss did? I'd be wary, too—"

"Tell me why you're so hung up on *your* rules. Is it because of what a *client* did to you?" I lashed out, terrified of how effortlessly he was probing beneath my skin.

A muscle rippled in his jaw. "We're not talking about me."

I forced a laugh. "That tells me everything. Who was she?" I pressed.

His whole face grew taut. "Nobody you need to concern yourself with," he bit out.

The confirmation that someone somewhere had affected him enough to drive his guard up hit me with unnerving disquiet. Nearly as much as his accurate divining of my panic.

"Fine. Can we leave now?" I cringed at the stress in my voice.

He inhaled slow and deep, and then pulled out his wallet.

"I have an account here. They'll put it on my tab," I said.

He scowled as he placed a couple of hundred dollar bills on the table. "I brought you to lunch. I'm paying."

Outside, the brilliant sunlight reminded me it was still daytime. That I had many more hours of work ahead of me.

About to get in the SUV, I caught Caleb scanning the street, his gaze alert. I knew he had men out there but the fact that he was in fixer/protector mode despite the turbulence between us shook loose something I hadn't felt in a long time.

Warmth.

The memory of it was ephemeral—the contented seven-year-old tucked in her mother's arms with no clue that a mother's love could be temporary like everything else.

You're truly losing it.

I slammed the door and shook my head.

Like the outbound journey, neither of us spoke as we drove back to SDM but I knew I had to say something as he pulled up into my parking space.

I undid my seat belt, faced him and opened my mouth. He grabbed me and pulled me across the center console.

"I know it's insane, and we'll both probably regret it, but fuck, I need to kiss you again," he breathed roughly against my mouth.

Before I could take a breath, his tongue slid into my mouth. Wet and insistent and carnal. It was the dirtiest promise of sex I'd ever known. Over and above every inappropriate sexual thing he'd said to me since we met, it was that decadent slide of his tongue against mine that did me in. My hands returned to dig into his waist, my torso straining across the small space to slide against his.

He banded one hand around my waist and lifted me over to his side. And just like that the heat of his cock was a living thing against my ass, announcing its insistent virility. I moaned, half-ashamed at how easily I'd fallen into the kiss, half-fearful of his sensual power over me.

Slowly, that fear built, insidiously reminding me that this was no longer my default setting. I was so close to true freedom for the first time in my life. I couldn't become a slave to my hormones or my emotions.

I pushed at Caleb's chest before the hand sneaking up my waist could cup my breast. "Stop!"

He froze immediately.

I took a breath. "Let me go."

He stared at me for a full minute, his chest rising and falling in harsh pants. Then his hands dropped from my body.

I hopped over into my seat, struggling with my own breathing.

"Jesus," he swore under his breath, slammed his head against the headrest and closed his eyes. After tense seconds he opened them. "I'm…" He stopped and gritted his teeth. "Hell, I suppose you want an apology?" Before I could answer, he continued, "You're not going to get one because I'm not sorry. You, with that tight, gorgeous body and that bruised, ripe mouth, are fucking irresistible," he growled.

My lungs deflated in a giddy rush. Heat spiked through my blood, and my panties grew shamelessly damper. Every atom in my body strained to jump into his lap and continue where we'd left off. I curled my nails into my palms until tiny bites of pain brought a little clarity.

"I'm afraid you'll have to resist."

To my surprise, he nodded. "Understood."

My jaw threatened to drop. I caught myself, then shifted my gaze from his face. Now I'd successfully drawn the line, I didn't know what to do next.

He answered by stepping out and escorting me inside.

In my office, he calmly returned to the sofa. While I spent the next hour rewriting the same code.

I called it a night at six. He drove us home after stopping to pick up the takeout I'd ordered.

Over dinner, he asked me a bunch of work-related questions, probing my routines and those of my team. Any trace of the fever that overtook us in the restaurant and the parking lot was wiped from his features as he listened and made notes on his laptop.

Just before nine, he sat back in his chair, his eyes on his screen. "That's enough for today. I'll see what I can dig up with this info." His tone was impersonal as he stood and picked up the plates and empty cartons. He helped clean up and stack the dishwasher, maintaining a chilly distance that made my stomach muscles tighten.

You wanted this. Professional distance is good.

When we were done, I turned to leave.

"Remember, you need to let me know if you're going outside," he said.

My face felt stiff so I didn't even attempt a smile. "I haven't forgotten."

He stared at me for a beat then nodded.

In my den I made a stab at work for a solid hour before giving up and giving in to a burst of resentment. I swiveled in the seat and stared out the window.

Caleb probably thought he was only doing his job, but his interrogation had peeled back a thin layer of memories I wanted to keep buried.

Boston. My mother.

Frustration threatened to build as I paced from window to wall and back again. My restlessness eventually drove me to the cinema room and I halfheartedly settled for a new rom-com I wasn't really in the mood for.

I startled awake to a blank screen and a sore neck. When my disorientation cleared, I noticed a blanket that had been draped over me and there were cushions I'd dislodged in my sleep, which weren't there before.

My heart lurched as that warmth encroached again, teasing me with its comfort. I pushed it away, got up and stumbled upstairs to bed.

Caleb Steele, like everyone in my life, was a transient, *paid* presence.

Nothing else.

Sunday was a repeat of Saturday, minus the mind-melting making-out sessions, the probing questions into my sex life and the sexually loaded banter.

That set the course for the next three days.

On Thursday we returned to the Japanese restaurant and picked our way through an uncomfortable meal.

As he wove through light traffic on the way back to SDM, I glanced at him, that little morsel he'd let drop on Saturday returning like a nagging toothache.

Who was the client who'd triggered his rule? Was he or, as I suspected, *she*, still in his life?

At a stoplight he speared me with dark blue eyes. "Something on your mind?" His tone was cool. That plus the absence of his mocking eyebrow lift rattled me more than I cared for. It was like he had become a different person after the episode in the parking lot.

I reminded myself that I'd only known him for a handful of days.

That first night and day had been...out of the norm. Intense. We were both fighting for control. We'd reached an understanding and now he was focused on what he came here to do.

This was the real Caleb Steele. End of story.

So this unsettled sensation that had carved a small hollow in my stomach was misplaced. Right?

I looked away from his piercing eyes. "Nope. Nothing at all."

He drove on, dismissing me as coolly as he'd done for the past few days.

Unfortunately, the sensation knotted inside me wasn't as easy to dismiss. Admitting I wanted the dirty-tongued, brooding-eyed Caleb back was...hard.

I glanced out the window, frowning at my reflection when I caught myself biting my lip. I had more important things to dwell on than which version of my fixer I preferred. Besides, what the hell could I do? Crawl into his lap, drag my fingers through his hair and kiss him the way I'd wanted to do on Saturday before sanity returned?

The dragging sensation in my belly gave me the answer.

I avoided his gaze for the remainder of the journey.

The fretful but excited buzz in the air when we

reached my floor was a great excuse not to hunt for an answer right then.

"What's going on?" Caleb asked as we entered my office.

"We're presenting a midseason upgrade on two SDM products to the board tomorrow. The day before is always a little frantic."

His gaze narrowed slightly as he watched me. "That doesn't include what you're working on, does it?"

"No. That's still confidential. But I'll be giving a presentation of my own to three of the board members tomorrow, too."

"Which members?"

"Chance and two of his colleagues." I couldn't keep the stiffness out of my voice.

He noticed. "He's coming here?" he rasped.

I swallowed at the volatile vibes oozing from him. "Yes."

His gaze narrowed on me for several heartbeats. "Okay, I'll need the names of the colleagues."

I gave him the names, unable to stop the chill spreading over my nape. "Why?"

His stare was direct. "Everyone who has access to you is a suspect until I catch this asshole. Don't underestimate anyone, Lily. And if you can help it, don't trust anyone, either. That way you'll avoid any nasty surprises."

He turned away but not before I caught a flash of pain in his eyes.

Add the confounding emotions coiling through me, it rooted me to the spot for several heartbeats until a knock on my door snapped me free. By the time I finished dealing with my team member's query, Caleb was on his phone.

We worked late into the night, then headed down to the seventh floor where the in-house catering staff had laid out a buffet-style meal in the dining room.

Although Caleb stayed close by, he didn't engage in conversation. I tried not to glance his way, but it proved almost impossible. Especially when Miranda slid into the seat next to him, and he gave her one of those smiles that had been absent for almost a week now.

I turned away, finished the chicken parmesan I didn't really want, while doing my best to reassure the two tech newbies on either side of me that they wouldn't tank their presentation tomorrow.

I wasn't sure what made me glance over at Caleb halfway through my conversation. His eyes were fixed on me, a ripple of muscle ticking in his jaw as he clenched his teeth.

Abruptly, he stood and walked around to where I sat. "Are you done eating?" He glanced pointedly at my plate.

"Yes."

"You ready to head out?" he asked, flicking a cold glance at one newbie, who cowered away from the arctic mountain glowering at him.

I considered calling Caleb out on his rudeness, but it had been a long, draining day. I really wanted to get out of here. And it had absolutely nothing to do with wanting to get him away from Miranda, who was eyeing Caleb with barely disguised hunger.

I swallowed a knot of irritation. "Don't stay too long, Miranda. I need you back here by seven."

Her gaze swung to me, and I swore I caught a flash

of something nasty in her eyes. A moment later it was gone. "Sure thing, boss. I'll make sure you're all set to go."

Caleb's impatient hand gripped the back of my chair, and I rose.

Maybe it was the don't-mess-with-me vibes he gave off as we left the building, but nobody approached to talk to me. I continued with last minute prepping on my tablet right until we drove through the gates of my house. And then I couldn't hold back the grain of irritation that had grown since dinner.

I cleared my throat. "I need a favor," I said briskly.

He paused with a hand on the door. His eyebrow twitched but didn't exactly lift. "Normally, a request like that is couched in a more...friendly tone."

I fixed my gaze somewhere around his chest to avoid New Caleb's cool, disinterested expression. "Tomorrow is an important day for me. So I need you not to..." I paused, a little annoyed with myself for needing to utter the words.

"It would help if you actually complete the sentence?"

The mild mockery lacing the words made me forget not to look into his face. His eyes weren't disinterested. They were neutral. Enough to make that odd little band around my chest tighten.

To hell with this. "Stop flirting with my assistant," I snapped.

He sat back in his seat, his eyes narrowing. "Why?"

"Excuse me?"

"What do you care who I flirt with?" he drawled.

"You're supposed to be a professional. Do I really need to point this out to you?"

He gave a careless shrug.

"Fine. Your…attention hasn't impacted her work. *Yet*. But—"

"You're worried she's becoming preoccupied with getting into my pants and you have a problem with that?" The words were delivered with a little more of that zing I was used to.

Hot little fires began licking through my veins, sparking electricity that engulfed my breasts, stung between my legs. "I only have a problem with how it pertains to my work. She needs to be on her A-game for tomorrow. So, yes, I'd be grateful if you'd dial down the low-voiced charm, and all that *smiling*."

The smile I'd just denigrated lit up his face. It was slow and deadly. It was also so drop-dead magnificent that I couldn't look away. Couldn't breathe. Couldn't do anything other than absorb it. Bask in it and God help me, grow intensely, claws-out possessive over Caleb smiling at another woman like that. And right in that moment of admitting that I was mindlessly attracted to him, I wanted to die.

Especially when that smile turned stupidly smug.

"Why, Lily, if I didn't know any better, I would think you were jealous."

CHAPTER NINE

Caleb

I WATCHED HER stalk to the front door, her body stiff with outrage.

My smile dimmed as my gaze swept feverishly over her, greedily taking one of the few long glances I'd been reduced to stealing all week. A part of me remained pissed off that she'd put the brakes on what had seemed like a slam-dunk acceptance of the green light I gave her.

Hell, three insanely hot make-out sessions in twenty-four hours was a record, even for me, although that first time in the restaurant had been a simple exercise in taking her down a peg or two, but had quickly escalated into something mildly earthshaking.

Okay, nothing about what happened between us could be classified under *mild*. I would've fucked her in broad daylight in the front seat of my SUV if one of us hadn't come to our senses.

Still. The part I was having a hard time dealing with was how hard it'd been to stick to my own rules this week. I'd spent more than a few sleepless nights reliving Lily's taste, enduring a raging—pun intended—storm in my cock I was yet to get under full control.

As I watched her stab the code to turn off the alarm, though, I couldn't help my gratification at this latest revelation.

"I'm not jealous," she denied hotly as if she'd read my thoughts.

I shut the front door and slid home the dead bolt. "Really? You're sure acting like it."

Her grip tightened on the satchel she never left home without. "Of course you would think that."

I strolled over to her. "I did wonder why you felt the need to instruct Miranda to come in on time tomorrow when she's never been late."

"And how would you know that?" she challenged huffily.

I cracked a little smile, watched her eyes drop to my mouth before she averted her gaze. The slow, torturous burn in my loins intensified. The wall I'd deliberately erected between us to help honor her wishes crumbled a little. I was tempted to give it a healthy kick, but deep down I knew she was right to want to keep things professional between us.

Besides, I wasn't sure I wanted to test my control just yet. Lily was as sensational as I imagined she would be. And that was with barely a taste.

"I know how to get the information I need," I answered her question.

Her eyes narrowed. "Was that what you were doing tonight? Gathering information?"

I shrugged. "Sometimes it's best to use honey, not vinegar."

She nodded and turned toward the stairs.

"Are you going to bed?"

Her eyes met mine for a second before she looked away, the pulse at her throat picking up speed. She let go of the satchel to drag her fingers through her hair. At some point this week, she'd repainted her short nails a dark purple shade that looked almost black. Something about the way it contrasted against her shock-white blond hair raised my temperature.

"No. I was thinking of going for a swim. I need the exercise to...de-stress a little."

Fuck, I had a dozen positions in mind to help her de-stress. And that was for starters. I forced the lid back on my runaway libido. "You nervous about tomorrow?" I asked.

She knew I was asking about Chance and tensed for a moment, and then she deliberately avoided the subject. "I shouldn't be. The code is working perfectly. But..." She shrugged.

I'd been looking into Chance Donovan and had a few thoughts on the bastard CEO. But I didn't want to add to her stress.

So, even though Lily in a sexy swimsuit and within touching distance was so not a good idea, I jerked my head toward the stairs anyway. "Go get changed. I'll meet you in the living room."

"Thanks," she said, looking relieved that I'd let the matter drop.

I stayed at the bottom of the stairs, unable to take my eyes off her perfect ass as she sprinted upstairs. Yeah, I was a glutton for punishment.

That punishment increased a hundredfold the moment she entered the living room. My hand froze on the French doors, and I swallowed hard.

She was wearing a see-through black mesh T-shirt over a burnt-orange bikini. Two things struck me hard just then. First, that while her signature black suited her alabaster complexion, the dark orange was even more flattering, drawing attention to her pint-size perfection.

Second, that the wall I'd built to contain my insane attraction and strict rules didn't stand a chance of staying up.

"Everything okay?" she asked, her eyes a little wide as she took in the joggers and T-shirt I'd changed into. *Fuck, no.* "Sure." I held the door open for her.

She walked past me, trailing light, sensual perfume that made me want to bury my face in her neck. Her back view was just as spectacular as her front, the tight globes of her ass barely contained in the bikini bottom.

A dangerously high percentage of blood rushed south, emptying my head of every thought except the one that fixated on what I wanted to do to her body. "How long do you need?" I croaked, dropping onto the lounger and hitching up one leg before she turned and saw the steel rod tenting my pants.

She paused at the edge of the pool and glanced over her shoulder. The setting sun's rays worshipped her cheek, her arms, her stomach and thighs. "I normally swim a hundred laps. So…forty-five minutes?" she murmured.

"Yeah. Fine." *Wow, you'll be drooling like a brain-dead idiot next.*

She grabbed the bottom of her T-shirt and pulled it over her head. A groan rumbled up my throat as she dove cleanly into the water with the smoothness of a practiced athlete.

It took twenty laps for me to get myself back under

acceptable control. Of course she chose that moment to pause at the far end of the pool to smooth back her wet hair and slowly swivel her head until her gaze rested on me. Her lips parted as she sucked in air to regain her breath.

She didn't utter a word. Neither did I. And yet, a thousand conversations passed between us.

Later, I would appreciate that this was the moment we both accepted that we were far from done with each other. That the rules and barriers and words we'd thrown up in an attempt to stop this sexual juggernaut stood no chance.

She clung to the edge of the pool for a full minute, her sexy green eyes never wavering from mine. Then with a lithe twist of her body, she dove underwater.

Every cell in my body wanted to join her. If for nothing else, to cool down before the top of my head blew clean off. But I stayed put, counted down her laps until she reached ninety-eight.

I jumped up, grabbed a towel from the stack next to the lounger and was waiting when she climbed the shallow steps.

Just like last time, delicious droplets clung to her skin. I wanted to lick each and every one off, then concentrate on licking her between her legs.

Instead, I held out the towel. Her eyes met and clung to mine as she accepted it and wrapped it around her body. "Thanks."

My eyes drifted to the wet curl clinging to her cheek. Unable to resist, I smoothed it behind her ear, then went to retrieve her T-shirt.

"Let's get you inside." I didn't give one tiny shit that my voice was a gruff mess. Or that my cock still stood at attention. I saw her eyes drop to it before, reddening, she glanced away.

She followed me inside and lingered in the living room as I locked the doors. "Drink?" I needed one badly before I did something foolish.

She passed the towel through her hair before lowering it. "Umm... I shouldn't."

I handed back her T-shirt. "That doesn't sound like a definite no," I said, then held up my hands. "But I'm not trying to corrupt you or anything so if you want to head up to bed, don't let me stop you." The breath trapped in my lungs told a different story to the words falling from my mouth. I wanted her to stay. Badly.

She dropped the towel on the coffee table and shook her head. "No. I'll just lie in bed worrying about stuff. Or I'll be tempted to tinker with the code some more. Bad idea," she said with a laugh.

It was the first time I'd heard her laugh. The soft, tinkling sound hooked into me, feeding a need to hear more of it. "Okay, so what do you do to distract yourself?"

She looked away, fidgeted, then dragged the T-shirt over her head. "I normally read. Or watch a movie downstairs..."

It was an easy decision. "I vote for downstairs." She had a bar down there, after all. "I'll have a drink. You can join me. Or not." I cocked an eyebrow.

The barest hint of a smile curved her mouth as her gaze touched on my brow. "I get to pick the movie."

I shrugged. "Your theater, your choice. I'm just coming for the booze."

Her smile widened a little more.

We went down together, her bare feet slapping

lightly on the polished wood. I crossed to the bar shelves stacked with expensive alcohol. She went to the sweets stand and returned with a large cone cup filled with assorted candy.

She popped a pink marshmallow into her mouth, then held out the cup to me. I chose a jellybean and pointed it at her. "These things will rot your teeth."

"Luckily I have an excellent dental plan." Her sexy grin exhibited perfect teeth.

I refocused on pouring my bourbon. "You sure you don't want anything?"

She inspected the row of drink bottles behind me. "Okay, I'll have a lemondrop martini, please."

I laughed. "You folded much easier than I thought you would."

She plucked another marshmallow from her supply before placing the cup on the counter. "I rarely fix it myself because it never comes out right. You look… comfortable behind the bar, like you know what you're doing."

Our eyes met. Locked. "So this is a test?"

Her lips slowly parted. "Maybe."

"And if I pass?"

Her gaze swept down for a moment before stunning green eyes met mine again. "I'll let you help me pick the movie."

I slowly set down the bourbon, biting my tongue against spilling what I really wanted for my prize. Hell, she knew it already. Knowledge flamed in her eyes. Whether she would choose tonight to do something about it was another matter.

I gathered the ingredients and watched her watch me

fix her drink. I slid it across the counter to her, lifted my glass of bourbon and waited.

She picked up her glass, took a delicate sip. Her tongue slid across her bottom lip. My cock jumped. "It's good."

"Just good?"

Again, her eyes flicked to my raised eyebrow, and her mouth twitched. "Okay. It's perfect."

"You're welcome." I reached into the freezer, plucked out two ice cubes and dropped them into my drink. Anything to lower the inferno raging in my groin.

Grabbing her candy and drink, she hopped off the bar and headed for the red leather lounger with drink holders on either side.

Perfect for two.

On Saturday night, when another damned nightmare had ripped me from sleep, I'd wandered downstairs, heard the movie running and came to check on her. I'd toyed with waking her but with tensions running high, I thought it best to leave her alone. As I'd made her comfortable, she'd made a small, forlorn sound that ripped through me.

As I joined her now, questions crowded my mind. Asking more personal ones would mostly likely hurl us back onto the battleground. So I stuck to a less volatile one.

"I've ruled out most people on the list." Including her ex. A discreet probe into Scott Wyatt's activities showed he'd been mostly out of town in the weeks before the stalking started, and was currently engaged in a long-distance relationship with a new woman in Seattle. He was lucky he was out of my reach.

A trace of unease flitted over Lily's face. "Okay. So who's left?"

I paused. My answer could risk her acting differently around the people left on the list. "I haven't been able to rule out Nordic Razor yet. Could he have seen what you were working on when you were online?"

She tucked her legs underneath her, rested sideways on the lounger, and took another sip of her drink. "No. I use a separate computer for social activities."

I set my glass in the holder. "Why Q?"

"What?"

"Cipher Q. What does the Q stand for?"

She toyed with a damp strand of hair. "What do you think it stands for?"

"I thought it was Quantum. But I'm going with Queen," I replied.

Her head dipped, that hint of shyness and innocence adding to her appeal. "It's silly, I know. And vain. But…"

"But you wanted to feel empowered at a time when things felt out of control?"

Her mouth dropped open a few seconds before she shut it. "I don't like it when you do that," she murmured.

"Do what?" I asked gently.

"See…too much."

"I won't hurt you, Lily. Not with any information you give me. I can promise you that."

After a moment, she nodded.

Grasping that tiny leeway, I probed softly, "How old were you when you started hacking?"

She looked a little trapped by my question, but she answered, "Thirteen."

"I'm guessing it was your stepfather who made you feel…less?"

A shadow crossed her face and she remained silent for a long time before she nodded. "He was saddled with me after my mom left. Every now and then he would let me feel his displeasure."

My fist tightened. "Did he hurt you?"

"Physically? No. In other ways…yes."

I took a sip of bourbon just for something to do so I didn't drive my fist through the wall behind me. "Tell me what he did."

Her nostrils quivered as she sucked in a breath. "I don't have all night."

"Then tell me exactly how you got involved with Chance."

"When I was fourteen, I hacked him. I was good back then, but I wasn't great. He hired another hacker to find me, and turned up at my house with the cops. He gave me a choice, work for him or go to jail."

"Your stepfather didn't tell him to get lost, I take it."

She gave a bitter laugh. "Not when Chance started throwing money his way, he didn't."

She flinched at my tight curse. I reached across the counter and placed my hand on hers. She stared at it with a sad smile before she inhaled long and deep.

"Anyway, between them they hammered out a deal that he'd pay my stepfather a monthly fee for my maintenance, then my college tuition fees on condition that when I left MIT I'd devote all my time to developing something big for him."

"The algorithm?" I asked, my chest and throat tight with the effort it took to keep my fury inside.

She nodded. "I had the beginnings of the idea back then."

"Why didn't you walk away when you turned eighteen or even twenty-one?"

Her lips tightened and she shrugged. "I gave him my word I wouldn't."

A simple answer, but such a powerful statement as to the true depths of Lily Gracen. I would've thought it impossible, but I grew even more attracted to her in that moment.

"And the Scott thing? How did you find out?"

She smiled unapologetically. "I hacked his phone records and confronted him."

"How did Chance take it?" I realized I was searching for another reason to punch the guy's lights out when I met him tomorrow.

"He claimed he was looking out for me. I called bullshit and threatened to walk then. He promised it would never happen again." The information was coming out in charged little bites.

"Lily—"

She shook her head. "No more. You're ruining the mood."

I cupped her cheek, my thumb caressing her lower lip until she had herself back under control. "Don't feel bad about letting me in. I know a little about how that feels like."

Wide green eyes locked on mine. "Really?"

I heard the throb of pain in my voice and inwardly grimaced. I could've answered differently, thrown her off with a shrug or said nothing at all. Instead, the last word I expected to say surged from my throat. "Yes."

She waited. Then a breath huffed out. "That's all you're going to give me?"

Curiosity swirled in her eyes, making my chest pound for a different reason. "Yes. I don't want to ruin the mood, either."

Her breath grew shaky. As did her hand when she raised her glass to take a healthy gulp. She stared at me for several heartbeats. Then, visibly shaking it off, she grabbed the remote and aimed it at the screen.

"Lowlights." Her command activated the lights, dimming the overhead lights and leaving only a set of lowlights running along the floor.

Onscreen, the system had grouped her entertainment into genres and then favorites. She clicked *favorites*. A long list rolled down the screen.

"These are all your favorites?" I asked skeptically.

"Uh-huh."

The title she clicked on caught my eye, and another raw memory spiked through me. *"The English Patient?"*

She glared at me. "It's a classic."

"If you want to weep into your martini glass the whole time then fall into a coma from boredom, sure."

"You've seen it?"

My teeth clenched as I toyed with evading. "Yeah, I've seen it. It was my mother's favorite, too."

Naked, hesitant curiosity lit her eyes. *"Was?"*

I threw back the remaining bourbon. What the hell… "She died. Fifteen years ago." Because she fell through the cracks. Over and over again until she hit rock bottom and never rose. I swallowed my bitterness as Lily leaned closer.

"When you were fourteen?"

I jerked out a nod. Silence throbbed between us,

then I indicated the screen. "Are we gonna watch this movie or what?"

Her head swiveled to the screen, then back at me. She held out the remote. "The deal was you could help me pick. You've vetoed my first choice. Show me what you got."

I accepted it, allowing my fingers to graze hers. She exhaled sharply.

God, I wanted to feel that puff of breath on my face. Reluctantly, I turned to the screen. Surprisingly, only half of the movies were chick flicks. Top-notch detective movies and psychological thrillers had made the cut.

I frowned as the list kept going. "There are over a hundred here. How can they all be your favorite?"

She stared at me. "Is it too difficult? I can help you out if you want?" I caught a hint of teasing challenge.

I snorted and selected one.

She grimaced. "Uh, no. I love Bruce Lee but not tonight. The sound effects alone will give me a headache."

I scrolled some more until she laid her hand over mine. "This one," she breathed.

"Revenge?" It was the original movie with Anthony Quinn, Kevin Costner and Madeleine Stowe. I couldn't remember the plot line but I'd probably seen it. Movies had been a huge escape for Mom the few times depression released her from its merciless talons. To be honest, they'd been an escape for me, too, because for a blessed stretch of two or three hours, I could stop worrying about her. She'd even summoned a laugh when we watched a comedy.

"Yes. It doesn't have a high rating but I love it. Unless you want to find something else?"

I tore myself from the past. "This will do." I hit Play and pointed to her empty glass. "Do you want another?"

She stared wistfully at the martini glass. "No, I better not. I'll take a soda, though."

I grabbed a soda for her and bottled water for myself. She broke the tab, curled her lip over the top and drank half the contents, while I forced myself not to stare at her throat.

The movie's plot became clear within twenty minutes. Sex. Corruption. Forbidden lust. Betrayal.

I settled in and tried to give it my full attention. Lily set the cup of candy between us and stretched out her legs. She ate another marshmallow, then held out a jelly bean to me. I took it, chewed, and steeled myself not to stare at her exposed thighs. Or her flat belly beneath the mesh top. Or the slight mound of her pussy.

Jesus.

A few minutes later she shifted again, turning onto her side to face me as she slid one leg up against the other.

She rested her head on one arm, and started toying with the ends of her short hair.

Hell, something about the way she played with those white-blond tips turned me on beyond comprehension. A moment later her other hand dipped into the candy cup. She didn't pick one, just rummaged through it, her gaze still fixed on me.

"Are you going to settle down or are you planning on fidgeting through the movie?"

Dark-tipped fingers traced the edge of the cup.

"I still feel…wired," Lily stated, her voice hardly above a husky whisper.

Alcohol, sugar, unscripted revelations and lust didn't sit well together. Add the flimsy top and bikini she wore, and it was an explosion waiting to happen.

I grabbed the candy cup and moved it to the other side of my seat. "Maybe you should stop stuffing yourself with sugar, then."

Her lower lip protruded in a sexy pout, drawing my eyes to the luscious curve.

Lily made a small, muffled sound under her breath. "Caleb."

God, *now* she chose to say my name voluntarily. In that damn dirty, cock-stroking voice.

Her free hand dropped onto the space between us, then drew tiny circles on the leather.

"Maybe it's time to call it a night." I didn't mean it. At all.

She dragged her lower lip between her teeth. "No. I…can't. I'm wound too tight," she whispered.

"Tell me what you need." *Hell of a time to be the better man, Steele.*

She blinked slowly, sultrily, and her hand bunched into a fist. A moment later her gaze swept over my chest, then dropped lower to caress my rigid cock. She took a deep breath. "I've decided to accept that pass."

I stopped breathing. "What?"

Beautifully lusty, gorgeously defiant eyes met mine. "You heard me. You gave me a loophole in your rule. I'm taking it."

Filthy little fires leaped through my body. "What exactly are we talking about?"

A wickedly saucy smile curved her lips. "You'll see. Wanna get my Bob?"

Shit. My cock was very ready and extremely capable. I gritted my teeth for a second. "Your little pink toy. You sure?" I rasped.

"I need release and the way I see it, I have two choices. I can let you fuck me or help me some other way. I'm not ready for the first one yet."

What the hell did she have in mind? "Lily—"

"Are you in, Caleb?"

As if I could answer any other way. "Where is it?"

Hectic color stained her cheeks as she nodded to the small bathroom next to the bar. "Under the first blanket in the closet," she whispered.

I sucked in a sustaining breath and rose from the lounger.

Fuck, I pushed her into testing my self-control. Now my cock was hard enough to hammer nails, and my balls were on fire.

Way to go, champ!

I entered the bathroom and tossed the first blanket. The bright pink sex toy gleamed at me. I wanted to leave it there, tell her I didn't find it.

I could easily give her what she craved with my mouth. My fingers. My tongue. But I knew I wouldn't be able to stop there.

I grabbed the gadget and returned to find her half sitting up, her breathing elevated. That mesh top was driving me nuts. As for her bare, supple thighs and the shadowed space between them—

"We need some ground rules," she blurted. "We keep our clothes on, no matter what. Deal?"

Her eyes were wide and shiny, and goddamn it, she

was the most beautiful I'd ever seen her. And I wanted to see her come so badly, my back teeth hurt from the need. "Deal," I croaked.

I crawled back onto the lounger and laid the vibrator between us.

She looked down at it, and fresh flames lit up her alabaster cheeks. "Caleb—"

"I'm yours to command, baby. Just tell me what you need."

"Kiss me," she instructed.

God, yes.

Spiking my fingers through her hair, I yanked her down and fused my mouth to hers, heard her sexy little whimper, right before she melted into me. I didn't need to cajole my way in. She opened her beautiful mouth and I licked my way inside, unable to stop from groaning as I got another taste of Lily.

She eased back against the seat. I followed until my chest was pressed against hers, her firm, plump breasts rubbing against me as she breathed.

I deepened the kiss, sliding my tongue against hers, biting the tip of it when I recalled how much she liked it last time. She rewarded me with a moan, the hands exploring my back quickening their caress. Her fingers traced the waistline of my joggers, then tentatively dropped to my ass. I bit gently on her top lip. Her nails dug into my ass, even as her legs parted to accommodate me.

The flames licking through my veins intensified as I broke away and glanced down between us. Less than six inches separated us. I only needed to drop down a fraction for my cock to brush her bikini-covered mound. And if I angled downward I would easily slide between her legs, rub the underside of my cock against her clit. Get her off that way.

My breath shuddered out as I glanced into her glazed eyes. At her bruised lips.

Fuck me.

She was in charge, and as much as it unsettled me, it was also the headiest thing I'd ever experienced.

Slamming on the brakes was hard. But I planted my hands on either side of her head, increased the gap between us and drew up my knees to bracket her thighs. From my position, I had an intoxicating view of her from head to toe.

"What now?" I rasped.

One hand scrambled blindly for the vibrator. Then hesitated.

"Go for it, sweetheart. Before my good intentions take a flying leap." Her breath kept hitching as if she couldn't catch it. When her gaze dropped to my mouth, I dropped my head and delivered a quick, hard kiss. "Now, Lily," I commanded hoarsely.

She brought it up between us, and flicked it on with her thumb. Noticing the low setting, I raised my eyebrow.

"I've never used number three before," she blurted.

I put my thumb over hers and flicked it up two more. "Then I'm glad I'm here for your first time." My grin felt as tight as the pressure in my groin as I returned to my original position. And waited.

Slowly, she lowered her hand, and then paused with the sex toy above her belly. Then she raised her gorgeous eyes to me. "You do it."

Fuck. I drew in a strangled breath. "You sure?"

She caught her lip between her teeth and nodded

jerkily. She handed me the vibrator, then lowered her hand and drew aside the crotch of her bikini.

At the first sight of her pretty pink pussy, I nearly lost my mind.

Fighting the irrational jealousy rising within me, I slid the vibrator against her wet clit. A sharp gasp broke from her lips as her back arched off the lounger.

My arms shook with the effort it took to stay upright. "Fuck."

"Oh…God." She shuddered as I pressed the vibrator harder against her clit. "Ahh…"

The scent of her wetness rose between us, triggering fresh agony in my balls. "God, your pussy smells incredible, Lily."

Another set of shudders unraveled through her, ending in her undulating her hips against the pink toy. Beneath the mesh and bikini top, her nipples were hard little points that begged to be tasted.

Saliva filled my mouth as I fought with the rampant urge to rip her clothes off and do just that. Instead, I contented myself with planting openmouthed kisses down her satin-smooth neck, licking the frantic pulse racing at her throat. Biting her earlobe.

"Caleb. Oh." The groan was dragged from her as her face pinched and her eyes rolled shut.

"Are you close, baby?"

She shuddered, her hips moving faster. "Yes… Yes!"

"Open your eyes. Look at me. I want to see your gorgeous eyes when you come," I instructed, barely recognizing my own voice.

Her lust-glazed eyes met mine. "Caleb… I'm coming," she said in a hushed whisper. "Oh!" Her hips exploded and she screamed.

My fists bunched hard, tension screaming up my spine as I locked my knees to stay put.

Dear God, she was glorious.

I lost the fight halfway through her release, and slanted my mouth over hers. Her lips clung to mine as I devoured her every panted breath, desperate not to miss a moment of her glorious climax.

After an eternity, her convulsion died down. That was when I realized her arms and legs were locked around me. When the smell of her hit me, I knew I was in deeper trouble.

Clamping an arm around her waist, I lifted her off the lounger and staggered for the door.

"Caleb?" Her voice was still slurred.

"I'm taking you to bed," I said through clenched teeth.

Her breath hitched. "No."

"Don't worry. I'm not going to pressure you. You're going to bed alone. And we're definitely going to fuck," I promised, "but not until this shit is taken care of."

Her legs clamped tighter around me. Which delivered the fresh hell of having my eager cock sweetly cradled by her very wet pussy.

I stumbled on the stairs as she buried her face in my neck and gave a low moan. "But...what about you?" she whispered, performing a slow, torturous grind against me.

"I'll take care of it...later." My mouth drifted from the corner of hers to the delicate shell of her ear. "Or I'll save it for you."

She whimpered. A glorious sound. I tunneled my fingers in her hair and pulled her head back.

"Would you like that?"

Her blush deepened, but she met my gaze. "Yes."

I groaned, tightened my hold on her and vaulted up the stairs.

In her room, I pulled back the covers and set her down in the middle of the bed. Her legs stayed locked in place for a beat before she released me. I kissed her soft lips and reluctantly stepped back. "Get some sleep. I'll see you bright and early."

Resolutely, I headed for the door.

"Caleb?"

My hand tightened around the door handle, and I squeezed my eyes shut for a bracing second before I looked over my shoulder. "Yeah?"

She twisted a corner of the duvet between her fingers, making no move to cover herself. "Thank you. For…tonight."

My fevered gaze scoured her body to the shadows between her legs, unashamed of the savage hunger most likely blazing on my face. "Don't thank me just yet. I intend to fuck your lights out the second this shit is handled. And it won't be a nice, gentlemanly fucking. Good night, Lily."

CHAPTER TEN

Lily

MY INNER ALARM nudged me awake just shy of 5:00 a.m., after the soundest sleep I'd enjoyed since my stalker problem started. I stretched, rolled over and froze as memories of last night flooded in.

Heat surged through my body, pooling in my pelvis, before rushing up to engulf my face.

OMG!

I lay there, breath held, bracing myself for extreme vulnerability slash acute mortification. I'd bared parts of my past I'd never told another soul to Caleb. And then I'd let him use my vibrator on me!

Weirdly, neither sensation arrived. Emotionally, I felt unburdened, like a heavy cloak had been lifted off my shoulders. And neither by word nor deed had Caleb judged me.

Sexually, I felt…sensational. Like I'd won a grand prize in a contest I didn't even know I was competing in.

Great sex had always felt like a gift granted to other people, a sleight of hand everyone else had mastered but me. I wasn't ashamed to confess that was the reason why I invested in the very best sex toys. But… last night…

I came harder than I ever had…and we didn't even have sex. I was one hundred percent sure it had nothing to do with the higher setting on my vibrator. The only other time I'd tried the highest setting, all I could think about was the noise and what possible damage the overload of electricity was doing to my clit. It ruined the experience.

But last night I unlocked a previously unknown inhibiting door and been rewarded with an amazing experience.

The memory of him crouched over me, big, hot, wild, with barely restrained hunger stamped on his face, his hand between my legs, and dirty, beautiful words pouring out of his mouth…

Yeah, that certainly guaranteed the unforgettable encounter my instinct had been nudging me toward from the start.

I felt empowered, like I could do it all over again, no problem.

I gulped down the moan rising in my throat.

Despite laying down the caveat, there'd been a moment, right before that incredible climax hit me, when I'd wanted to beg Caleb to pull out his thick cock jutting boldly against his pants. Beg him to *fuck my lights out*.

His gruff, sexy promise echoed in my head, ripping free a ravenous moan. I wanted that. Badly.

Except it wouldn't happen until my stalker was caught.

My stalker.

My code.

The SDM presentation.

Reality drenched me like an icy waterfall, catapulting me out of bed and into the shower. Someone was still out there, watching, waiting for me to slip up. I clenched my teeth against the skin-crawling sensation that threatened to ruin my day and tried to regain my buzz.

I never quite got it back. My mood plummeted further when an email from Chance buzzed on my phone just as I was heading downstairs.

I entered the kitchen to find Caleb at the coffee machine. In the few seconds before he turned around, I hungrily ogled his V-shaped torso draped in a fitted navy blue shirt, tucked into tailored pants that framed his mouthwatering ass.

The ass I'd gripped all too briefly last night before he'd called a halt to my exploration.

He turned, two mugs of coffee in his hands. We both froze as his eyes met mine.

The memory of last night pulsed between us, hot and heavy. His heated gaze swept down and up my body, its intensity heightening with each pass. I was glad I'd taken extra care with my attire.

My black dress was a combination of a corset top and flared skirt, which I teamed with three-inch-heeled ankle boots. My makeup was flawless, too, with an added confidence-boosting layer of eyeliner and mascara, topped off with my favorite scarlet lipstick.

"Good morning," I murmured, eager for something to dissipate the charge rippling between us before I did something embarrassing, like stare at his crotch and wonder if he'd given in and jacked off last night or whether he'd kept to his promise to save it for me.

"Morning," he responded, striding forward to hand me the coffee.

We drifted to the center island, both lifting our mugs to take an idle sip while his eyes made another pass over my body. Then he reached out to touch the silver star dangling from the middle of my lace choker. "You look…incredibly beautiful," he said throatily.

My whole body reacted to his words, going from zero to furnace-hot in seconds. "Thank you."

His eyes slowly narrowed. "Something's wrong."

I waved my phone. "Email from Chance. He's bringing someone else to the meeting today."

He tensed. "Who?"

"He didn't say."

"Has he done that before?"

"Not at the last minute, no." I took another sip of coffee, swallowing it down with my anxiety.

"And you're worried," he observed.

I shrugged. "I can do without the extra pressure."

He set his mug down and cupped my cheeks. "I've watched you all week, batting away problems from your team without so much as pausing to look up from your keyboard. You'll kick ass today. I've no doubt."

Like last night, his gentle touch, together with the encouraging words, sent fierce prickles to my eyes. I blinked rapidly, dead certain I didn't want to cry in front of Caleb. "Thanks."

One thumb drifted along my jaw. "You're welcome," he murmured.

His gaze dropped to my mouth, and a different emotion swirled around us.

He stepped away first, picked up his cup and finished his coffee. "You ready to go?"

My nod was as shaky as the emotions zipping through me.

In the hallway, he picked up the waist-length jacket I dropped next to my satchel and held it out for me. I stood in front of him, put my arms through the sleeves, secretly breathing in the heady scent of aftershave and pure man. When I went to do up the single button, he brushed my hands away, pulled the lapels close and secured it.

Then he gripped my waist tight and pulled me back into his body. "I don't know how well you slept last night," he breathed in my ear, "but mine was pretty damned fucked because all I could think about was how magnificent you looked when you came. Just thought you should know."

I was struggling to breathe as he shrugged into his leather jacket and we left home without exchanging another word.

What could I say? That knowing he hadn't slept made my panties wet? To hell with waiting for my stalker to be caught. I wanted him to pull over and bang me on the backseat.

Conversation became redundant as his phone blared to life. He reached for it, his brows creasing when he looked down at the screen.

"Ross," he answered with a cool voice. "Yes, Maggie told me you've been trying to reach me. I've been a little busy." His eyes flicked to me before returning to the road. "What can I do for you?"

Traffic was light, and with the radio in the SUV set to low, I heard the other voice on the line. "The band won't take me back."

Caleb suppressed a sigh. "Have you been showing up for rehearsals like we agreed?"

"Every day. I even blew off my weekend plans to put in some extra work. They said it was too little, too late."

"It's only been a week. Maybe they're testing you to see whether you'll disappoint them again. Where are you right now?" Caleb asked.

There was a moment's hesitation before Ross-who-ever-he-was answered, "At the Beverly Hilton."

A muscle rippled in Caleb's jaw. "Didn't we agree you wouldn't go back there again?"

"Yeah, but if the guys won't take me back then what's—?"

"You better not be thinking of pulling that stunt again or I'll hang up right now and block your number permanently," Caleb interrupted harshly.

"I won't… But it's hard, man," the other man whined.

"That's what happens when you let people down, Ross. They stop trusting you." His voice gentled. "If you really want this, you just have to keep trying. They'll come around eventually."

"And if they don't?"

"Then you have to find answers elsewhere. You're talented. You just need to take a little more responsibility for your life. Ultimately, it's down to you whether you want to succeed or fail."

"I…want this. The band," Ross said.

"Then you know what you have to do."

A sigh echoed down the line. "Yeah. Umm…thanks, man."

"You can thank me by checking out of that hotel and getting your ass back home." He hung up and slid his phone back into his pocket.

Silence throbbed through the vehicle for a few blocks.

"You're good at this... Being a fixer."

The corners of his mouth lifted, but the smile didn't quite reach his eyes. "Thanks. That's high praise coming from you."

"I mean it. It can't be easy dealing with people who aren't always receptive."

He eyed me. "Are you including yourself in that?"

I hid a grimace. "Maybe. But what you said to him, just now...is that why you're a fixer? Because people let you down?"

His face tightened. "That's too heavy a conversation for this time of the morning, sweetheart."

"You're avoiding."

"And you're searching for something to take your mind off your meeting. This subject isn't it, Lily." There was a touch of warning in his voice.

"Why not? I've told you my secrets. You owe me something. *Quid pro quo.* Isn't that what it's called?"

His lips flattened. But he blew out a breath a moment later. "Yeah, a bunch of people let me down. But more than that, they let my *mother* down when she needed them the most. It's not a good feeling, being that helpless, so fixing became my thing."

"When did you start?"

"Officially? When I was twenty. Unofficially, shortly after my mother died. There was a lot of fixing to be done in Trenton Gardens." There was a hard, bitter note in his voice that drew shivers down my arms.

"I don't know where that is."

"Consider that a good thing, baby."

I looked at his rigid profile, and burning with a need I couldn't suppress, I tapped the name into my phone.

And grew colder. "Trenton Gardens, home of the most notorious gangs in South Central LA. Five people are killed there *every week*!" I read out loud with growing horror.

A flash of anger lit his eyes as he glanced at the phone, but then he gave a grim shrug. "Not exactly fairy-tale reading, is it?"

I put my phone away, my chest tightening with sympathy for this man with the hard exterior and flashes of tenderness. I wanted to know more, uncover his layers.

"I hear you sometimes," I murmured.

His body tensed. "Excuse me?"

"In the night. You don't sleep very well, do you?" I probed gently.

"What makes you think I'm not checking on things? Keeping you safe?"

"Are you?"

His fingers tightened around the steering wheel. "Leave it alone, Lily."

"My mother left just before I turned eight. I didn't sleep through the night for a year," I blurted. "My stepdad and I woke up one morning and she was…gone. Left a note to say she was never coming back and we shouldn't try to find her. Even after we received papers the next week from her lawyer granting my stepfather full custody of me I still thought she would come back. Stephen was sterile and couldn't have children of his own. That's the only reason he kept me."

Caleb cursed under his breath. "That's his loss, Lily, not yours."

I attempted to shrug his sympathy away, but my

shoulders didn't comply. "I wasn't entirely blameless. It...hurt, knowing my mother could leave without a second thought, and my stepfather would've walked away if he had children of his own. I acted out. Sometimes."

"That's still not an excuse for what he did."

"I know, but..." I shrugged.

"Deep down you wish things had turned out differently," he said.

I sniffed away the unexpected tears. "Stupid, right?"

"No. Not stupid at all," he murmured, reaching out to glide a finger down my cheek.

Damn, there he went, being all gentle again. A fat drop rolled down my cheek.

He cursed again as he turned off the ignition. A distracted look outside showed we were in SDM's parking lot. It was still early enough that there were only a handful of cars around, the nearest one six bays away.

When his thumb brushed my chin, I tried to pull away, more than a little terrified of the softening happening inside me. He clamped his fingers in my hair, forcing me to look at him.

One brow was cocked, but his eyes were gentle. "I told you this was too heavy for this time of the morning. You should listen to me more often."

Another tear slipped free. I tried to laugh it away. "I have no idea why I'm crying. I'm over all of that. Counting the days until I put him and Chance in my rearview."

His fingers tightened on my nape. His other hand patted his lap. "Come here," he commanded.

My breath caught. "Why?"

"So I can make you feel better," he answered, his

voice lower, deeper, curling around my turbulent emotions.

I shouldn't.

I really, *really*, shouldn't.

My hands slowly went to my seat belt, freeing it despite the voice screeching warning at the back of my head. Caleb's seat, already extended fully to accommodate his long legs, afforded me plenty of space as I crawled into his lap.

The hand on my nape speared into my hair and the other clamped one hip.

"Open your jacket," he instructed.

Hands shaking, I complied.

The sun wasn't fully up yet and the tinted windows shielded us as I braced my knees on either side of him. The moment my hands landed on his shoulders, he pulled me down and fused his lips to mine.

Caleb ravaged my mouth like I was his last meal, and I was more than happy to be devoured.

Between my legs, his erection thickened, pressing insistently against me. Shamelessly turned on, I ground against him, earning his tortured groan. We kissed until the need for more oxygen forced us apart. He kneaded my ass, encouraging me to grind against him. The feeling was intensely exquisite.

God, I could come from just rubbing my clit on his cock.

The thought drew a hungry moan but when I tried to dive back into the kiss, he stopped me.

"I didn't see a zipper on your dress when I helped you with your jacket earlier. Where is it?" he demanded hoarsely.

I motioned dazedly to my left rib cage.

"Take it down for me, baby," he said, his eyes still consuming me.

My racing heart tripled its tempo but I couldn't have stopped myself if a freight train was bearing down on me. I lowered the zipper until the corset gaped to reveal my breasts.

Caleb stared at me for another tense second before his gaze dropped. He exhaled sharply. "Fuck." His hand dropped to brush the back of his knuckles over one tight nipple, making me jerk against him. "I wondered whether these would be pale or dark." His gaze flicked to my face, absorbing my reaction as he repeated the gesture over the twin peak. "I have no clue which I would've preferred because seeing them now…they're fucking perfect." The words ended in a groan as he yanked me forward and clamped his mouth around one tight bud.

"Oh, God!"

He suckled me, hot and urgent, then flicked his tongue mercilessly over the sensitive bud, all the while dragging my damp center back and forth over his erection.

He transferred his attention to the other nipple, catching the freed, wet bud between his thumb and finger.

Stars exploded across my vision. "Yes!"

My fingers dug into his hair, desperate to keep him right where he was. I threw my head back as my hips took on a life of their own, fixated on riding him to the bliss that hovered on the horizon.

"Holy fuck, you're beautiful," he groaned against me, staring up at me with an intensity I couldn't fathom.

"Caleb…"

"You have no idea how gorgeous you are, do you?"

I couldn't breathe. This man was unraveling me, piece by piece. Body and soul. And I couldn't think of a single reason to stop him.

My body was a knot of seething sensation, waiting for some unknown directive to explode. Caleb wrapped one hand around my throat, restricting but not hurting. The other slipped beneath my dress and nudged my panties aside.

My fingers dug into his shoulders.

"I wasn't going to. But I need to feel you, Lily."

"Yes." Agreement was as easy as breathing, my need unstoppable.

His eyes hooked into mine, Caleb dragged his tongue across my nipple as he sank one thick finger inside me.

A tight scream erupted from my throat. He added a second finger and pleasure rained on me, quickening the movements of my hips as I chased ecstasy.

"Damn, you're so fucking tight," he exclaimed harshly, his breathing a ragged mess. "I can't wait to bury my cock inside you."

"Caleb…" I couldn't form any other words other than his name as he drove me insane with his fingers.

Sweet vortex swirled closer, sucking me down.

The hand around my throat bore me down onto piston-fast fingers. His thumb circled my clit and pleasure like I've never known before completely unraveled me. I came hard.

Somewhere in the midst of blinding ecstasy, Caleb covered my mouth with his, riding the waves with me until my convulsions ebbed away.

I collapsed in a boneless heap on top of him, panting like a bitch straight out of heat. He rained kisses on my neck and jaw, his hand caressing my ass.

"You okay?" he asked gruffly in my ear.

I hummed, mindlessly floating on a sea of bliss. The fingers inside me crooked, making me gasp one last time before he pulled out.

He gently nudged me upright, made me watch as he put his fingers in his mouth and licked off my essence. A fierce blush lit up my skin as he pressed his mouth against mine. "You taste even more sublime than I thought you would. The list of what I'm going to do to you is growing by the hour, baby. I've just added eating your pussy for hours to it."

I groaned, my senses firing up all over again. Before my orgasm-addled brain could return to reality, I scooted sideways and reached for his belt.

He tensed. "Lily?"

Maybe it was the orgasms that made me bold. Maybe it was his words of praise that tapped into a reserve of strength inside me. Either way, I slowly brushed my fingers over his mouth before replacing them with my own. "Shh," I whispered. "You're not the only one who gets to bestow awesome gifts this morning. I'm feeling generous, too."

His eyes widened a touch, right before his gaze dropped to my mouth. And locked, with blazing hunger flaring in his eyes. "Lily…" Hoarse anticipation thickened his voice.

"Will you let me, Caleb?" I lowered his zipper and slipped my hand beneath the waistband of his boxers. "Make us both feel good?"

He slammed his head against the headrest and

groaned, long and hard and pained. "Do you really expect me to refuse an offer like that?"

I pulled him out, gasped and just...stared. *God.* He was huge. Thick and hard and insanely hot. Caleb's cock was everything I'd dreamed it would be and more. "You're beautiful." Tentatively, I stroked his hard length.

A rough sound erupted from his throat. "Dammit, Lily..."

Trepidation threatened to overcome me as the difference between watching a few porn clips and giving my first blowjob hit home.

I stroked him harder, loving the velvet-steel feel of him, loving the way his teeth gritted and his cheekbones flushed with color.

Lost in my ministrations, I startled when he cursed, "Fuck, stop licking your lips like that and put your gorgeous mouth on me before I come."

Heart racing, I slowly lowered my head and kissed his crown. A hiss flew from his lips as his hand slid up my back. I trailed kisses over his length, and then dragged my tongue up the underside of his cock, earning myself another deep groan.

Still sliding my hand up and down his glorious shaft, I flicked my tongue in rapid succession over his slit. His hips jerked against my mouth and frantic fingers dug into my hair. "Fuck!"

I sucked and pumped him with long, even strokes, establishing a rhythm that drew harsh pants from him.

"Yes! Fuck, yes, just like that," he croaked, his other hand fumbling for my breast.

Sensation curled through me as he fondled me almost frantically, his movements growing jerkier as I kept up a relentless pace on his cock.

A glance up showed his eyes squeezed shut, his chest heaving as he sucked in desperate breaths.

I reached between his legs, stroked his balls, and his fingers tightened painfully in my hair.

"God, Lily, don't stop. Don't fucking stop."

Impossibly, he thickened in my mouth. I drew him deep, right to the back of my throat and held still, glorying in his utter lack of control when he ground himself mercilessly against me.

"Take it. Fuck, take it all," he panted, right before a pure, animalist growl rumbled from his chest, then erupted in a hoarse shout as he came furiously in my mouth.

I swallowed him down, the salty muskiness of him weirdly addictive. When his body sagged against the seat, I licked him clean, then allowed him to pull me upright.

"Jesus, Lily. That was sensational," he breathed against my mouth.

The smile that curved my lips was pure feminine power. My first blow and I hadn't sucked at it. A wicked little laugh broke loose before I could stop it.

"Enjoying your power, are you?" he croaked.

"Maybe," I replied breathlessly.

He pulled me in for a deep, long kiss. When we parted, we stared at each other for several heartbeats, both adjusting to the shifting landscape beneath our feet.

His gaze scoured my face; then his thumb brushed my lower lip.

After he zipped himself up, he reached into the center console and handed me packet of tissues. I took one and reached between my legs.

He caught my wrist. "No. Not there. I want you to walk around the office today with a reminder of how good this moment felt. Each time you get anxious, remember this moment. Remember that you're phenomenal. Okay?"

The huge lump that rose in my throat prevented me from speaking. After I nodded, he took the tissue from me, and gently wiped my smeared lipstick. Then he wiped his own mouth before reaching for my satchel and the small makeup bag I kept in there.

He watched as I repaired my makeup, his intense gaze fixed on my face. Only then did he zip me back up, button my jacket and let me slide back into my seat.

"You ready?"

I took a deep breath and let my gratitude show in my smile. "Yes."

His return smile was gentle if a little dazed around the edges. "Let's go."

The morning presentation went without a hitch, with an eager audience comprising the tech media and bloggers, applauding when the two-hour event was done.

Over the years, Chance and I had perfected the art of being in the same room but speaking only the barest minimum to one another.

Afterward, I returned to my office with Chance. Caleb had grudgingly agreed to keep out of sight while I dealt with Chance but I knew he was nearby, and that gave me a layer of comfort I didn't know I needed till it was time for the second presentation.

The beta test started off well, my tweaks making the algorithm as fast as I promised it would be.

Right up until the moment the compression sequence slowed to a crawl. My heart jumped into my throat. Seventeen excruciating seconds ticked by before it sped up again.

But the blip was the only thing that mattered when the screen turned black and the lights went back up in the conference room.

CHAPTER ELEVEN

Lily

"I CAN FIX IT," I blurted. "It's just a small area of the code."

Chance looked furious. "We thought these wrinkles would've been ironed out by now."

"I still have three weeks of beta testing before the final deadline."

Walter Green, the man Chance had brought with him, frowned. "You said it would be ready, Donovan."

"I was assured it would be," Chance responded.

I ignored the men and fired up my laptop. Scrolling through the code, I zeroed in on where the problem was. Heart pumping, I forced myself to analyze it line by line. After forty lines, I stopped. "It's fixable," I repeated. "But I'll need time."

"How much time?" Chance snapped.

I bit my lip. "A week. Ten days, tops."

Silence greeted me.

Walter Green rose and left the room without saying a word. The other SDM executives also left.

Chance Donovan's gray eyes lanced me. The rest of him looked as harmless as a middle-aged CEO with a wife and three kids could look. But from the moment we met, I'd glimpsed a layer of menace in his eyes that pushed all my self-preservation buttons. "This is disappointing, Lily," he rasped.

I forced myself not to waver. "Who's Walter Green?"

"He's the guy who decides whether SDM sinks or swims. Delivering this algorithm, correctly and on time, and earning the freedom you claim to so badly crave, feeds directly into that. Is that clear enough?" he said.

"Yes," I murmured.

"Good. Now, what's this I hear about a new consultant?" he asked.

I struggled not to tense up as I trotted out the line Caleb and I practiced. "He's from LA. He's helping me with preliminary info on a possible gaming app my team is working on."

Suspicion flickered through his eyes. "Why don't I know about this? And why is he staying at your house?"

Why wasn't I surprised he knew Caleb was staying with me? "Because this is still *preliminary*. And because I don't need your permission to have a houseguest."

His eyes narrowed and he didn't speak for a long time. "Remember what's riding on this project, Lily," he warned, then left without further comment.

I buried my face in my hands.

A minute later Caleb arrived, swiveling my chair to face him before tugging my hands down. He'd been listening on my laptop so I didn't need to repeat what had happened. His solid presence took away some of my apprehension.

"Apart from my regret that I wasn't here to punch

that asshole in the face, the problem is only a minor bump in the road, right?"

"Maybe. Maybe not."

He frowned, crouching down in front of me. "Meaning?"

"The mistake looks…sophisticated. I triple-checked everything yesterday. I could've missed it—"

"You think you were hacked?" he asked.

The icy hand on my nape wouldn't let go. "I don't think so but it's possible…" I stopped as another thought occurred to me.

"What?"

"I added a last-minute tweaked version this morning from the team."

"Which team?"

"Sanjeet's team. But—"

His fingers brushed my lips, halting my words. "You want to think the best of everyone. I don't want to take that away from you, but you have to accept sooner or later than not everyone is decent."

My heart lurched. "I know, but I trust them."

"Give them the benefit of the doubt if you want. Let me worry about who's at fault here. Okay?"

Chest tight, my gaze settled on my laptop. "What's their end goal, Caleb?"

"The stalking is most likely to keep you off balance while they try to get their hands on what you're working on."

The thought drew a horrified shudder. "That can't happen."

"It won't," he ground out. With a decisive click, he shut the lid. "It's almost eight. You've been up since five this morning. I'm taking you home."

I shook my head. "I can't. The team always goes out to celebrate after a presentation. They'll expect me to be there."

"Where's it happening?"

"Q Base in Cupertino."

He pulled out his phone to relay the instruction to his security team. Then he cupped my shoulders. "You're officially clocked off for the day. Understood?"

Feeling numb, I nodded.

I was grateful when Maggie called and kept Caleb on the phone for most of the time it took to drive to Q Base.

Thumping music when we entered the club further prevented me from making meaningful conversation with Caleb or my team.

I exchanged high fives with anyone who stopped at the VIP lounge reserved for SDM, but the first chance I got, I headed to the main bar.

"You want a lemondrop?" Caleb leaned down to ask in my ear.

Memories of last night flooded in, knocking aside a bit of my melancholy. "Not unless you're making it," I said before I fully grasped how revealing my answer was. His lips curved in a smug smile. "They don't make it that well here. I'll have a noche azul," I added in a rush.

He ordered my drink and bourbon for himself.

Since it was early by clubbing standards, we had most of the dance floor to ourselves. But an hour later the place was packed.

I excused myself to go to the ladies' room, and returned to find Miranda seated next to Caleb. Frozen, I watched her lean in close and whisper in his ear.

A smile crept up his face but he shook his head. She leaned in closer, her bare leg sliding against his.

Hot, green bile curdled in my gut, merrily aided by the two cocktails I'd consumed. I wanted to stalk over, uproot her by the hair and lay my claim on him.

But other than the two orgasms he'd given me, a few shared confidences and a promise to screw each other's brains out sometime in the future, what hold did we have on one another? For all I knew, Caleb could be gone from my life this time next week.

The thought slashed through me, sharp and unexpectedly agonizing.

I made a U-turn, heading for the bar. Someone stepped in front of me. He looked familiar.

Mark, the ex who'd turned out to be harmless.

"I thought that was you," he said.

"Hi." I summoned a bright smile.

"Long time, no see."

"Yeah…"

He cocked his head at the dance floor. "Wanna dance?"

I looked over my shoulder. Caleb's eyes were fixed on me, narrowing as it flicked between Mark and me. Even from across the wide space, I witnessed tension climbing into his body.

I turned back around. "Sure, why not?"

Mark grinned. We headed to the dance floor and, with a sense of wild abandon, I threw myself into the dance. Seconds later Caleb materialized beside me.

"You. Beat it," Caleb snarled at Mark.

Like a true analyst, Mark assessed the situation, saw he was on a losing streak and beat a hasty retreat.

Furious blue eyes glared at me. "What the fuck are you doing?"

I lifted an eyebrow. "I should ask you the same thing. You just deprived me of my dance partner."

"You said you were going to the bathroom," he accused.

"I did. Only when I returned, you seemed...busy."

His jaw clenched. "So you decided to let some punk drool all over you?" he bit out.

I shrugged and his gaze dropped to my cleavage. I discarded my jacket a while ago, and without it my attire had transformed from quirky but acceptably professional to risqué.

"Not just some guy. I let my ex *dance* with me. Now that you've driven him away, are you going to take his place or just growl at me? You're certainly putting on a great show for our audience."

He didn't so much as flick a glance at said audience. He stepped closer, towering over me. I tilted my head, met his furious gaze full-on. Then I placed my hands on his waist. He tensed. Still watching him, I began to move, swaying my hips to the slower tempo of the song now playing. Then I added subtle shoulder shimmies.

His gaze dropped again to my cleavage and a light shiver rolled through him. I dragged my nails across his abs as I swayed deeper. His hand landed on my back and yanked me closer.

"Are you trying to make me lose my shit, Lily?" he rasped in my ear.

I pouted. "I'm just trying to *dance*."

He stared down at me for tense seconds. "Fine. Let's dance."

Over the next five songs, Caleb effortlessly proved

how incredible he was on the dance floor. Smooth moves drew increasing attention until every pair of female eyes was fixed on him.

His wicked smile flashed with increasing frequency, until I was turned on beyond belief.

Enough to make me forget my disgruntlement. Enough to make me grip his hand tight as he led me off the dance floor.

"Want another drink?" he asked as we found a quiet spot near the bar.

"No, thanks."

"Okay." He smoothed a lock of hair behind my ear, then caressed my jaw.

I looked into his gorgeous face and smoldering eyes.

Heart hammering, I bit the inside of my cheek. It was now or never. "Caleb?"

"Yeah?" His voice was gruff, as if the feelings swirling inside me gripped him, too.

"I don't want to wait."

He pulled back, blue eyes piercing as they searched mine. "If this is because of what happened at your presentation—"

"No, it's not." I swirled my tongue over my lip, nerves consuming me. "Please, Caleb. You said you wouldn't hurt me with anything that happens while on this case. I'm saying the same to you. I want you..."

Then he leaned in, one hand braced on the wall above my head. "Just so we're clear, you want me to what, exactly?" he demanded.

I slid my hand up his chest, over his shoulder to his nape and drew him down to me. "I want you to break your rule and take me home," I whispered in his ear. "I want you to take my panties off. I want you to undress me. Or I... I can keep my dress on if you want. And I want you to fuck my lights out. Like you promised."

A deep shudder rolled through him. He continued to stare at me for several heartbeats. "Jesus." He buried his face in my neck, breathed out harshly, then plucked my hand from around his neck. "I knew I wouldn't be able to hold out for much longer. Are you sure?"

"Yes."

His jaw clenched as he tried to fight it for one more minute. Then: "Let's go."

Each mile from Cupertino back home felt like an eternity.

I was hot, getting hotter and wetter every time I glanced at Caleb's tense profile. At the thick rod of his cock pressing against his fly. He changed lanes suddenly, his thighs flexing as he stepped on the gas.

"I like the way you drive."

He flicked me a heated glance. "I like the way you're looking at me."

On impulse, I reclined my seat by thirty degrees and propped up my legs on the dashboard. The skirt of my dress slid down to midthigh.

Heat turned to flames. "Christ, Lily, you're going to get me arrested. I swear to God, if I get pulled over before I've fucked your phenomenal pussy, I'll spank your sweet ass until you can't sit down for a week."

Why did the thought of that sound insanely heavenly? "I have bail money. I'll help you out," I said, sliding my skirt higher.

He swerved into the faster lane, splitting his fevered attention between the road and my thighs. Then he groaned. "Stop. Please, baby, let me get us home in one piece. Then you can show me this insanely sexy, naughty side of you."

My fists bunched. "I don't know if I can wait."

"Well, I'm not fucking you on the side of the road our first time, that's for damn sure," he growled. He reached over and gripped my thigh, pressing my flesh a little roughly before snatching his hand away. "Behave." His terse plea almost made me smile.

"Okay." I released my skirt and draped my arms around the headrest, exposing a generous amount of breasts.

"For fuck's sake! You think that's better?" he rasped hoarsely.

"Hmm. Maybe I'll take a nap. Wake me up when we get home?"

He cursed again as I closed my eyes. A few sharp turns threatened to dislodge my feet from the dashboard. My saucy smile melted away as the minutes ticked by. By the time we arrived home, I was as breathless and as on edge as Caleb.

He turned off the ignition without glancing my way. Stepping out, he stalked over to my side and yanked the door open. His chest rose and fell rapidly as he scoured my reclined body.

Slowly, his eyes locked on mine, he reached over and unsnapped my seat belt. When I attempted to rise, he pressed a hand against my midriff. With his other hand, he trailed his fingers down my inner thigh. Torturously, he slipped beneath my skirt, just as he did this morning. When he reached his destination, his fingers fingers boldly against my mound, cupping me through my panties.

"Jesus, Lily, you're fucking soaked," he muttered with a groan.

He circled his fingers, applying pressure over my engorged clit. I whimpered before I could stop myself.

The sound triggered him into action. He scooped me up, kicked the door shut and strode to the front door. Opening it, he set me down and deactivated the alarm. "Stay put."

The security check took less than five minutes. Anticipation had me breathless by the time he trotted back downstairs. On the second to last step he stopped, hands clasped behind his back.

"Come here." The order was gravel-rough.

On shaky legs, I teetered over to him. With his elevated position, my eyes were level with his fly. And excruciatingly aware of what lay behind it.

He stared at me. Then he nodded at his crotch. "See what you've done to me?"

My head bobbed up and down.

"What are you going to do about it?" he demanded thickly.

I swallowed as a dozen erotic images flashed through my mind, all starting and ending with my hands on his body. My hands found his chest, felt the hard muscles shift beneath my touch, then trailed over his abs to his waist.

Then, breath held, I slowly slid his belt free. Twisted open his button and lowered his zipper.

His broad chest expanded in a deep intake of breath, his eyes dark pools of hunger tracking my every move. Whether it was those incisive eyes or my own insecurities that suddenly pummeled me, I wasn't sure. I froze, my mouth drying as I struggled to breathe.

* * *

With a snatched breath, I slipped my hand beneath his waistband and closed my fingers around him.

His breath hissed out between gritted teeth. He swallowed hard but didn't move an inch. I tugged his pants and briefs lower, exposing the cock that had fueled more lurid fantasies all day.

I stroked him once. Twice. He grew thicker, his dick pulsing in my hold. Emboldened, I tightened my grip, pumped him a few more times.

A tortured groan rumbled from his throat as his fingers sank into my hair. "Fuck, Lily, that feels so good."

I stepped closer, breathed in his earthy scent. But it wasn't enough. I wanted more. I wanted to devour him. I yanked down his pants, cupped his heavy balls. He groaned again, a drop of precum glistening at his broad head.

I flicked my tongue against his slit and he jerked against me. I went to taste him again, but his fingers clenched in my hair, pulling me away.

"No." The denial was torn reluctantly from his throat.

My fingers tightened around him, making his abs clench hard. "Caleb, I… I want you in my mouth." This morning hadn't been enough. I wanted more.

He shuddered, but still shook his head. "I'd love for you to blow me again, sweetheart, but right now, I'm dying to be inside you."

Before I could protest, he scooped me up again like I weighed nothing, pivoted and hauled ass up the stairs. The hallway passed in a blur, the door to my bedroom slamming shut to his kick.

He set me down on the side of the bed. Eyes pinned to

mine, he made short work of his buttons and shrugged off his shirt. He was ripped and tanned all over, hairless except for the thin strip of silky hair that arrowed from his belly button to frame his groin.

"You're so hot," I gushed, unable to stop myself.

Dark color flared across his cheekbones, and his nostrils flared as he toed off his shoes and socks. "Keep talking like that and you won't get to walk straight for a week," he growled.

The very idea made me weak. I sagged onto the bed with a pathetic whimper.

With a smug smile, Caleb bent over me, pressed his forehead against mine as he nudged me backward onto my elbows. He grabbed my knees and made room for himself between my thighs, then fused his lips with mine.

The kiss was ravenous to the point of decimation. Strong fingers kneaded my calves, then drifted down to tug off my shoes. He continued kissing me as his hands reversed direction, trailed up my thighs to slip beneath my dress. He started to pull down my panties, then halfway through he muttered under his breath and ripped it free.

At my gasp, he smiled against my lips. "Sorry."

"You're not really, are you?" I challenged between kisses.

"No," he confirmed, then sucked my tongue into his mouth in a move that melted my brain.

God, the man could kiss. I'd lost the ability to think straight when he pulled away. From his back pocket he took out a pack of condoms and tossed it on the bed.

I was staring at the box, wondering if I would be lucky enough to get through the pack by morning, when he grabbed my thighs and dropped onto his knees. Utterly captivated, I watched Caleb trail his tongue slowly up one inner thigh, then the other, but maddeningly staying away from my needy center.

"Get the lights up in here. I want to see your beautiful pussy properly," he said as he bit lightly on my flesh.

Pleasure shivering through me, it took a moment to realize the only light in the room was the one on my dresser, set to come on automatically at nightfall.

My breath puffed out as my lungs remembered how to work. "Lights," I croaked. Nothing happened. I cleared my throat. "Lights."

The lamps on my nightstand flared softly, chasing away the shadows. Baring me to Caleb's avid gaze. His mouth dropped open, a hot breath escaping as he stared.

And stared.

I squirmed. "Caleb…"

"Shh. Give me a moment," he rasped.

A moment to what? I squirmed harder.

He lifted his gaze and his eyes were on fire. "You're fucking exquisite, Lily." Hunger and worship throbbed in his voice.

In that moment I knew it was entirely possible to orgasm from dirty talk alone. Except it wasn't just dirty talk. Because my heart was flip-flopping in my chest in a weird, terrifying way.

This was just sex. My heart shouldn't…couldn't get involved. No way—

Fear melted into pleasure as his tongue licked me in one long sweep.

Sweet. Heaven.

My eyes rolled as I collapsed onto the bed. He repeated the caress several times, then spread me wider and went to town.

Caleb was a connoisseur, using every part of his mouth on every part of my pussy until I was one delirious mess.

"Please, Caleb," I begged when he drove me to the edge for the umpteenth time, only to withdraw. My fingers speared into his hair, tightening when he started to pull away. "Make me come. *Please, please, please.*"

"Fuck," he groaned against me right before he sucked my clit into his mouth.

I shot off like a rocket, my legs fighting to close as fireworks exploded behind my closed lids. He kept me wide open, working me into a frenzied orgasm that felt like it would last forever.

Convulsions were still rippling through me when I felt him tug on my zipper and remove my dress.

"Caleb," I sighed.

"I'm right here, baby. Hold on." His voice was tight. Edgy.

The sound of ripped foil preceded a hiss from him as he rolled it on; then he crawled over my body. One arm circled my waist, and he tossed me higher up the bed.

"I've been craving this since the moment I saw you," he said, his tongue sliding over one nipple.

My nails dug into his shoulders as fresh waves of pleasure washed over me. "Me, too."

His mouth curved in a smug smile. "How hot were you for me?" The question was rasped against my throat as he grazed my skin with his teeth. He was marking me. I didn't care one little bit.

"Umm…"

He paused and tracked the blush creeping up my neck. "You wanted my cock pounding your pretty little pussy even as you were snapping at me, didn't you?"

I wriggled, half-shamed, half-impatient. "Yes!"

"Don't fret, baby. You're going to get it exactly as you wanted it."

He matched words to action.

With one hand planted next to my head, he trailed the other over my breast, my quivering belly to my pussy. He slid two fingers inside me, his eyes absorbing my reaction. His face tautened at my gasp.

"Please, Caleb, I'm ready. Don't wait."

His teeth gritted, but he continued to fuck me with his fingers, stretching me for another minute before he drew my leg higher, and nudged my entrance with his cock.

Slowly, excruciatingly, he pushed inside me, filling me, stretching me to the point of pain. "God, you're so tight."

He withdrew. Pushed back in. I bit my lip to keep from crying out.

He tensed. "Lily?"

I shook my head. "I'm good."

"You're not good. You're so fucking small," he bit out tersely.

I dug my nails into his back. "Don't stop! Please don't stop." I clamped my legs around him, raised my hips to meet his next thrust. Pain and pleasure collided and I screamed.

"Shit!"

"More," I begged.

A wave of uncertainty flashed across his face. Then it morphed into something else. Something hot and dangerous and guaranteed to send me to another strato-sphere. Incredibly, it made me wetter. He felt it on his next thrust when his cock seated deeper inside me.

A mini-roar erupted from his throat. "Jesus, you're incredible."

I hauled myself up on one elbow, fused my mouth to his for a hot moment before dropping back down. "More, please, Caleb."

He didn't need any more begging. He fucked me until my vision blurred and my heart pounded against my rib cage. Until sweat dripped from his body to mine, and my screams mingled with his thick groans.

Until one last series of pounding ripped me from reality and I blacked out from pleasure. I wasn't sure how long I blissed out. But when I resurfaced, he was still a hard, unspent presence inside me.

Tension still gripped him and sweat dotted his upper lip. "Did I tell you how much I love watching you come?" he rasped.

I shook my head, stunned by his control.

"Well, I do. I could watch you all day." He started to move inside me again.

"Oh, God... I can't."

He kissed me, hard and quick. "Wrap your legs around me and give me one more, baby. Just one more."

He caught the heels of my last climax minutes later, unraveling me as he roared his own release. I was fairly sure I passed out again.

When I came to, I was stretched on top of him, his arms clamped around me with his chin resting on top of my head.

My hand trembled as I caressed his chest. "Caleb?"

"Hmm?"

"I… I don't think I can move."

A low, deep laugh rumbled from him. "That's okay. I can't move, either."

A happy little note strummed in my heart, the first warning that I had let in a seemingly harmless virus that could potentially compromise my very existence.

Because as I drifted off to sleep it struck me that I would be totally okay if he didn't move from my bed.

Not tonight.

Not tomorrow.

Not ever.

CHAPTER TWELVE

Caleb

IT WAS SEVEN o'clock and I'd been up for an hour. I should get up. Draw clear lines by returning to my room.

I didn't engage in cozy heart-to-hearts. I never fell asleep in a woman's bed. Or, worse, woke up and... *lingered*.

Yet I couldn't move.

Because I had no clue where the line was anymore. I'd given Lily the green light to blur it, and I'd completely obliterated it by sleeping with her.

And hell, I'd barely scratched the surface of my need for her. I couldn't get enough of Lily. Her silky softness. Her smell. The way her eyelids fluttered as she dreamed.

I breathed out slowly, reluctant to wake her even though my eager dick was raring to go again.

One taste and I was addicted. Enough to remain in her bed, enjoying her slight weight draped over me as I waited for her to wake up so I could indulge all over again.

Despite being more than a little rattled that I'd also

experienced the soundest, nightmare-free sleep in years. The jagged, heart-pounding images that usually taunted me with how I failed to save my mother were so inherent I'd accepted their presence.

Last night they didn't materialize. It was disturbing to even consider that Lily had anything to do with it. That something as simple as sharing bits of our past with each other had achieved this result.

It was absurd, right?

Unbidden, other moments filtered through—her pain during our first lunch in the restaurant. Her tears when she told me about her stepfather. Exposing her vulnerability at the possibility of one of her team sabotaging her work.

After the sort of childhood Lily had experienced, many people would've cut their families out of their lives and closed themselves off.

I was surprised she hadn't.

Stephen Gracen parked himself on his favorite bar stool in his favorite Irish pub most days before noon and stayed till closing, his tab settled courtesy of the money he'd made off his stepdaughter's talent. The guy I sent to Boston to check him out had reported that while Gracen hadn't exactly talked trash about Lily, he hadn't been complimentary, either.

Gracen was either too bitter or too stupid to realize the gem he had in his stepdaughter.

I'd met several Silicon Valley types who thought they were hot shit because they could string code together that baffled the common man.

In the past few days I'd discovered that Lily, despite being a highly intelligent woman who was mostly likely being paid millions for her professional skills, wasn't in any way a pampered princess.

She was caring and considerate.

And she'd shared her deepest pain with me.

Scattered across several events, they'd seemed minor but put together they were huge. Put-your-trust-in-another-person huge.

When was I remotely okay with being that guy?

I eyed the bedroom door, wondering again why I wasn't hightailing out of it.

Because you want the same from her.

The sharp ache in my chest answered the inner voice.

I shifted again, uncomfortable at the fresh turmoil churning inside me.

This was why I didn't do feelings. So far, every encounter between us had come packed with them, even the moments she'd accepted my help to ease her stress sexually. They were all emotional land mines that usually had pushed my eject button.

I gritted my teeth. I liked her. A hell of a lot. But feelings and fucking didn't mix well. Period.

She stirred against me. I looked down and saw her watching me with contemplative eyes. It was that same look she'd given me before prying secrets from me yesterday in the car.

"You look seriously...*serious.*" Wary questions lurked in her eyes, traces of unease and all those pitfalls I suspected came with the morning after a night of earth-shattering sex.

"For a genius, I expected more eloquence than *seriously serious.*" I kept my voice light.

Her hand drifted up my waist to my chest even though her eyes remained dark, searching. "Okay, how about this." Her thigh brushed my hard-on. "Is that one of my sex toys in your lap or are you just extremely happy to see me?"

Sex. This I could handle.

Talking about my mother and how I would have her back in a heartbeat, if only for a chance to do things differently, push harder, shout louder until my voice was heard, until she got the help she needed, I most definitely couldn't.

I smiled past my disquiet, willing my emotions to detach again as I rolled her over and slid two fingers beneath the choker we never got round to taking off last night. "In case I need to spell it out, your battery-operated boyfriends have had their privileges revoked for the foreseeable future. I'm taking care of your every need from now on."

The words echoed with an unnerving sense of permanence, sending another spike of unease up my spine.

Something flitted through her eyes before her lids swept down, cutting me off from her expression. When she looked back up, her eyes contained nothing but hot sexual promise. "If it's going to be anywhere near as good as last night…"

I brushed my lips over hers, teasing even though I wanted to plunge in and devour. "That better not be a challenge, baby. Or I'll be forced to give you a demonstration."

Her breathing picked up, her pulse racing against my fingers. "Yes, please."

Before the words were out of her mouth, I was sliding my tongue between her lips, giving her a vivid taste of what was coming.

A moan rolled from her throat as her fingers dug

into my back. My dick jerked, homing in on that place between her open thighs. When her eager wetness greeted it, my vision blurred.

For the first time in my life, I wondered what it would be like to take a woman bare, to glide skin on skin. To come at the gateway to where a new life could be created—

Christ, what the hell is wrong with you?

I dragged my mouth from hers, scrambling for sanity before I did something unthinkable, like ask if she was on the pill. If another man had ever been with her the way I suddenly craved to be.

Irrational jealousy bubbled up, joining the deranged carnival going on inside me. The hand fondling one gorgeous breast tightened.

She inhaled sharply. "Caleb?" Bewilderment laced her lust-soaked voice.

Get yourself together!

I dropped a contrite kiss on her mouth. "Shower or pool?" In the hour before she woke, before perplexing thoughts ruined my mood, I listed all the places I wanted to fuck her.

She blinked, then murmured, "Shower."

Thank fuck. I didn't think I'd make it to the pool.

I scooped her out of bed, grabbed a condom before walking us into the bathroom. Like mine, there was a huge copper roll-top bathtub and a separate shower stall.

I held her against me as I turned on the shower and adjusted the temperature. When my hands slid from her ass to her waist to set her down, the arms around my neck clung, forcing me to look into her face.

"Caleb, are you okay?" she asked, still a little hesitant.

Hell, no, I wasn't. But I wasn't going to attempt to explain something that puzzled the shit out of me. "You took your time to wake up. I've been rock-hard for you for over an hour," I deflected, cupping her breasts and mercilessly teasing her nipples.

The tactic worked. Her head dropped back and she whimpered. I continued to fondle her as I nudged her against the wall, watched the spray hit her chest and cascade down her body. I'd never seen anything more beautiful.

She made another innocent, dirty sound and I couldn't help but press my mouth against her, gliding my tongue against hers to devour the sound.

My hand slid down her belly, through the trimmed thatch of hair to her sweet, soaked pussy, before inserting two fingers inside her.

Her hand fisted my hair as she gasped.

"Good?" I demanded against her mouth.

"So, so good," she moaned.

I finger-fucked her slow and steady, until her eyes rolled and her thighs shook. Until her cries echoed through the steam.

Only then did I slide on the condom and flip her around. "Brace your hands on the wall and arch your back for me, my dirty little angel."

A smile laced her arousal. "I see you've started with the pet names again."

"I never promised I would stop. Besides, you could lead a man straight to his doom."

She sent me a sultry glance over one shoulder. "Just a man?"

Something bit hard inside me. "Fine. You could lead

me straight to the gates of hell. Is that what you want to hear?"

Her eyes searched mine. "Maybe."

I hooked one finger into the choker, using the leverage to bring her head back to align her face with mine. "That back still isn't arched. Do I need to spank obedience out of you?" I growled against her throat.

Her whole body shook. Then, with a slow sensual stretch that wouldn't have been amiss on a mermaid, she curved her spine, until her gorgeous twin globes perfectly framed my cock.

I looked down and nearly lost my mind. "God…Lily. You know exactly how to drive me insane, don't you?"

Her answer was to rise on her tiptoes. "Fuck me, Caleb."

With a less than gentle touch, I grabbed her hip and yanked her back onto my waiting cock.

She screamed. My insanity tripled. I forgot to breathe, forgot to think. Forgot everything but the need to bury my cock inside her over and over again.

"Yes. Yes! More," she panted, delirious in her pleasure.

"You're a greedy little thing, aren't you? Always demanding more."

Her fingers clawed the tiles. "Don't stop. Please don't stop."

She continued to beg. I gave her everything until we were seconds from imploding. Then she reached up, covered the hand I had on her choker, locked her eyes on mine and croaked, "Tighter."

A little shocked and a hell of a lot more turned on than I'd ever been in my life, I hooked another finger beneath the tight lace.

She started to come. Endlessly. Gripping me with muscles that demanded my complete surrender. I clung to sanity just so I could watch her for one more soul-shaking second. And holy hell, Lily Gracen, lost in ecstasy, was beyond magnificent.

In that moment before the bottom fell out of my world, I wished I could freeze time. Wished this transcendental moment would never end.

Transcendental. Soul-shaking. *Feelings.*

The next shudder that gripped me had nothing to do with my phenomenal orgasm and everything to do with *emotions* attempting to shift the center of my gravity.

Enough.

The stern warning didn't stop me from kissing her crown and sliding my hand down her back before I pulled out. We both groaned and subsided into silence, words seeming superfluous in this aftermath. I disposed of the condom, turned her around, then directed the flow of water over both of us.

Her eyes were still glazed, but as I reached for the simple lock that secured her choker, her gaze darted to mine.

I froze, waiting for her to speak.

Her nostrils quivered as she sucked in a breath. "I… want you to know…I've never done that before," she muttered. "I was just…"

I brushed my fingers over her lips, absorbing the electric delight that lit through me. "You don't need to explain, sweetheart. If it helps, the effect on you was fantastic for me, too."

A deep blush swept over her cheeks as she caught my hand in hers and kissed my knuckles.

The move was unexpectedly sweet. For a split second, I wanted to succumb.

I returned to my task and undid the choker. Red marks ringed her neck, a perfect imprint of the lace pattern. I trailed my lips over the mark, still caught in the cycle I couldn't break free from, feeling a little perverse that the sight of it aroused me.

The gel I picked up smelled like Lily. I washed her from head to toe, lingering in places that made her gasp.

Then she held out her hand for the bottle. I handed it over and braced my palms over the wall above her head. I was hard again before she was halfway down my chest.

I didn't reach for her. I needed a moment to regroup, to make sure I could emerge from whatever was happening between us with my faculties intact. When she sank onto her knees, I squeezed my eyes shut and locked my jaw as her small, wicked fingers washed my cock, my balls, then finally moved lower.

I was so focused on not grabbing her for another mind-blowing fuck, I didn't realize she'd ducked under my arm to wash my back until she gasped.

Shit. The scar.

Gentle fingers touched my left shoulder blade where the bullet grazed me. "What happened?"

Her soft sympathy reached inside me, further weakening rigid foundations. My shrug didn't hit the offhand mark as I turned. "Trigger-happy client. Let's get out of here and I'll tell you the full story over breakfast."

She looked disappointed but she didn't say anything as I rinsed off and grabbed a towel. In the bedroom I gathered my clothes, aware that her gaze grew more guarded with each passing second.

I tightened my gut against the urge to reassure her. It was better this way. I wasn't about to break open a box of hearts and flowers. Even if I once possessed such a box it had been smashed beneath the reality of repeated promises made and broken with callous indifference. Every single promise made to help my mother had been broken.

Then Kirsten came along and drove the knife in deeper.

I wasn't about to speak words I didn't mean or give reassurance that I couldn't back up. "I'll see you downstairs in ten?"

She blinked, then jerked out a nod.

I walked out, suspecting that the word *bastard* was lit up in Lily's mind right now. I slammed the door in my room, then stood frozen in place. Could I have handled it better?

No. Maybe. Minutes ticked by, then I heard her walk past my door.

Fuck it. I threw on fresh clothes with an urgency I didn't understand, and rushed downstairs to find Lily hovering by the front door wearing a tight black T-shirt that ended where a pair of leather shorts started. Those shorts ended at the top of her thighs, leaving an indecent amount of leg showing. She wore minimal makeup, but her eyes were darkly outlined, and her lips gleamed a faint pink. The wrist cuffs were back in place, as was a new, broader choker.

God, if she was trying to torture me, it was working. She looked phenomenal.

I swallowed my tongue, spotted the keys in her hand and realized she was dressed for *outside*.

"Where are you going?"

Her chin lifted. "For breakfast. Where else?"

"Lily—"

"Oh, and I'm driving this time." She twirled the keys. "You can come with me or you can follow me."

My jeans and T-shirt were okay to go out but I would've followed regardless. She stepped outside and hurried to the garage.

"Lily, let's talk about this—"

"Let's not," she snapped. "And if you even *think* about physically restraining me, I'll rip your balls off."

I believed her. But I still shook my head as I followed her to the garage. "No can do, baby. I catch the smallest sign of danger and I'm getting *very* physical. Count on it."

I let her glare at me for a full five seconds before opening the Mini's door for her. She slid behind the wheel. Going around I said a prayer and contorted myself into the passenger seat.

She drove fast without breaking limits and considerately without being a pushover. Me, she completely ignored. We passed several respectable cafés before she stopped at an upmarket bistro. She surprised me by bypassing the parking lot and heading for the drive-through lane. It wasn't your average drive-through. Shiny food trucks displayed glorious baked goods, bacon, cheeses and everything in between.

Two guys and a woman manned the trucks. The woman smiled when she spotted Lily. "Hey, girl." She handed over two big paper bags with the bistro's logo on it.

"Thanks," Lily replied.

I deposited the bags on the backseat and reached for my wallet, but she was already driving away.

In between ensuring I wasn't blocking the blood flow to my legs and trying not to drool over her legs, I decided to maintain silence. Ten minutes later she pulled up to an abandoned lot with a tall wall erected on the south edge. She drove to the center, stopped next to a bench and turned off the engine.

I stepped out with our food and looked around. "What's this place?" I asked.

"It used to be a drive-in theater." She reached into the bag and started setting out the food. Bacon. Bagels. Cream cheese. Coffee.

I had zero appetite but I accepted the coffee. She laced hers with cream and sugar, took a sip and set it back down.

"Who owns this place?"

"For now, the original owner. Next month, maybe me."

I nodded at the food. "Why the drive-through? Why here?"

She stared into her coffee. Then shrugged. "Your guys didn't have a chance to check out the bistro first. And I knew I could be alone here."

I. Not *we.*

I waited a beat. "You're pissed."

Her mouth firmed. "Give the man a prize."

My jaw clenched. "Enough. You've made your point with your little tantrum."

Anger flashed across her face. I watched her rein it in. "Fine. Talk to me, then, Caleb. Convince me I didn't

just sleep with an asshole who couldn't even be bothered with conversation after he fucked me."

"Jesus…"

"Leave him out of it. This is between you and me."

Absurdly, I wanted to smile. But her beautiful face
was a picture of hurt she was trying to hide. I dragged
a hand down my stubbled face. "Full confession. What
we did kinda…blew my mind."

Shock replaced hurt, and then her expression slowly
softened. After a minute she nodded. "Me, too," she
whispered, blushing fiercely.

"Okay. Now that we've got that squared away, how
can I make you feel…less pissed?"

She grabbed a sliced bagel, tore a piece, but didn't
eat it. "I want to know you, Caleb. Tell me something."

I took a deep breath. "You know I grew up on the
rough streets of LA."

Her hand trembled as she stared wide-eyed at me.
"Yes. Was it after you lost your mom?"

Christ. I weighed the option of evasion against the
return of her hurt, and grimaced inwardly. "It was before. And after. She was a manic-depressive. The moments of light in her darkness were very few but for
the first nine years of my life she had medical insurance and a decent doctor to prescribe her the right
medication."

"Caleb—"

My fingers brushed her lips, silencing her. "I don't
like telling this story. Let me tell it once and be done.
Okay?"

A small nod.

My chest tightened as memories flooded in. "She
lost her job and the domino effect of no insurance, los-

ing our house, ending up at a halfway house, then a shelter, sent her into a deeper hole. I was eleven before we were assigned a place in Trenton Gardens."

Lily winced but I couldn't let her sympathy affect me.

"But it was too late. She'd lost the will to..." I took a breath. "I was the only thing she fought for. Every time social services tried to take me away, she would fight to keep me. I've no idea how she did it, but she won. But then she would spiral back into darkness. I couldn't help her. I called every helpline I could find, wrote a dozen letters every week to anyone I thought could help. The doctors we managed to see were hopeless. Twice, she tried to end her life. Every time they sent her home from the hospital with a damn leaflet. I even pawned her jewelry to pay for an appointment with a private doctor. The pills he prescribed helped. When she ran out I called my social worker and asked her to help me get her more. She just...laughed at me." Anger and despair I hadn't felt in a long time swelled inside me. I withdrew my hand from Lily's, clenched it in my lap and took another breath. "Anyway, she succeeded on her third attempt."

"Oh, God..."

Tears spilled down her cheeks. I opened my mouth to tell her not to cry for me. Then stopped. I *wanted* her soft sympathy. It was a salve to a wound that had never healed. Shedding tears for my mother was one of the many things I hadn't been able to do for her. Maybe Lily's tears would be enough to let her know how sorry I was for failing.

Lily got up, walked round and slid into my lap. "I'm so sorry." Her arms circled my neck. I hugged her close, breathed in her goodness. And just like in the bathroom, I never wanted this moment to end.

I never wanted to let her go.

Which was crazy. We'd only known each other for a week. And...dammit, I didn't do feelings!

I looked around and grimaced. "Can we continue this at home?" I said, raising my eyebrow.

For some reason my cocked eyebrow made her smile. "Too wide-open-spaces for you?"

"Something like that," I said, looking down at the table. "Breakfast is ruined, though."

She shrugged. "I wasn't that hungry anyway."

I scowled. "A woeful waste of good bacon."

Her smile widened as she stood up. "We have bacon at home," she suggested.

Unable to keep my hands off her, I grabbed her and trailed my hands up her thighs. "Is there an offer in there?"

Her fingers tunneled through my hair, gently massaging my scalp. "If you want. But I don't break out my culinary skills for just anyone."

I caught a trace of pain through the flippant words. "Why not?"

Green eyes darted away, then came back. "Stepdaddy issues. In return for him...tolerating me, I had to cook for him. It made me hate cooking."

I caressed her damp cheek. "He doesn't deserve your love. Or your pain."

Her eyes misted. "It's not easy to brush it off."

True. I'd lived with guilt and anger for so long it was fused into my DNA. "I get it."

"Caleb?"

"Yeah."

"I was thinking…maybe your presence has achieved the opposite of what we hoped. Maybe instead of bringing my stalker out into the open, he's given up?"

"Sorry to disappoint you, but assholes like that don't go away easily. I'm close to catching him. Trust me. Okay?"

Small, soft hands framed my face. "Okay."

My hands coasted higher, brushed the underside of her breasts. Her breathing altered. "Let's go home."

She nodded.

We threw the uneaten breakfast in the trash. I winced as I folded myself back into the car. "This is the second thing I'm punishing you for when we get back."

Her eyes widened. "What's the first thing?"

"Driving me insane with those fucking shorts," I griped, reaching down to adjust my hard-on. "That was the intention, wasn't it?"

Pink flared in her cheeks. "Maybe."

"Well, you are *definitely* getting your ass spanked for it."

Hot anticipation washed away the last of the sadness and pain in her eyes.

When she pulled up at a stop sign, I dragged my gaze from her slim thighs to her face, then her hair. "Has your hair always been this color?"

She shook her head. "It used to be dark blond." She grabbed a lock at her right temple. "This part started turning whiter when I was twelve. It was cool at first. Then I got tired of it. So I went white all over."

"I like it. A lot."

Her gaze latched on to mine. We stared at one another, pure electricity zinging between us. The driver behind us honked impatiently. She jumped, then laughed. Her laughter triggered mine, easing the tension of the past hour. The lightness stayed as we drove through the gates. As I threw her over my shoulder and rushed through the front door into the living room.

Maybe this…unburdening thing wasn't catastrophic after all.

Maybe breaking my rule for her wasn't the end of the world.

Maybe—

We froze as the TV flicked to life of its own accord. Except that was impossible. Not without electronic intervention.

That intervention arrived in the form of neon green bits of code raining down the screen, then a masked face framed by a black hoodie. I pushed Lily behind me as if it would protect her from the loud, distorted voice that filled the room.

"Hello, Lily Gracen. First of all, congratulations. You're very close to achieving perfection with your code. Don't be frightened. I represent interested parties wishing to form a partnership. Apologies if I've made you a little…uncomfortable lately. But I urge you not to give the code to SDM or I'll have no choice but to stay in your life a while longer. Think about it. I'll be in touch. Oh, and tell that fixer to go home to LA. He won't be of much use to you."

The strangled sound Lily made cut to the heart of me. I took a step toward the TV just as it went blank.

A loud pop shot through the house, then an eerie silence echoed in its wake.

CHAPTER THIRTEEN

Caleb

"WHAT ARE YOU DOING?"

"We're getting the hell out of here." I spotted an overnight bag and handed it to her. "Pack what you need but do it fast."

She reached for my hand. "Caleb—"

I turned away, fist clenched, the need to punch something running wild through me. "Lily, the asshole hacked your Wi-Fi, sent the transmission, then hit the house with an electromagnetic wave that killed the electricity on the whole street. You're not staying here. Not until I have my hands around his fucking throat."

To her credit, she didn't dawdle. She stuffed clothes into the bag, added essentials, then grabbed her satchel and purse.

Ten minutes later we were driving away from the house.

"Your guys searched the area. Did they find anything?"

My security team's presence had provided some reassurance, but not enough to close the horrified black chasm in my stomach at the thought that from the moment we returned to the house, we were sitting ducks. It snatched my breath. Reminded me of the consequences of dropping my guard.

"Caleb?"

I gathered my scattered thoughts. "They found motorcycle tracks behind the house."

She flinched at my cold tone, but said nothing for a couple of miles. "Where are we going?"

"To the airport."

"And then?"

"We're swinging by my place in Malibu. Then I'm taking you to the safe house in Lake Tahoe." I should've done that in the first place. Regardless of the fact that bringing her home had produced the desired effect of drawing the stalker out, the flip side was much worse. The EMP blast could've been knockout gas. Or—

"So you still don't know who it is?"

My fingers tightened on the wheel. "No."

She didn't speak much after that. Neither did I. I was too busy playing worst-case-scenario.

Anything could've happened to Lily.

My jet was ready when we arrived at the airport. We took off immediately. Leaving Lily in the club chair upfront, I retreated to the back of the plane and dialed Maggie.

She answered on the first ring. "Boss, how can I help?"

"I've left three guys in Palo Alto to track down this bastard. I need another team at the Reno safe house."

"I'll get right on it."

I hung up, then went through my contacts. Every favor owed to me, I shamelessly called on. By the time we landed in LA I was in a better frame of mind.

My house in Malibu was set on a bluff that overlooked a private beach. The helipad that came with the property had been used only a handful of times. Today it came in handy as a way of avoiding LA's horrendous traffic.

I walked in and my steps slowed. The last time I was here I was in complete control of my world, my only focus on being bigger, better, *badder*.

In the space of seven days, the ground had shifted beneath me, attempted to change my orbit. All because of the stunning woman who stopped beside me, her eyes lighting on the space I'd claimed, possessions that proclaimed my success. That fierce yearning to hang on to her clobbered me again. I smashed it to pieces.

No more breaking rules.

"Hang tight. I'll be right back." I sprinted upstairs to my bedroom to retrieve the weapons I kept in the safe.

I came down to find her at the window, staring at the ocean with her arms wrapped around her middle. She turned at my approach. "Can't we just stay here?"

The urge to say yes pounded me. "No. This place is secure enough but it's in my name. Any fucker with a computer can find it. I need you off the grid."

Resigned, she nodded.

We headed outside and reboarded the chopper.

"Chance will need to know I'm going off-grid."

My teeth gritted. "No, he doesn't. You still have time before your deadline. And frankly, I don't want him anywhere near you right now."

Again, she didn't react as expected. She was either in shock or afraid. Neither of the two sat well with me.

"Lily…"

Her fingers curled in her lap. "What if it's someone close to me? What would that say about my judgment?"

"You're not blaming yourself for this." That ball was squarely in my court.

"Since you don't know *who* it is, that's easier said than done," she murmured.

I had no answer to that so I remained silent as we reboarded the plane and took off.

There was very little in the way of conversation during the flight.

Many times I opened my mouth to say something, then decided against it.

Action, not platitudes.

Maggie had lined up another SUV for us, and I hightailed it out of the airport with one eye on the police scanner on the dashboard. I wanted to get us to the cabin on the Nevada side of the lake as quickly as possible without attracting attention from the cops for speeding.

Twenty minutes later I breathed a sigh of relief when I spotted the turnoff for the dirt track leading to the cabin. I'd kept it overgrown on purpose. There were no signposts or no trespassing warnings to attract inquisitive neighbors.

The Jeffrey pines lining the track and surrounding the property were ideal for mounting security cameras and other intruder-warning triggers.

I pulled up in front of the cabin in Knots Peak, killed the engine and glanced over at Lily. She was staring at the log building that would be her home until I came through with my assurance to catch her stalker.

My gaze slid past her to the three-leveled property. The one-bedroom dilapidated structure I bought five years ago had been expanded into a no-cost-spared piece of real estate worth ten times its original price.

It was one of three safe houses I owned around the country. The other four were overseas but this was my favorite. On the rare occasion I took downtime from fixing other people's problems, the cabin was my first choice.

There would be no downtime, though. I'd dropped my guard, messed around with a client and the bastard had gotten close.

Fury and guilt bubbled inside as I threw open the door. "Let's get you inside."

I grabbed her bag and walked her to the front door. A palm print and alphanumeric code released the lock.

Rugs spread out in the wide hallway and over polished wooden floors throughout the cabin muffled our footsteps. Exposed oak beams propped up high ceilings in the living room, and light filtered in from a wide window facing the lake.

I stashed her bag in the bedroom before returning to the living room. Still clutching her satchel, she stood at the window, lost in the view.

"The window is one-way glass so no one can see inside. Even at night you'll be able to see the lake. That should help a little." Shit, I sounded like a damn realtor.

She turned, wary eyes catching mine. "Help with what?"

I shrugged. "Not everyone likes being stuck in the middle of nowhere. The lake will give you something to look at."

"I'm okay with it," she replied, although her sleek white throat moved in a nervous swallow. I dragged my gaze away from the smooth landscape of her skin. Giving in to those insane yearnings was what had landed us here.

"Good. Security-wise, the outer doors are made of solid oak. It would take a very large ax or a sizeable explosive device to breach it. The woods for half a mile radius are part of the property. There are a few booby traps to prevent intruders."

She frowned. "What kinds of traps?"

"Very effective ones," I gritted out, partly to reassure her, partly to reassure myself.

She flinched; then her lips pursed.

I dragged my hands down my face and walked over to her. Every cell in my body was dying to touch her. But I'd already let too much *personal* get in the way.

It was time to revert to Caleb Steele, Stone-Cold Fixer.

Jaw set, I moved toward the French doors. "I need to go through the cabin's security with you. Familiarize yourself with the property."

"Why are you being so cold?"

Her soft, bewildered words were like a punch to the gut. I steeled myself against it before turning to face her.

"You wanted to know what happened to my shoulder? I got involved with a client. Kirsten was an actress, one of my first clients. She'd made a couple of wrong choices in the past. The studio she was working with was threatening to fire her over some revealing pictures. She begged me to help. She was beautiful and I was young, foolish and…into her." Lily's gaze dropped and a look I couldn't fathom crossed her face. "When she needed a car, I gave her mine. When she needed a place to stay, I asked her to move in with me." My bitter laughter seared my throat. "Hell, I believed we were in a *relationship.* Right up until I found her banging the director. Even then I thought she was the victim. I

punched his lights out and caused general mayhem that
ensured my fledgling career tanked before it'd taken
off properly. And Kirsten's response? She went off her
head because I'd just ruined her chances for another
movie and decided she didn't want me in her life after
all so she tried to fucking shoot me."

Lily blanched. "Oh, my God!"

I shrugged despite the fury of bitterness and anger
dueling inside me. "Luckily, she was a very lousy shot.
Anyway, if it hadn't been for Ross's father, I'd still be
fixing problems for gangsters back in Trenton Gardens.
He gave me a piece of advice, one I'd already figured
out the hard way—never get involved with a client."

A horrified little sound escaped her throat, scraping on my nerve endings. "S-so you think this is my
fault?" she whispered.

I opened my mouth to say *hell, no*, but then stopped.
She was partly to blame. She'd gotten under my skin
with her soft sympathy and her flashes of innocence
and her incredible inner strength in the face of adver-
sity and her gloriously tight body. Even now, she continued to drive me insane with her jaw-dropping beauty.

"I think my point has been proven conclusively that
shit happens when you break the rules," I said. "Besides, you were on a mission of your own, weren't you?"

She gasped and her eyes darkened in pain. I turned
away. My point was made. And I still had a stalker
to catch.

"Security tour. Now." I crossed to the French doors
on the other side of the living room and stepped out
onto the porch, not looking back to see if she was following.

The sky was a clear blue, and the cool air was drifting in from the lake. It was all so fucking idyllic.

When I heard her behind me, I went down wooden stairs leading to a sloping garden. A staggered limestone feature tumbled water into the rock pond one level lower and stopped next to a covered hot tub. I bypassed it, trying not to think of Lily immersed in the swirling bubbles, completely naked, with the setting sun gleaming on her glorious skin.

A few hours ago I would've said, *forget the fucking tour, let's go to bed*. But my sex-addled brain had put her in danger.

We skirted the garden and the high stone walls to stop at the side gate. "This leads down to the lake. And a boat for a quick getaway if you need to. The code is 40998061."

Fear sparked through the shadowed swirls in her eyes. I forced myself not to react to it.

After a few beats she placed her thumb against the panel, and the gate sprang open. The scent of pine and earth grew as we stepped onto the uneven path and walked in silence to the jetty. "Have you driven a boat before?"

"No."

"The keys are hidden beneath the sixth slab…right here." I tried to ignore the feel of her silky skin as I caught her arm and pointed to the wooden plank. "It's screwed in but loose enough to pry apart in a hurry if you need to."

The boat was a few years old but was kept in good condition and fully fueled at all times.

She hopped down before I could help her, and then took a step away from me. I gritted my teeth against the grating discomfort in my chest and pointed to the ignition. "Twist to the left and hold. Engine should kick in. Then push the lever. Ignore everything else."

"It looks pretty straightforward."

"It might not be if you're panicking," I bit out.

Her cheeks lost color, but she nodded. "Understood."

We returned to the house and I took her round the lower level to another door. "Same code as the gate but backward."

"16089904," she repeated instantly.

Hell, even scrambling to maintain distance, I couldn't help but admire her incredible brain.

The large room that doubled up as a games room and gym took up most of the square footage of the cabin. It was also self-contained enough to use as a sleeping place for the odd bodyguard or two when needed.

I bypassed the doors connecting the short hallway to the stairs leading up and headed to the far wall. When she joined me, I pushed on the fourth wooden panel. A five-foot partition sprang open to reveal a small spiral staircase. "This takes you straight up into the kitchen. After you."

She sprinted up lithely on the balls of her feet. I took the stairs much slower, unable to take my eyes off the ass that'd cradled my cock in the shower this morning.

Her steps slowed as she neared the top.

"Is there a problem?" The question emerged with a tight croak.

I stopped two steps below her, keeping us at eye level. Close enough for me to lean forward and taste the sinfully gorgeous mouth currently pinched with tension. I locked my knees hard and reminded myself that my wayward cock had brought us to this.

"You didn't bring in your bag from the car. And you've just given me a very detailed tour. Why?"

Chains shackled my chest. "Because I'm returning to Palo Alto."

"You're leaving." The statement was final and chilled. Unaccustomed dread slowly filled my chest.

I'd pushed her into accepting that what happened with us was a mistake, and yet seeing that acceptance in her eyes had lodged a cold, hard ball in my gut.

I braced a hand against the banister as another truth bit me hard. I'd told her to *trust me*. And had done zero to back it up.

My failures, rehashed just a few short hours ago, slashed me in half.

Bitter laughter seared my throat as patterns were laid bare.

My success rate with jobs that didn't require emotional expenditure was near perfect. Those I allowed myself to care about were doomed to failure. My mother. Then Kirsten. Now Lily.

And yes...I cared about Lily. Hell, I was damned sure *caring* was too mild a word for it.

I gathered every last scrap of emotion, knotted it into a cold ball, and buried it deep. Then I forced a nod, despite my veins beginning to fill with icy water. "I can't find your stalker stuck here with you. I need to get back, rattle a few cages."

Her eyes, no longer that gorgeous shade of green I loved, shadowed even further. Then she gathered that admirable strength and nodded. "I see. You better get to it then."

Something that tasted uncannily like anguish billowed up from my feet to lodge in my throat. No amount of bracing myself could prevent it saturating every corner of my being as I watched her walk to the sofa and snatch up her satchel.

"Lily." I said her name for the simple, selfish reason that I couldn't bear the distance between us.

She glanced impatiently at me. "What?"

I pointed to the fridge. "You didn't have any breakfast. You need to eat something."

Her gaze swung blankly to the fridge. Then she frowned. "I'm not hungry."

"Well, eat anyway. You'll need—"

"I'm not a child. I'm capable of feeding myself when I need to, thanks."

I opened my mouth. My phone beeped. I read the message and my heart sank.

Me, the man of action who abhorred drawn-out goodbyes, was reeling that his time was up with Lily Gracen. "Your security team is here."

She nodded stiffly as I introduced her to her three minders. Two disappeared to take up positions around the perimeter. The one tasked to stay inside with her at all times retreated to a respectful distance.

"Was there anything else?" she asked coldly.

There were a thousand things. But everything started and ended with the fact that I'd failed her. So not a single word emerged.

Slowly her eyes grew colder, her face a mask of disappointment as she strutted to the door and pointedly threw it open.

"Goodbye, Caleb." The echoing finality behind her words stayed with me long after my plane soared into the sky, racing me away from her.

CHAPTER FOURTEEN

Lily

HE WAS GONE.

Forty-eight hours later I still couldn't believe how quickly everything had turned to ash. When Maggie called last night to ask if I needed anything, I had to bite my tongue hard to stop myself from asking about Caleb.

What good would it have done? He blamed me for pushing him into territory he'd never wanted to revisit. And he was right. I'd taken advantage of our insane chemistry just so I could prove I was in control. And I was the one bleeding with no end of the ravaging pain in sight.

The truth wasn't hard to accept. The pain that came with it was.

I'd allowed myself to hope. To care.

If only I hadn't let the moments of gentleness and protectiveness weave into my heart. If only he hadn't opened up at the drive-in...

If only the phenomenal sex hadn't left me raw and reeling and craving the impossible.

From the start he'd made it clear sex was off the

table as long as I was his client. And I'd seen that as a challenge.

Misery clawed through me. My heart shuddered and I blinked to stop the fierce prickling that preceded tears.

God, was it even possible to fall in love in seven short days?

My inability to catch my breath, the endless turmoil in my mind and the anguish coursing through my body, screamed *yes*. Butting heads with him at the start had been my mating dance. Giving him my body had gone hand in hand with giving him my heart. A heart left battered even before it'd had a chance to soar.

If I had to pinpoint when it was well and truly doomed, it was the moment he confirmed why he became a fixer.

I couldn't even hate him for that. He'd never hidden himself from me.

Maybe it was better this way. Having happiness snatched from me before I truly tasted it would be a blessing somewhere down the road.

I stared at the horizon, watching the fingers of dawn trail the inky blue sky. Down by the water I spotted Kurt, the minder who'd pulled lake duty. I didn't sleep a wink last night. Surprise. But I managed to snatch moments of lucidity, long enough to confirm that it was Sanjeet's code that sabotaged the beta test.

Further anguish weighted my heart, but I was thankful I didn't have to deal with him just yet. I would repair the code on my own and test it vigorously before the next meeting.

Because now more than ever, I needed total control of my life. I had a feeling I'd need it because this ravaging pain wasn't done with me by a long stretch.

Caleb

I jerked awake from a sleep filled with alternating images of losing my mother, then Lily. As I watched, screaming, their images blended, then drifted farther and farther out of reach.

I dragged myself upright to a sweat-soaked T-shirt and guilt-laden relief that immediately morphed into pain.

It'd been like this for the last four interminable days. In the cold light of day, I could distract myself with something else, although success in that area was dwindling. But in my dreams I was helpless against the savage craving; helpless to fight the powerful emotions that poured out of my soul, wrenched me from sleep only to mock me with the emptiness of my reality.

I stared out the window of the cabin's guest room, the peace I usually found here shattered.

Why the hell did I put her in my bedroom?

So you can torture yourself with visions of her when she's gone, why else?

Perversely, the thought that I'd have *something* to hang on to soothed me a little.

Jesus.

I rose, changed my T-shirt, added sweatpants and grabbed my phone. As I approached the door, my heart began to race.

I told myself the smell of coffee didn't mean a thing. Lack of sleep and the couple of drinks I had on the plane equaled a foggy brain. I could've set the coffee machine myself when I rolled in at...whatever o'clock.

I entered the living room, saw her, and thoughts of time dissolved.

She sat cross-legged on the sofa nearest the window, beneath the worshipful rays of the morning sun.

The leather and lace comprising her usual work attire had been swapped for a less dramatic getup of black T-shirt and jersey shorts. But a choker still circled her neck, cuffs binding her wrists.

She hadn't seen me yet. I needed an uninterrupted minute to imprint her on my memory. Some of the things I said couldn't be taken back.

Hell, my behavior had been beyond shitty. So yeah, the chances of her being gone by nightfall were extremely high.

But God, I needed another minute, because I'd missed her beautiful face...her body...so damn much.

She was spectacular, if elusive, in my dreams but the reality was infinitely better. I approached, the contrasting black-and-white vision of her a magnet I couldn't resist.

She was completely absorbed in her work, her fingers dancing in a hypnotic blur over the keyboard. Earbuds firmly in place cut her off from me.

But then, greedily, I wanted those beautiful green eyes that had invaded my dreams every night since I left on me.

As if she heard my thoughts, her fingers froze.

Her head snapped up, her eyes widened, then dimmed. Her resting expression was a punch in the gut. I tried to absorb it as I strolled closer.

"Hey." She eyed me warily as she plucked her earbuds out. "I didn't…when did you get back?"

"Very late. Or very early."

Her eyes grew more guarded. "Is…everything all right?"

I hesitated.

The moment I answered, it was over. There would be nothing keeping her here. A shamefully large part of me wanted to stall, like I'd wanted to freeze time in the shower, and at the drive-in. Hell, every moment with Lily deserved to be preserved in amber.

But the universe selfishly ticked forward. Gritting my teeth, I indicated the sofa. "May I sit?"

She stared blankly at me, then down at the space before shrugging. "It's your house, Caleb." Her voice was a chilled rasp.

I ignored the ache sucking oxygen out of my lungs and sat down. When she tensed and tucked her legs firmer beneath her, I bunched my fist on my thigh.

Wow, you blew it good this time, Steele.

"Caleb?" Her fingers were curled tensely around the lid of her laptop.

I cleared my throat and fired up the video app on my phone. In a dark gray room, across a desk and two chairs, two men faced each other.

I pointed to the younger man. "Do you know him?"

She set her laptop aside. "No. Should I?"

"His name is Eric Vasiliev. He works for Baitlin Tech."

She blinked. "Baitlin was on the list I gave you."

I nodded. "He's also Sanjeet's roommate."

Alarm widened her eyes. "Okay. Who's the other guy?"

"A friend of mine. He's in law enforcement. He did me a solid."

"How?"

"He interviewed the remaining people on the list, helped me fill out a few blanks."

Her breath caught, hope filling her eyes. "Are you saying... Have you caught my stalker?"

I smiled. "Yes. You don't need to worry. They're in custody. And your algorithm is safe."

Relief drenched her face. She covered her open mouth with one hand. "Oh, my God," she whispered.

I wanted to touch her so badly my hand burned with the need.

She took a few more breaths, and then her gaze returned to the screen. "Did Sanjeet have anything to do with it?"

"Not directly. But he unwittingly started the whole thing. Eric saw what he was working on during a FaceTime call and asked a few questions, enough to get an idea of what you were working on."

"But Sanjeet was just a third of the team, and the others didn't know about each other."

I hit the second video in the folder. "They didn't, but she did."

Lily stared at the video, hurt and anger flashing across her face. "Miranda?"

"Yeah. She had access to you. All she had to do was listen and watch and tell Eric when to strike."

"But...why?"

The throb of anguish in her voice cut through me. I wanted to absorb her pain. "Money. She was dating Eric. They hatched the plan together. All they had to do was destabilize the team, stalk you in the hopes of you making a mistake. If that didn't work they were going to move to outright blackmail to get the code. They had a bidding war going with six countries."

"She told your friend all of this?"

I nodded. "We got it all on tape."

"Oh, my God." Her eyes filled with tears.

Unable to hold back my need, I reached for her. She flinched away, jumped to her feet and paced to the window.

I threw my phone on the coffee table, swallowing the boulder of pain in my throat.

After a minute she swiped her eyes. When she faced me, her face was a controlled mask. "So it's over. I can leave?"

Every ounce of power concentrated in keeping my jaw clenched just so I didn't have to answer. But the part of me that yearned to give her what she wanted forced my head to nod. "The police will need a statement from you at some point, but with the confession they have it should all be straightforward."

Then, unable to sit still, I surged to my feet. "Lily—"

"I want to leave. Now. Please."

No. *Hell, no.*

One look at her face showed my firecracker was back, ready to rain fire and brimstone on me if I didn't grant her wish.

"Lily, we need to talk."

She shook her head. "I need to pack." She darted down the hallway so fast she was a blur.

I followed because, fuck it, I was tired of feeling like shit.

I knocked. At her silence, I entered. She was hold-

ing a top, staring blindly into her suitcase. I took another moment to memorize her face.

Her head snapped up, and her face tightened. "What
do you want, Caleb? We said everything that needed
saying last time."

"No we didn't. I have more to say."

She looked mutinous for a moment, and then her
cute chin lifted. "Fine, let's hear it."

My fists tightened, the magnitude of my need an
overwhelming weight pressing me down. But I pushed
ahead. "I don't want you to leave. We're not done. Hell,
we barely even started. I want you back."

A look flashed through her eyes but it was gone
too quickly to read. "Wanting me back suggests you
had me in the first place. Did you?" she queried almost carelessly.

"What?"

She threw the top into the suitcase. "Let's forget
that for a minute. You want me…back…for how long?"

I frowned. "Lily—"

"A week? A month? Two months?"

I shrugged. "It's something we can figure out together."

She laughed, an acid-tipped sound that whipped
blades through me. "How? What criteria would you
use? When the sex isn't so hot anymore? When your
next exciting case came up?"

"If you want a time frame I'm not going to give
you one," I snapped with more heat than I'd intended.

She paled. I reached out. She flinched. This wasn't
how I'd intended it to go. At all.

"Lily, I—"

"Why did you become a fixer, Caleb?" The question

walloped me from left field. Her voice was wooden but her sharp eyes were prying beneath my veneer.

I didn't want to be analyzed. Not while this rawness lived inside me. "Why the hell not?" I snapped again.

"That's not an answer. Shall I tell you what I think? You enjoy the control it gives you. But more than that you enjoy the transient nature of your work. You don't have to invest in the long-term. You go in, all guns blazing, you fix whatever's wrong. And then you *leave*. Don't you?"

I stared at her, trying to summon fury and detachment. All I achieved was a widening of the chasm between us. Fuck it. "Yes," I threw out.

It was the truth, after all.

She whirled to face the window, then almost immediately turned back again. "Well, there's your answer. You can't guarantee anything beyond your next *fix*. That's what you live for. That's all you'll ever care about. But you know what else you can't guarantee? That your neat record will hold out. Sooner or later you'll have to accept that some things can't be fixed."

The raw ache intensified. "What the fuck are you talking about?"

She sighed. "It doesn't matter. I just know that I don't want to be your next fix, Caleb."

Somewhere beneath the roaring in my ears, I heard the sound of her suitcase zipper and the echo of her footsteps down the hallway.

Moments later an engine started, revved, then slowly faded away.

CHAPTER FIFTEEN

Caleb
One month later

"WHY ISN'T THE Landon file on my desk? I asked for it twenty minutes ago. What's going on?" I snarled as Maggie hurriedly slammed her laptop shut.

"Nothing!"

I eyed her, the irritation that had been living beneath my skin for weeks threatening to erupt. "If you want to watch porn, do it in your own time, not on company property. And seriously, I thought you were a much better liar than that?"

"Okay, first of all, ewww. Second of all, double ewww!"

"You have five seconds to fess up before I fire you for inappropriate use of office property."

With a long-suffering sigh, she opened her laptop, and hit Play.

The sweet, sexy voice that lived in my dreams flowed through the speaker. Heart lodged in my throat, I rounded Maggie's desk.

And there she was.

Lily. Giving another interview.

I'd taken pains to avoid all forms of tech news since she left me in Lake Tahoe.

I tried to summon the anger I'd carried with me since she walked out. All I managed was the ashen aftertaste of a poorly handled situation.

I don't want to be your next fix...

I snorted under my breath. Lily Gracen had proven that she was one long fix, one I couldn't get away from whether I was awake or asleep.

She'd burrowed herself firmly beneath my skin, made it so I couldn't take three steps before she crossed my mind. I wasn't sure whether to be pissed with her or feel sorry for myself for allowing her close.

Some things can't be fixed...

Ironically, in letting her smudge the lines, she'd forced me to redraw my rigid boundaries, forced me to examine the hard chains I'd wrapped around myself since my mother died. A few had been rusty, surprisingly easy to break, letting me breathe easier than I had in a very long time.

Some others not so much.

All in all, she'd forced me to examine far too much. Which was why I was still leaning heavily in the pissed column.

And there she was, without a fucking care in the world.

Stunning in customary black. With...a pair of stylish, boxy glasses perched on her nose.

Holy fuck.

That last day in Silicon Valley, sitting in the passenger seat of her cramped-as-hell little car, watching her laugh while wearing those saucy shorts, I thought she couldn't get any more sensational.

I just discovered she could.

"Umm...boss?"

I scowled. "What?"

"Just checking that you're breathing, is all."

I wrenched my gaze from the screen. "I'm not paying you to sit around watching online videos all day, Maggie."

She nodded sagely. "Then I guess you won't want the thing I just sent to your phone."

My scowl deepened. "What thing?" I pulled my phone from my pocket.

It was an invitation to a black tie event. Hosted by SDM. Five thousand dollars a plate. Starting at 8 pm. Tonight.

A tremble rolled up my arm and down my body. "Why the hell did you send me this?"

"Because I'm terrified one of these days you'll develop actual fangs and claws and all my parents will find when they come looking for me is a dried up husk."

"Trust me. If I turned feral you wouldn't be my first choice of a meal."

I knew someone who tasted sweeter. Glorious, in fact. Someone whose every breath I would die for, given half a chance.

"Fine, but just FYI, this is her last gig for SDM. Who knows where she'll disappear to afterward?"

The words struck pure dread into my heart, pissing me off even more. I stomped back into my office. "Can't go. I'm busy."

"Actually, you're not. But okay."

I threw myself into my chair, vowing not to look at the invitation. I lasted five minutes. "Maggie!"

"Yeah, boss, I have your tux right here."

Great. This was my chance to rectify a few things with Lily Gracen.

Once and for all.

Lily

The terrace of the Griffith Observatory was great for many things, including its stunning views of nighttime LA. But decked out in spotlights and caviar towers and champagne fountains, it was magnificent. That was before the celebrities and Fortune 500 CEOs who'd flown in from around the globe added their dazzle to the occasion.

After two weeks of hard publicity, tonight was the official launch party stroke fund-raiser for SDM's compression algorithm. And my final appearance as the ambassador for the most talked about development in the tech world. After tonight I was free. I'd never need to set eyes on Chance Donovan, or my stepfather again.

Even though the latter thought brought a pang of pain, I was okay with it. For the first time in my life, I could truly move forward with no baggage.

I closed on the sale of the abandoned drive-in movie theater today, and immediately applied for permission to convert it into offices. I was starting my own tech company and even though I was scared spitless, I was also excited.

If nothing else, starting a company from the ground up would take my mind off thinking about Caleb.

Whoever said time healed all wounds was a dotard. With every passing day, the hole in my chest grew wider, deeper. There were times when I feared the thing could just expire from the brutal trauma it endured daily, simply because it craved one night of perfection that would never be repeated.

But did you make absolutely sure it couldn't be repeated? Or did you shut the door because you were hurt and never looked back?

Those lingering questions were the reason I hadn't erased his last message from two weeks ago from my phone. Or maybe I was just a glutton for punishment.

Had he moved on? Was he currently buried neck deep in a new exciting case?

"I have no idea what it does, but I hear it's revolutionary. What did they call it again?"

"They called it the Angel Algorithm," a deep, magnificent voice said.

Dear God. His voice...

"Why *Angel*?"

"Because it's the creator's middle name," Caleb replied.

"Oh, how special," the female guest gushed.

"I couldn't agree more. She's one of a kind."

Heart in my throat, I turned around. He stood six feet away. Resplendent in a black tux and snowy white shirt. His face looked a little thinner but the designer stubble and slightly windswept hair worked for him so splendidly, I couldn't have pried my eyes off him if an earthquake cratered the ground beneath my feet.

The crowd seemed to part between us, and he loomed, magnificent, over me. "That was right, wasn't it?"

Breath totally depleted, I nodded. "Short for Angela. Chance let me name it." After witnessing the code that would make him and his company billions, he'd been so ecstatic he'd allowed me to name it. Regardless of how our relationship had begun, it was ending on my terms, with an achievement I was proud of. I'd chosen to let go of all grudges.

"It's a beautiful name." Caleb's voice was a little gruff, his eyes a fierce blue that blazed over me from my crown to my feet and back again. "Hello, Lily."

"Hi," I whispered.

"You look...incredible."

"Thank you." In honor of tonight, I'd gone a different way with my clothes. Dressed top to toe in white, the only splash of color were the red soles of my white platform heels. Diamond-and-pearl pins secured my slicked back hair, and even the choker around my neck was white leather.

Caleb's eyes lingered there the longest, setting my body aflame. "Lily, can we talk?"

Say no. Save yourself more heartache. "Yes."

Relief drenched his face. He started to reach for me. Someone bumped into me, sending me one stumble forward.

"Okay, enough of this shit," Caleb growled. He relieved me of my half-finished champagne glass, meshed his fingers with mine and tugged me through the crowd.

"Where are you taking me?"

"You'll see."

"But...I can't leave the party."

"You've given Donovan the algorithm. You've done his speeches. You don't owe him a thing. Besides, we need to revisit our last conversation in Lake Tahoe. There are a few things I never got around to saying."

He gripped me tighter as I navigated the steps to the lower level, then increased his pace again.

"God, I haven't missed this bossy side of you at all." I tried to project irritation but the wild hum in my veins wasn't anger. It was...*joy.*

"Sure you have. Or you wouldn't be hurrying to keep up with me."

He was right. I would go anywhere with this man, but at what price?

"I still want to know where we're going."

"We're here," he replied in a hushed voice, then pushed the door open.

I entered, and gasped. "We can't be in here," I whispered halfheartedly. But my excitement tripled as I gazed up at the stunning constellation splashed across the planetarium roof.

His fingers trailed up my wrists, my arms, to cup my shoulders. I redirected my gaze to his, saw the raw emotion stamped on his face.

"I'm fucking pissed at you."

I gasped. "What?"

"You heard me. But God, I've also missed you. So much," he confessed raggedly.

I stopped myself from blurting out that I'd missed him, too. "Have you? You were shitty to me."

His face clouded with pain. "Believe me, I know. I'd do anything to take it all back."

My throat clogged. Excitement faded and harrowing pain rushed at me. "Would you? Why?"

"Because you didn't deserve it. Not a single one of the things I threw at you."

"Are you sure? Because there's no shame in admitting you don't have room in your life…for me." It hurt me to say it, but it needed to be said.

He shook his head vehemently. "That's not—"

"I saw how devastated you were when you told me about your mom. You blame yourself for her. You moved heaven and earth for her and she still died, and after that you were never going to become so wrapped up in anyone else. Am I right?"

He stared down at me for the longest time. Then he exhaled harshly. "Yes. I'd love to say I fought hard to shut people out, but…after she died, it was easy to close the door, to bottle the pain and become the lone wolf no one depended on. Until Kirsten."

My heart twisted with pain for him. For me. "And she let you down, too."

His mouth tightened. "I don't want to talk about her. She's not important. Not anymore. She was just another crutch I used to distance myself. The option to walk away on my own terms before things got heavy with anyone was mine alone. I was okay with it. Until I met you. You forced me to take a long, hard look at myself."

My lungs flattened. "Caleb…"

"Walking away from you was the hardest thing I've ever done, Lily," he confessed forcefully.

Remembering brought more pain. "Then why did you?"

"I let my guard down with you. My instincts warned me about Miranda but I saw how close you were to your team. To her. I knew you would be hurt if it was her and I didn't want you to experience that pain. I hesitated when I could've acted sooner. Then the breach happened and all I could think about was that I could've lost you. In the end I did anyway by pushing you away, when I should've pulled you close."

"I thought you were into her. Miranda."

Caleb's fingers brushed my throat and I realized I was clinging to his wrists. "I'm into one particular pint-size blonde, with a heart of gold, the courage of a lion and a body designed to stop traffic."

"She's into you, too, but she was terrified all you'd ever want was to be a fixer. That she wouldn't be able to compete with your calling. You chose to do what you do to help people but also to stay connected to your mother. I... I didn't know if I could compete with that."

"The moment you walked into my life, the competition was over. I would've come after you whether you were a client or not. My heart and my soul craved you even before I knew what was happening. That second time in Lake Tahoe was my piss-poor way of telling you I couldn't live without you."

"Oh, Caleb."

"I've been wretched without you. The thought of waking up every morning for the rest of my life without you..." He stopped and shook his head, urgent hands cupping my cheeks to tilt my gaze to his. "If there's any part of you that feels a fraction of that, please give me a chance to make us both happy."

Bright, shining hope billowed through me. "Do you mean that?"

"With every bone in my body," he breathed.

"Oh, my God."

Fevered eyes pierced me. "Is that... Are you considering it, Lily?"

"I don't need to. I was thinking of what it would be like to wake up each day with you."

His fingers trembled against my cheek. "And?"

"I would love that, Caleb. So very much."

A blinding smile erupted. "God, Lily... I love you."

Hope turned to joy, filling my battered spaces with new, vibrant life, and my eyes with tears. "I love you, too," I wailed.

Caleb stared at me for a stupefied moment; then my big, magnificent man snatched me in his arms, but not before I caught a suspicious sheen in his eyes.

He fused his lips to mine, and my heart sighed with happiness. Still bound in his arms, I felt him moving. Felt him sink into a seat before he placed me before him.

His hands worshipped my face, my neck, my fingers. Adoring eyes pinned me as he slid his hands under my dress.

"I saw you on TV." His fingers drifted up my thighs.

"Yes, I've been doing a lot of that lately," I whispered.

He nodded. "You looked...incredible."

"Yes, you said that already," I teased.

He hummed as he skimmed the edge of my panties. "I had this fantasy as I watched you give that *Tech-Crunch* interview."

"Yeah?" I was beginning to pant and I didn't even care.

He hooked two fingers into the lace and dragged it down my legs. "Hmm. You were rattling off all these big tech words and numbers. And I promised myself if I ever got you back, I would have you recite the Fibonnaci Sequence while I fucked you long and slow."

My gasp echoed around the large room. "Oh, my God."

He tapped my legs. I stepped out of my panties, and he stuffed them into his jacket pocket. "That's not all. You would be wearing nothing but a choker, those boxy glasses and black heels you wore for the *Wired* cover shoot when you announced you were starting your own company. I'm incredibly proud of you for that, by the way."

My heart threatened to burst with happiness. "Did you watch *all* my interviews?"

"Every single one. Twice. I bought all the magazines, too. I've had a very busy afternoon." He plucked a condom from his wallet, handed it to me, then reached beneath his cummerbund and lowered his zipper.

"Wow. If I didn't know better, I'd say you were obsessed with me, Mr. Steele."

His eyes clung to mine. "It's more than an obsession. You're my reason for breathing."

My fingers shook as I tore open the condom. Then the shaking suffused my whole body as he took out his big, beautiful cock.

I leaned over him, kissed his gorgeous lips before bending lower to kiss the crown of his penis. His strangled curse was music to my ears.

The moment I glided the condom on, he pulled me close, tugged my legs on either side of his lap, and he stared up at me with eyes shining with unfettered love. I braced my hands on his shoulders and sank down, slowly, excruciatingly impaling myself on him. His groan mingled with mine.

When he was fully seated inside me, he held me still.

"There are over a billion stars above our heads right

now. But I bet we could touch every one of them if we tried really, really hard."

I cupped his jaw in my hands. "I'd love nothing better than to reach for the stars with you. Oh, Caleb. I love you."

"I love you, too. I'm going to spend the rest of my life making you incredibly, sublimely happy," he vowed.

I sealed my lips to his and silently promised that, for as long as the sun rose each morning, I would love and worship him, too.

* * * * *

GETTING LUCKY

AVRIL TREMAYNE

MILLS & BOON

For my wonderful, supportive, honourable husband,
without whom there would be no books.

CHAPTER ONE

ROMY RANG THE DOORBELL, and a few seconds later, heard a "Cooooomiiiing," from somewhere inside.

It was hard to believe that this house—or was *mansion* the correct word for Russian Hill?—was Matt's. To say it was a departure from his usual student-like accommodation was a whopping understatement.

An inside door slammed. A closer "Gotta find the keys" was called out, followed by an even closer, much louder "Fuck!"

Okay, it was *definitely* Matt's place.

She ran a neatening hand over her hair while she waited for him. Unbuttoned her overcoat. Brushed at the flared skirt of her new red dress.

Stupid, really. Matt never noticed what her hair looked like or what she was wearing. He saved such observations for women he wanted to have sex with—and Romy had come to terms with not being one of those women ten years ago.

Still, her natural inclination was to look immaculate-but-fashionable for business discussions, and the deal she'd made with Matt on the phone two weeks ago was definitely in that category, despite the chaos of that crazy call. Serious enough to warrant a flight from London to San Francisco to dot every i and cross every t.

Footsteps on floorboards. A fumble at the lock. Another "Fuck" that had her battling a giggle, because it was so typical of Matt to be impatient with a door that didn't open fast enough. A click, a swoosh…and there he was.

Six feet three of lean, hard muscle looking rebelliously casual in just-snug-enough jeans and a just-tight-enough T-shirt; hold the footwear because he never wore shoes unless he had to. Good-looking in a boy-next-door-meets-fallen-angel way. Thick waves of red-blond hair, sharply alert green eyes, incongruously olive skin. Tick, tick, tick, tick and tick—Matthew Carter was a prime genetic specimen.

"Good evening, Mr. Carter," Romy said, tamping down another giggle at the absurdity of assessing Matt's attributes like he was breeding stock. "I'm here to discuss your sperm."

Matt gave her a censorious tsk-tsk at odds with the twinkle in his eyes. "I hope you don't say that to *all* the boys, Ms. Allen!"

"Only the ones with a really big— Matt!"—as he yanked her over the threshold and into a fierce hug.

"A really big what?" he asked, digging his chin into the top of her head. "Go on, I dare you to say it."

"Cup, you pervert," she said, dissolving into laughter even though her bottom lip was suddenly trembling from the emotional toll of being on the cusp of something momentous with him. "A really big *cup*!"

"Cup?" he scoffed. "More like a bucket! We're talking serious size and don't you forget it!" He released her, looking down at her with a grin that promptly faded. "Uh-oh, do *not* cry! You know you look like a troll when you cry!"

"Trying not to," she said shakily. "It's just…you're just…you're going to hate me for saying it again, but you really are my— Hey!" as he dragged her in for another hug.

"If you call me your fucking hero one more fucking time I'll squeeze you hard enough to crack a fucking rib!"

"Okay, *okay*!" Watery chuckle. "Enough fucking!"

"There's never enough fucking to suit me, you know that." And as she chuckled again, "But I mean it, Romy. It's one hybrid kid. Not like we're spawning a dynasty of Targaryens to rule the Seven Kingdoms."

"Except I feel like I'm carrying the iron throne in my briefcase," she said, wrapping her arms around his waist. "Weighs a ton."

"Briefcase?" He half and half laugh/groaned. "Tonight is going to suck sooo badly."

"A briefcase *which you made me drop*. Serve you right if it gouged a hole in your floorboards. And you're squeezing me hard enough to crack *two* fucking ribs, by the way."

He dug his chin into the crown of her head again. "Keep complaining and I'll bench-press you!"

"You'll give yourself a hernia."

"I've been working out—I can take you."

"You haven't seen my backside lately! It's expanded. Way bigger than anything you're used to."

"I'll look at it if you want me to, but as an expert in all things posterior I usually start by copping a feel," he said.

"Hmm, well, I've eaten enough to feed an army in

the past two days and I'm fit to burst out of my clothes, so maybe just take my word for it. I wouldn't want to shock you."

"You always eat enough for an army, so don't try using that as an excuse for your butt—*or* for not cooking the paella you promised me, if that's where you're heading."

She choked up again, because paella was a pathetically inadequate thank-you for what he was doing. She searched for words to express her gratitude more eloquently, but she knew he wouldn't let her say them—he *never* let his friends thank him, always brushed them off, said it was easy, he was doing it for himself, no big deal, anything to shut them up—so she simply rested her cheek against his chest and...ahhh...breathed. In, then out, in, out.

"It'll be all right, Romy, I promise," he murmured into her hair.

"You always say that," she said huskily.

"Because it's true."

Romy smiled against his chest. Matt's *It'll be all right, I promise* had become a group slogan in their Capitol University days. He'd said those words to her, Rafael, Veronica, Artie when he couldn't run away fast enough, and even the older and more rational Teague, whenever he was trying to convince them to do something off-the-wall. Skydiving, bungee jumping, that outrageous sex-in-a-public-place challenge, the horrendous pub crawl during a near blizzard, flying all the way to Sydney, Australia, for a *weekend* to support Frankie the Aussie barmaid when her bastard ex got married, skateboarding down Lombard Street the time they'd all come to San Francisco to hear Matt speak at that tech conference and he needed to release some energy. An endless stream of dares that had them following Matt like lemmings off a cliff because whenever he said *It'll be all right, I promise*, they believed him. And even though such adventures mostly *didn't* end up all right in the end, they'd lemminged after him the next time anyway, because Matt was invincible.

But this time, *this* dare, the consequences were forever. And while Romy wasn't so much willing to embrace those consequences as desperate to do so now the carrot had been dangled in front of her, she couldn't bear the thought that this might be the one time Matt wound up regretting something.

Already, though, she was ready to believe things would be as all right as Matt promised. That was the effect he had on her, probably because he was always picking up her pieces, whether they were fully broken, slightly chipped or just a little bit scratched.

She closed her eyes, blocking out everything except the smell of the arctic pine soap he always used, the feel of his chest rising and falling with his breaths, the well-washed texture of his T-shirt beneath her cheek, his hand pressing between her shoulder blades, bringing her closer. So close her heart felt bruised against his hardness. No...not bruised, squeezed. Squeezed until it was pounding. Pounding until she was dizzy.

And then she realized Matt's heart was pounding, too, and the world tilted. A rush, a swirl, a blaze of heat, and she was in territory that was both familiar and *un*familiar—like she'd been pitched into a color-saturated virtual reality. A picture darted into her head. The two of them chest to chest and hip to hip against the wall, Matt's mouth on hers, his hand fumbling her skirt up out of the way, his fingers tugging at her underwear, and then… Oh God, *God*, he was big and hard and sliding into her until she was full of him, stretched and throbbing and wildly wanting. *You want my sperm, then take it, Romy, as much as you need, take it all, but take it like this.* Her legs wrapping around him, jerking in time with his thrusts. *Yes, please, Matt, please.*

"Matt, please!" she whispered, tilting her hips into his as though what she saw in her head was hers for the asking, for the *taking*.

Matt went perfectly still, and so did she as reality clubbed her back to her senses.

Long moment of nothing but hectic heartbeats and held breaths. And then he let her go so suddenly she stumbled back and almost fell over her briefcase. He grabbed her arm, righted her, released her abruptly again.

Romy, frantically replaying that fantasy in her head, knew how that breathy *Matt, please* must have sounded—like a woman on heat. Nothing new for Matt, who'd been beating women off with the proverbial stick ever since she'd known him, but definitely new between the two of them. And Matt's holy-fuck-help-me expression was telling her their status quo wasn't about to change.

"Sorry, jet lag," she said—the first excuse she could think of. "It kicked in last night, and I barely slept so I've been feeling light-headed all day. I guess when you squeezed me like that, it made me a little…a little woozy. A little…breathless…?"

Okaaay, best case scenario would be for Matt to grab her in a headlock, rub his knuckles against her scalp and tell her to stop bullshitting him, because she'd been flying between the UK and the USA for ten years without suffering from jet lag, so she should just confess—ha-ha-ha—that she'd thrust her hips at him like a nymphomaniac because she wanted his body. To which she'd respond—ha-ha-ha—that being part of a harem wasn't her style and he should stop wanking over himself. The same comedy routine they'd been doing since the night they'd met to ward off any vaguely sexual frisson that might oscillate between them.

Worst case scenario would be… Hmm, well, that would be what he was doing now. Closing his eyes, then bolt-opening them as though he'd seen something horrific behind his eyelids. Smiling like he was trying not to throw up. *Agreeing* with her, "Yeah, jet lag's a bitch." And then reaching past her to close the door with the air of a guy who'd dislocate his own arm if necessary to avoid contact with her.

About the only good thing to be said for such a response was that he was obviously intent on ignoring her momentary lapse into oversexed insanity—praise the Lord!

She bent to fiddle with the clasp on her briefcase, buying herself a minute to recover, reassuring herself that all she really had to do to get past this episode of utter mortification was not thrust her hips at him like a nymphomaniac *again*. Should be easy enough: she'd had ten years' practice pretending not to lust after him.

Fixing a smile on her face, she took her briefcase by the handle and straightened—and if she was daunted to find that Matt had taken himself out of touching range, presumably for his own safety, at least she had enough self-control to keep smiling.

"We'll talk in the library," Matt said, looking at her

right eyebrow. "Through here." And he opened a door to the left of the entrance hall and fled.

Romy dropped her briefcase again—and her smile with it—covering her face with her hands to trap the groan she just couldn't keep inside. She wasn't sure she'd cope if he started addressing all his remarks to her eyebrows. Deep breaths. More deep breaths. Phew. She slowly lowered her hands—and then drew in a few *more* deep breaths as she finally noticed the grandeur of her surroundings, which were definitely in the mansion-not-a-house category.

The floors were a chocolatey-dark wood, the walls painted low-sheen gold. Two impressive staircases curved their way to an upper floor. Behind and between the staircases were two massively proportioned doors, closing off what she presumed was the living area. To the right was a door matching the one Matt had gone through to get to the library.

She tilted back her head, expecting to find a chandelier hanging from the ceiling, and even when that was exactly what she found, she couldn't quite believe it. All that was missing was a gigantic vase of exotic flowers on a marble table and Matt's entrance hall would rival the lobby of the five-star hotel she was staying in. Her entire flat, with its jammed-together living, dining and kitchen areas, would fit into this one space.

She tried to imagine the library, using this as an example, and decided she couldn't actually get past the fact that Matt *had* a library. He only read ebooks! How did an e-reader require an entire room?

Of course, Matt had only moved in a week ago; the first she'd heard he was even looking for a place was when he'd emailed her three days after her fateful phone call, asking what he'd need to set up his new kitchen. So the library was probably just an empty room waiting to be repurposed. Or maybe it was nothing but a grandly named study housing a desk, a couple of chairs and his computer paraphernalia. Because *libraries* weren't Matt's style. *Libraries* were what the Teague Hamiltons and Veronica Johnsons of the world had in their homes. And not because Teague and Veronica were any more loaded than Matt—by his twenty-seventh birthday last year Matt had made a fortune selling the online payment software he and Artie (his partner in all things geek) had built while still at college. It was more that where Teague and Veronica carried the suggestion of the bred-in-the-bone wealth that went with stately homes, self-made Matt was just Matt. He still drove a beaten-up Toyota, still wore Levi's, T-shirts and Vans when barefoot wasn't an option, still drank Sam Adams.

A curse floated out to her through the doorway on the left, followed by a thud.

Ha! And he still swore like a sailor and had the patience of a gnat.

She reached up a hand to pat at her hair. Took off her overcoat and gave her dress a more thorough brush down. Adjusted the silicon-lined band at the top of one of her thick black thigh-high socks, which had slid down half an inch. Re-pasted her smile. Picked up her briefcase.

Showtime.

CHAPTER TWO

FUCK, FUCK, *FUCK*.

It had seemed so easy two weeks ago. A favor to a friend. On par with what he'd done for Romy back in their Capitol U days, when they'd all lived on top of each other in Veronica's town house and there'd been no hiding the fact that menstruation was more a feat of endurance for Romy than a normal bodily function.

He, Veronica and Rafael had taken turns refilling her hot water bottle, making her cup after cup of Lapsang Souchong, breaking the megawatt-but-useless painkillers out of their blister packs, restocking her why-are-they-disappearing-so-fast sanitary items. Even Teague had taken a few turns, despite not living with them—during *and* after his brief stint as Romy's boyfriend.

So when Romy had called two weeks ago to update him on where she was at with getting her whack job of a uterus fixed, it was pretty much a case of business as usual.

Or it *would* have been, if Camilla hadn't answered his phone.

Women he was fucking always seemed to need to do that when Romy's name flashed up, so it wasn't the act of answering the phone that bothered him so much as the way she'd said, *Oh, it's your Romy*, before swiping to accept the call.

His Romy? Fuck that! Romy was just Romy.

And then Camilla had told Romy that Matt would call her back, and that was a step too far in the proprietary stakes so he'd pulled the phone out of her hand fast enough to give her whiplash of the wrist and taken it into another room.

Camilla had looked mightily displeased, but it was poor form for a guy to ask a girl about her menstrual cycle in front of someone she'd never met, so he'd left Camilla to it and launched straight into it with Romy via a short, sharp opener: *Enough of this bullshit, how do we fix it?*

We can have an ablation, she'd said.

Then have one, was his response.

She *couldn't* if she wanted a kid one day—which she definitely *did*, she'd explained—because there'd be no having one afterward.

So have a baby now, he'd said, what was stopping her?

Little problem of no man in her LIFE! And yes, she'd screamed the last word, because a cramp had ripped her in half at that exact moment.

He'd paced the floor while she'd breathed through the pain, and then said, fuck it, *he'd* give her a baby— why not?

And she'd said, *Why not?* Because it was a big deal requiring more than the *one minute's* reflection he usually afforded life-and-death decisions.

And he'd told her it sure as hell didn't require her usual *one thousand years'* reflection, *and* that it would

make the top ten list of easiest things he'd ever fucking contemplated: a quick ejaculation on his side of the
Atlantic, a turkey baster on hers, a courier in between,
a baby at the end and Yippie-Kai-Yay motherfucker to
the problem.

She'd laughed so hard at the *Yippie-Kai-Yay motherfucker* she'd snorted, but she was crying at the same
time, and then she'd said he was the next best thing to
Captain America to offer, even if she couldn't accept.

And *he'd* snort-laughed then, insisting that Captain
America was a *virgin* as well as not being the mastur-
batory type, whereas Matt had shot out so many gal-
lons of semen over the years—with and without the
assistance of a second party—he could have his own
page in *Guinness World Records* so where was the
comparison?

And somehow during the ensuing argument over
Captain America's sexual expertise—or lack thereof—
which they'd been having forever—Matt's sperm offer
had been accepted and general terms for proceeding
agreed to, and he'd felt pretty damn happy with himself because hey, he was going to be a father, which
he'd *never* thought he'd be.

Correction: godfather.

Because *obviously* he couldn't be a *real* father.

By that stage Camilla had left, presumably in a huff
since he hadn't heard from her since, and Matt had figured that was just as well since she probably wouldn't
appreciate his commitment to impregnating another
woman even if he wasn't actually coming within spurt-
ing distance of Romy's fallopian tubes.

And now here they were, and he felt pretty sure
Camilla had jinxed him with the *his Romy* bullshit

because *his Romy* wasn't the Romy he'd opened the door to.

His Romy had obviously been kidnapped by aliens and replaced with a metamorphosed porn star version who looked exactly like *his Romy*—neat and chic, clean and bright—but was on a mission to drive him out of his fucking mind with the need to get his hands on her. Which he *could not do*, because *his Romy*, his *real* Romy, was off-limits.

He wasn't *allowed* to imagine taking *his Romy* against the wall energetically enough to shake the crystals off that god-awful chandelier. He would never have flung *his Romy* halfway across the hall for fear of what he might otherwise do to her! Because he would never have mistaken *his Romy's* breathless *Matt, please* as an invitation to enact that shameful scene in his head when it was really nothing more than a plea to stop his rampaging dick from stabbing her in the stomach—and thank God she hadn't called him on that but had taken pity on him by blaming a mythical case of jet lag for the whole damn disaster.

And okay, taking the blame for him was something *his Romy would* do, which meant she really *was his Romy* and his alien abduction theory therefore was a bust.

The only other explanation for this whole phenomenon was that it was an aberration brought on by his two-week sexual hiatus—and the fact he'd lasted two weeks without sex, ever since Romy's phone call, was the equivalent of *him* being abducted by aliens and replaced with a *choirboy* version of himself!

Matthew Carter a choirboy? Now, *that* was an aberration.

As he'd hurried into the library and manhandled his chair into the best position for hiding the beast in his jeans under the desk—not without a certain amount of cursing and desk-related violence—he'd decided it probably wasn't unusual for sex addicts to crave the first available person they saw during periods of deprivation. Didn't mean he was going to act on it, though. He'd been keeping Romy safe from his perversions for ten whole fucking years and that's how things were going to stay if he had to lock a chastity belt onto her himself!

What the hell was keeping her, anyway? They should be halfway through her first document by now. The tedium of paperwork would put a stop to any weird-ass sexual cravings, so he wanted those damn documents stat! Bring them *all* on, the whole fucking briefcase full!

He checked the time on his cell phone. She couldn't be lost between the entrance hall and the library— only one door in the corridor was open and she'd have to see not only the glow of the lights but feel the heat from the monstrous fucking fireplace that was slowly stewing him in his own juice.

Maybe he should go and find her.

Take her by the hand...lead her upstairs...into his bedroom...strip her...lie her across the bed. Ash-brown hair tangled on his pillow...eyes a glitter of hazel from beneath those heavy, tilted lids that made her look perpetually, deceptively sleepy...mouth slightly open as she panted for him...tongue darting to lick her top lip...breasts round and heavy...beige nipples jutting proudly...thighs opening to reveal her pink, juicy core...waiting for his fingers...his tongue...his cock.

A whimper, a moan, as he slid inside her...clenching around him...hips rising to meet his thrusts...

Oh God, he wanted to come...needed to come.

His heart was thudding the way it had in the entrance hall when he'd had his arms around her, his shoulders tightening, thighs clamping, his dick straining for release. And then the hairs on the back of his neck vibrated themselves upright as though a lover's finger were trailing down his spine, and he realized he was no longer on his own in the room.

He focused his eyes on his cell phone, counting out the seconds, willing himself to get it together before turning to confirm Romy's presence behind him... aaand go...

He swiveled his chair, and lust rushed at him like a bullet. He wanted to suck the breath out of her, rip the clothes off her, lick the scent from her skin.

What the fuck was happening to him?

"Sorry to make you wait," she said, her trying-but-not-quite-making-it smile telling him she felt his tension. "I had to call Lennie to report on last night's restaurant."

She'd taken off her overcoat, and when she paused on her way to the desk to drape it over a chair he saw what she meant about bursting out of her clothes—her bodice was skintight, and she looked ripe as a ready-to-eat-immediately peach. He really didn't think he was going to survive tonight.

"It's two in the morning in London," he said, the snap in his voice a symptom of his overwrought edginess.

"So?"

"So don't try telling me you called Lennie." Not that

it was anything to *him* if she called Lennie at two in the fucking morning.

"I...I did," she said, and blushed, defensive. "Chef's hours. I couldn't have called him any earlier."

"Yeah, well, Lennie's an asshole, expecting you to report in after every meal," he grumbled, and swiveled his chair back to the desk, because the blush pissed him off and he didn't want to see it. Not that it was anything to him who she blushed over, but she shouldn't be blushing over Lennie of all people. "You're a restaurant consultant not a slave."

She'd reached the desk and took her seat, holding her briefcase on her lap as though it were that chastity belt he'd told himself she needed. "You know I have to jump when he says jump."

"I know you can't trust a guy who fricassees garden snails," Matt said, because *he* didn't trust Lennie. Lennie thought he owned her.

She gave an agitated little huff that told him he was being a dick. "And here I was thinking you might have given up burgers for escargot."

"Why would I do that?"

"The house...this room." She looked around. "Your tastes have changed."

"It's just a library."

"Yes, and it's very *library*-like," she said, looking around again. "Hmm. It reminds me of the library in Teague's family's place in the Hamptons. All those shelves full of...of books."

"Hel-lo! Library!"

"Yes but the chairs, tables, Persian rugs, velvet curtains. That fireplace! Big enough to incinerate an elephant!" She laughed, but it sounded forced. "Remember that time we were all invited to the Hamptons for the Hamiltons' Fourth of July ball? Even Veronica was wowed by the library!"

"You went into raptures over it, too, so what's the problem here?"

She grimaced—*grimaced!* What the fuck!

"I just...wondered if you'd bought the place already furnished, that's all," she said.

"Why? Because I don't have Teague's good taste?"

"Well, you *don't*, actually. Nobody does! But what I meant was that not even *you* could get all this done in a week."

"Oh." He shrugged, suddenly self-conscious that it *hadn't* been furnished, that he'd hired people to do it, that he'd told them to copy Teague's style and to get it ready in a week in time for Romy's visit. The library, the kitchen, two bedrooms—his and a spare in case she decided to stay—and an outdoor table, two chairs and a patio heater so they could eat breakfast on the deck tomorrow, because the deck wasn't as oppressive as the rest of this fucking ginormous house. And now it felt all wrong. "Look, are we going to spend the night talking about decor or can we get on with the business at hand?"

"Okay!" She huffed a breath in and out as she pulled a sheaf of pages out of her briefcase and put the briefcase on the floor beside her chair. And then she frowned at him. "You know all this paperwork is only to help you make an informed decision, right? I'm not here to torment you with red tape."

"I'm not tormented."

"You sound tormented. You look tormented. You—"

"I'm not tormented!"

Pause. "Let me put it a different way."

"Fuck!"

"If you're having second thoughts about giving me your sperm, I'll let you off the hook, no questions asked."

He almost laughed at that! "Romy, I'm having so many thoughts about giving you my sperm I can barely keep up with them—but not one of them involves being let off the hook."

"I just want us to be...you know...normal."

"So we make that a nonnegotiable condition, okay? We stay normal or it's off."

"Yes, but—"

"Jesus, Romy, move things the fuck along or I'll think *you're* having second thoughts!"

She opened her mouth, closed it, opened it, closed it, opened it, and all that drawing attention to her mouth was not helping because it made him want to kiss her! And then, "Fine!" she said. "Fine. If you're sure." She sorted agitatedly through her paperwork. "Here," selecting a page and holding it out to him as she placed the rest on the desk in front of her.

He took the page. "What is it?"

"A waiver my lawyer drew up for your protection."

"Protection from what?"

"From me. Think of it as the prenup you have when you're not getting married."

"You've got to be kidding me!"

"I'm not going to have people say I baby-trapped America's favorite dot-com billionaire."

He stared at her for one long, fraught moment. And then, "Okay," he said, and read the document. "Right." Looking up. "Got it."

"Read it again."

"I don't need to read it again, Romy."

"Yes, Matt, you do. You make decisions too quickly. And this is important. Important enough that you might want to have your lawyer read it. In fact, you *should* get your lawyer to read it."

"I don't need my lawyer to read it, because I'm not signing it."

"Well, of course I'm not expecting you to sign it right this minute."

"I'm not signing it, period."

"What?"

"Will this make it easier to understand?" he asked— and ripped the page in half, dropping the two pieces back onto the desk.

"Why did you do that?"

"Because if you think I'm going to sit here on a fortune while my kid lives on a budget on the other side of the world, you've got rocks in your head. I may know fuck-all about being a father, and we both know I'd be a shitty role model for a kid—"

"You would not!"

"—but one thing I *can* do, and do easily, is money."

"I don't want your money, Matt."

"The money's not for you, so get over it. You're getting just about everything you want out of this deal, Romy, and that's fine. That's great. I'm cool with it. But for the love of God, stop rubbing in the whole I-don't-need-you-Matt thing."

"Rubbing—? Need—? I don't—!" She peered at him as though trying to dive into his brain. "I don't understand. All I'm trying to do is protect you!"

"I don't *want* to be protected. I just…" He stopped, dragged in a slow breath. "I just…want to do this."

"You *are* doing this. You're providing half the chromosomes."

"Yeah, anyone with a dick can do that."

"But I want *your* dick," she said.

They looked at each other in shock—and then they both burst out laughing. And God it felt good. Back to normal. Almost.

"Is that a Freudian slip?" he asked. "Because hey, come on over to my side of the desk."

"Oh, shut up."

"Look," he said, "seriously, what difference is it going to make if I fling you a few dollars? I could support a hundred kids and not notice the outlay."

"It's not supposed to be about buying a baby."

"I'm not selling one."

"It's not *fair* to you. Not when you'll have a real family one day."

"You *are* my real family. You, Rafael, Veronica, Teague, crazy Artie."

"You know what I mean. What happens when you get married?"

"I'm not getting married. No other kids. This is it for me. My one chance. So don't take it away from me over something stupid like money."

"Are you blackmailing me?"

"I'm appealing to your kind heart."

"You are so full of it!"

"Okay, I'll switch to blackmail if you're going to be mean about it. I'm making it a nonnegotiable condition of my participation. No money, no kid." He picked up the pieces of paper. "Now, are we starting negotiations on the same torn page, or not?"

"Blackmail isn't a negotiation."

"Ticktock, time's a-marchin'."

"Yes, but it's my clock that's ticking, not yours. You have all the time in the world to have other kids."

"Don't want others. I'm good with clocks. Might as well synchronize my alarm with yours. Are we on? Decide."

"I don't— I can't— I'm not...not *like* that. I don't make decisions on the fly."

"But I *do*, Romy. And things work out just fine for me. So decide. Now."

Long, long moment. And then, "Okay," she said, the word sounding as though it had been dragged out against its will. "I'll take the money, but I want it tied up in a trust. I mean it, Matt. No sneaky stuff. No saving me from imaginary destitution on the sly. I'm getting my lawyer involved—I'm warning you."

He dropped the paper pieces. "Just so you know, I've already got my lawyer on the case, and I'll bet she's scarier than yours. If I want to sneak money to you on the sly, it'll be done before you know it's happening and there'll be nothing you can do about it."

"Now you see, that's your inner superhero waving his flag. You think you're saving a damsel in distress, but I promise you, I'm not in distress."

"Have you thought that maybe this isn't about you, it's about me? How do you know I'm not the one buying a baby?"

"What? No!"

"And if I told you straight out that I am?"

"I guess I'd ask why you chose me."

Their eyes met. Held. Something flashed inside him. Hot. Vivid. "And I'd answer...*because* it's you," he said. And the instant the words were out, he knew they were true. He was doing this not only *for* her, but because it *was* her. Because she was the one pure thing in his life and he needed her and if they shared a child he'd always have her. And his child...? Well, of course he had more to offer his child than money: he had *her*. Her light, to cancel out his darkness.

"Oh!" she said, blinking furiously.

Shit! "Don't go troll on me," he warned.

"I won't. I promise. It's just...nice. To hear that."

"Yeah, well, don't get sentimental about it. It's to my benefit to give my kid a good mother. Less chance it'll want to come and live with me one day."

"Oh!" she said again, and gave a tiny sniff that freaked him out.

"Jesus, Romy! Get a grip. Are you on hormones or something?"

"No. No, no, that's just nice to hear, too. In a...a twisted kind of way."

"That's me—twisted."

She gave him that peer-into-your-brain look again. "Why do you always do that, Matt?"

"What?"

"Make yourself something...less."

He hunched a shoulder. "I'm not doing anything except reminding you there's something in this for both of us. Right, we still have a hundred documents to get through and I'll be ripping up any that have a tear splotch on them, so get it together."

She wiped a finger under each eye. "It's not a hundred, it's fifteen."

"That's my girl! Precision document preparer." He laughed. "We'll get through a paltry fifteen like a hot knife through butter."

He hoped she'd laugh, too, but she didn't. She was watching him, her forehead creased as though she wasn't sure whether or not she should be frowning, and Matt felt panic edge its way up his spine because maybe she was about to call things off—and suddenly, unexpectedly, he knew he'd move heaven and hell to keep the deal alive. "Are we good, Romy?" he asked.

She bit her lip, and he did his best to make himself look nonthreatening. If he could have willed the right response out of her, he would have—he certainly directed every synapse in his brain at her as he silently urged: *Say yes...say yes...say yes, damn you.*

"Yes," she said, and his limbs went weak with relief. "Yes, we're good."

"So," he said, as nonchalantly as he could manage. "What's next?"

She flipped a page, another, another, muttering something under her breath. He knew what she was doing. Sorting the documents, easiest to hardest, building her case. The muttering thing usually made him want to get her in a headlock, rub his knuckles against her scalp and warn her she was talking out loud, not in her head. But not tonight. Tonight, for reasons he *did not want to face*, it made him want to take her on his lap like he used to do at college when something was worrying her. But this was different from college. Because he didn't just want to reassure her, he wanted to kiss her.

He forced his eyes away from her mouth to her hands, and the platinum signet ring on her right pinky finger caught his eye. She'd worn it every day since Teague had given it to her for her twenty-first birthday seven years ago, and he barely noticed it anymore. But now he wanted to rip it off her finger and throw it into the fire. What a fucking crazy upended night this was turning out to be.

"This one," she said, and picked out a page.

The ring caught the overhead light, distracting him. "Huh?"

She held the page out to him. "Timing."

He ignored the page. He wanted this done. Wrapped up. Settled, before she could change her mind. "Choose any time you want—I'll fit in with you. Next."

Flip. Shuffle. She held out another page. "Clinic options in San Francisco."

He ignored that document, too. "Mark your preferred one and I'll make an appointment. Next."

New page—held out. "The process."

"Fuck, Romy. I grab a girlie magazine and jack off. Do you really think I need instructions? Next."

She chose a new page, held it out to him, then pulled it back and put it on top of the pile. "You know what?" she said, neatening the edges of her documents as that fucking ring flash-flash-flashed at him. "Let's stop pretending you're interested in the paperwork. Just point me in the direction of the kitchen so I can make your *fucking* paella! And *then*, since your mind is clearly on what time Camilla's arriving and not on me, set the table for the two of you, *not* all three of us, and I'll go back to my hotel, and that way—"

She broke off as his hand shot across the desk and latched itself around her right wrist, shocking the bejesus out of both of them. He watched her fingers curl, then flex, then curl again—but she didn't break his hold the way she should have if she had any sense. He imagined her feeling the tremor that was shimmering through him and working out what it meant, then blushing for him the way she had for Lennie. Her slumberous eyes half closing as she offered herself to him. He could see her on the desktop, raising the skirt of her cherry-red dress...see himself taking off her black stockings, sliding her panties down her legs. One lick, to taste her. *Do that again, Matt...lick me... I want you to do everything to me...anything you want...*

"Matt," she said, in that same breathy whisper she'd used when he'd hugged her too hard in the entrance hall, and he released her just as suddenly as he had then. He had to get his shit together. Stop the Jekyll and Hyde fuckery.

He put his hands palm down on the desk, ordered them to stay there. Splayed his fingers, then brought them in again, splayed...and back. Breathing, breathing, breathing through the moment of holy-hell panic and trying to remember the last thing she'd said and how he was supposed to respond. Something about the documents...kitchen...paella...Camilla...

"Why would you think Camilla was coming for dinner?"

"Because your girlfriends always do."

"Point of clarification, Romy—I haven't had a 'girlfriend' since I was seventeen."

"Well, *whatever* you call them, they're always joining us for dinner or lunch or drinks or something."

"I *call* them by their name."

"You know what I mean."

"Hookups, then. I call them hookups."

"I'm talking about women who are *more* than casual hookups."

"They're *all* casual hookups."

"Um…no! You met Camilla a week before Thanksgiving, and I called you two weeks ago—five weeks *after* Thanksgiving—and you were still with her. That length of time with someone does *not* equal a casual hookup."

"What would you call it?"

"An affair, maybe?"

"Affair? Fuck!"

"What's wrong with *affair*?"

"*Affair* is so *bourgeois*," he said, and immediately recognized *bourgeois* as one of his father's words. *Why be bourgeois, Matthew, when you can be bohemian?* How many times had he heard variations on that theme? And now he was parroting his father to Romy! What the hell was wrong with him tonight?

"Well, how *'bourgeois'* is it to answer a guy's phone for him?" Romy asked. "Casual hookups don't answer your phone."

"Yeah, well, she was on top, it was easier for her to reach it," he said, goaded by who-knew-what into yet more assholery.

Her eyes went wide. "You spoke to me in the middle of having *sex* with her? You—you—"

"Bastard? Is that the word you're looking for? Because *that's* bourgeois." Her eyes were still wide, and her naïveté provoked him into wanting to shock her further. Shock her…show her who she was dealing with here. "It's just sex, Romy, and nonexclusive at that. *Hookup* fits better than *affair*, trust me on this.

And since Camilla hasn't called me since that night, whatever she *was*, she's not *it* anymore."

"Not exclusive?" Pause. "You mean exclusive as in—"

"Monogamous."

"You were hooking up with other women simultaneously?"

"Not at *exactly* the same time, if you know what I mean."

"Well, that's…something. I guess."

"Although I have in the past. There's nothing quite like a threesome."

"Oh," she said faintly, "I see. But…but not with Camilla. But doesn't that mean—?"

"Camilla, of course, was hooking up with other men—she's not at all bourgeois."

"I see."

"Good," he said. "Now you know."

"I just thought…"

"What? That I was an innocent, clean-cut boy?"

"I thought…at least you used to be… I was *sure* you were…monogamous."

"Still am, on request. You want monogamy, you got it. That tends to get the cardinal rule broken a little faster, though, and that's always the end," he said, threading his voice with amusement.

"Cardinal rule? How do I not know about a cardinal rule after ten years?"

"You don't know because you don't break it, Romy. You don't *say* it."

"Say *what*, Matthew?"

"That you love me."

Romy had this thing she did when she was trying to make sense of something that did not compute: a raised-eyebrow blink in slow motion, which he called her blink of insanity. She did it now. "A woman tells you she loves you, your instant reaction is to *dump* her?"

"I don't like the word *dump*. It's more what I'd call a withdrawal of interest."

"Now, you see, I think a woman might still regard that as being dumped."

"Then she'd be wrong, because dumping implies there was a relationship. And, like I said, I haven't had one of those since I was—"

"Seventeen? She must have been some girl, the one you were with at seventeen, to be so hard to replace."

"Oh, yes, Gail was some girl, all right," Matt said, and although his voice was steady, the old sick rage he thought he was done with welled up in him.

Romy saw it, too. Or sensed it. He could tell. Ah shit. He braced for follow-on questions, holding his breath as she did the open-shut mouth routine...

But she must have decided that was one story too many, because with a slight shake of her head, she changed tack. "So when you *are* monogamous," she said, "they fall in love...when? Are we talking days? Weeks? Months?"

He managed an almost-natural laugh. "You think I keep track?"

"Too many to keep track of? Maybe you and Artie could invent a track-keeping app."

"Smart-ass."

Pause. "So...how long does it take *you* to fall in love, Matt?"

"What is this? The Spanish Inquisition?" He tried out another laugh, but this one missed natural by a mile.

"Just a simple question."

"Then here's a simple answer—I don't."

"Not since you were seventeen, I suppose."

Back to that. He pushed his chair back from the desk, then pulled it straight back in. Restless. Agitated. "It's like this: both people in a...a..."

"Relationship?"

"...*situation* need to want the same thing or someone's going to get hurt."

"Are you saying you never want the same thing they do?"

"No, sometimes we want *exactly* the same thing, and that's great."

"But it's never love?"

"Search your memory for a contradictory example, Romy. You won't find one."

"Well, that's a shame, because you've gone out with a lot of wonderful women." She sighed. "I hope you at least warn them up front what to expect."

"Oh, I make it clear, what's in it for both of us."

"Sex."

"*Good* sex. And fun. And respect. I'm not jealous or possessive, which means they can leave whenever they like, no questions asked. No stalking or bad-mouthing or revenge porn when it's over. Friendship if they're up for that at the end, although very few are and that's okay, too. I just...don't want them to love me."

"And yet they *do* love you, Matt. I've talked enough of them off the ledge at the end to know it."

He shook his head, dismissive. "They don't stay on the ledge for long. And that's because although they *say* they love me, they really don't."

"You can't know that."

"I know they almost invariably speak those magic words at the peak of an orgasm, which tells me it's about sex. And if they think sex is the way to my heart, they sure as fuck don't know me well enough to love me. In fact, I'll let you in on a deep dark secret about the way to my heart, Romy." He leaned across the desk, confidante-style, and lowered his voice. "There *is* no way, because I don't *have* a heart."

"If that were true I wouldn't have trusted you all these years and I wouldn't be here now. I trust you, Matt. I trust you absolutely."

"Trust in anything you like except my heart. Or my soul, come to think of it. I definitely don't have one of those. It's the Carter curse, inherited along with the hair. So don't look into my eyes for too long or I'll steal yours." He leaned back in his chair and smiled mockingly. "Have you thought what'll happen if you have a red-haired, soul-stealing kid? Will you reject the baby?"

She looked directly into his eyes. "I like your red hair. I want the baby to have it."

That look, so serious and compelling, was like a blow to the chest, and it took Matt a moment to absorb the impact. Trust, she'd said she trusted him. And it was in her eyes. Even after everything he'd just told her. She was a babe in the woods, wandering through the forest in her red dress with no idea wolves were lurking behind the trees. She needed to be protected from the likes of him.

"Yeah well, I suggest you look past the red hair," he said, "and understand that the only thing I have to offer is a very big cock."

She surprised him by not flinching, by looking at

him just as steadily, as seriously, as trustingly. "And if I were to say that I *love* your red hair? That I love *everything* about you? What would you do, Matthew? Would you dump me? And…and Veronica and Rafael and Artie and Teague? Would you dump them, too? Because I—they—*we*—all love you! How could we not, when you push and pull us to do things we never would otherwise? The baby you're giving me, for starters."

"I told you—that's for me."

"Then what about the time I couldn't afford the air-fare to Sydney for Frankie's wedding, and lo and behold, a ticket materialized."

"Air miles—it cost me nothing!"

"And Artie—the software that would have stayed in your heads if not for you. You made him rich."

"Made me rich, too, and it wouldn't have happened without his brain."

"Then what about the Silicon Valley tech hub you set up and dragged him into."

"That's a partnership, benefiting me, too."

"You pushed Rafael into entering that international writing competition, which he won."

"He didn't take much pushing."

"You got Veronica the gig with the university's Student Healthcare Outreach program because she needed a good deed on her CV."

"Stop!"

"And Teague only snagged a spot crewing in the Sydney Hobart Yacht Race because of you."

"Teague almost drowned!"

"He loved every minute of it! And he loves *you*. Like a brother. He's told me so."

"Goddammit, Romy." He looked away from her,

because that shook him. Teague. *Teague*, who'd seen more than the others, who'd guessed it all, who fucking *knew*. Teague might be the closest anyone had come to sainthood, but he wasn't stupid enough to want a brother like Matt. Romy was deluding herself. He brought his eyes back to her. "You're wrong. All those things...they're nothing. I've done other stuff you wouldn't congratulate me for, believe me."

"What stuff?"

He had to force himself not to look away again; to do so once was barely acceptable; twice would give too much away. "Stuff you don't need to know."

"Why can't I know?"

"Because you'd back out of this deal if you did."

For a long moment she just looked at him. And then she sighed. "How am I supposed to understand why it's so hard to accept that people love you if you won't tell me?"

"You don't have to understand, you only have to accept that to me, love is nothing but an overused word," he said. "I love ice cream, oysters, pizza. I love cooking, sailing, camping. How's anyone supposed to take that word seriously when it's thrown out about anything and everything? So I'm asking you not to say it, the way you haven't said it for ten years."

"I *must* have said it before."

"Not to me. And I figure if you were ever going to say it, you'd have said it by now. I don't *want* to hear it, Romy, so don't say it now." He stopped to take a calming breath. "There are other words for what we have. More meaningful words. Words that can't be desecrated. Words like *friendship*, *camaraderie*, *affection*. Be as creative as you want. Just don't call it love."

"Okay." She held up her hands, palms out, surrender. "This is me not calling it love."

"Good."

"I hereby promise not to love you."

"Great."

"I refuse to love you."

"Okay, I get it, Romy, give it a rest."

"It's not like I was going to propose marriage."

"Fucking fantastic. Go you. Now, moving *on*!"

She snatched up the page on top of her pile. "Visitation," she announced. "My lawyer thinks—"

"Not interested in anything your lawyer says," Matt interrupted irritably. "I'll just tell you what I want—access without restrictions when I'm in London."

"I'm sure we can come up with a form of words to that effect," she said, all business now. "You're only in London for one week a year, so give me advance notice and I'll make sure I'm not out of town."

"It'll be more than once a year. I'll be over in four months' time to look at premises, and then again two months after that to sort out tenancy agreements."

"Premises? What have I missed?"

"Artie and I are opening a tech start-up hub in London similar to the Silicon Valley one. He's taking the lead so he's already over there, but once it's up and running, I'll be there on and off for the first year at least."

"Okay. No problem. Like I said, advance notice, and I'll make it easy for you to see the baby." She shot him a curious look. "If that's really what you want."

"Why wouldn't I want it?"

"You indicated on the phone you were looking for a no-strings godfather role. It's a little…confusing, I guess, to hear you talk about unrestricted access. And

I...I just think it's a good idea to start as you mean to go on."

"What does *that* mean?"

"That you don't keep changing your mind—like, one year you decide to come every month, the next year you come once in the whole year. Children need certainty."

"Okay then, how about we leave it at once a year, scheduled, and you decide whether or not to allow other visits on a rolling basis."

"Fine. Then let's move on to—"

"I'm not finished."

She waited, watching him warily.

"The kid's going to be half-American," he went on, "so if I'm only going to be guaranteed one visit a year, you need to bring it out here once a year. For...I don't know...heritage purposes."

"Easy! I'm already here once a year—and I'll be over more often if I land Suzanne Plieu as a client. She's keen to open a fine dining restaurant in New York and we've had a preliminary chat about what I can do to help her find a partner."

"New York is Teague's territory, not mine."

"Well, yeees." That same curious look, as though she were trying to work him out. "And if Suzanne needs a lawyer, he'd be—"

"I'm not talking about Suzanne's restaurants or legal needs. I'm talking about you being needed in San Francisco with me, the kid's father, not in New York with Teague."

"It's going to depend on whether I can afford it."

"*I* can afford it."

"My clients pay for my travel here and you're not my client."

"Then start working on your aversion to staying with me. No accommodation costs, and I won't *feel* like your client when you sashay in with your briefcase."

"I can't stay with you, Matt."

"Why not? You stay with Teague when you're in New York."

"Only when my work is finished."

"Should I point out that you're not working tonight?"

Pause. He knew that slight twist to her mouth. She was working out what to say. "Teague's apartment is... spacious. It's easier there."

"And I now have a large house. So when you come with the kid, you stay. As long as your 'form of words' contains that, we're good."

"We're not good in that case."

"Why not?"

And she was up, out of her chair, walking over to the fireplace, dragging her hands through her hair—which she never, ever did.

"Why not?" he asked again, when she just stood there looking into the flames.

"It won't work."

"Asking again—why not?"

Shake of her head.

"Romy, what's going on? Why did I buy a house with a million rooms if you and the kid are going to stay in a hotel?"

She turned to face him then. "But th-that's not why you bought the house!"

"Isn't it?"

He saw the breath she took, and prepared himself for an argument.

"Okay then, Matthew," she said, "in the spirit of negotiation—"

"It's not negotiable."

"—I'll *agree* to stay here, on the condition that I know in advance who else will be here and I can opt out if I'm uncomfortable."

"Uncomfortable?"

"I don't want to impinge on your lifestyle."

"My 'lifestyle'?"

"There'll be times it won't be appropriate for me to stay, depending on…on who…"

He shot to his feet. "Who I'm *fucking*? Is that what you mean?" He realized he'd yelled that, but couldn't get the anger under control enough to care.

"If you'd let me expl—"

"You think I'm going to have someone stashed in my bedroom for after I've finished reading my kid a bedtime story?" Yelled again.

"I wouldn't put it quite like—"

"Will I have to fill out a form? Name, age, occupation, social security number? Nominate what nights of the week I intend to fuck them?"

"Oh, for God's sake!" she said, firing up at last and yelling back at him. "I already *know* what nights of the week! *Every* damn night of *every* damn week! That's the problem!"

"I'm glad you appreciate my stamina!"

"That place we shared back in the day had paper-thin walls! We *all* appreciated your stamina! Veronica and I used to joke about buying shares in Durex, you went through so many jumbo boxes of condoms!"

"So you counted my condoms and listened in? Interesting."

"Sadly, the pillow I jammed over my head to filter out the moans, grunts and squeals didn't quite block everything."

"What can I say? I do a good job. A better job than Teague, now I think of it, since he didn't ever stay with you overnight."

"This isn't about Teague."

"No, it isn't, is it, or maybe *I* would have heard something."

"Not over the racket going on in *your* room!"

"Jealous?"

She raised her chin. "Just over it! Okay? I'm over it! I don't *want* to hear you anymore! I've had *enough* of hearing you!" And she was on the move again, storming over to the drapes, trying to drag them open as though their very existence was cutting off her oxygen supply.

He stalked across the room, reached her, spun her. "Then how about you stay tonight and test the sound-proofing? In the absence of my usual fuck noises you can listen for the loud howl of sexual frustration that'll be coming out of my room because I haven't had sex for two fucking *weeks*! Does that scare you, Romy?"

"Why should it scare me?"

"Because you're here alone with me and I...I... Arrrggh! It's dangerous, can't you see that?"

"Dangerous how?"

"Jesus, Romy, how naive *are* you?" Matt said. The room was hot, stifling, claustrophobic. He needed air, needed...*something*! "Fuck this!" He reached past her, grabbed a handful of velvet, yanked on it, heard a satisfying rip, and then the drapes dropped to the floor. He kicked them for good measure. "When are you going to accept that I'm not your damn hero, Romy? I'm not like Teague. I don't *do* chastity, and yet I've just told you I *have* done it, for *two weeks*."

"So *what*?"

"So I'm a *sex addict*. And you're *here*."

"A sex addict would have made a move on me the night we met! God knows I gave you the chance! So don't talk to me about not 'doing' chastity when you've been nothing *but* chaste with me for ten years!"

"You're not like the others!"

"Well, that just goes to show that you're an *idiot*! Because I *am* like the others. I'm *exactly* like the others. I want what *they* want, damn you!"

Sudden, charged silence.

Matt's skin prickled, his senses going on high alert. "Tell me what you mean," he said, breathing the words. "What you want."

She closed her eyes. Heartbeat. Opened them. "You know what I mean. You of all men *know* what women mean!" And it was as though the angry energy drained out of her, even though her hands had clenched into fists by her sides. "What I want is you. I want...you."

CHAPTER THREE

TEN YEARS OF not saying the words, and now they were out, hanging between them.

Romy's heart was beating hard enough to leap out of her body. And Matt looked rigid enough to bounce the poor thing off his chest. Like a stone column. Or... or petrified wood.

Petrified being the operative word.

She choked down a rising bubble of hysterical laughter at the notion that big, bad Matt could be scared of her. *She* was the one who should be scared. Scared he'd tell her no and leave her with nothing: friendship in tatters, no baby and still no clue about what it was like to...to *be* with him like all those other women.

"You don't know what you're saying," Matt said.

And on the spot, she consigned any last vestige of caution to hell. For ten long years she'd been subjugating her lust for him. That was long enough! "Yes, Matt, I do," she said. "Exactly what I *did* say. I want you. But you can call it Plan B if that's easier for you to deal with."

"Plan B?"

"I need to get pregnant. You offered to provide the sperm. We've discussed the turkey baster method—

Plan A—but there's no reason it can't be done the old-fashioned way—Plan B."

"Old-fashioned way."

"We have a window of opportunity here. It's almost like fate stepped in."

"Window of opportunity," he said, like he was having trouble keeping up.

"Neither of us has someone in our lives—a minor miracle in your case. You said you were sexually frustrated, so you need a release valve, and here I am offering to be it."

"Release valve."

"From my perspective, it's cheaper than IVF. It's certainly more *efficient*. Like a direct deposit, cutting out the middleman."

"Direct deposit."

"Oh, for God's sake, stop repeating everything I say," she semiexploded as her resolve frayed around the edges. "It's easy to understand, isn't it? It's just a one-night stand! We've already been through your ground rules about not mistaking sex for anything more, so don't worry that I'll be expecting a bourgeois romance. And you're not the only one who knows what it is to be sexually frustrated, because it's been a while for me, let me tell you, and I daresay it'll be a much *longer* while once I'm pregnant."

"One-night stand."

"Yes, one night. No encore required. If it doesn't work, we simply revert to the turkey baster/courier option and…and…and aren't you going to say something?"

"No encore."

"Something that's *not* a stupid repeat of what I've already said."

She waited; he stared.

Romy couldn't recall an instance in which Matt had taken this long to make a decision. She wondered if she should shorthand the argument by taking off her dress.

"Matt..." she said, reaching for the zipper at her left side—but before she could touch it, a log fell in the fireplace, jolting the momentum out of her so that she lost her nerve. "Forget it. It was just a suggestion. If you can't bring yourself to do it, there's nothing more to be said. Plan A it is."

"I'm pretty sure I can bring myself to do it," he said, and then he started laughing as though she'd told the funniest joke on the world.

She drew herself up, glaring at him. "I'm glad I've managed to amuse you."

She tried to push past him, but he blocked her. "Wait!" he said.

"We've wasted enough time. We need to go back to the paperwork."

Again he blocked her. "I said wait. Let's at least *talk* about Plan B."

"I'm no longer interested in Plan B."

"Why not?"

"Because you've just reminded me how it ends."

"How can that be when it hasn't happened yet?"

"It'll be a carbon copy of the time I told you Jeff Blewett kissed like his mouth was an octopus suction cup and you dared me to let you demonstrate the way you imagined that to be. I was stupid enough to say yes because I thought...I thought...never mind what I thought, it doesn't *matter* what I thought, because at the last minute you changed direction and gave me a hickey right here…" jabbing at the center of her forehead "…and no amount of makeup would cover it up so I went around for two days looking like I'd been hit by a cricket ball and you thought it was all hilarious."

"So how about I try it now?"

"I don't need another forehead hickey, thank you."

"I mean I could kiss you for real. And then…well, then you could decide if we go ahead with Plan B."

"It'd serve you right if I said yes."

"So say it."

Romy licked her lips nervously. "Be careful, Matt, or I really will call your bluff."

"Call it. I dare you to."

"After the forehead hickey, you're going to have to convince me you'll be able to get it up at the crucial moment before I go any further," she said.

He took a step back from her, which she didn't consider promising. "One look at me will tell you that's not going to be a problem. So go on and look."

She examined his face, trying to gauge his seriousness. She was so keyed up, she'd rip his throat out if she saw so much as a glint of humor in his eye.

"Lower," he instructed.

Her eyes dropped to his chest.

"Jesus, Romy, are you doing this on purpose? Lower!"

To his jeans. "Oh."

"Bingo," he said.

She raised her eyes to his face again. "I've heard that's always there."

"Are you fucking nuts? I'd never function as a human being if that were the case." He reached for her then. "But it's been there since you walked in tonight." Folded her into his arms. "So if you're telling me you didn't feel it in the entrance hall, I'm going to think I've shrunk. And I know I'm ten years past my sexual peak, but it seemed to work very...*sizably*, shall we say, two weeks ago."

She choked on a laugh. "Your ego is gargantuan."

"My ego isn't the thing that's gargantuan. Although if you really didn't notice the size of my cock when you first arrived, it's going to need some stroking."

"I hope you mean your ego."

"Actually, I really do mean my cock. So stay riiight...theeere, ahhhhh, that feels good." Nudging his cock against her. "Think about what it means vis-à-vis your question about whether or not I can bring myself to do it."

"What it means..." she breathed out, fairly sure she could orgasm just from what he was doing here and now.

"It means yes I can, and when I do it's going to be amazing. I'll make it amazing for you, Romy. The moment you say yes."

Same man she'd been friends with for ten years, same man who'd hugged her, tousled her hair, dragged her onto his lap, forced her earrings through her ill-pierced left earlobe. But this was different. *He* was different. And she had a premonition that he would always be different, from this moment.

The fear of losing him if she said the "yes" he was asking for was real, because women in whom Matt had a sexual interest were never around for long. The only women who lasted in his life were those who dated his friends—like Veronica, whom he treated like a sister even after her split from Rafael. And wasn't that at least one reason Romy had transferred her starry eyes from Matt to Teague in their freshman year? Not only because Teague really was perfect but because Matt had *brought* him to her, thereby marking her place in Matt's life while she got her head around consigning Matt to the friend zone?

How long would she last if she stepped out of that zone? Matt had said friendship at the end was possible with women he'd had sex with but that most didn't want it. Why would she be any different from all those other women?

The baby, of course. The baby made her different. But the baby made her vulnerable, too, because it was precious not only for its own sake but because it would be a part of Matt that would always belong to her, a part she was allowed to love. She so wanted to believe Matt would come to love the baby, which would be like loving a part of her, even if he didn't call it love.

Impossible to risk all that for one night...and yet just as impossible *not* to after wanting him for so long. Oh, how she wished she could blur the line between sex and friendship instead of stepping over it, keeping everything in its proper place.

If the sex was awful, she probably could. They'd laughingly accept that they'd given it the old college try and there was no harm done whether she was pregnant—experiment concluded successfully—or not— back to Plan A.

If it was awful...

But Romy knew it wouldn't be awful.

The tightness of her skin told her that. Her racing heart, too. The way the smell of his pine-tree-scented soap made her want to lick him.

Those were the feelings lovers had, not friends.

Lovers.

Love.

Don't call it love. Call it anything *except* love. Friendship, camaraderie, affection. A window of opportunity. A cheaper, faster, more efficient method of sperm insertion. Release valve. Direct deposit. Plan B. Sex, just sex.

If she kept all those descriptions in mind, surely she could do this. She could blur the line, she *would* blur the line, and she'd survive the end.

"All right, yes," she breathed, both brave and terrified.

He pulled her in even more tightly. "Then I suggest we go upstairs immediately because it's not your forehead I want to suck right now, and if we don't move, I'm afraid I'll drag you down to the floor and have my evil way with you right here."

She huffed out a desperate laugh. "Evil is fine by me."

He rubbed his cheek across the top of her head, and she felt him sigh even though she didn't hear it. "Careful what you say, Romy."

CHAPTER FOUR

ROMY MADE IT to the entrance hall—and stopped.

"The stairs on the left." Matt, behind her.

She hesitated. "Do you really think we can be friends at the end of this?" she asked.

"That's the idea."

"It didn't work out that way for Veronica and Rafael. They haven't spoken to each other since graduation."

"Those two weren't friends to start with, Romy. They were a Molotov cocktail from the night we all met, hell-bent on being in love. But you and I are a whole different ball game. We've got our plan straight."

"Plan B," she said. What a time to realize that for once in her life she didn't *really* have a plan—not for the mechanics of what would happen next. She was far from having an encyclopedic knowledge of the *Kama Sutra*—whereas Matt, whose sexual prowess was the stuff of legend, probably had his own annotated version.

"What is it?" he asked.

"Nothing," she said in a small voice.

Pause. "Do you want to stop?"

"No." Same tiny voice.

"Because if you've changed your mind, this would be a good time to tell me."

"I haven't changed my mind," she said, and made it to the base of the stairs before stopping again. Oh God, what if she couldn't even get him to have an orgasm and he ended up just as sexually frustrated at the end as he'd been at the beginning?

Matt's hands landed on her hips. She expected him to urge her to go up, but instead he pulled her back against him as though they had all the time in the world. She swallowed a mouthful of saliva as she felt his erection prodding against her back. He'd said he had a very big cock and he wasn't kidding. If its size really was illustrative of Matt being ten years past his sexual peak, he must have had the penis of a freaking giant at eighteen.

"Romy?" he said, with a tingle-inducing nudge at her ear. "Be certain you want this, because there'll come a point when I'll stop asking and you'll have to *tell* me if something's bothering you."

"There's no problem," she lied—because she wasn't going to ask him if he'd ever been bored enough to fall asleep halfway through sex—and headed up the stairs, only to stop again at the top.

Matt must have reached that point where he stopped asking, because all he said was, "To the left, fourth door, the open one."

Inhale, step, exhale, step, inhale, step, exhale.

Just the feel of his hands on her hips was making her lust for him in a way she'd never thought possible. What would she do for him when his hands were on her naked flesh? Anything, she suspected. Anything at all. Everything he asked.

Now breathe. Because they'd reached the bedroom. The final frontier.

She stepped over the threshold. Dark floorboards, white walls, a night view of San Francisco Bay in the distance, through curtains opened wide. There was an inner door she assumed led through to a bathroom. Aside from a built-in wardrobe, the only furniture was a gigantic bed and one armchair—a scarcity that amplified the room's size.

"It's big," she said.

"So all the girls say."

And somehow, that made her laugh as she turned to face him, despite her anxiety. "Are you obsessed with size?"

"Only with what I can do with it."

"Don't overpromise, Matthew."

"Not an overpromise," he said huskily, and ran his hand over her hair—a sensual stroke that made her breath catch in her throat. "Are you nervous, Romy?"

"No," she said—but a tic jumped to life at the side of her mouth and gave the lie to that. "Not...really."

Matt pressed his thumb over the tic. "We'll take it as slowly as we need to. I'm not going to do anything I think you won't like, I promise. Stop me anytime. I won't be angry. I won't argue. I won't pressure you. We'll just find another way."

She gestured to the bed, so nervous she could barely stand. "Why don't you tell me what position you want me in so we can get started?"

"Romy! We're not even naked yet."

"I'd rather have it worked out in my head before we take our clothes off so we don't get...you know... distracted."

"Getting…you know…distracted is kind of the aim. So why don't we just play it by ear?"

"By ear?" She reached up and touched her left earlobe, the one he'd nudged with his nose, feeling a residual tingle. "No, that won't work."

He looked at her for a long, quiet moment. "If you don't want to touch me, Romy, there's no point to this."

"I do want to. But I…I just know I could prepare myself better if I knew where we were headed."

"You're overthinking it."

"But what if I suck?"

"Then that'll be perfect."

"Oh!" She laughed. "You know what I mean."

He sighed. "I want you, Romy. I *want* you, *however* this unfolds. I'm telling you that straight. And you know how important you are to me outside this room, which means I have to know this is what you really want. So tell me. Tell me you want me."

"I already t-told you."

"Tell me again. Make me believe it. Or this stops now."

Her pulse leaped—fear, excitement. "I want you."

"Tell me you want me to not only make you pregnant, but to make you come."

Another leap. "Oh God."

"Tell me."

"Fine. I want you to make me come, and come, and come." She rolled her eyes at him. "There. I said it. Now can we get on with it?"

"Come and come and *come*," he repeated.

"Well…yes."

He smiled. "Pfft."

"Pfft?"

"Three orgasms is for amateurs. Let's make it four." He turned her to face the bed. "You want to talk positions? This is how I want you. Go and lie facedown across the bed with your hips at the edge."

Her hands went to her zipper. "Should I—?"

"Leave your clothes on. We'll do this first orgasm fast so you can relax."

Romy went to the bed and took up the position Matt had instructed her to take, her heartbeat now at a gallop. Oh God. Oh God, oh God, oh God, this was going to happen, it really, really was. She was about to find out why all those girls had followed him all over campus, why so many women since had put their lives on hold waiting for him to come back to them even though history told them he'd never do it. She'd know the secret to being the one for him, and she didn't *care* that it was only for one night, she *wouldn't* care, wouldn't stop to think, wouldn't stop at all. She'd waited too long for this.

"And don't worry, you don't have to prepare yourself," he said, coming up behind her, "because *I'm* going to prepare you."

Next second, he was easing her slightly backward and opening her legs. She felt a rush of moisture between her thighs, readying her for what would come next.

"Good," Matt said, as though he'd seen that gush, and Romy *wanted* him to see it, wanted him to *feel* it, wanted him to *taste* it. The anticipation was already better than anything she'd actually experienced.

He raised the skirt of her dress, hissed in a breath, slid his hands around the bands of those black socks that suddenly seemed erotic rather than fashionable. "These stay on," he said huskily.

"Whatever you want."

"You have no idea how much I wish…"

"You wish…?" she breathed, doing some wishing of her own—that he'd finish what he'd been about to say so she could tell him yes, do it, do anything, do everything; it was one night and she wanted it all.

But he didn't complete the sentence. Instead he moved his hands to the bare flesh of her upper thighs above her socks, and Romy lost interest in anything but his stroking fingers.

"You are so absolutely perfect," he said, his voice a raw note off an actual throb. "Now open your legs a little more." She obeyed, only to be told, "Wider, I need room to kneel behind you so I can get my tongue in."

Tongue. She started to tremble, and bit at her bottom lip, determined not to moan. *Tongue*. God help her, she was going to come the moment he touched it to her. She gripped two handfuls of his duvet in preparation.

"Ordinarily I'd suck you through your panties before taking them off," he said, causing another gush. It was a reflex action, to close her legs and contain it, but he laughed, low and strained, and said, "Oh no, you don't," and pushed her thighs wider apart. "But I want my tongue right on you, so I think…yes, I think I'll leave those snug panties of yours on and just move them…" sliding his fingers under the crotch "…so I can see them as I lick you. Win-win for me."

He grazed her with his fingers, only *just* touching her, making her gasp before she could catch it back. Then one quick tug, and Matt hissed in another breath, groaned this one back out. How did she look from back there, with the soaking-wet crotch of her lilac panties shoved aside? What was he thinking, seeing her like that—half on display, half hidden, swollen with need? Ah God, who cared what she looked like or what he thought, as long as he touched her.

"So pretty—more than I could have imagined," Matt said, and next second he was kneeling between her open thighs. "Better than I deserve." That was added so softly, her heart thumping so strongly, Romy wasn't sure she'd heard him correctly. It didn't make sense, that he could not deserve her. Not when she was so sure she didn't deserve *him*, when she'd somehow tricked him into this.

"Wh-what?" she asked, but his answer was to tug the crotch of her panties still farther aside.

His answer was to lick all the way along her sex with the flat of his tongue so that she jerked and cried out, her hands twisting in the duvet, her leg muscles quivering, and she cared about nothing except that he keep going. He licked her again, and again and again, until she was pushing herself against his mouth. *Harder, harder.* She screamed it only in her head, but it was as though Matt heard her, because he settled into a rhythm, directing his assault at her clitoris now, alternating the flat of his tongue with the tip. Strokes and flicks, changing the pressure from hard to soft and back, increasing speed. Faster, faster, faster. It was coming, she could feel it, she didn't even have to reach for it, didn't have to will it. She had no control. One, two, three harder licks, and he sucked her clit into his mouth. He kept sucking until she was ready to bang her head on the mattress, so great was the effort it took not to humiliate herself by begging him to finish it.

Her breaths were ragged, hips thrusting convulsively back and forth as though he were actually fucking her and she was meeting each lunge of his cock, but his mouth stayed with her, winding her tight like a key in a toy. *His* toy.

Something had to give. Something had to break. Something had to—

"OooohhhhhmyyyyyGoooooooood." The cry wailed out of her as the orgasm slammed into her, crashed over her, zigzagged through her like burning, bright, hot lightning.

Matt had to know she was coming, she was rigid with it, pulsing under his mouth, but he didn't stop. He kept tonguing her, going at her until her twitching body went limp. She was still gasping for air as he slowed and finished with one opulent lick. And then…hold, hold, hold, his fingers still on the panties he'd dragged out of his way. He was looking at her, she knew he was, and she had neither the strength nor the desire to stop him. His labored breathing, rough and fast, made her long to know what he was thinking.

But one more lick, a quick kiss, and his thinking was over. He turned brisk, repositioning the crotch of her panties, pulling her dress down to cover her, standing.

"Two minutes and twenty seconds," he said. "Was that fast enough for you, Romy?"

His words settled into her fried brain. Lodged there, stuck there…*stung* there.

She got off the bed, brushed at her dress with an unsteady hand. Saw that he was…smirking? Oh no. No, no, *no*! No smirking allowed. This wasn't going to turn into an octopus hickey moment.

"Yes, that was fast enough," she said briskly, "but that wasn't the deal."

Up went Matt's eyebrows. "I said we'd make the first one fast. You didn't complain."

"About the orgasm, no. But there was no semen, therefore no sperm inserted. So although it was good in terms of elapsed time, it was also a *waste* of time."

"Elapsed time? Wow! How...technical. Okay so I'll be technical back and tell you that happy though I am to oblige your demand for multiple orgasms, men have to pace themselves through four orgasms when they'll only get to two or three for themselves."

"Yes, but in this instance it's not like you need to recharge since that was all about me."

"Nooo, but think about it like...well, like a restaurant meal. Appetizer, main course, dessert, petits fours. Cunnilingus is the appetizer. Good to start with, not going to fill me up."

"But what you just did could have been the petits fours—not everyone gets to them, and they're hardly essential to a satisfying meal."

"Er...you know, I'll try almost anything once, but there's one thing I won't do: drink my own semen. Not going to happen. Hence...appetizer. Gotta get the order right when you're not wearing a condom."

A laugh exploded out of her before she could stop it.

Matt grinned. "I see you understand."

"I'd offer to drink it for you, but it would be a—"

"Waste of sperm. Sad but true. For now, though, you can taste yourself." And he stepped right up to her and cupped her face in his hands.

Why hadn't she ever noticed how big Matt's hands were? How big *he* was, compared to her. She was a woman who liked food and she was no twig—so why did she suddenly *feel* like a twig? Small and snappable. She wanted to fold into him but at the same time pull back, run away, protect herself. Because she was already in danger of wanting more than he was willing to give, and it was hard to remember that whatever was happening now wasn't real. Reality would come roaring back later. Outside this room, outside this moment. When this night out of time was over and they were just friends again.

He tilted her head back so she was looking into his eyes, which had gone dark, the pupils having taken over almost all the green. One of his thumbs moved to her mouth, dragged roughly across her bottom lip. He was going to kiss her. She stiffened, afraid to risk the intimacy of a kiss, wanting to hold herself back from it. She tried to form a phrase with the word *no* in it, one that wouldn't betray her confused sense of truth. But all she could find to say was, "Kissing isn't required." A stupid, mood-shattering thing to say.

"I thought we had a dare going."

"D-dare?"

"Octopus kiss."

"You said you weren't interested in my forehead."

"I'm interested in every part of you."

"If that were true you would have kissed me back then."

"Ah, but if I'd kissed you back then, where would we be now?"

"I think..." she whispered. "I think we'd be nowhere."

"Nowhere..." he repeated, and the way he looked at her was as melancholy as a goodbye, even though they'd barely begun. "I don't like that thought, Romy."

"Neither do I, so let's not think," she said, wanting to take away that look. "Go ahead and kiss me. Do it."

"Forgive me for it first."

"For what?"

"Just...say that you do."

"I'll forgive you anything, always, you know that."

She looked into his eyes as he smoothed his thumbs across her cheeks. And then he gently rested his mouth on hers, and even though he went no further, the moment felt more serious than anything he'd said or done so far. She was balanced on the knife edge of that line she *could not blur*, and one wrong move would slice her in two. Friend...lover. Which was more important to her? Which would Matt choose to be if he couldn't be both? Which would she *want* him to choose?

"Romy," he breathed against her mouth, and she wound her arms around him, held on to him, as though she'd save him from whatever it was that was chasing him. She wished she could pour herself through his skin and comfort him from the inside out, but all she could do was let him take whatever it was he needed from her, the forgiveness she didn't understand.

She knew then there was no choice to be made. She might not know what she'd end up being to him after tonight, but at this moment she would be whatever he wanted her to be.

He tightened his hands on her face and rubbed his mouth across hers, side to side to side, and she catapulted over that damn line into something that was more than friendship and way more than sex.

She parted her lips, inviting him in, expecting a swoop of tongue, a conquest. Instead, he licked at her top lip, then sucked it into his mouth. She opened wider, desperate now for his tongue against hers, and at last he fitted his mouth on hers, tight as a seal. And there it was, his tongue, inside her. Heady, heady moment, the taste of him at last. Unfamiliar—and yet as right as though she'd been expecting exactly this forever. He made a sweep of her mouth, and while her senses were still absorbing the feel of that, he came in hard, his tongue demanding a response from her so that she clung to him and kissed him back, wanting the moment to go on and on.

When he eased away from her and looked down at her, any hint of gentleness was gone. Something in his eyes she couldn't decipher made her skin prickle all over with heat.

"Orgasm number two coming up, Romy," he said, and there was the promise of something wild in his voice. "And this time, by God, you'll get the sperm."

CHAPTER FIVE

"THAT'S...GOOD," Romy said, and she sounded so breathily gorgeous, Matt wanted to kiss her again.

And maybe he would have, if he didn't have so much more he wanted to do to her.

It had been so damn *hot* to take her mouth like that, with the salty, lemony butter from between her thighs still on his tongue. How had he overlooked the blatant sensuality of her mouth for so long? He figured it was because her lips were almost colorless so there was a hide-in-plain-sight thing going on, but that seemed a piss-poor excuse now he'd kissed her. Everything about her mouth was sexy as hell. Wide bottom lip, top lip almost unnaturally heavy. Lickable. Suckable. If he'd known how it would be, he'd have kissed her ten years ago, fuck his good intentions.

And then, of course, they'd be exactly where she said they'd be: nowhere. Because he'd barely known her, and he would have turned her into a hookup and it would have been over within days and he wouldn't have had the past ten years of having her look at him the way she always did, like he could slay dragons.

Of course, she had no idea that the biggest dragon in her life was him. Which was why his conscience kept tap-tap-tapping at him, telling him that even one night had consequences.

But it was too late to listen to his conscience and so he told himself that since it *was* only one night, the risk was limited. And if he fucked things up…well, hadn't Romy just said she'd forgive him? If she could forgive him anything, surely he could forgive himself for taking this one night. Anyway, he *couldn't* stop now. Not after the way she'd kissed him, like she was making up for those ten lost years. Enticing him to give more, to take more, to devour her mouth, until it was pink and swollen and wet.

Pink, swollen, wet. Like the luscious place between her legs—mysterious, like a dewy flower, its petals closed, peeking out from around the barrier of her panties.

Burrowing his tongue between the petals, searching out every fold, had been an adventure in eroticism. Hidden secrets, buried treasures. And he would use his one night to find every last concealment and plunder it.

How he wished he'd plunged his tongue inside her, but she'd come before he'd had the chance. She was so effortlessly sensitive, it had taken almost no time to get her there. It was like she was made for his mouth. For his cock, too, judging by the way it had throbbed all the way through, demanding its turn. It was a miracle the poor thing hadn't exploded, depositing a gallon of semen through his jeans.

Wasted sperm, Romy would have called that. And so would he. He wanted to be buried all the way inside her when he lost it the first time. And maybe if he was lucky—really, really lucky—the time after that, she might take him into her mouth before she remembered *that* would be a waste of sperm, too. But hell, one suck, one lick, even the briefest kiss, would get him ready to do whatever she wanted. Just the *thought* of seeing her lips wrapped around him was enough to make him wild. It was going to take some willpower to not fall on her like an unrestrained caveman when her clothes came off.

He sent a quick message to his dick: *control yourself.* His dick twitched in response, which Matt interpreted as the penile equivalent of being flipped the bird.

"So...what do you want me to do?" Romy prompted, making him wonder how long he'd been standing there arguing with himself. "Do I take off my clothes now?"

Matt shook his head, closing the small distance between them. "I'll do it," he said, because he needed his first touch to be controlled and once she stripped, all bets would be off. He reached for her zipper. "All you have to do is kick off your shoes."

She kicked. And waited.

He unzipped. And hovered.

Stop, breathe, swallow, control yourself. "Lift your arms," he said.

She did as he asked, and he drew her dress slowly up and off, tossing it in the direction of the chair without taking his eyes from her. He was going to need every ounce of self-restraint he could muster, because he'd never seen a hotter sight than Romy in her underwear. The contrast of the opaque black of her stockings against the matte cream of her upper thighs and the translucent lilac of her panties was pin-up-girl sexy. The neat little patch of brown hair he could see through her panties had his fingers twitching with the need to touch it. Her bra was ivory lace, her full breasts pushing against the cups as though craving both release and his hands, the pastel-pink areolae showing through the material longing to be licked.

"Shall I...?" she asked, reaching behind her for the clasp of her bra.

"No!" Too harsh. *Stop, breathe, control yourself.* "I'll do it." Better. Just.

She nodded, her hands falling to her sides—a simple movement that told him she was ceding herself to him. He liked the idea of her giving her body wholly into his care a little too much for it to be healthy, but he was in thrall to the idea of it nonetheless.

He circled her, drinking in the sight of curves delectably full and lush. He wished he could ravish her a thousand times all at once, in her underwear and out of it. He unclipped her bra, drew the straps down her arms, let it fall to the floor. One long look at her milk-pale back before allowing his eyes to dip lower. When he reached her generous bottom, which was stretching out the lace of her underwear to the limit, he wanted to sink his teeth into her. His hands were shaking as he reached for her panties to push them past her hips, down her legs.

He was glad she wasn't repeating her earlier question about what position he wanted her in; he wasn't sure how he'd frame an answer that included every position known to man. On her back, on her knees, on her side, on top, underneath him, straddling him, sucking him off, on his tongue, in his mouth, hanging from the fucking chandelier. He was past desire; what he felt for her was darker, like a craving—and he knew it was that darkness he had to control at all costs. He *would not* tarnish his bright and brilliant girl.

She stepped out of her panties and he picked them up, sifting them through his eager fingers before throwing them who-the-fuck-knew-where because it struck him that he might savage a hole through the lace—a dead giveaway that he wasn't in control.

He came around in front of her. If she felt uncomfortable wearing nothing but those black stay-ups in front of him, she didn't show it. She looked like she belonged exactly like that, waiting for his touch. Like she trusted him—exactly as she'd said she did—to take care of her.

She reached out a hand, fingertips on his chest, frustratingly tentative. "What about *your* clothes?"

He'd intended to strip off pretty damn quick, but when he looked for outward signs that Romy was as aroused as he was, he got such a shock his hands stopped midaction. Her face was appropriately flushed and her breathing was revealingly fast and shallow—but her nipples were steadfastly flat.

He'd been so busy imagining her breasts with nipples jutting out as per his steamy daydreams in the library, it took him a moment to process that there was no jut. No jut *at all*.

Romy gave a sigh that could only be described as long-suffering. "They're inverted," she explained. "And I'm guessing you haven't seen their like before, despite your revolving bedroom door."

"Inverted. Does that mean…? What does that mean? I mean, I know what *inverted* means but does it… mean…" *Oooooh, shit.* "Does it mean you don't like them to be touched?"

"No! I mean…no."

Thank you, God.

"They're actually super sensitive," she continued, blushing. "It's just not easy to guess how I'm…you know…"

"I know?"

"How I'm…*feeling*, okay?"

God, did she think that was a problem? Because he fucking *loved* the idea of having to work hard to make her show herself. He wanted to work over every inch of her until there was nothing he didn't know. One night. He wanted it all.

He leaned in for a groan of a kiss. "I guess that means I'll have to check how you're *feeling* by doing this…" Sliding his fingers between her thighs to swirl them around her clitoris before slipping them inside her. "Mmm. I think you're almost ready, Romy."

"Not almost. I am. I am ready…I am…I am… ooooh…" she said between pants, and clenched around his fingers as they pulled out of her, as though to keep them inside her. "Oh, please!"

Much as it thrilled Matt that she wanted him to stay there, though, that wasn't the game now. "I *will* please you, Romy, I promise. But first, I want to play with these." His hands went to her breasts, thumbs rubbing over their mysteriously hidden nipples. "Do they ever come out?" he asked, intrigued.

"Sometimes," she said, and arched her back, thrusting her breasts into his hands. "Depending…"

"Depending on what?"

"What you do."

No way was he going to turn down that invitation to experiment!

He pinched around her areolae. "Do you like that?" he asked, and when she groaned and nodded, he said, "Me, too." Only it came out more like a growl, like something feral, so he paused for a moment to rein it all back.

And then he started pinching again, feeling what he couldn't see, the hardness secreted inside. Another buried treasure, waiting to be coaxed out of hiding. Irresistible.

He lowered his head to lick over the top of one nipple, then the other. Her gasping breaths told him she liked that, too, so he kept going. One then the other, back and forth, over and over. She leaned into him, enticing him to more. Her hands were on his hips, gripping hard as he kept licking, experimenting with his tongue. Flat, pointed, lines, circles, hard, soft. What did she like?

The answer was everything, judging by the way she kept shifting from foot to foot, pressing her thighs together, then releasing, then pressing. When he put a hand around each breast and squeezed, narrowing his focal point so he could intensify the pressure of his tongue, she actually moaned. It was hot, hot, *hot*, to hear her. Hot, hot, hot to taste her. He *liked* wanting her like this. The insistent kick of lust, the anticipation of what was to come without knowing quite what path they'd take to reach the cliff, taking her with him every step.

He raised his head, stared into her heavy eyes. "Shall I test again?" he asked, and without waiting for an answer, released one breast, sliding that hand down her body, slipping his fingers between her thighs again. Her clit felt like a small oiled pearl, and as he rolled it between finger and thumb he imagined dropping to his knees to suck her there. But before he could turn the thought to action, she tensed, gasped and—bang!—she came in a clenching rush, the act of it, the *force* of it, taking Matt completely by surprise.

As she collapsed against him, Matt couldn't think past the ease with which he'd gotten her there. Either she was the most responsive woman he'd ever had or he was a fucking magnificent foreplayer. Whichever, he was euphoric. He loved that her sleepy eyelids were even sleepier, loved the way her breaths were still more like pants, loved the way her nails were digging into his hips. And then she topped it all by nestling her face into his chest and biting him through his T-shirt, and his dick leaped like an animal.

"Two down," he said—no, *snarled*, like a beast. "Two to go."

One more twirl of the fingers that were still between her thighs because he simply couldn't resist. And then he started stripping with a vengeance. Thank God he was barefoot; if he'd had to bend down to take off shoes, he was pretty sure his dick would see it as an opportunity to wrap itself around his neck and strangle him—revenge for making it wait.

His T-shirt was wrenched up and off. Jeans and underwear shoved down, kicked aside. A glance showed a damp patch on his boxer briefs. He'd been leaking precum for so long his poor imprisoned penis had had just about enough. He reached for her, but she stepped back. Prime position to be tumbled on her back on the bed, exactly where he needed her. He reached again.

"No," she said.

Freeze. "No?" It came out disbelievingly.

"Not *that* no," she said. "I mean no as in wait." Her eyes dropped to his dick, which all but lunged at her. He needed a leash for it, that was becoming obvious. "Wait because I want to look at you. First time, you know?"

Jesus God yes, he knew. He took a deep breath to curb the rush in his veins. He could wait while she looked him over. He fucking *loved* that she was looking him over. Another deep breath to calm his body, which had broken out in a sweat.

"Can you make it fast? The looking?" he half asked/ half pleaded. "Because I'd like to move on to some mutual touching."

Her eyes raced over him as he started counting in his head. *One, two, breathe, breathe*, as her eyes snagged on his lower abdominals and she licked her lips. He went taut as a bowstring as he pictured her licking her way up and down the V framing them. *Three—God- help-me—four.* She reached out a finger, touched the top of his dick where more liquid was leaking. *Holy- Mary-mother-of-God—five—six.* She raised her finger to her mouth and sucked it inside.

"Mmm," she said.

And the bowstring twanged, whip-fast, sending his arrow flying. "Fuck this," he said, and launched himself at her.

She landed on her back on the bed, Matt on top of her. A keening moan—hers. A ground-out curse—his. She tried to put her arms around him but he stopped her, forcing them over her head so that her big, beautiful breasts were thrust up at him. He leaned in for one more lick of each nipple, shuddering as her back curved up off the bed, offering him more. His thighs settled between hers, knees splaying to open her, spreading her wide. His hips were pistoning even before his cock was in position. He was so hard he knew he wouldn't need to guide it in. It knew where it had to be and was in a fever to go there. One thrust, and he was inside her, her legs wrapping around him. On his third stroke he felt her heels digging into him, encouraging him to go harder.

He tried to kiss her, but he was too far gone to manage anything except a riotous assault of lips and tongue, goaded on by the fact she was attacking him right back. He was sweating enough to make sliding off her a real possibility, so he let go of the hands he still had pinioned above her head and wrapped his arms around her, burying his head between her neck and her shoulder, dragging her in so close they were plastered together tightly enough that a tornado wouldn't separate them. Pulse thundering in his ears. Romy almost sobbing as she spurred him on—heels *and* words. "Matt, I'm going to come. Make me, make me, make me come."

And as he felt her internal muscles start to contract around his cock, he unleashed himself, hands moving beneath her bottom, angling her hips, surging into her, aiming for the spot he knew would tip her over.

"Yes, there," she gasped, grinding against him. "God, right *there*."

Thrust, thrust, fucking thrust, and he felt his own orgasm zap through him. She spasmed around him, crying out his name, and it was as though she'd set a torch to him, so sudden was his eruption, like a gush of lava bursting from a volcano. Gush...then scorching flow. An endless stream, endless pour from him to her. Hot, wet, tight. Delirium.

He stayed, hips bowing into her, as the almost pain-ful tension finally started to drain out of him. He real-ized he was shivering, but he was still so hot. He had no control over his body, even in the aftermath. Dis-tance. He needed distance. But when he tried to roll off her, she tightened her arms and her legs around him and clung.

"I'm too heavy," he said.

"One minute," she said, her voice muffled because she'd buried her face against his chest. "Just one."

And so Matt stayed on top of her, caught between helplessness and dread at the terrible, aching, never-before closeness. He was relieved when she finally relaxed beneath him, unhooking herself, freeing him.

"I'm fine now," she said, and he eased off her to lie beside her, staring up at the ceiling, not knowing what came next.

She propped herself up on an elbow. "How long do you need to recharge, Matt?"

He angled his head toward her, uncomprehending.

"I'm flying out in the morning, remember, so I need to get back to my hotel soon," she explained. "I need to check my notes for Lennie, and pack, and...and double-check the time of my transfer to the airport. All the things an overthinker does. So if we're going to do it again..." She offered him a tremulous smile. "Well, we're up to petits fours, right?"

Flying out in the morning. Flying. Out. "I thought—" He stopped himself. One night, she'd said. That didn't have to mean *all* night.

But...but he'd thought she'd stay.

Stop! He didn't care if she stayed. It was better if she *didn't* stay.

Safer.

How many goes did it take to get pregnant, anyway? Okay, stupid question. He knew it only took one. It was just a matter of *which* one. A matter of what point in the cycle she was at, and whether the stars were aligning and shit like that.

He thought back to her phone call two weeks ago, when she'd been on day three of her period. If he used that as a guide, they were damn close to target. And when you combined that timing with the fact that he'd shot off inside her like a NASA-grade rocket, she was probably already pregnant. He'd probably given her *triplets* to match the three orgasms. She didn't even have to stay for her fourth…fourth orgasm…if she didn't…want…oooohhhh.

Brain slowing down. Blood, heart, nerves, seizing up. *Back up a step. Back up.*

She was probably already pregnant. Already…pregnant. Already…

Matt reached out a trembling hand, laid it low on her belly.

Romy stopped breathing, stopped everything, looking at Matt's hand on her.

She knew what he was thinking, and now that he was thinking it, she was thinking it, too: she might already be pregnant.

Way to change the dynamic! A few minutes ago, it was all about sex. Now it was about more.

She put her hand over his. "So?" she asked softly, searching his face.

He kept his eyes on their hands. He said nothing but she felt the shiver that ran through him all the way to her bone marrow, as though he'd become a part of her. She wanted to warm him, to rub away the crease between his eyebrows, tell him everything would be okay.

Except that everything wouldn't be okay. His silence told her that, and the look on his face—a look she'd never seen on him before. Haunted. Hunted.

They hadn't blurred the line, and they hadn't crossed it; they'd drawn a new one. And it wasn't a situation that could be withdrawn from. It was real, and it was forever. He'd become hers in a way that was different from before, and she had a sudden insight that he always would be hers, whether she was pregnant or not, no matter what happened in her life, or who else she slept with. And that was more than he'd bargained on and *way* more than he wanted.

"So," Matt said, and took a deep breath as he eased his hand out from beneath hers. "I'm recharged—let's go for broke this time."

Fast, practiced, blank-faced, he stripped off her socks, and even *that* seemed portentous. Because it felt as though they were no longer erotic—they were just something in his way.

CHAPTER SIX

MATT ENJOYED MORNINGS AFTER. When he was alone, sated, relaxed and a little nostalgic for the previous night's experience even though the details were already hazy.

But this morning, standing in the kitchen Romy hadn't seen even though he'd kitted it out especially for her, he was neither sated nor relaxed. And the details weren't hazy—each one was crystal clear.

Romy, so hesitant going up the stairs.

Romy, diffident and wanting to get it over with once they'd reached the bedroom.

Romy, talking about returning to her hotel room after he'd gone at her like a battering ram.

What did that fucking *tell* him? That she wasn't his speed!

Why hadn't he fucking *listened*? Because he was a fucking monster!

What had he done about it? He'd forged ahead and done her again! Shoving himself into her deep and hard and relentless, wringing a double orgasm out of her, making her beg for it!

And his reward for that brutality was for her to jump out of bed even before she'd stopped gasping his name, grab her clothes as though he'd steal them if she wasn't fast enough, and run for the shower like she couldn't wait to wash him off her skin.

That's when he'd seen the purple marks on her hips, and he'd thanked God she wasn't staying the night after all because he'd have marked her black-and-blue and scraped her raw all over by morning.

He'd pulled on his clothes and waited impatiently for her to reappear from the bathroom, rehearsing apologies, explanations. But when she'd resurfaced, scrubbed and dressed, paper white and jittery, he'd known there was no excuse that would make it right.

"Well, that's that, then," she'd said. And the look on her face as she'd said it had ripped a hole in him. Like she was going to cry, like she was going to *break*.

And so Matt had called her a cab, and trailed after her like a stray dog all the way down that overwrought staircase, and fetched her overcoat and briefcase from the overstuffed library while she waited in the pretentious entrance hall of his mausoleum of a house. And then they'd stood by the door and stared past each other for a million fucking years until the taxi arrived. Then she'd said, "I'll know one way or the other in two weeks, so I'll be in touch then." And with a restrained, chicken-like peck on his cheek, whoosh! She was gone, the door had closed, the taxi was driving away.

Matt had stayed at the door, and it wasn't until three minutes had passed that he'd realized he was waiting for her to come back. Because she *never* left him without hugging him like a maniac and ruffling his hair. He'd actually rested his hand on the door handle, preparing to wrench open the door the moment he heard the cab pull up.

Another minute—no cab.

His knuckles had turned white as it registered that she wasn't coming back. That the peck on the cheek was all he was going to get. That it might be the last thing he ever got from her. And he'd raced up to strip his bed, as though by doing so he could rip the experience out of his room, out of his house, out of his exploding head.

That was when he'd spied the tiny ball of lilac, scrunched up behind the armchair. She'd been so eager to leave, she hadn't even looked for her panties; she'd gone commando—something *his Romy* would never, ever have done because she'd have been all, *What if I get hit by a bus?*

And even knowing that that meant she had to have been in a panic to escape him, he couldn't stop himself from picking up those panties and sniffing them like a sexual deviant, which triggered a leap in his cock that *infuriated* him because those were *Romy's* panties! *His Romy's* panties that he hadn't let himself near for ten fucking years!

He'd grabbed the sheets, screwed them and the panties up together, strode into the bathroom and shoved the lot into the laundry hamper so hard he pushed his hand right through the wickerwork, giving new meaning to the term *basket case*—which he clearly still was the morning after a sleep-deprived night because here he was standing in *her* kitchen, his dick throbbing like the devil, willing her to come back even though he knew she was already in the goddamn air.

"Fuuuuuuuuuuuuck!" he yelled, and when that didn't release enough pressure, banged his fist on the counter. "Fuck." Bang. "Fuck." Bang. "*Fuck* this!" And he swept

an arm across the kitchen counter, knocking the coffee
he'd made for himself but hadn't drunk into the sink.

Fuck the coffee, too! Why was he drinking coffee?
He needed an anesthetic, not a stimulant. He wrenched
a beer from the fridge—and he was beyond fucking
caring that Romy always tsk-tsked him out of drinking beer in the morning—and made his way out onto
the deck because it was past time for his dick to start
behaving like a regular body part and not a Viagra-
fueled nightmare and he hoped the frigid wind would
knock an inch or two off his erection.

Throwing himself into a seat at his purpose-bought-
for-Romy outdoor setting, he took a vicious swig of his
beer and forced himself to look out toward San Francisco Bay, where he was going to keep looking until
he calmed the fuck down.

An intention that lasted forty seconds, when he
experienced an overpowering need to check his cell
phone just in case he'd missed a text message from
Romy.

Aaaand nope. Moron. If he hadn't gotten a text
by now he wasn't going to get one, because she was
already-in-the-goddamn-air-how-long-did-it-take-to-
get-that-through-his-head!

He tossed his phone onto the table, only to pick it
up again immediately to call up the message Romy
had sent him after their phone call two weeks ago—
the selfie, in which she was blowing him a kiss. "My
hero" was the text that accompanied it. He'd rolled his
eyes at that, but he'd laughed, too, because her mouth
was too wide for that expression to be anything other
than comical. Maybe seeing it now would give him

hope that the two of them might laugh about last night in due course.

But when he pulled up the photo, instead of laughing at her duckbill lips, he found himself running his fingertip over them while his breathing went haywire and his heartbeat went bump-bump-thump and he could almost...taste her.

He snatched his hand away from the phone, picked up his beer, took another swig. But swilling the beer around his mouth did nothing to disperse the taste of her, which seemed to have drenched him at some cellular level.

She should be here, telling him he was still her hero even though he knew he was an asshole. She should be here, forgiving him the way she said she always would. She should be here, easing his rage the way being around her always did—that bitter strangle of fury he'd been carrying inside forever, forever, for ever, at what his parents had turned him into. This...*thing*, dark and twisted and disgusting, that made him not good enough for her.

"Fuuuuuuuuuuck!" Another gut-wrenching yell. Because he wanted her here...and yet he should be glad she wasn't. He'd spent ten careful years keeping her away, blocking every sexual thought of her, trying not to ruin what he'd felt that first night he'd met her, that glimmering sense of comfort she gave him.

It was ever-after stuff, what he'd felt that night. And what he'd felt for her had stayed in the realm of ever-after through three and a half years' living in the same house, through six and a half years' living on different continents, through the past two weeks of knowing the baby was his gateway to a permanent link with her because she'd have only one child and that child would be his and whoever came after him could therefore *never* take his place in her life.

If he were a decent human being, he would have told her everything about himself and given her the chance to find better sperm. But he could live with not being a decent human being. He'd lived with it a hell of a long time now.

He reached for his beer, saw that his hand was shaking and took a long, painful breath.

If he'd succeeded in accomplishing the ultimate betrayal and impregnating her, would she hate the thought of having his child, after last night? And if she *wasn't* pregnant, would she write him off and look elsewhere?

Two weeks, and he'd know. Two weeks—that's when she'd said she'd be in touch.

Although he could contact her, couldn't he? He could text her now, if he wanted to.

He picked up his phone again, racking his brain for something funny to say. Maybe something about preparing the kid for a lifetime of dealing with redhead jokes…?

But…no. She might get all serious and tell him again that she loved his red hair. Loved his hair…loved everything about him…loved…him…?

No!

No, she couldn't tell him that. He wouldn't let her tell him that.

The text would have to be something simple like checking she got home all right. He always sent that text when she was flying home. And it never mattered that he sent it while she was in the air, because she got it when she landed and she always responded straightaway and that way it would be only hours—not two weeks—before he heard from her.

He tapped out the message...and then froze.

What the fuck was he doing?

She'd said two weeks. The inference being she didn't *want* to be in touch until then.

Was he going to start hounding her when she didn't want to be hounded? After he'd *told* her he didn't do that stalking shit? Why make her more uncomfortable with him than she already was?

Nope. Delete. Delete that message. Delete, delete, DELETE, GODDAMMIT!

He realized he was about to crack the case on his cell phone, and forced himself to ease his grip. He threw the phone down, got up and strode over to the edge of the deck. The view was the only thing he liked about this house. He should be out on that damn bay, kayaking. It would be worth freezing his ass off to get out of the house.

He strode back to the table, scooped up his phone—in case a message came through—shoved it in his pocket—because he knew it wouldn't—and headed inside to the library to find his kayaking map because no way was he taking his cell phone with him; odds were instead of using it to check his coordinates he'd obsess about text messages he wasn't getting and didn't want to *think* about getting.

But once in the library he was drawn to the desk, where Romy's paperwork was, and he lost interest in looking for the map. He could see her, even with his eyes open, muttering to herself as she flicked through pages. And when he closed his eyes... Oh God, the images. Furtive flashes of naked bodies, eager thrusts, cries and tongues and fevered flesh.

His eyes bolted open. "Jesus Christ, stop!" he cried.

And as if in answer to a prayer, his cell phone pinged with an incoming text.

Bump-bump-thump went his heart.

Romy!

So she hadn't caught her flight. She was still in San Francisco.

He put his hand over the phone in his pocket and smiled. She'd forgiven him.

Call or text back?

Call, he decided. He'd suggest she come over and hang out here, strictly friend zone now their one-night stand was over. He'd remind her about the paella she owed him and then help her make it, and they could eat it while watching a movie—there was a TV behind a panel in this godforsaken library and it didn't get more innocent than watching a movie; they always watched movies together when she was over. He fumbled the phone out. He'd get her new flight details, drive her to the airport at the appointed time the way he usually did, when she wasn't running for her life. And if she didn't hug him goodbye he'd headlock her!

He swiped his cell on. It would all be back to norm—

"Shit." As he saw who the message was from.

Not Romy, Camilla.

Coffee? Can meet you in ten.

Coffee. Camilla's daytime euphemism for sex. Nighttime was margarita.

Well, obviously *that* wasn't going to happen. A guy

who'd offered to impregnate a friend didn't fuck his way around town until the job was done. Still...hmm... any red-blooded man would get a libidinous spark at the thought of sex with Camilla—so why wasn't he?

He tried picturing Camilla. Honey-blond hair; aquamarine eyes; sharp, high cheekbones; pouty mouth; curved in all the right places and perfectly proportioned. A very beautiful woman. She was fun, too. She laughed a lot; she ate like a normal person and drank beer. She was even clued up on tech talk, unlike Romy, who thought the only Java that existed was an island in Indonesia. He *liked* Camilla. They were good together. They thought alike. And she was the type to flay the flesh off a guy—literally, not metaphorically—which was exactly what he needed at that moment, a physical pain to replace the other kind.

He tried to coax some hot blood into his veins, some rigidity into his cock. But it was no use. His veins remained disinterested. His penis positively *un*interested—in fact, it was...deflating...? Oh God, he really was deflating!

He sighed, and sent back a simple text to Camilla of the sorry-no-can-do-some-other-time variety. Then he stared at the phone some more, but no matter how long he stared, no text from Romy materialized.

He shoved the phone into his pocket. He was going to go back to his bedroom. He was going to take the sheets out of the hamper and rip the fuckers in half.

He was three strides to the door when he recalled that there was a pair of lilac panties in with the sheets and—whooshka—up came his dick, like an amphetamine-loaded cobra from a snake charmer's basket. Un-fucking-*bearable*.

He whirled again, returned to the windows, desperate to calm down, but there was no calm to be had out there. Swollen gray clouds were gathering over the bay, like they were building apace with his turbulent mood. The weather wouldn't stop him taking out the kayak—in fact, he relished the idea of carving through the water in a storm.

He watched until the first raindrops dotted the window...gathered power...started pelting. He turned into the room, strode to the desk, looked down at those motherfucking pages. Their only saving grace was that Teague hadn't drawn them up; he'd hate to have to beat the crap out of Teague for getting between him and Romy.

Not that the documents really mattered. The crux of the deal was that Matt's name wouldn't be on the birth certificate. He didn't need fifteen documents to confirm he wasn't going to be a real father.

He picked up a three-page document at random and ripped it in half. An action that reminded him of what he wanted to do to his sheets, so he ripped it again. Again. Again. He hated those fucking pages. Rip, rip, fucking rip. To the next document. Rip. Rip. Over and over and over, page after page.

He was breathing heavily by the time he'd finished his harried tearing and looked at the pieces scattered across the desktop. What a mess. An all-round fucking mess. On the desk, and in his head.

It wasn't meant to be like this. It was meant to be easy. A carefree donation of easily produced body fluid. So why had it felt like something else, something more, last night?

Oh God, why could he *see* her so clearly? His red-haired, hazel-eyed daughter, looking at him with the same quiet trust he'd seen in Romy's eyes last night.

He didn't know how to banish that image; he didn't know how to fix him and Romy; he didn't know how to stop wanting forever; he didn't know how to reconcile all those things into a way of existing that didn't feel like he was being ripped into pieces, like those fucking pages on the desk.

He rubbed his fingertips up and down his forehead, trying to ease the ache that was building in his head. His sinuses felt swollen. The back of his nose was stinging. He blinked hard and swallowed against a sudden lump in his throat. Swallowed again, but the lump remained.

He imagined getting Romy's regular parcel of photos, and that in with the shots of her parents, a guy she might be dating, restaurant dishes she was about to consume and shoes she needed a second opinion on before purchase, were photos of his daughter. The birth. The home-from-the-hospital shot. First tooth. First crawl. First birthday. First walk. First day at school. First French fucking snail being eaten. Photos of a normal kid, who had a normal mother and normal grandparents. A normal, innocent childhood.

He spun away from the desk, strode to the window, kicked aside the ruined curtains, stared out. The rain was pelting down now. "If only…" he said, conscious of a horrible, clawing, push-pull need in his life for less… and yet more. He placed the palms of his hands on the glass, wishing he could feel the storm. "If only…" But he blocked the thought before he could finish it. No point in going there.

The back of his nose was stinging again, and there was a crushing ache in his chest.

There was no use pretending he didn't know what it was.

It was grief.

And it was out of his control.

CHAPTER SEVEN

NOT PREGNANT.

Not.

A month had passed since San Francisco, and Romy, sitting at her computer with her email account open, knew she could no longer put off telling Matt.

She should have done it the instant she'd gotten her period two weeks ago, but she'd had a minimeltdown in the bathroom and bawled her eyes out instead.

And then the cramps had hit, the pain going all-out to completely incapacitate her as though punishing her for daring to do what she'd done with Matt—and surely agony was a valid excuse for delaying the call.

Disbelief had come next. With all Matt's potency, delivered at the right time of the month, it was *inconceivable* that she wasn't pregnant. So maybe her uterus was playing a last, loathsome trick on her and she *wasn't* not-pregnant after all.

That had bought her a week.

But today, when Lennie had called to ask her to return to San Francisco because he'd finally made a decision and needed her to scout out a definite location for his restaurant, it was a case of time's up. Within

two minutes of peeing on the stick of her home pregnancy kit, she'd burst into tears again.

And now, sitting at her computer, she knew there'd
only ever been one honest reason for not telling Matt two
weeks ago: fear that the instant he knew, she'd lose him.

Okay, that wasn't quite true. It was more that the instant he knew, she'd have to accept that she'd *already*
lost him. She could even pinpoint the exact moment it
had happened: when he'd put his hand where their baby
might have been and what he'd done had become real.

The mind-blowing sex he'd almost immediately
launched into made no sense after that...but Romy
had a nagging feeling that if she figured out what had
motivated him to "go for broke" following that club
to the head, she'd have the key to the tower Matt kept
himself barricaded in.

Not that she'd had time to test any locks! The vortex
into which he'd hurled her had been so wild, she hadn't
been able to so much as catch her breath from start to
finish. No words, no instruction, no invitation—just
his touch driving her inexorably on until her eyes rolled
back in her head and her toes curled. The crescendo?
Two soaring, thrilling orgasms, the last one adroitly,
effortlessly, synchronized to his own.

And yet despite his almost slavish attention to her
pleasure, and despite that careful synchronization she
though may well have curled his toes, too, she'd felt...
alone. Flung away, like an electric guitar that had been
played for maximum flash and drama before being
pounded onto the stage and obliterated.

Her self-preservation instincts had kicked in, and
she was up, preparing to leave, desperate not to face
being Matt's first-ever regret.

She'd reached for her mobile phone so many times

that night, wanting to jump back over that crossed line and at least open the door to reclaiming their friendship, but every time she'd started a text, she'd lost her nerve. There'd been no adequate words for what she was feeling. Or at least, none he'd want to hear. Don't call it love, he'd said, and she hadn't, she wouldn't. But she had no other words, either.

So here she was, still with no words, effectively in limbo, with Matt's email address staring accusingly at her from the To box above the blank message space.

She scrubbed her hands over her face. Had it really been only six weeks since that phone call, when Matt had assured her having a baby would be the easiest thing in the world?

She closed her eyes, steeling herself to call up the image of his face after he'd come inside her that first time—the bleakness of it. To remember the way his expression had changed to something cool and calculating as he'd said, *I'm recharged—let's go for broke this time.* The silence as he'd walked her downstairs. The desolation in his eyes when she'd kissed his cheek—as though in going for broke, he'd broken *himself.*

And she knew what she had to do was formally, officially, let him go.

She opened her eyes, and started typing.

Hi, Matt
The big news is I'm not pregnant, so no Yippie-Kai-Yay motherfucker just yet.

Been thinking that with you there and me here and all that paperwork we never got to the end of, a donor closer to home makes more sense. So consider this an official notification that Plan A is extinct—in other words you're off the hook, services no longer required.

She paused there, not sure how to sign off.

Would these be her last words to Matt? If so, she knew what she'd want them to be. She'd broken the cardinal rule before she'd known it existed and said them in her heart ten years ago. She may not have said the words aloud but she wanted to. She was *tired* of keeping them inside. So tired, her fingers trembled on the keyboard with the need to type them...

I love you

Almost by magic the words were there on the screen. Her heart raced as she read them; she knew if she sent them it really would be over.

In which case, wouldn't the words be useless?

If she wanted to get him back into her life she had to be more strategic. She had to let him know there was a cleared path back to their old friendship...but only if he chose to tread it. And so she deleted those three words and tapped out a new closer. Light and bright and cool and unthreatening:

But I owe you a favor of your choice for giving it the old college try. If you're still hankering for paella, I've got a new twist on the old recipe so give me a shout when you're next in London if you'd like to collect.
Romy
X

And then she hit Send, closed her laptop and burst into tears.

CHAPTER EIGHT

"I NEVER PRETENDED to be a computer whiz," Romy said, bringing Teague's fourth cup of coffee over to him.

"Neither did I," Teague said, "so say a prayer that between us we haven't lost everything while you *open that damn door*! With any luck it'll be Matt, come to save us."

She checked, but only for an instant, at hearing Matt's name. "It won't be him." She plonked Teague's coffee on the dining table beside her laptop, within reach of his hand. "So keep going. And remember, you can lose anything you like as long as you find the—"

"Romy—the door—I beg you."

"—Lennie_SanFrancisco file," she finished, before heading for the door, calling out an en route "Keep your shirt on!" to whoever was outside.

She swung the door open…and her mouth snap-froze in a gape.

Her heart jolted, then hammered, as Matt—it really, astoundingly, unbelievably, *was* Matt!—lowered the clenched fist he'd raised as though preparing to pound a hole through the wood.

When had she sent her email? She counted back, lightning fast. Less than twenty-four hours ago. If her email was responsible for rocketing Matt across the Atlantic, was that a positive, negative or neutral development? She didn't know, couldn't work it out because her thoughts were flying past each other, refusing to land.

"Keep my shirt on?" Matt asked, sounding oddly breathless, and when one corner of his mouth quirked up in a rueful smile, her thoughts stopped flying and stuttered to a halt. "You sure about that?"

Shirt. On. Here. London. Matt! Gorgeous.

Her brain was too mangled to form actual sentences and her mouth was too dry to say them. She was reduced to stepping back and vaguely beckoning with her hand, a mute version of *Come in.*

Matt stepped over the threshold, and ever-careless of his possessions, ignored the coat stand to drop his overcoat on the floor along with his duffel bag. For a hopeful moment, Romy thought he was going to pull her into his arms, but a sound behind her—Teague's chair scraping against the floor—distracted him.

"Yay! The hero arrives!" Teague said.

Shock sparked in Matt's eyes as he looked past her, but when Romy turned to uncover the problem all she found was Teague looking at them over the top of her laptop screen.

"Uh-oh," Teague said.

Uh-oh? Romy's eyes went from Teague to a now-expressionless Matt.

"Just to be clear, Matt," Teague said, "all I was doing was reinstalling Windows for her."

"I'll finish it," Matt said.

"It's finished. But by all means check what I did."

Romy looked from Matt to Teague this time. Something was wrong.

Teague closed her laptop and made his way over to them.

"But…are you leaving?" she asked him as he retrieved his overcoat from the stand.

"Yes, Romy, I am."

"Where are you going?"

Shrugging into his coat. "Back to my hotel."

"Why?"

Grabbing his scarf. "Because dinner appears to be canceled."

"It's *not* canceled!" Romy said, and turned to Matt. "Tell him to stay." Getting nothing from that quarter, she tennis-balled back to Teague. "Teague!"

Teague laugh-winced. "Are you trying to get me killed, Romes?"

"What? No! I mean— What?"

Teague's response was to look squarely at Matt as he draped his scarf around his neck. "Just one thing," he said. "Prove to her I've recovered the Lennie_San-Francisco file or you'll have a meltdown on your hands. She's got a meeting with him tomorrow."

"Fuck Lennie!" Matt said with extreme loathing.

Teague grinned. "He *wishes* she would, anyway!" He knotted his scarf. "But it's your job to rescue her if Lennie steps out of line, isn't it?"

Matt's eyes narrowed. "What's that supposed to mean?"

"It means you'll swoop in to save Romy's day, as usual."

In the hanging moment that followed, Romy found herself holding her breath. She could feel tension rolling off Matt in thick waves, but his voice was calm when he asked, "Do *you* want the job, Teague?" Almost *too* calm.

"Oh, I can't do *that* job," Teague said. "Lennie's not scared of me."

"What makes you think he's scared of *me*?"

Teague kept his gaze steady on Matt. "Intuition."

Matt made an infinitesimal adjustment to his stance. "Are *you* scared of me, Teague?"

"No," Teague said. "Because *I* know *you* know I'm not a threat."

On the verge of passing out from oxygen deprivation, Romy took in a tiny breath, then held it again when Matt made a sound like a cut-off growl as Teague pulled her into his arms for a hug.

"Call me if you need me, Romes, okay?" Teague said in a stage whisper, before letting her go. "But now, if you'll excuse me…"

"Wait!" Romy cried, and caught Teague's hand. "You don't have to leave!"

Teague squeezed then released her fingers. "Yes, Romy, I do."

"Then…then at least let me walk with you to the train station and…and explain," she urged—even though she didn't know what the explanation *was*.

Teague touched her cheek briefly. "I don't need an explanation. And I'd prefer it if you stayed to soothe the savage beast." He flashed her a whiter-than-snow smile. "For *all* our sakes, hmm?"

And then he clapped a hand briefly on Matt's shoulder, said, "Play nice with my girl," and left.

Romy stared at the door after it clicked shut behind Teague, trying to figure out what had just happened.

She sensed Matt moving, heard him settling into

Teague's chair at the dining table. *Play nice with my girl*, Teague had adjured him. But Matt didn't appear to be in a "nice" mood.

Or maybe...thinking back to Matt's smile as she'd opened the door...maybe seeing Teague had *changed* Matt's mood. It had certainly upped the testosterone quotient. But that would mean Matt was jealous, wouldn't it? And he was *never* jealous. He didn't *care* enough to be jealous. Or maybe...maybe he did...?

She turned, intrigued by that notion, to find Matt tapping away at her computer, and cleared her throat to get his attention.

Matt ignored her. And that was interesting, because he'd never ignored her before and she was *p-r-e-t-t-y* sure he hadn't flown all the way from San Francisco just to do so now.

So why *was* he here? Question of the day.

She took two steps, and cleared her throat again. "Are you going to tell me why you're here, Matt?"

He stilled, eyes on her keyboard. "Are you going to tell me why *Teague* was here?" And then he raised his eyes, pinning her in place. "Because fixing your computer is *my* job, isn't it?"

Okay, that definitely smacked of *some* kind of jealousy, and it made her heart flutter like a leaf in a storm. "You were in San Francisco."

"I've installed updates on your computer remotely before."

"It's just...he was here."

"So I noticed."

"For dinner."

"So I gathered."

"He's working on a big corporate merger, and one of

the parties is British so he's here for a couple of weeks and he called me and I offered to cook—just like I do for *you* when you're here. And when he arrived, I mentioned my computer problems, and..." She stopped, threw up her hands. "Why am I explaining this? I've done nothing wrong."

"Why *are* you explaining, if you've done nothing wrong?"

"Probably because you're glaring at me, making me *think* I've done something wrong. He came—he saw—he fixed. The end. Unless you want to know the dinner menu, in which case it was supposed to be steak and ale pie."

Matt leaned back in his chair. "Let me ask a different question. When did he arrive in London? Could it possibly have been *yesterday*?"

"Yes, so what?"

"So that gives me some context for that 'closer to home' reference in your email."

"You mean...? No, you *can't* mean—! *Teague?* Teague lives in *Manhattan*. How's that close to London?"

"He's here now. Ergo, close."

"As are you—so *what?*"

"So it finally makes sense why you took so long to contact me."

"You mean...?" But she shook her head. "*What* do you mean?"

"I mean I hear nothing from you for a month, but then Teague arrives and—wham!—notice to terminate my services comes flying through cyberspace."

She stared at him while that sifted through her foggy brain. And then, "Oh. My God!" she said. "You cannot be serious."

"And yet I am."

She came storming over to the table as four weeks of pent-up emotion ruptured. "You *dare* to tick me off for not contacting you? You didn't send me one text! One email! I didn't get a phone call, a Facebook message, nothing! I had to fill the void by overthinking every damn thing that had happened in San Francisco until I thought I'd go crazy!"

"I've been hanging on the edge of my fucking seat waiting for two fucking words from you—not pregnant. A few seconds is all it would have taken!"

"Oh! Oh! You were *not* hanging on the edge of your seat! You made it crystal clear you'd lost interest in the whole thing even before I left your house! I saw your face, Matt, when it hit you—it hit you like a ton of bricks—what you'd let yourself in for, that maybe, just maybe, that boring paperwork I wanted to go through with you was worth reading after all!"

"I tore up that paperwork!"

"You—you—"

"*Bastard* is the word I think we agreed on in San Francisco."

"You bastard!" she rapped out.

He set his jaw. "Which doesn't change the fact that *you* were supposed to contact *me*, goddammit!"

"And I *did*!"

He banged his hand on the table. "Two weeks *late*!"

"Well, excuse me for not being buoyed with optimism by your last words to me. 'Let's go for broke this time'! It took me the whole month to get over that!"

He pushed his chair back from the table, jumped to his feet. "I told you to stop me if you didn't like what I did!"

"It wasn't that *I* didn't like it, it was that *you* didn't. That last time was a performance—a bravura performance but definitely a performance, even if you didn't really want to give it."

"That wasn't a performance, Romy, that was me. What I *am*. What I *like*."

"You didn't like *anything* after you realized I might be pregnant. You couldn't even muster up a goodbye when I left!"

"You didn't give me *time* to say goodbye. You ran out on me like your ass was on fire."

"You could have stopped me!"

"I don't stop women from leaving me, remember? You want to leave, you leave!"

"If you believe that, why are you here?"

Split second while he stared at her. And then, "Good question!" he snarled, and strode for the door.

She hurried after him. "What are you doing?"

"Figure it out," he said, and reefed his overcoat up off the floor, one-handed.

"Matt!"

Up came his bag. Flung over his shoulder.

She grabbed his arm. "You're not leaving until we talk this through."

He jerked away from her. "Read your own fucking email. You talked it through for both of us."

"What is the problem? If you want to try again, we'll just…try again!"

"No, Romy, we won't. It's too dangerous. *I'm* too dangerous." And he turned to the door again.

"No!" she cried, and dragged his overcoat from him, threw it back on the floor. "What are you talking about?"

"I saw the bruises, okay?"

"They were nothing!" Romy cried.

He reached for his coat again—she blocked him. "If that's really what's bothering you—a few love bites— I'll put some on you right now and we'll be even."

"That's not funny."

"No, it's not funny, if you think I'm some delicate flower who can't handle some enthusiastic sex! So read my lips: You. Didn't. Hurt me. You didn't. And you're not going to leave me like this after keeping me hanging for a month."

"You left *me*, Romy," he said to her.

"Only because you *wanted* me to go."

"Bullshit. I asked you to stay the night."

"That was *before*."

"Before *what*? Before you moved the goalposts? Before you replaced ten years with one night on a fucking *whim*? Plan B! Jesus! What made you think that was going to work with someone like me?"

"Someone like you? What does that even mean?"

"It means your email hit the nail on the head—I'm *not* the man for the job. I don't *want* the job. So…so sign Teague up! I don't care."

"What *is* it about Teague tonight? It's just Teague— same old Teague! But it's like you're suddenly jealous of him!"

He recoiled. "I'm not jealous of Teague."

"Then what was all that about when you arrived?"

"Not jealousy. Not…what you think."

She rolled her eyes. "Okay."

"I mean it!"

"Okay!"

"I *mean* it, Romy! I'm the opposite of jealous! I *want*

him to have you. I *always* wanted him to have you.
That's why I introduced him to you in the first place.
He's a fucking saint! There's no one better for you."

She blinked at him—once, twice, slowly—and she
finally understood why Matt called it the blink of insanity when she did that: because she was blinking
at a stark, staring madman. "Oh my God," she said.
"You want him to *have* me? What am I? A reward for
good behavior?"

"You've got it ass-end around, Romy, I want *you*
to have *him.*"

"And what about what I want for myself?"

"We're *talking* about what you want—a clean-cut,
solid-gold hero."

"No, Matt. If we were talking about what I want,
we'd be talking about you."

"Romy, you only *think*—"

"*Don't* tell me what I think! If I wanted to have sex
with Teague I'd have done it when we were dating!"

"But this is about more than sex. It's about sharing
a baby, raising a baby, providing the best for a baby."

"And if I'd wanted to have a *baby* with Teague, I'd
have turned down your offer and called him straight
up to ask him!"

"So ask him! Go on! You know it'll be better with
him."

"And if I asked him, what do you think he'd say?"

"He'd say yes." He tore his hands through his hair.
"Ah Jesus, he'd say yes."

"He'd say *Let's wait, Romy,* that's what he'd say.
He'd say *Let's think it through. Let's do the* math. *Let's
get the fucking* paperwork *in order. And meanwhile,
Romy, why don't you get your own lawyer to look into*

precedents, even though I'm a lawyer myself, because two lawyers are better than one, and maybe go back to the doctor for some stronger painkillers and bleed your goddamn life out while I think it through, and then when you're sure *you're sure and I'm* sure, *we'll get married and* then *we'll start trying.*"

"And that's what you wanted—due process."

"No! No! I don't want another version of myself! I want what *you* did! What *you* offered is what I want. Fast and brave and unthinking and…and fuck-it-all, let's just do it. That's what I want. And you! I wanted *you*! I want you still."

"Stop, Romy!"

"No, I won't stop. You turn up here, all but scare Teague out of the flat for what reason I have *no fucking idea* since you're *not fucking jealous*, and then you tell me I'm supposed to fall into Teague's arms because you think that'll work better for me? Well, the answer is no! I'm not doing it. I remember very well that you got me and Teague together in college. I also remember you never asked why we split up."

"Because it didn't matter why."

"Of course it mattered! But I think you *knew* why we split up. And I think you didn't want to face it. Well, I want you to face it. So in case you *don't* know, I'm going to tell you—it's because I couldn't love him. And the reason I couldn't love him is because I already loved—"

"No!" he said, cutting her off.

"Why *not*?"

"Because it'll be the end. Don't. Say it. Don't, Romy."

"Not saying it out loud won't change the truth."

He grabbed her right hand, lifted it. "Wanna know

about love? It's *this*. He gave you his dead sister's ring even though you'd been broken up for two and a half years. What does that tell you?"

"That he knew I'd cherish it."

"The way he cherishes *you*."

"No!" she said.

"Not saying it out loud won't change the truth," he said, throwing her own words back at her. "You want love—he'll give it to you. I won't."

"We're friends. Teague and I are *friends*."

"What do you think you and I are?"

"I don't... I want... I don't know anymore."

"Having sex didn't make us more than friends, Romy—all it made us is friends with *benefits*. Benefits that were supposed to accrue to *you*. And who knows? If you'd stayed the night those benefits may have had more of a chance to accrue. Well, spilt milk, water under the bridge, whatever—you cut things short. So stand by that decision, because your instinct was right—I'm not the best man for this. And if the friend dynamic is what's bothering you about Teague, let me tell you that I've had sex with friends before and I will again. So I suggest you accept that you *can* have sex with friends, take another look at Teague and the next time he gives you a ring it'll have a whopping big diamond in it."

"I don't want a diamond."

"Yeah, well, even without the diamond, compare his platinum ring to what I gave you for your twenty-first birthday. A computer game. I mean, seriously! There's the difference between him and me right there on your finger."

"You gave me *shares*, Matt, not a computer game.

Shares in Artie's start-up gaming company. Shares he wanted to be *yours*, not mine."

"They were worthless."

"And now they're not."

"Yeah, well, as I've said before, money's an easy thing for me to give."

"Those shares weren't money to you. They came from that soul you say you don't have."

He flung her hand away. "Oh, for fuck's sake! Don't worry about my soul, Romy—protect your own. Or I may yet give in to my baser urgings and steal it."

"Oh, Matt, can't you see? You don't *have* to steal my soul. I'll give it to you willingly. I'll *gift wrap* it for you. I'll change it to suit you, twist into any shape you want, paint it any color you like."

He grabbed her by the upper arms and pulled her in close, looking down at her with such an intense mix of fury and fuck me, a sliver of almost-pleasurable fear shimmied down her spine. "Make it pitch-black and we might have a deal," he said.

"I said any color—I meant it."

"I've told you before, Romy, be careful what you say. What you open the door to. There are wolves out there—wolves like me."

"Then teach me to be a wolf."

"A kitten can't become a wolf."

"What can I do to convince you?"

"Nothing."

"What about if I…if I bite you?"

He laughed.

"I mean it. It's what I've always wanted to do. Bite a man through the skin until I draw blood. There. That's my deepest, darkest fantasy. What do you think about that?"

He released her, stepped back, tilted his head to one side and dragged at his sweater, the T-shirt beneath, to expose his neck to her. "Go ahead, Vampira."

She swallowed. "I..."

He laughed again. Released his sweater. "You're *not. My. Speed.*"

Her eyes flickered downward, to the front of his jeans. "I don't believe you."

"As you said—that's always there."

"As you said—you wouldn't be able to function like a human if it was."

"I'm not much of a human. And my services are no longer required, remember?"

"And yet, knowing that...here you are."

"I came because we had unfinished business."

"Then finish it!"

"It was finished the minute I walked in the door and saw him."

"Prove it's finished. Kiss me."

"No."

"Then don't kiss me. Fuck me."

CHAPTER NINE

"ASKING TO BE fucked isn't enough to bring you down to my level," he said, but although his voice carried the right amount of sneer, desire raced through him so fast he trembled with it.

She straightened her spine, and it made his heart lurch. God, she'd always been a straight arrow. The straightest. "Then tell me what will," she said.

He retook her right hand, brought it to his mouth, licked the problematic platinum band, then sucked her pinky finger into his mouth. He watched her as he sucked, as he kept sucking. *Stop me, stop me, Romy*, he pleaded silently, because he hated himself for what he was about to ask.

But she didn't stop him. She did nothing except close her eyes, and then open them as though she wouldn't allow herself that weakness. He slipped his mouth from her finger, slowly, insolently, but kept hold of her hand. "Taking off his ring will be a start. Do that and I'll fuck you."

He saw her eyes go wide, the swallow she took. But she tipped up her chin and threw his challenge back at him. "I won't make what's between us about Teague. It has *nothing* to do with him."

"It has everything to do with him. I'm the bit of rough you have on the side—he's the one you go home to. You don't take off the ring of the man you go home to."

"I came home to *you*, Matt. For three and a half years I came home to you. After every man, I came home to you. And you...you came home to me."

"Oh, Romy." He had to touch her. Had to. Just once. So he cupped her cheek, even though he knew she'd feel the fine quivering in his fingers. "I could count your men on one hand. And there's the difference. Do you have any idea how many sex partners I've had?"

She brought her hand up to cover his, keeping it there. "I only care that it took ten years to make me one of them."

"But you were only one of them for a night," he said. "And you won't be again unless you take off his ring."

"If it's so important to you, *you* take it off. Take it to Teague. Tell him everything. Tell him the reason I always wear it is because I feel guilty for not...not loving him the way you seem to think I should. But do it *after*, not before, so I know this is about me, not him."

"And if I insist on doing it now?"

"You won't. I know you won't. You stopped me so many times in San Francisco, making sure I was okay, making sure I hadn't changed my mind. You said you wouldn't do anything I didn't like—and you didn't. I know you won't do anything I don't want you to do now, either. You're not the man you're trying so hard to tell me you are."

And that was when he lost it, as though he could hear a snap in his brain, and he crushed her against his chest. How could he want to be her hero and yet simultaneously need to show her that he'd be her downfall? He was confused, and crazy with lust for her, and so damn tired of not having her.

"So be my type all the way now. *Mine*, not his," he said, and ground his cock against her to let her know exactly what his type was.

And *God*, she felt good. Plump and fragrant and perfect. A delicious tremble ran through her and he loved the feel of it so much he ground his cock against her again.

"Do you like that?" he asked.

"Yes," she gasped.

"My cock?"

"Yes."

"You can't even say the word, can you?"

"Cock. Your cock."

"And if I said I wanted to see you on your knees for me, with my cock in your mouth, sucking?"

"I'd do it."

"Say it, Romy."

"I want to suck your cock."

"Would you do anything I ask?"

"Anything!" she moaned, her hips arching helplessly into him as he rubbed himself against her again. "Oh God, it isn't fair to torment me like this."

His mouth hovered over hers. "You want fair? Then hear me. I don't care about your heart, or your soul. I care about your body, for a limited time only. And all that's of interest to me right now is if..." grind "you're..." grind "wet!"

A whimper reached past the whoosh of his pulse in his ears, but no words. He wished he could see her eyes, but they were tightly closed now. It was hard to see her so lost in passion, knowing he wanted to be more for her, to be better for her, and yet be unable to convince himself that was possible. But he was helpless. He would take her, lost or found, his or Teague's or anyone else's, any way at all, even though he didn't deserve her, and pray that this time he'd get her out of his burning blood so he could leave her alone.

He ground himself against her again, more urgently now, and she edged her thighs slightly apart. "Tell me, Romy. Hurry. Tell me you're ready, you're wet and ready enough for me."

Her eyes bolted open. "I'm not telling you—you'll have to find out for yours—"

It was as far as she got, because Matt found he couldn't wait another second to put his mouth on hers. Not gently. He couldn't be gentle. He wanted her too much. No more words. No taunts. No dares. No time. He needed her on his tongue, needed her limbs and her breaths tangled with his. He needed to be closer, surrounding her, inside her.

For the longest moment she stayed with him, and then she moaned against his mouth and it seemed to snap her back to reality. She bolted against him and struggled free, and then stared up at him, her breaths coming in sharp bursts, her magnificent chest heaving.

Had he scared her off already? "Romy," he said. Just her name, but there was a plea in it—a plea both to stop him and to not stop him.

She gave a cry of surrender, flung herself into his arms again, kissed him so hard their teeth crashed together and he fucking exulted in it. It wasn't anything soft that she was offering, nothing comfortable. No more stopping. No backing out. So when she eased slightly away, a murmur of apology for hurting him on her lips, he used his hand on the back of her head to jam her mouth against his and instantly she gave herself up to him. A drench of heat, back and forth between them. He shoved one thigh roughly between her legs, and she surged against him. A drugging, sucking kiss. A wanton, blazing kiss.

When he broke to breathe, he kept his mouth close enough to taste her. "Tell me it's me you want, that I'm the only one."

"Yes!" she said, surging against him. "You, I want *you*, any way you want to be."

"Only me."

"Only you." She shoved his chest. "There." Another shove. "Satisfied? Now do it!"

God, the triumph of it! He didn't care if she shoved him through the nearest wall as long as she meant those words. It was wrong to want to hear them, worse to *ask* to hear them, but he needed them. A kind of forgiveness, permission to be exactly who he was, to be only what he could.

"Am I satisfied?" he asked, and framing her face with his hands, he kissed her harder still. "I won't be satisfied until I'm buried inside you."

Another rough kiss, hot and wet. Her hands were at the front of his jeans, unbuttoning, unzipping him, and he wondered how long he'd last when he'd been starving for her for so long. Mouths crushing, bruising, a clash of teeth and tongue, his heartbeat going crazy, excitement fizzing in his blood.

He kept kissing her, couldn't seem to stop, as he dragged her jeans halfway down her legs. Unable to wait another inch, he ripped off her panties. He wanted to tear every stitch of her clothing and rend from her life everything that had kept her from him for four unfathomable weeks, for ten clueless years.

Romy's hands were under his sweater, under his T-shirt, skating up his chest. He wished she'd rake him with her nails and make him bleed for her. And as if answering that need in him, she dug her fingernails in. He drew back, not to stop her but to see her as she marked him, and the ferociousness in her face made him kiss her again. Wanting him made her angry. Well, he was with her there, furious at how much he wanted this with her. So if a bit of fierce would bring them to terms with what was between them, then he'd *give* her fierce.

He untethered the last of his restraint, hauling her to the floor and under him, his cock lunging even though her legs weren't open to him. He was going to take her here, now. He was going to pretend there was no choice, even though he knew the choice would be waiting at the end of whatever they did.

Her jeans were manacling her legs, but he couldn't bear to let her go long enough to release her from the bind. His cock wasn't going to wait; it was weeping for her already. He'd have to take her as she was, even though she'd be so tight in that position he'd likely explode the moment he was inside her. He tore his mouth free and dragged in a tortured breath.

"Hurry, hurry," she pleaded, struggling against the stubborn jeans that wouldn't let her open her legs for him. "Oh God, hurry!"

She craned upward to lick his lips, and he kissed her again, easing a hand between their bodies, sliding it down, down, tangling his fingers in her pubic hair.

She sobbed out a breath, raised her hips in encouragement and he delved lower, pushing between thighs that were almost clamped together. She started to shudder, her hands pulling at the hip band of his jeans, trying to free him.

"Make me come," she said. "Do it."

"I will," as he plunged his fingers into her.

"More, I need more."

But he stayed there for a maddening moment, loving the silky moisture against his fingertips, playing in her heat, absorbing the little shivers of her body.

"Matt!" she cried.

He eased off her, barely enough to free himself while one hand continued to play in her wetness. He jolted as his naked cock nudged at her opening, so eager for her he fumbled uncharacteristically as he slid his fingers out, pushed his cock inside. The fit was so snug he thought he wouldn't make it all the way in. But one thrust and he was there. *Fuuuuuuuck.* He stopped to absorb the dizzying sensation of being one with her as she whimpered and gasped and gripped him. A blinding, heaven-hell moment. It was tight, so tight, having her thighs almost closed.

"God, you feel good," he gasp-groaned.

"So do you. Right there. Exactly there, exactly like that. Stay there. Fill me."

He tried, he really did, despite his cock demanding that he move into the age-old rhythm. He dropped his head to her shoulder, panting through the need. But it was no use. "Romy, I have to move. Just…oh God… once. Just once."

"Then do it, but hard, I want it hard. Fill me up, and up, and up." So he withdrew all the way, then pushed all the way in again. Stop. Counting in his head to try to control the animal urge. "That's sooo good," she moaned out, and he withdrew again but try though he did to regulate himself, when he plunged into her again he went so violently she shifted a foot along the floor. He stopped again, fearful that he'd been too rough but she didn't flinch and she didn't let go of him and he sure as hell wasn't letting go of her.

And then it was on. Ruthless. This was more than wanting her. He was claiming her as his so that whoever came after him could never own all of her. One, two, three, five, ten thrusts. Stuffing himself inside despite the constriction of her almost-closed legs, thankful for her drenching moisture but for which he could never have found his way. Whatever was happening, it was tighter, hotter, wilder than anything he'd ever experienced.

Missionary position. As vanilla as you could get, but this was *hot* vanilla. Hot and intense, like a secret flavor, hidden away for only him to taste.

All too soon the rush was there. He threw back his head, a "Gaaaaah" tearing from his throat as he tried to stop himself from coming and then he felt her inner muscles clamp. Another cry ripped out of him, like an endless death, in sync with her own, and he was coming and coming and didn't want to stop, never, ever stop. Didn't want to leave her heat. Never...ever...leave.

CHAPTER TEN

ROMY FLOATED BACK to earth slowly, breaths settling inhalation by exhalation, heart rate decelerating beat by beat.

She wanted the world to stop so she could keep savoring the feeling of Matt still inside her, his head nuzzled between her neck and her shoulder.

Her limbs felt heavy, her eyelids, too; she was warm and drowsy and replete.

She almost couldn't believe the things she'd said, telling him to go deeper, to stay there, to fill her. Unfiltered demands she couldn't imagine making of any other man. She felt a laugh burble up, because the moisture coating the inside of her thighs told her he'd taken her at her word and filled her all right.

He raised his head and looked down at her, and for a moment his eyes told her he could belong to her, and only her, forever. His eyes told her that he loved her.

She held her right hand to his face, and he turned his mouth to it, kissing her palm.

"Take it off," she said.

"Hmm?"

"The ring, take it off."

And in the time it took her to blink, the poignant

tenderness she was so sure she'd seen in his eyes was gone and in its place was that other look, the one full of despair at what he'd done, what it meant. But that was just as fleeting, replaced by an emptiness so icy it made her shiver.

Funny how the springlike warmth their friendship had basked in for so long had transitioned so quickly into a season of extremes—the sear of summer, the frost of winter, no temperate zone.

Matt removed her hand from his face, withdrew from her body swift and hard, and stood. One hand hitched his underwear and jeans back into place. And it seemed they were back to square one: she may or may not be pregnant; he may or may not be interested; and sex was definitely not love.

Unutterably depressed, Romy moved more slowly— getting up off the floor, refastening her jeans, plucking the destruction that was her blue silk underwear off the floor and stuffing it out of sight in her back pocket because she didn't think he needed the reminder.

And then she fixed her eyes on him. "If you didn't really want me to take off the ring, what was the point of demanding that I tell you I want you, only you?"

He hunched a shoulder. "They're just...words."

"Just words," she repeated. "I see. Like love. And saying them during sex makes them meaningless?"

He took a step toward her. "Romy, I just—"

"No!" Pulling back.

"I wasn't going to— Ah, Jesus! I just— I want you to know that whatever applied before still applies, that's all."

"What does that mean?"

"Arrangements. The trust fund."

She took a slow, do-not-punch-him breath. "You know what? Go ahead and set up the trust fund—or not. I don't care. See your lawyer—or not. I don't care. I don't even care if you've been with fifteen women in the past month, as long as you give me a shout if you discover you've caught something nasty."

"I haven't."

"Caught anything? Good to know."

"*Been* with anyone. I'm monogamous on request, remember."

"I didn't request it."

"It was implied."

"Well, good for you, but like I said, I don't care."

"It's the truth."

"How many ways can I say I don't care?"

His jaw had tightened. "Just so you know, Romy, *I'll* care."

"You'll—?"

"If you're not monogamous, I'll fucking care."

"My, my, how *bourgeois*! But I suppose you have to have some guarantee that valuable trust fund won't be supporting another man's child, right?"

"I don't give a fuck about the trust fund."

"For someone who doesn't give a fuck about it, you talk about it a lot. But anyway, back to the new plan."

"We don't need a new plan."

"Sure we do, Matt, because whatever we've been doing for the past ten years isn't working for me anymore. For ten years, I've wanted you. And you've known it, and ignored it, because I guess you wanted me just as much as I wanted you but in a different *way*."

"Romy—"

"Please, just…let me say this. Think of us as actors

in a movie, filming a scene that goes on way too long because nobody's prepared to call 'Cut.' You, our hero, are walled up in a castle tower surrounded by a moat. One by one, the best and strongest women in the kingdom have been diving into the moat and swimming across to the tower hoping to scale your impregnable wall, yet not one of them has made it inside.

"Enter the heroine of the piece—that's me, in case you're wondering. I've been assessing the structure of your tower for ten years, learning the makeup of the stone and waiting for the perfect moment to make my own attempt. And a window of opportunity opens, and I can see you framed in that window. So I jump into the moat and swim like crazy, but the water is murkier than I expected, choked with weeds, so it's hard work—so hard, I'm exhausted by the time I get to the tower. I don't care, though, because I've found a gap in the stonework at last, and even if it's not quite big enough to slip through, it's there, and I figure if I scrape and claw and gouge and dig, I'll find my way in. But it takes me a while to realize I've torn open my flesh trying to reach you, and my heart…my h-heart is on display. But when I look up to the window in that tower to ask you to open the drawbridge, because my heart needs you, and I know you can see me, clinging to the wall with my heart *bleeding*, Matt, bleeding for you…you turn away, even though you know I'll drown if I fall back into that moat."

"Stop, Romy."

But she wouldn't stop. She couldn't. "So I think we need to recut that scene, change it from a heart-wrenching drama into a fun comedy. Which is what we've done for the past ten years so it should be easy—

all we really have to do is go back to being just friends. We even have a new window of opportunity, because you're here and I'm here, but this time, we need to stay here, as in *together*, so as to avoid any unfair accusations about who hasn't contacted whom in two weeks' time when I find out if I'm pregnant. My plan—let's call it Plan C—has two possible outcomes. One—I'm pregnant: we draw up new paperwork according to the level of friend zone success we've achieved. Two—I'm not pregnant: you go home and keep the hell out of my life." She offered him a wintry smile. "Deal?"

"No," he said, and picked up his duffel bag. "Contrary to what you seem to believe, I don't enjoy seeing you bleed, and whatever happens, Romy, you *will be in my life.*"

"I won't be in your life if you walk out that door, because I will never see you or speak to you again."

"That's not fair."

"Your definition of fair doesn't suit me. I've spent too long waiting for you to see me."

"I *do* see you, Romy."

"You see what you want to see, but I dare you to look harder. I *dare* you, Matt. Stay and play it out."

"Jesus!" he said, and picked up his overcoat.

Romy said nothing, did nothing. Even though she knew it would half kill her if he left.

And then he yelled, "Fuck." He glared at her. "FUCK!" He threw his overcoat and duffel bag across the room. "Fuck this, and fuck you for doing this to me."

Up went her chin. "You won't be fucking me, Matt, but other than that, I'll take your response as a yes."

CHAPTER ELEVEN

Plan fucking C.

Matt gave his duffel bag, sitting innocently on the floor of the spare room to which he'd been relegated, a savage kick.

Fun comedy—so why wasn't he laughing?

Just friends—when it was fucking obvious that things had changed and he'd just made it fucking obvious to both of them the only way he could keep his hands off her was to do it from the other side of the fucking Atlantic!

He didn't know how to describe the way he was feeling. Like he desperately wanted to get away from her…yet he was terrified of not being with her. Like he was a wolf baying for a mate…but strangling himself to silence.

Excruciating. Agonizing. Confusing. Bewildering. All of those things together. With an overlay of panic that in two weeks' time she'd be pregnant…but maybe she wouldn't. That he couldn't control what happened, and couldn't even blame her for taking control out of his hands because he'd made a fucking mess of things in two countries!

Ha. To think he was in this latest mess all because

of an *X* in an email. That pathetic *X* of a kiss, which was the way Romy signed off her emails to everyone— even that prick Lennie—and to which Matt had taken exception on the basis he wasn't going to start being an "everyone" to Romy after ten years' being number one with her!

And then to get to her apartment, and see Teague and…and resent him, in part because Teague was so damn perfect he *hadn't* slept with her when he'd had the chance?

Up came his hands, fingers rubbing at his forehead.

It was going to be a struggle to live with Romy in this tiny place for two weeks. She'd complained about noises through their old thin walls, but she'd hear his *thoughts* ticking in this apartment—and his thoughts were far from celibate. God help him if she came into this room, because there was barely room for the two of them to stand. He could probably cross it in three strides.

He took one long step past the single bed to test that theory, another, stretched his arms out and up and… stopped, mid-third-stride, because his hand had hit something.

He looked up and saw the mobile hanging from the ceiling—silver-and-white stars.

With a sense of foreboding, he turned a slow circle, taking in the freshly painted walls—a silvery gray with a scatter of white stars on one wall, the small rug on the floor with the same white stars on a gray background, a new white bureau against one wall.

Bump-bump-thump went his heart.

Because he was standing in the nursery.

He'd be *sleeping* in his baby's room.

He looked around the room again, soaking in the details. Typical of Romy to have the interior decorating under way before she was pregnant. Not that there was a lot to see other than the paint scheme and the star/moon theme. A lamp sitting on his bedside table—a full moon—was clearly intended for the baby. And the bureau, in white—that had baby clothes written all over it.

Curious, he went over to it and opened the top drawer. "Oh!" he breathed, as he saw the cache of tiny garments.

He lifted out a minuscule white cardigan, raised it to his face, rubbed the wool against his cheek. Soft as a cloud.

One by one, he opened the drawers, taking out all the other perfect things, holding them to his face, inhaling their pure scent. Three sleeper suits. Two pairs of knitted booties. A cap in white wool that matched the cardigan. Baby vests and leggings and tops. Wraps and rugs, a small fluffy towel. The tininess of each item as he carefully placed each item back in its spot squeezed his heart until he felt like it had been pushed up into his throat.

When only the little white cardigan remained, held against his chest, Romy knocked on the door. "Matt?" she asked. "Dinner will be ready in twenty minutes if you want to grab a shower."

He couldn't speak.

"Matthew?"

He took a moment to reel everything back in, hand rubbing his throat to ease the choking sensation there, and then forced out a "Got it."

Pause. "Are you okay?"

"I'm fine," he said. Because he *was* fine. Just fine.
If you didn't count that stinging at the back of his
nose and the longing to tuck that tiny white cardigan
under his T-shirt, right against his still-throbbing heart.

CHAPTER TWELVE

DINNER WAS...NOT GOOD.

Oh, not the steak and ale pie, which was as it always was, but the general atmosphere of *What the hell are we doing?* that had pervaded the flat.

Or perhaps the more accurate question was *What the hell am I doing?* because Romy knew very well she was the one who'd pitched them into this awkward hell. *She'd* wanted to have sex; *she'd* blackmailed him into staying; *she'd* positioned her heart ready for a trampling at the end of the two weeks when Matt left—as he would do, no matter which of her two scenarios came to pass.

She might have enticed him into having sex with her—twice, now—but the scalding truth was that she loved Matt and he didn't love her.

Love? Ha! He didn't even *like* her anymore, judging by his nonexistent dinner conversation. Her own dogged attempts at it—questions about Matt's flight, the chaos of Heathrow, the weather in San Francisco, his new business venture with Artie—were met with such headache-inducing vagueness, Romy almost wished for a return to the rage that had had her fearing he'd spontaneously combust before she'd shown him to the spare room and left him to froth at the mouth in peace.

When Matt opted to work in his room straight after dinner, Romy was relieved but also apprehensive. From tomorrow, she'd be at work during the days so the after-dinner hours would become important harbingers of the direction their relationship would take. Two weeks suddenly seemed a very short time to navigate their future as potential parents—it would be even shorter if they spent every possible minute of that time avoiding each other.

Romy didn't expect to fall into an easy sleep—and she didn't. Dreams of Matt had haunted her ever since she'd left San Francisco, and his presence in the flat acted on those dreams like an injection of steroids, supersizing them. The taste of his mouth, the feel of his hands, the way he fit inside her—they were all there. Right along with the things he'd said to her that night, which played in her head over and over... *If I said I wanted to see you on your knees for me, with my cock in your mouth, sucking... All that's of interest to me right now is if you're wet... I won't be satisfied until I'm buried inside you...*

No romance, not love words, but dear God, so indescribably, feverishly arousing she had to struggle not to go to him and tell him she was ready to suck anything he wanted her to suck.

Such a night left her ill prepared for seeing him in her kitchen the next morning. He'd gone for a run—as he always did—and looked so sweatily, deliciously scruffy as he scrambled eggs, she didn't trust herself not to lick him so she mumbled an apology about being late and left the flat without eating.

And despite lecturing herself half the day about Plan C's restrictions, when she arrived home that night all it took was one look at Matt sitting on her couch with a beer in his hand to knock her straight into the same state of salivating hunger in which she'd left that morning.

Matt's eyes locked with hers, the beer he'd been raising to his lips stalling halfway to its destination. He got to his feet as though hypnotized and the air thickened so that it would have taken a chain saw to cut through it—and Romy's briefcase slipped from her now-nerveless fingers and hit the floor, jarring them out of a trance that had nothing of friendship about it and everything about sex. Saved by the briefcase!

Romy blurted out something about chicken curry, Matt said he'd set the table, and they proceeded to keep out of each other's way until dinner was served.

They set the pattern that night for the rest of the week. A stilted conversation over dinner, followed by watching a movie on TV while occupying uncomfortably opposite-end-of-the-couch positions so as to avoid accidentally touching. Not exactly a return to their old friendship.

Matt gave up halfway through the movie, citing the need to check in with the manager he'd left in charge of his San Francisco hub, and Romy surrendered to a tension headache and went in search of painkillers and a restless night's sleep.

The next morning, when Romy cried upon waking at the prospect of seeing Matt in his running gear and actually touched the walls in the shower as she imagined soaping Matt's naked body, she knew she wasn't going to survive two weeks of living this way.

It was with considerable trepidation that she ventured out to the kitchen, where she found Matt looking hotter than sin. He plonked a plate of scrambled eggs and a mug of steaming coffee on the counter for her, giving her a rusty "Good morning" that melted her insides. Thankfully he then promptly took himself off for his turn in the bathroom, leaving her to choke down her breakfast around a mouthful of drool.

As she paused outside the flat and laid her palm on the wood of the door like she was trying to feel Matt through it, she knew a storm was brewing between them and it was going to either break or suffocate them.

Something was going to have to give, and give soon. The only question about it was which of them would be the catalyst.

Matt had no idea how he was going to reclaim his position in the friend zone when he was fucking Romy all night in his sleep and thinking about fucking her every moment of the day.

His solution was to distract himself by invading Artie's Wimbledon house. Annoyingly, he could think of only two business matters for them to discuss, and both were finalized by 11:20 a.m. on Matt's first day.

At that point, Matt decided he had no option but to confess to Artie that impending fatherhood was responsible for his earlier-than-expected arrival in London. He felt a surge of energy after getting that off his chest, and urged Artie to join him in some steam-releasing activities. But he was doomed to disappointment. Artie, never the most intrepid of adventurers, was uninterested in abseiling down the ArcelorMittal Orbit, rap jumping down a tower or kayaking on the

Thames, and informed Matt that he got all the dare-devilry he needed from his DIY obsession: in fact, his only recent hair-raising stunt had been making a bird-house in his mantuary—a.k.a. backyard shed—during which he'd narrowly avoided slicing off an arm with a circular saw.

Which was when Matt had the brilliant idea of making his baby a crib. What better way of a) keeping himself from going stir-crazy in that Romy-saturated apartment, and b) demonstrating to Romy that he didn't *really* think fatherhood was all about slinging money at the kid?

By one o'clock, he and Artie had downloaded a design for a crib in a half-moon shape with cutout stars on the sides to match Romy's nursery decor, ordered wood and paint, familiarized themselves with the necessary tools and were ready to blaze a home handyman trail starting Tuesday morning.

And thus, the pattern of Matt's temporary life with Romy was set.

He'd go for his morning run, then make and eat his own breakfast. When Romy headed for the shower, he'd scramble her eggs the way she always made them, with mayonnaise, Parmesan and basil. She'd come to the kitchen counter, they'd exchange a subdued "Good morning" and he'd leave her to eat while he took his turn in the bathroom. By the time he was done Romy would have left for her Islington office and he'd be ready to head to Artie's to get macho with the power tools. He'd then be back at the apartment showering off man-cave grime before Romy left her office at six o'clock for the trip home.

When she arrived, Matt would be reduced to farcical TV Sitcom Land, making use of anything readily available to hide his exhibitionist dick—his laptop, Romy's *London AZ* guide, a cushion. If she'd had a damn pot plant in the place he may even have snapped off a frond and tied it around his groin! He'd get a reprieve while she cooked dinner, because she'd banned him from helping her in the kitchen on the—correct—grounds there wasn't enough room for the two of them.

They'd eat dinner while making inane conversation, then watch TV until the rigidity of perching as far away from her as possible without falling off the damn couch gave him an actual pain in the neck. At that point, he'd excuse himself to catch up on his San Francisco projects while the time zones were favorable, after which he'd dream about Romy all night and wonder if she was dreaming about him.

In other words, it was Hell. On. Earth.

And then, on Friday night, everything changed.

CHAPTER THIRTEEN

THE CRADLE WAS finished on Friday afternoon.

Artie was jubilant that they'd completed it with only one trip to the emergency room to get his forearm stitched.

Matt *had* been jubilant because he'd thought it looked fucking amazing…until he saw it in situ and by comparison to Romy's pristine paint job on the walls, realized it was in fact fucking crap.

He pictured Romy coming into the room in all her chic neatness and zeroing in on that drip of silver paint that he'd thought was unnoticeable but could now see would be visible from Jupiter using nothing but the naked eye. He envisioned her comparing his amateurish jigsaw-cut stars to the perfection of the ones painted on the wall. He imagined her waiting impatiently for Matt to leave London before she threw it out.

And then it sank in that he probably wouldn't *know* what she did with the damn cradle, because given the way things were going between them the chances of her inviting him anywhere near her for the rest of their lives seemed remote.

He thought back to what he'd said to her when she'd put Plan C to him—that whatever outcomes her Plan C covered, she'd be in his life no matter what. The truth was he needed that guarantee; it was what had driven all his decisions about Romy from the night he'd met her. Her, in his life somewhere.

And not the way they were at the moment. That wasn't having her in his life; that was *losing* her from his life—piece by piece, a little more every day. And it was going to have to stop.

He was going to fix whatever was wrong. Change the dynamic between them. There could be no more meaningless conversations over dinner. No struggling to keep their limbs separated on the couch. No more scheduling of morning showers to avoid contact. They had to have contact! They'd *always* had contact. Except for those four weeks after she'd flown home from San Francisco when he'd heard nothing from her, and he couldn't take another month like that. Nor could he wait another nine days to find out what sort of contact they'd have in the future. He had to know now, tonight.

Babies needed certainty, she'd told him. And he was ready to do his bit to guarantee their baby had it, via parents who would never give up on each other! If his gruesome parents could stay together for thirty years, he and Romy had to be able to manage some kind of longevity, didn't they?

Restless, he gave the cradle a gentle push with his fingertip to check the way it rocked on the nursery floor. Another push. Another. Picturing his tiny daughter in it.

He wondered if Romy had any names picked out. He kinda liked the name Rose… Similar to Romy, and yet…different. Pretty. Sweet. A little serious. He liked the idea of a serious kid.

Okay, it was a little crazy to be thinking so far ahead. The kid was still only a blastocyst, if she was here at all!

Still, he wondered what Romy would look like pregnant. As chic as ever. Beautiful.

He hoped she wouldn't get morning sickness. That would suck after all the pain she'd already been through. Morning sickness could be serious if you got it bad—like that type the Duchess of Cambridge got. She'd have to move in with her mother if she got that kind because it would be impossible to live alone and suffer like that. Or she could go into the hospital.

He'd better check out the hospital she'd chosen for the birth, now he thought of it. In case other serious shit happened. Blood pressure problems. Gestational diabetes...

Miscarriage. Twenty percent of women had miscarriages.

Or—hang on—did women still die in childbirth?

Jesus, he hadn't researched that one! He was going to have to look into it.

Because fuck.

Like...fuck.

No. Just no. Not going to happen.

He realized he'd stopped rocking the cradle and looked down at the sweaty palm he'd been gripping it with. He swallowed, breathed deeply, but the questions wouldn't leave him. Pregnancy, childbirth, the things that could go wrong. He was going to have a stroke thinking about this stuff when he was back in San Francisco.

Which...meant...ooooh. Holy shit! He was going to have to *not be* in San Francisco—he was going to have to be *here* for the next nine months to make sure nothing went wrong.

For a moment, he felt disorientated, and had to sit on the edge of the bed and breathe through it. Ha! Anyone would think he was having sympathy contractions nine months early!

Nine months. Living with Romy for nine months... Was it possible?

Well, yeah! Perspective! He'd lived with her for three and a half years, hadn't he?

And all right, that was different. He hadn't even caught an accidental bathroom flash of Romy's body in all that time, and now he'd had sex with her twice and could visualize every damn inch of her skin. That made it a little harder to maintain a hands-off friendship.

Also, he was having a kid with her, for Christ's sake, so...so...ooooh. He was sleeping in the nursery, and he'd have to *get out* of the nursery so he and Romy could get the nursery finished, which meant there was only one place to sleep and that was with her.

He stared around the room, seeing nothing, as he assembled thoughts and then disassembled them. He wasn't flavor of the month with Romy—she'd told him sex was out of the question and she looked a lot like she wasn't intending to back down on that anytime soon. And he had no intention of backing down on it, either.

But...but...would it be so bad? If they put strict rules in place? It was only nine months, just until the baby arrived, and she could put together whatever legal documents she wanted to regulate the arrangement, couldn't she?

He had to shake his hands at that point to release some tension, then rub them on his jeans because his palms were sweaty again. Oh God. God! Whichever way you sliced it, this was a big deal. Huge! This was *not* a hookup. This was an affair. A real, bourgeois affair. He had to think this through. Maybe…maybe set the arguments out the way Romy did and try them on her tonight, easiest to hardest, no rushing his fences the way he usually did. He'd call it a Plan D.

He got up, went over to the cradle, set it rocking again, picturing a little tuft of red hair, a mini version of Romy's pursed duckbill lips.

He smiled. That kid was going to be *cute*!

CHAPTER FOURTEEN

MATT FIRED HIS opening salvo over their evening meal of spaghetti with ricotta, prosciutto and arugula pesto—"You look tired."

And okay, that statement wasn't going to set any woman's heart aflutter, but it was harder than he'd anticipated to think of something scintillating to say after five days of cold shoulder.

Romy didn't even look up from twirling a piece of spaghetti around her fork. "That's because I am."

Matt waited for her to finish eating that forkful, and tried again. "Tiredness is common when you're pregnant."

She paused, another forkful halfway to her mouth.

He gave her a weak smile. "I...er...read up on the symptoms, that month in San Francisco. Just...just in case."

The fork continued its journey in silence.

He cleared his throat. "So? Do you think you're... you know...*tired*?"

Aaand she laid down her fork. "I have no idea if I'm pregnant. If you're impatient for an answer because you're ready to call it quits and go home, however, I can grab a no out of the air for you. Or you could just *go*!"

"I'm not leaving, Romy," he said, which of course was exactly the point he'd been intending to work up to, but before he could elaborate she tossed her napkin on the table and stomped off to her bedroom.

Okay, that hadn't gone exactly as he'd planned. But he had a Plan E.

He cleared the table, stacked the dishwasher, sat at the dining table with his laptop, pretending to work in case she came out but in reality checking what was on TV because he knew Romy would be out eventually to watch it with him—she'd been making a point of *not* running away from him as though it were a badge of honor to suffer his company.

Sure enough, twenty minutes later she emerged in sweatpants and a loose T-shirt that screamed *I am in the friend zone* but which nevertheless set him on fire.

Out of the corner of his eye he watched her hesitate at the couch, then take up her usual position on the extreme right end, pick up the remote, turn on the TV and start changing channels at a rate of knots.

He took a couple of deep-but-silent breaths, adjusting his dick for the millionth time to try to give it a little extra room in his jeans, then he grabbed a beer for himself and a glass of water for Romy and made his way over to the couch. He deposited the drinks on the coffee table and took his allocated place on the extreme left.

Immediately, his penis eased out of the position he'd forced it into, making him squirm.

Romy looked at him, frowning. "What is it?"

"Just a twinge. In my...hip," he said, and grabbed the nearest cushion to thrust over his lap with a telepathic order to his dick to behave because he was *not* going to rush his fences!

"I've got some Deep Heat in the bathroom if you need something for it."

He almost burst out laughing at that. Deep Heat on his cock? That'd serve the bastard right. "No, I'll be... fine," he said, and he let himself look at her, really look at her, in a way he hadn't allowed himself for five days.

Every cell in his body seemed to vibrate with the need to touch her immediately. The idea of never touching her again was unendurable. And he didn't want to build an argument rationally—he just wanted her. Fast-tracked.

Okay, he was going to rush a fucking fence.

He threw his lap-covering cushion over the back of the couch. "Romy?"

She turned to him, her hand tightening on the remote. "Yes?"

"Stick a fork in me—I'm done."

CHAPTER FIFTEEN

"A WHAT?" Romy asked.

"A big, sharp fork. Or your teeth if you prefer."

She choked on the breath she'd been taking, coughed, wheezed, grabbed for the glass of water on the coffee table and took a massive gulp. *What* had he just said?

He grinned at her. "I can do kink, you know."

And she choked again, this time on the water, and coughed up half a lung.

"You okay?" Matt asked. "Maybe you need some of that Deep Heat."

Deep Heat? Yes! *Yes*, she needed deep heat. The deeper the better.

"But if you're trying to change my channel," he said, with a half laugh, "it's too late. It's preprogrammed."

"Wh-what?"

He gestured to the remote, and she looked down at it as though she'd never seen it before.

"Here," he said, taking it from her and pointing it at the TV. "Let's agree that the next channel switch we stick with no matter what."

But when he jabbed his finger on the remote and

somehow found *The Proposal*, she wanted to snatch the remote off him and try again.

She and Matt had watched *The Proposal* together the night she and Teague had broken up. February 14, nine years ago to the day. Not that Matt would remember that. But it was etched in her mind as the date she finally accepted Matt didn't know she was equipped with boobs and a vagina.

"What is it about this movie and Valentine's Day?" Matt asked.

Blink of utter, *utter* insanity. "You *remember* watching this?"

"Well, yeah! *I* wasn't the one who drank a whole bottle of red wine on my own—my memory is unblotted. Now shh, we've already missed half of it." And he fixed his eyes on the screen while simultaneously reaching out a hand and yanking her close to him.

What the *hell* was going oooon—dear God, he'd put a hand on her thigh.

She waited for him to move it. One…two…five…ten seconds… But his hand stayed where it was.

What was she supposed to do? Leave it there? She tried to think if she'd felt this hot and bothered in the old days when they'd watched a movie and he'd casually touched her, but her body had gone into free fall and there was only now. A deep, painful longing for him suffused her. She'd sit through anything as long as he kept his hand there—golf tournament, snooker, home shopping channel, even *The Proposal*.

"So," he said, his eyes still on the TV screen.

"Yes?" she breathed.

"Back to that fork…"

The fork. Ha! Stick a fork in *him*? Stick a fork in

her! She was so done she was like a slab of overcooked pork crackling!

Matt hooted out a laugh as though he'd heard her thoughts, then gestured to the TV. "Do you remember this bit?"

She forced herself to focus on the screen. Ugh. "Unfortunately, yes. You made me get up and chant to the universe and dance around the living room."

"You didn't take much persuading."

"Red wine."

"Wanna have another go—without tripping over the coffee table this time?"

"Thank you, no."

"Then shh," he said, and as he refocused on the TV, he released his grip on her thigh and pulled her under his arm instead.

Romy kept watching the screen, conscious of the need to appear like she was just…well, breathing. Like a normal woman would breathe when she was jammed under the arm of a guy she was gagging for!

But she was struggling to take in anything, because she was seeing instead Valentine's Day evening nine years ago…

Matt and his date *du jour*, Kelsey, were going to a brasserie. Rafael and Veronica were at a diner because Rafael was broke and his pride wouldn't bend by so much as a quarter inch when it came to Veronica contributing funds toward their date nights. Romy, who'd been dating Teague for two chaste months, didn't know where Teague was taking her because it was a surprise, but she knew if she was ever going to sleep with him this was the night. She might have actually gone through with it, too, if he'd booked any old restaurant.

But the moment she'd seen it was the exclusive, expensive Catch of the Day—which she'd been dying to try but couldn't afford—she'd had a crisis of conscience. Going to bed with Teague after such a meal would feel like a dinner-for-sex trade, and she liked him too much to go through with it. So she'd put her hand on his arm to stop him from entering the restaurant, and he'd given her his gentle, crooked smile and said, "It's okay, Romes. Apparently Valentine's Day breakups are almost as common as Valentine's Day engagements."

And they'd hugged, and she'd tearily rejected his what-the-hell-it's-Valentine's-Day offer of as much lobster and champagne as she could consume, and thirty minutes later Romy was back in the town house with a take-out pizza.

She'd been about to indulge in her first bite when Matt walked in, looked at the pizza in its box on the coffee table, at the glass of red wine beside it, and asked, "What's with the pizza?"

"Can't a girl order a pizza every now and then?"

"Not when the girl is you."

"I don't cook *every* night."

"Yes, Romy, you do. You're *obsessed* with cooking." And he'd swiped a slice, sampled it, grimaced, picked up the pizza and taken it to the kitchen, where he threw it in the garbage.

"I haven't eaten dinner!" she complained.

"If you want pizza, I'll take you to Vendetta's."

"It took so long to get into this dress I can't be bothered getting out of it just to go for pizza. The whole point of takeout was that I didn't *have* to."

"Yeah, I guess you do look overly trussed for a pizzeria."

"A real man wouldn't be deterred by a few buttons."

"*Any* man would be deterred by three million of the things, so to save us both the effort..." dragging her off the couch "...I'll make you something to eat instead."

He'd tugged her to the kitchen counter, got a beer for himself, poured her a fresh glass of red, tapped the neck of his bottle to her glass, taken a quick swig and started gathering ingredients.

Recognizing the makings of Matt's infamous cheese, bell pepper, chili and Henry's Hot Sauce omelet, Romy had spared a mournful thought for her trashed pizza capricciosa. But she knew Matt only made this particular omelet when someone was miserable—there was something about hot sauce and egg that helped take your mind off your troubles, he insisted, to everyone else's disbelief—and so she'd said, "What happened?" preparing to take one for the team and help him eat the damn thing.

"Huh?" As he roughly chopped the pepper.

"Tonight. What happened with you and Kelsey?"

"Nothing." Shaking out a ton of chili flakes.

"Nothing as in...nothing?"

"What?" he said, distracted by cracking eggs into a bowl and whisking enthusiastically. And then he paused and looked at her. "Oh no, I don't mean *nothing* nothing. I mean nothing *interesting*."

He mixed the cheese, chili and pepper chunks into the egg, tipped the mixture into the pan and pushed it around with a spatula. A couple of minutes later he scraped what looked like a lumpy red-and-beige splotch onto a plate. Without ceremony, he poured the hot sauce over it, threw a knife and fork on top and slid the plate across the kitchen counter to her.

"Where's yours?" she asked, dismayed at the gargantuan size of the thing.

"Shit, *I* don't need to eat." He grabbed for his beer and took an enthusiastic swallow. "I had to eat Kelsey's dinner *and* mine because she's on a diet." Another slug of beer. "Fuuuucking hell, Romy—a diet!"

"She's a *cheerleader*, Matthew," Romy said, and shoved a valiant forkful into her mouth. She swallowed with some difficulty, then grabbed his beer off him, needing a sip to extinguish the flame in her throat. "She has to wear skimpy outfits, and people have to toss her in the air and…and things. You're the American—you know this stuff better than I do."

"So what?"

"Sooooo she can't eat like the rest of us—she has to keep her weight down."

"Oh. Yeah. I guess."

"And come on, you *know* girls don't look as good as Kelsey without a little self-deprivation."

"Who cares about looks?"

Romy choked on the bite of omelet she'd just taken. Took another sip of Matt's beer. "Name one nongorgeous girl you've been out with."

He grabbed his beer bottle back off her. "Names aren't important. And neither are looks."

"Ha ha."

"I'll qualify that—looks are a drawcard, but not if the rest of the person is annoying."

"Yeah, well, your problem is you're spoilt for choice. You get the pretty ones and the creative ones and the smart ones—all the ones."

"At least I don't get the nasty ones like you! Don't

make me regret wasting the Omelet of Compassion on you, Romy."

Romy slowly lowered the laden fork that was half-way to her mouth. "What makes you think I'm in need of compassion?"

"Er…the pizza? Obvs!"

"Try again."

He ran a hand behind his neck. "Well, you're here, and Teague's not."

"How did you know I'd be here?"

Another rub of his neck. "I saw Teague at Flick's."

"Flick's? *Teague?*"

A look of annoyance crossed Matt's face. "It's not a den of iniquity you know, it's just a bar that happens to show films on Wednesday nights. They went anti-Valentine tonight with some godawful indie horror film. *Lots* of people were there."

"Yes, but Teague?"

"Why not Teague? At twenty-one he doesn't even need a fake ID, even if they could be bothered card-ing us, so—"

"It's not that! It's just… I don't know. It doesn't *seem* like him. It has a bit of a reputation."

"Oh, so Flick's is good enough for me but not for him? Yeah, well, he *was* there, halo and all! So I asked him why you weren't with him and he told me you two had called it quits."

"And you assumed I'd be in need of an omelet! Well, let me assure you the split was amicable." She pushed her plate away. "I promise you it wasn't worth leaving Kelsey unsatisfied."

"As it happens, smart-ass, we'd already done the satisfying stuff before dinner." He grinned. "*And* after.

We were just out for a postcoital drink and the movie, and to be honest I was looking for an excuse to skip the film because there's a scene with an eyeball being chewed in *close-up*. Blech."

"I'm glad I didn't *completely* ruin your evening," she said drily.

"You don't *look* glad."

"Because you threw out my pizza!"

"Hey, I was going to take you out!"

"Oh, great—me eating and you watching!"

"Well, I… Sorry. I got a little ahead of myself with the pizza."

"That's because you always act first and think later. But since I don't need a babysitter, please take yourself back to Flick's."

"Don't make me go back there, Romy! I've got a DVD of *The Proposal* for us to watch instead—much better than a chewed eyeball. Kelsey said you'd like it and she's a film major so she'd know. She says it's perfect for V-Day."

"*Kelsey* suggested it?" Romy didn't know how to feel about not being considered a threat; she was *living* with Matt, after all!

"Come on, Romy, you know how squeamish I am. I can't take the eyeball. Don't make me go back there."

And so she'd laughed—of course!—and let him pour her more wine and put on the movie and tuck them both under a blanket on the couch. And then he'd poured her *more* wine, and made her do the chant-dance, followed by more wine…

And then came the scene with the ivory satin wedding dress and Romy had started to cry, and as though Matt had been waiting for exactly that, he'd scooped her up and sat her on his lap and patted her back and she'd snuggled against him.

Matt made stupid *It's all right, I've got you, You've still got me* murmurs into her hair, and even stupider than what he was saying was that she'd fallen asleep. Cradled on Matt's lap *she'd fallen asleep*! What a waste!

When she woke up, she was sprawled on Matt on the couch, and for the longest time she'd watched him sleep. Awake, he was always so sure of himself, and yet asleep there was something defenseless about him that made her want to hug him.

She'd felt an insane desire to take his face between her hands and rub her lips against his to see what it was that he gave to other women that he wouldn't give to her. It had shocked her, how much she wanted to do it, not only because it felt wrong to break up with one guy and kiss another all in the one night but because she hadn't allowed herself to think about Matt like that since that first night they'd met, when they'd *almost* kissed.

Whatever the reason, she'd sucked in a breath and the small noise woke him. For a moment, he'd stared at her, and then his eyes heated, and hooded. The hands that had been loosely crossed over her back tightened and he'd pulled her in close and she'd felt his erection.

Time stopped. She'd sensed rather than felt his heartbeat, steady and strong. Or maybe it was her own she was in tune with: it was telling her to kiss him, kiss him now because she might never get another chance.

"One thing I noticed last night..." he'd said, and she'd held her breath, dying to know. And then he'd grinned. "You look kind of like a troll when you cry."

"Oh, you...you bastard!" she'd exploded, whacking him in the chest and oofing her way off him.

"Hey, it's cute," he'd insisted, laughing at her disappearing back as she stomped to her room, where she told herself that she was to Matthew Carter what Teague Hamilton was to her. A friend you liked too much to love. A friend you needed in your life but not your bed. A friend, nothing more.

And now, so many years later, nothing had changed...and she still wanted him anyway...

"Hey—remember this bit?" Matt, giving her a nudge and bringing her back to the present. "Betty White trying to find Sandra Bullock's boobs in that dress. You started crying and said your boobs were too big, so you were going on a diet like Kelsey to shrink them."

"Yep, got it, thank you."

"And I had to lift you onto my lap and cuddle you."

"Aaaand you can shut up now."

"And I said I'd take a look at your boobs for you and give you an honest appraisal."

"Shut *up*, Matthew!"

"And you started undoing those three million buttons on your dress."

"Yes, I *remember*," she said, exasperated. "I also remember that you stopped me."

He looked at her, eyes heating. "I was a moron. How about I check your boobs now?"

Oh God, oh God, what did that mean? Fork. Done. No! If she asked about it, it would probably turn out to be something about barbecued steak! "Very funny."

"Except that I'm not laughing, Romy."

For one perilous minute, she vacillated...but then she remembered that her buttons *hadn't* been unbuttoned that Valentine's Day nine years ago, and she turned back to the television.

"I can hear you sniffling, Romy," Matt said. "Just saying."

"I'm not sniffling."

"Are you, you know, hormonal?"

She looked up at him. "Am I *what*?"

"When women fall pregnant, they get sort of emotional."

"Oh, they do, do they?"

"Apparently."

"Shut up, Matt. And stop reading up on pregnancy. You won't be here, so you don't need to know."

"I could be here. If you needed me. If you...wanted me."

She swallowed, letting that sink in. "You can barely fit in this flat *before* I'm fat."

"I fit better if I do this," he said, and lifted her onto his lap. "Just like old times, huh?"

Old times? Not quite, Romy thought.

"And yet not like old times, is it?" Matt said, as though reading her mind.

"No, not like old times," she said.

"You see, Romy," he said, "I have a feeling the old times aren't coming back. Which leaves us with a choice of either no times or new times. And I...I don't want no times."

Breathless. Wanting. "So what do new times look like?"

"That's something we'd need to work out."

"How do we do that?"

"I don't know yet. What I *do* know is I still want you. I know, also, that if you didn't want me, too, you'd be down the other end of the couch. So I have a suggestion, if you're interested in hearing it."

Could this be real? Oh God, she didn't know what to think.

"Romy?"

"What's the suggestion?"

"That I give myself to you for the night, and you do whatever you want to me and we see how we feel at the end. And if it's good...I stay. But I stay in your room with you."

"Do you mean that?"

"Cross my heart, hope to die."

"Just so you know, I'll help you with the dying part if this turns out to be a joke," she said, and tilted her head, closed her eyes, waiting for the kiss.

Long moment of...nothing. And then Matt spoke. "Er, Romy...? I think you've got the wrong idea."

CHAPTER SIXTEEN

HER EYES BOLTED OPEN. "I knew it! I'm going to get the carving knife!" she said, as she started pushing off his lap—but he held her tight.

"You don't need a knife if you want to kill me," he said. "All you need to do is say no. Because I'll drop dead if you don't take me within the next two minutes."

"Take...you? Oh, take *you*! You mean I'm in control."

"That's what I mean."

"But why?"

"Because you said no sex, therefore you have to be the one to reverse that order. Because I like the idea of being your slave. And because...I trust you with my body, like I've never trusted anyone before."

She felt tears prickle, as they always did when he said something that moved her.

He groaned. "Hey! Cut that out. Tears aren't sexy."

"But big tough guys who turn to putty when they see them are."

"I'm scared of trolls, that's all," he said.

"I don't think you're scared of anything, Matt."

He cupped her cheek in one hand and looked at her, very seriously. "I'm scared of *you*, Romy, and that's the truth," he said. And then he gave a shaky laugh. "But here's a hot tip to help you with my seduction— I'm an easy lay—it won't take much to make me come. So the floor is yours. Or the couch. Too bad there's not a chandelier or you could—"

"Shut up and kiss me," she said, leaping straight into the fray before anything could snatch the chance from her—and almost before she finished saying it his mouth was on hers, his tongue in her mouth.

One, two, three seconds—and he sat back, took her hand, put it over his heart. "Feel that?"

"Yes," she said. "It's banging like a drum."

"I am going to come so hard for you," he said.

Oh God, just hearing him say that! "I'm going to make you," she said. "But first, I'm going to kiss you and you're not going to kiss me back—this is just for me."

He kept himself still as she brought her mouth to his. First she kissed one corner, then the other.

When she pulled back to look at him, he touched her mouth and breathed out slowly. "That's just the start, right?" he said.

Instead of answering him, she leaned into him again, trailing tiny kisses between those two corners, sometimes letting her tongue slide between his lips, sometimes not.

She pulled back again, watching for his reaction. "Well?"

"Well," he said, and licked his lips. "Am I allowed to ask for more? Because I want more, Romy. I want you to kiss me all night."

And with a little cry of surrender, she planted her

mouth over his. "Open," she said against his mouth. "Now you can kiss me back."

And obediently, he did, his tongue gliding deep and wet into her mouth, seeming to touch everywhere at once. She swiveled on his lap to straddle him, her arms twining around his neck, knees digging into the back of the couch either side of his hips as she brought her body snugly against his. Her hips moved back and forth, and so did his, as if their bodies were already planning to take over the show. He felt so good there, *her* toy now, and the thought that she could do whatever she wanted to him was an exhilarating one, even if all she really wanted to do was strip off their clothes and impale herself on him.

But she remembered how in San Francisco, when she was climbing the stairs, she'd wished she could be memorable for him, and so she forced herself to slow down, to throttle back. She would tell him what to do to her, because he wanted her to do that, he *trusted* her to do that—and being the one he trusted was already something memorable.

Her hands went to the hem of her T-shirt. "Do you know what I want you to do to me when I take this T-shirt off?" she asked.

"Tell me."

"I want your hands on my breasts. And then your mouth. I want you to coax my nipples out, to not stop until you do."

"Oh Jesus," he groaned. "I am so up for that."

She laughed, low and soft, and scooting back as far as she could on his lap, lifted her T-shirt up and off. Lowering her arms to her sides, she lifted her chin. Displaying the wares. Watching his eyes drop to her chest. Seeing him swallow hard. Her breasts seemed to swell from the heat in his eyes, begging to be released from the confines of her bra.

"Well?" she said.

"Well," Matt said fervently. "I could drool a fucking river looking at you."

"Hands. On me."

And as he raised his hands, placed them gently over her covered breasts and her heart gave a savage leap. He raising smiling eyes to hers and she knew he'd felt it.

He started to move his hands in circles over the white mesh of her bra, and her nipples tingled as though getting ready for him. One firm squeeze, and he pulled his hands back but only far enough for his fingertips to take over the work, drawing the lightest of circles around her areolae, which were on clear display through the mesh of her bra.

She huffed out a shuddering breath, so hot for him she thought she might scream. One more circle, another, another, each one infinitesimally smaller than the last, heading inward to his twin targets.

She squirmed on his lap, frustrated, and the way he laughed low in his throat told her he knew exactly what he was doing to her. Well, of course he knew!

But she wasn't entirely clueless, either, and when she made a little figure eight on his lap with her backside, using her hips to propel her, he actually gasped, his cock doing an involuntary lunge upward against her heat. "Ride me if you want, Romy. Do anything to me. Ask anything of me."

"Then...then I want your fingers on my nipples, right on them, right now, rubbing," she said.

"Your wish…my command," he breathed out, and used two fingers to rub each nipple through the white mesh. "Tell me when I can use my mouth."

A deep, drawn-out moan of a "Now" had him going straight to the job, holding her breasts in his hands and bending forward to lick around one areola, then the other, moving back and forth, back and forth again and again, before shifting to her nipples and using the flat of his tongue to lick her like an ice cream, then the tip to stab into the centers.

"Soooo gooood," she sighed.

"Don't I know it," he groaned, and gave each nipple a lightly sucking kiss.

"Take off my bra," she said. "I need you to touch me properly."

"How about I do it like this?" he said, and peeled the cups of her bra down. He leaned back to look at them, licking his lips as though he could taste her. "Ahhhh, God, it's a crime, how sexy you are."

She slipped her hands under his T-shirt, ran the palms up his chest. "You feel so hot."

"I am hot. Hot for you. Hot and hungry and ready."

She pulled her hands free, sat back to give him room. "Then take off your T-shirt."

He pulled it up and off lightning fast. "Romy, please touch me," he said. "Please."

She put her hands over his pecs, rested them there for long seconds, absorbing the thud of his heart and then moving her hands in the slow circles he'd used on her. "Are your nipples as sensitive as mine?" she asked.

"Find out," he said, and she moved her hands, softly, delicately circling them with her fingertips.

"Yes," she said. "They're hard. Oh, I wish you could feel mine."

"Say the word and I'll get back to work."

"First, I want to do this," she said, and leaned in so that her breasts were only just touching his chest. She closed her eyes, lost in the moment. "Oh, I like that."

He bucked against her, as though jolted by a burst of uncontainable energy.

"Don't," she ordered, even though she loved it. "Stay still and let me do this. It feels so wonderful." And it did, her skin against his, the crunch of his hair against her nipples, the graze of his own small nipples against her.

"Are you trying to torture me, Romy?"

"What do you mean?"

"Do you know how hard it is for me to wait?"

"Yes, because I've waited ten years for you, wanting this."

"So you're punishing me?"

"No," she said. "No, never. I would never hurt you. I want to give you everything." For an instant, she sensed a withdrawal in him, and the next moment his hands were in her hair, his forehead pressed to hers.

"Not those words tonight," he said.

"Why not, when I mean them?"

He released her, eased back, not answering. "Come on, get rough with me. I want you to fuck my brains out and make me beg."

Her hips moved, her core sliding over him, back and forth. "Does it feel good to have me do that?"

"Yes, you know it does—you can feel how hard I am."

"So say the words. Tell me exactly. I like it when you say the words to me."

He smiled again, a sexy curve of mouth. "It feels so good when you ride my cock. You make me so big and hard, I can't wait to be in you. I want to make you wet. I want to fill you up. I want to do you fast and slow and make you come all night."

"Yes," she panted, restless, seeking.

"So can I?"

"Not until you make my nipples come out. Undo my bra."

Swiftly, he undid the back clasp of her bra and stripped it from her.

"Get to work," she commanded.

He recupped her breasts with his hands, going straight for the nipples now, thumbing them gently, then harder, then pinching them between thumb and forefinger.

The air was full of small sounds. Sighs and moans and gasped-out breaths and tiny sucking sounds, rasps from his jeans against her as she writhed on his lap.

"Now your mouth," she said. "Lick them. Suck them. Say again you'll do anything, but this time I want to know it's only for me, no other woman."

"Only for you, Romy. Only ever for you will I do what I'm told, always you, only you, forever."

She closed her eyes, surprised that the words brought her pain, and he seemed to take that as his cue to increase the pressure because he went hard at her now, hands squeezing her breasts, settling in to suck on her, focused on only one, going hard, hard, hard, as though he were starving for her, so that she was arching her back and dragging his head closer and tighter. The intensity hovered just short of pain.

She let out a low, keening cry, and he went crazy,

his sucking almost frenzied. And unbelievably, with one last, long, luxurious suck, her nipple popped out into his mouth.

He pulled back, looked at it and she felt herself flame.

"I am so horny," he said, low and hoarse, as his fingers went to where his mouth had been, pinching and rolling. "I'm scared I might actually come." And he shuddered as though to underscore the truth of it.

"Suck me again," she said, and he bent his head and kept sucking, this time using his fingers on the other nipple as though to prepare it. And then with one final light bite, he switched sides, using the same technique, the same firm suction, the same concentration, and it happened fast his time, the nipple suckled into his mouth, eager and ready.

"Now," she said. "Now. I need you inside me now."

"Not yet," he begged, as he continued to lash one nipple with his tongue, twirl the other with his fingers, pinching, rolling, squeezing.

"Now," she said again.

"One minute more," he begged, and latched onto her nipple, sucking and sucking until she was shifting on his lap, whimpering, panting.

"I'm going to come if you keep going!" she cried.

"Good."

"No!" she said, and pushed against him so that she tumbled backward and would have fallen to the floor if he hadn't caught her hips, pulled her up, held her steady.

"You are driving me fucking wild, Romy," he said.

Their eyes clashed, warred. She undulated on his lap and a look of triumph came into her face. "Then kiss me, show me," she said, and he dragged her in, lunging his cock so high and tight against her she almost wished he'd take over, roll her under him and jam his cock into her. His mouth landed on hers, his tongue thrusting as though he were fucking her mouth, and she lost all sense of time and space until there was only heat and lust and musk.

Her slave. He really was her slave.

"Let me have you, Romy," he said against her mouth, between deep, drugging kisses. "Let me have you now."

And she was off his lap, dragging him up after her, kissing him again as her hands went for his jeans. Unzipping, hands diving, gripping him, squeezing him. "I want to see you naked," she said, and stepping back, she flicked a hand at his jeans. "Get them the fuck off."

"You bet," he said, and while he kicked his way free of his jeans and all but tore off his boxer briefs, she stripped off her sweatpants, her underwear.

And then she stopped to breathe before lowering herself onto the couch, where she laid herself out like a feast, and when he looked at her she felt a surge of power that this man, of all the men in the world, would want to be hers even for a fleeting moment.

As Matt looked at her, so confident on the couch, tenderness almost blinded him. She'd asked him to tell her he'd do anything only for her, no other woman.

To him it seemed so obvious, it didn't need to be said. Ten years of running only to her, ten years of doing whatever she asked. Even the fact that she'd asked him to take her, that night in San Francisco, the first time she'd ever outright asked, was proof. Because he'd held himself so rigidly back from her for so long—and yet he'd obeyed her. *Of course* he had. Here in London, too. It wasn't in him to deny her what she wanted. She'd always belonged to him, in every way but this—and now she was claiming this, too. Did she not see that he always would have done this for her if she'd asked? That he'd already done everything he could think of to keep her with him, even when the only way he could think of was to deny himself this final piece?

His body one giant throb straining toward her, held back only because he'd put himself at her command and she was reveling in her power over him.

Her silky light brown hair was spread out above her head. One arm was crooked beneath her head, the other stretching up the back of the couch, her hand flopping over the back of it. Creamy skin. Sleepy eyes. Mouth swollen from his kisses. Those small pink nipples, hard and impudent and all the more amazing because he'd had to work for them, and because she'd demanded he work hard. The tiny tangle of hair at the apex of her thighs, which made him want to fall to his knees and beg her to open her legs for him.

As though she'd divined that unspoken need, she spread her legs so that one foot was on the couch, the other on the floor. Like she was saying: yours.

"Ah, Romy," he said looking down at her. The moment felt too big for words, the air heavy with the promise of something special.

"Come," she said.

And slowly, he lowered himself on top of her, waiting for her arms to enclose him, folding his own tightly around her at the same time as he closed his eyes—the better to sharpen the moment. He stayed like that, quiet and still, for the longest time, absorbing her.

When he opened his eyes, it was to find her waiting for him. She strained up to kiss his mouth, deep and soft, and she kept kissing him as he slowly, so very slowly, entered her.

He stopped when he was all the way in, wanting to remember this moment because surely sex could never be so blissfully perfect again. And then he moved. Out, in, out, keeping it slow and rhythmic so she knew exactly what to expect.

Over and over he entered her, and she kept her mouth on his all the while. He wanted to take forever, wanted to immerse himself in the sound of sex, the arousing smell of her, the taste of her mouth, the pant of her quickened breaths, the feel of those delicious little nipples poking against his chest, the strength of her inner thighs gripping the outside of his as though she'd never let him go. But his cock was trying to slip the leash, desperate for the finale, and his orgasm was building, grabbing at him despite his efforts to slow it down.

Not yet, not...yet. He ground out the words in his head, but he knew it was a stroke or two only away. His breaths were heaving so much, he had to move his mouth off hers, gulping in air as his hips rubbed against hers. *Oh God, not yet, I want more.*

And then Romy's whole body went stiff. A gasp, and cry, her wet heat tightening around him as he sucked against her neck, then licked, then sucked, then licked.

"Let me say it, Matt," she said.

Oh God, he knew. Knew what she wanted. He shook his head, no. *No! Let me just have this.*

"I have to say it, Matt."

Panic. "No!" Aloud? In his head? "No, no, no, please no, just let me, let me, Romy."

But it was out of his control. Push, push, push, push, his body inside hers, owned. Her heart was thumping in time with his, the smell of her wrapping around him as surely as her arms. *Oh, please, no.*

"I love you, Matt," she cried, and the words pushed him over the edge so that he abandoned himself to the waves. "I love you, Matt. I love you, love you, love you. Ahhhhhhhh, I love you. Love."

Silence.

Full. Heavy. Lost.

His arms unwrapping, his mind unraveling, his body shivering.

He eased himself up over her, hands on either side of her, looked down into her face and all he could think was, *No, please don't say it*, even though it was too late.

She watched him. Boldly, unwavering, unapologetic.

Was she expecting him to say something? Because he had nothing to say.

He moved off her, stood, located his jeans and put them on. Found his T-shirt, dragged it over his head. He was covered, but he still felt exposed.

Romy sat up without taking her eyes off him. "What is it, Matt?"

"You know."

"Just words. Three little words."

"You promised not to say them, that night in San Francisco. You told me you refused to love me."

"And yet you knew I did."

"But you didn't tell me, you didn't say it. And then…

Ah Jesus. You said them like that. At that…that moment. That's not love, Romy."

"So if I'd said them over dinner, that'd be different? You'd have *welcomed* them over dinner?"

He shifted his shoulders. He felt worn out. Exhausted. "Well, doesn't matter, does it, because now I've heard them. So…thanks. I guess." He gave a throat-clearing cough, wanting his voice to be steady. "I'm going to catch up with Teague tonight, have a few beers."

More silence. Stretching, as she watched him.

Another clear of his throat. "You know, Teague…"

"Yes, I know Teague," she said. "Your friend. The man I'm supposed to be with. *That* Teague."

"He and I…" Pause. "We're going to…" Pause. "I'm…due there soon."

"And is it going to be an all-nighter with Teague?"

"Maybe."

"You asked me for tonight, Matt. All night."

Again, his shoulders shifted. "Plans change."

She sighed as at last she got off the couch. "Okay then, we understand each other," she said, and put on her sweatpants, her T-shirt—not hurrying.

"The whole…whole friend thing. We all need to get back to that. You. Me. Teague."

She sighed again. "You don't have to explain yourself to me, Matt. We…you and I… I guess we sorted out those 'new times' we were curious about, so we're good. On the same page."

"Are we?"

"Well, maybe the same book, different chapters. You gave yourself to me to do with what I wanted, I did what I wanted and now we both know what's what, how we feel."

"Romy—"

"I love you and want to have sex with you because of that. You want to have sex with me, but don't want to love me because of that. I guess that translates into you being at chapter five while I'm up to chapter twenty-five. But whereas I know I want to finish the book, you're bored with it and want to move on to a different story."

"That's not— I mean—"

"What? Did I misinterpret something?"

Matt tried to figure out how to say his feelings were more complicated than that, but when he thought of all the plans he'd made for himself just a few hours ago, all he could come up with was: "I need you, Romy."

She sucked in a breath, like he'd hurt her. "Yes, I think I know that. But I need you all the way, no secrets, no fears. And that's different from the way you need me." She smiled, with a roll of her eyes that managed to be both dismissive and defensively dramatic. "I shouldn't have called it love, I know, when you can't feel it, when you don't...don't know the...the *agony* of it. And it *is* agony, it really is. But I'm running out of nouns and adjectives, so you might have to give me some help there. I mean, we're not friends anymore, are we? I haven't been feeling much of a sense of camaraderie this week. I don't think what we just did was affectionate. We're not really having a casual fling because you're not using a condom the way you always do. So if you don't want it to be love, I don't know... Fuck buddies perhaps? Except that I've broken the cardinal rule so that's obsolete. How about ex-hookup?"

She ran her hand over her hair, smoothing a tangle. "How strange that I thought I was different, being the only female you weren't interested in fucking…and now I'm just like all the others. Right down to telling you I love you at the peak of an orgasm, like the worst cliché. But I understand it now, Matt. I understand all those women who choose that moment to do it. It's that gap in the tower wall, you see. We can't help saying it at that moment because you make us feel so close to you, like we really could slip inside and find you. I even know why they don't want to be your friend at the end—because it hurts to see you and not have you. And you know what? I'm glad I'm not different. I never *wanted* to be different. I *want* to love you. And *I* don't want to be your friend at the end, either."

She picked up her underwear and headed for her bedroom, saying over her shoulder, "Better get your skates on or you won't make it to Park Lane by eleven."

Ten minutes later, Matt found himself outside Romy's flat, leaning against the wall like a drunk, one hand over his eyes. The agony of love. She'd called it agony, what she felt for him. He stood there for a full five minutes, battling the stinging at the back of his nose he was starting to get used to.

And then he took a deep breath, and headed out into the night.

CHAPTER SEVENTEEN

ROMY SPENT THE first half of the night lying in bed, reliving Matt's reaction to her grand declaration of love—which was to look at her as though she'd stabbed him straight through the heart he professed not to have.

The second half of the night she spent pacing through the flat, wondering what she could expect from Matt when he eventually returned.

When there was no sign of him by nine o'clock, she switched to wondering *if* he'd return.

By eleven o'clock, she was convinced he wouldn't.

She'd gone to his room many times, hesitating outside, knowing one quick peek would tell her if he'd taken his duffel bag. But she hadn't been able to bring herself to open the door, instead hurrying to the kitchen to distract herself by making coffee—and for her to make coffee instead of tea was a true indicator that her state of mind was unsound.

By noon she'd drunk so much coffee she was totally wired—which she figured explained the sudden grip of terror that convinced her Matt was lying dead in an alley.

At one o'clock, she pulled up his number, ready to call him despite the fact that last night she'd told him he didn't have to explain himself to her…and then made more coffee instead.

At two o'clock, she had the brilliant idea of calling Teague to find out what he knew, and when he answered on the third ring she almost collapsed with relief.

"T-Teague?" she stammered.

"Romes!" he said. "Let me guess—you're calling to tell me all is well in the land of the lovers so I can stop worrying about you."

"You'd know more about that than me."

"Er…not following."

"Is Matt—? Did Matt—? Oh!"

"Still not following."

"Matt said he was spending the night with you, but…he didn't. Of course he didn't."

"Oh. Er…"

"Don't," she said. "Please don't cover for him. There's no need. It's none of my business where he spends his nights. I'm not his girlfriend. And that… that's not what's worrying me. It's just…you know how reckless he is, and I keep expecting to hear he's BASE jumped off The Shard and broken his neck or something, so—"

"Hang on, hang *on*! He's lying to you about where he's going, you're checking up on him and you're telling me you're not his girlfriend?"

"He doesn't have those."

"Well, you're not just friends if that's how you're both carrying on."

"We're not friends at all anymore, it seems."

"Oh, Romy, you two were never friends. Look, much as it pains me to do this, let me give you some advice—stop giving him so much rope, because he'll keep hanging himself with it."

"Rope?"

"Stop letting him come and go in your life as he pleases, see any woman he wants, do anything he likes. He doesn't want that freedom—not from you. Deep down, he wants you to give him boundaries."

"I don't...understand."

"Matt's problem is nobody ever reins him in. Not his friends, because we like him exactly the way he is—fast and brilliant. Not the women he attracts just by breathing, because they'd give him anything he asks for—which sucks, by the way, for guys like me who don't get a look-in when he's around. As for his parents—well, they don't want to rein *themselves* in let alone anyone else, and I don't think they'll be happy until they corrupt him absolutely."

"I don't—? His parents? I've never met them."

"Now you see, that's interesting. Ask him why. And while you're at it, *tell him* what you want from him, how you feel, lay it on the line—"

"Oh, Teague, I already told him how I feel." She closed her eyes as the heat of humiliation flooded her. "Last night I told him I loved him."

"Aaand it all makes sense. You told him—he ran away."

"What am I going to do?"

"Tell him again. Keep telling him. Keep showing him, too, but you've been showing him forever, so I have a feeling it's the telling that's going to get him."

"He doesn't like being told. I knew that, and I told him anyway."

"He'll hear it, from you he'll hear it, but you'll have

to make him hear it, and hear it, and hear it, because he won't believe it."

"And if I lose him for good?"

"Then at least it'll be an outcome, won't it? For you, if not for him. You can't keep limping around the edges of a relationship with him, Romy. If he really won't step up to the plate, it's time he let you go so you can find someone else. Someone who…who wants all of you, not just the parts Matt will spare."

"He'll say no—he won't step up."

"Then let him say no, and let him go. Look, just… think about it, okay?"

"Okay, I'll think about it…I think."

Teague laugh/sighed. "Okay, but while you're thinking about thinking about it, consider that every time you've needed him he's come running—and when I say running, I mean sprinting. You know, the night you and I broke up and I saw him at Flick's and told him we were through, he was out the door faster than a speeding bullet—"

"He hates being compared to superheroes."

"Then he should stop trying to save you. The point is, I was sure he was off to get the girl that night— but here you are, ten years later, still limping along the edges."

"Don't you think that means it's not supposed to be that way for us?"

"No, I think it means he's terrified. You're *different* for him, Romy."

"That's just it—I'm not different. I'm like everyone else who wants him but can't have him."

"I'm not talking about sex, except insofar as it took him ten years to get around to it with you—which *is*, in fact, the difference. He's scared to death of you, scared a wrong move will lose you, scared of his…his need for you to see him the way you see him. Because I'm telling you, he may not like you supersizing his heroism but he also kind of lives for it. He wants to be a hero for you, but deep down he won't believe he can be. He's scared—but don't you be scared, too, or you'll both still be limping around those edges when you're ninety. Anyway, enough Truth or Dare." He took a breath. "I'll tell you what I'll do. I'll text him, make sure he's alive, and then I'll text you so you can use your brain for more productive things than worrying about the idiot."

Romy received the "all clear" text from Teague half an hour later, but by four o'clock there was still no sign of Matt.

The time had come to make sure he hadn't moved out. Without hesitation this time, she opened the door to his room, walked boldly in…and her jaw dropped at the sight of a silver cradle in the shape of a half-moon.

She walked over to it, not quite believing it was real even though its slightly mangled cutout stars smacked of a DIY project so it was hardly a celestial gift beamed out of nowhere.

This was what Matt had been doing all week while she was at work? Not plotting a tech takeover of the world, but making his baby a cradle?

She blinked in disbelief as she ran her fingertips over the wood. As she gave it a little rock. And then she couldn't seem to stop blinking—not in disbelief anymore, but because tears had formed in her eyes. Everything about the wonky cradle moved her unbearably. Because she knew in that blinding, wrenching, heart-shattering moment that she'd gotten something very wrong about Matt and his motivations. He'd suggested giving her his sperm not as a favor to her, not to be a godfather, but because he wanted a baby. He'd wanted, specifically, *her* baby. He'd flown to London to stop her from finding a different donor because he *loved* their baby. He'd loved it then, when it didn't exist, and he loved it now when it *still* might not exist. He loved it even though he'd probably never be able to say the words.

And *she* loved *him*—so much in that moment she would have gladly cut out her heart and given it to him on a plate made of her own soul, painted not black but silver and white, to match the priceless, utterly wonderful gift he'd made for their child.

She put both her hands over her belly. "Please be there, my little one," she whispered. "For your daddy, if not for me, because whether or not he knows it, he needs you."

CHAPTER EIGHTEEN

THERE WAS NO sign of Romy when Matt opened the door at 7 p.m.—not even a wisp of aromatic steam coming out of the kitchen, which was where she'd normally be at this time of night.

He experienced a short burst of relief, followed almost immediately by a surge of panic.

But then he heard his name, "Matt?" called out like a question from her bedroom and the panic receded… and then surged right back, because he had no idea what he was going to do.

He'd had a turbulent night and a torturous day wandering the city, trying to work out why Romy's *I love you* was different from every other *I love you* he'd ever heard even though it *wasn't* different, why it made him want to stay instead of leave, why leaving therefore was exactly what he should do and why he needed to stay anyway.

Yeah, like any of *that* made sense.

"Matt?" she called again.

He opened his mouth to say yes, it was him, but when no sound emerged, he closed it.

And then she was there, in the room with him, smiling as though nothing had happened last night. "I'm glad you're back. I need you," she said, and walked over to him holding out something he accepted by reflex.

"Can you put that in for me?" she asked, and when he looked down at his hand he saw it was an earring. "The left ear is always tricky, as you know."

Of all the openings Romy could have given him after last night, this was about as far from his imaginings as it was possible to get.

"Matt?" she prompted when he stood there like his own mummified remains, and she moved closer so that their bodies were almost touching. And God, how he wanted to touch her, even if it was only her ear. He wanted to beg her not to hate him. He needed her to put her arms around him and hold on to him. He felt so lonely for her, which didn't make sense when she was standing in front of him.

She tilted her head as trustingly as ever, moving her hair out of the way. He started to put the spike of the earring through her lobe, but his fingers were trembling so much it took three attempts. "You need to get it repierced," he said—an excuse for his clumsiness.

She offered him a tremulous smile. "I'll get you a needle and you can do it for me."

"Needles hurt." He touched her cheek with his fingertips. "And I don't want to hurt you, Romy."

"So *don't* hurt me." Her smile failed. "Please don't, Matt."

He choked on what might have been a sob if he knew how to cry, and stepped back out of harm's way. And that's when he noticed she was wearing a silk dress and high heels. Her hair had been styled, her makeup carefully applied and there was a hint of Chanel in the air.

"You're going out," he said.

He saw her physically pull herself together. "My monthly dinner with my parents, which I completely forgot about until Mum called me this afternoon!" Pause, as she reapplied her smile. "If you want to come, I can wait a few minutes…?"

He swallowed. Shook his head. Took another step back, then stepped forward again because that was just too pathetic. What was he scared of—that she'd *love* him to death?

She took a gusty breath. "Okay then. I've left some menus on the kitchen counter—several restaurants nearby do home delivery. Or…or maybe you already have plans?" Pause, during which she very clearly braced while he said nothing. "Well, whatever. If you stay in and want to…to talk, about…about anything, I don't expect to be out too late."

She started to move past him but he stopped her. "Is Teague going to be there?"

"No."

"Has he met your parents, Romy?"

"Yes, he's been to a few of these dinners."

"So why did *I* never meet them on one of my trips?"

She looked at him for a long moment. He got the feeling she was choosing and discarding words. Then she shrugged and said simply: "Because it didn't work out that way."

"Why didn't it?" he pushed, because he wanted to know. Maybe it would help him to make sense of their relationship.

"Because we've never had the kind of…of friendship that would make such a meeting easy."

"How can he have been enough of a friend to meet them but not me?"

"Probably the same reason you took Teague home to meet your parents but not me."

"That's...different."

"Yes, and you and I are different from me and Teague or you and Teague. Or you and Veronica and Rafael and Artie and— Oh, Matt, can't you see that we're not friends in the same way? That we never were? We *couldn't* be, because I—" She broke off. Shook her head. "Look, you don't want to hear it and I'm late—I really have to go."

She tried to move past him again—again he stopped her.

"Do they know about me, Romy?"

"My parents? Yes. They know we were friends in college. They know we've been friends ever since. They know you're staying here. They want to meet you because they know about the sperm—in fact they half expect you to come with me tonight."

"Have you told them how we did it? The sperm? That it wasn't—"

"No. There didn't seem to be much point since... Well, let's just say I discuss almost everything with my parents, but not one-night stands."

"Three nights."

"Different number, same principle."

His head felt like it might explode. "I think..." Trailing off. Clearing his throat. "Doesn't matter. Have a nice time at— Where did you say you were going?"

"Petit Diable. I took you there last year, when I was dating the sous chef, Jules."

"Oh, Jules—yeah, I remember."

"That was the time you met Poppy." She took her overcoat off the coat stand by the door and slipped it on. "And you insisted Jules and I meet up with the two of you for brunch."

"Why are you mentioning that, Romy?"

She faced him. "Because I've decided there are some things I won't do anymore. Like having brunch or lunch or dinner or drinks or anything else with you and your latest hookup. I don't want to talk to them on the phone or see them on video calls or read their emails. I just…don't."

"You have to do that, Romy! I need you there."

"Why?"

"Stops them giving me ultimatums. Them, or you. I have to…to show them—"

"That I'm not a threat? Well, that makes sense. They meet me, they can tell what I mean to you and all is well in your world and theirs."

"I choose you. I *always* choose you."

She shook her head at him sadly. "Oh, Matt, that's not a choice. That's called having your cake and eating it, too. And I'm tired of being the vanilla sponge you refresh your palate with between bites of chocolate gâteau. I want to be the gâteau."

"That's not fair, Romy. I've never—"

"Don't!" She held up a hand. "It doesn't matter, Matt. It really doesn't." She opened the door, but stopped on the threshold, turned back. "You said something last night about old times and new times. Well, I'll find a way to accept that the new times are over—San Francisco, last night, done. But in return, you need to know that what we've had for the past ten years has to be over, too, because I'm not going back to the old times. I *can't* go back, even if what we end up with is nothing."

I can't go back, even if what we end up with is nothing.

Matt knew what nothing felt like—it was how he'd describe those four weeks after Romy had left San Francisco. But even in the midst of the full-blown freak-out that separation had brought on, he'd known that if he could have gone back and changed what had happened that night, he wouldn't have done it.

The miracle was that he'd held himself back from her for so long. He should have known he'd wouldn't be able to keep his hands off her forever. It was what he was like, the real him, not the hero she thought he was. *Of course* he was going to engineer a way to have her eventually. And the fact that she'd been the one to suggest that infamous Plan B didn't change it. He'd leaped at Plan B! And look what had happened when her email had arrived—not pregnant, off the hook! He should have taken that as a sign that it wasn't meant to be—instead he'd thrown the first things to come to hand in his duffel, snatched up his passport and headed for the airport to get to her and try again, and if Teague hadn't been there, he would have beaten his chest and dragged her by her hair to the nearest flat surface like a Neanderthal.

Hell, that's what he *had* done! He'd taken her on the floor like an animal. What more proof did he need that he didn't deserve her?

Ever since that night in San Francisco, he'd been trapped in a game of up and down. Take her, save her, take her, save her. It was a miracle her head wasn't spinning off her damn neck with how hot and cold he'd blown.

But she'd told him she loved him anyway.

Why couldn't he just accept that she did, no matter *when* she said it to him? What was the problem with her feeling close enough to him when they were having sex to say it then? He felt close enough to her when they were having sex to *merge* with her!

So...couldn't he *try* to accept it?

What if he asked Romy what he should do to be a better person? Already all she had to do was tsk-tsk him to get him rethinking shit like drinking beer in the morning. She could tsk-tsk him some more, couldn't she?

He could stop swearing as a first step. That'd have to go for the baby's sake anyway.

And he could take a few leaves out of Teague's book of saints—ones that didn't involve stealing the guy's interior-design flair. Teague had been to therapy after his sister died, and wasn't ashamed to admit it. So couldn't Matt give therapy a try—deal with his demons that way instead of locking himself in the tower? Wasn't Romy worth at least giving it a go?

What did he *want* out of the rest of his life, anyway? Not to fuck every girl he met the way he'd been doing forever—that was the way to turn into his father. Jesus! Scary.

The rest of his life... Forever... Ha. It was simple, really. His forever was tied up with Romy Allen—that's how all this had started. The baby was his gateway to forever with her. She'd said that night in San Francisco they had a window of opportunity that was like fate. Neither of them had someone in their lives at that precise moment when she needed him, they were together, she needed his sperm, he needed a release.

What if she was right about it being fate?

What if he ignored fate, and *didn't* get her into the tower with him and she got tired of trying to scale the wall and ended up with Teague?

Teague, who'd met her parents when Matt had not.

Well, fuck that! (Okay, stopping swearing would be a work in progress.) *He* should be the one meeting Romy's parents, not Teague. They were *his* baby's grandparents! And this wasn't petty jealousy, it *wasn't*. It was nothing to do with Teague personally, because he *liked* Teague, he did. No, it was about the past ten years and the past five weeks and…and finding his place in Romy's life and not letting her hate him and…and…and God, he needed a shower and clean jeans and a half-decent shirt and a taxi to Petit Diable.

And Romy, he needed Romy.

CHAPTER NINETEEN

MATT ARRIVED AT Petit Diable forty minutes later and looked in through the glass frontage until he found the Allens.

He watched for a few minutes, assessing the dynamics of the small group and growing anxious without understanding why—unless it was that they seemed so *nice*. Laughing, talking, helping serve each other from the platters on the table, focused completely on each other instead of the potential talent at other tables. Vastly different from the rare get-togethers he endured with his parents, during which the only indication they were a family came from his obvious physical resemblance to them both.

Romy didn't look anything like either of her parents—her father was stick thin and dark, her tiny mother looked like a damn movie star—but you could tell they were a solid unit. Assessing them, he wondered if the way he'd visualized his daughter, as a Matt/Romy combination with hazel eyes and red hair, might be way off the mark.

Something flickered through him like quicksilver—a sense of…disquiet. He stared at Romy's parents, trying to anchor the thought, but before he could latch onto it his view was blocked by servers clearing their table and he realized he'd have a better chance of latching onto whatever was bothering him if he actually joined them.

The moment he entered the restaurant, Romy looked straight at him—as though she sensed him. Her parents swiveled in their chairs to see what she was looking at, Romy dipped her head and said something to them, and next second they were on their feet, beaming at him.

Matt beckoned to the maître d' and after a quick explanation, the guy conducted some weird wordless cross-restaurant communication with Romy, and then he was allowed to make his way to them.

"Sorry I'm late," he announced upon arrival at the table.

Romy's father grabbed his hand and pumped it enthusiastically. "No need for apologies, son," he said.

Matt blocked a start at the "son" a fraction too late, and then started again when Romy's mother opened her arms. Shit. She was going to hug him. He didn't want that. He hadn't earned that. Didn't...*deserve* it.

Matt considered side-stepping her, making an excuse about needing the restroom, but it was too late; he was folded against her. And then that wasn't enough for her: her hands reached up, his head was dragged down and he was kissed soundly on each cheek. Another hug, and he was released, only to have both his hands held, gripped.

"I'm so very glad to meet you, Matthew," she gushed. "I've been wanting to thank you, personally, for what you're doing for Romy." And sure enough, there were tears swimming in her eyes! He wasn't going to cope with this. He shouldn't have come. He didn't belong here. He had to leave. But then she rubbed a rueful thumb against his cheek and said, "Lipstick, my darling, sorry," and his resistance melted because she was adorable.

His place setting was arranged as if by magic, his chair positioned opposite Romy and between her parents, and Mrs. Allen fussed him into his seat.

She smiled at her husband, who was seated on Matt's left. "Pour Matthew some wine, my love." Back to Matt. "Or would you prefer beer? Romy says you like beer."

"Wine," Matt said. "Wine is great, Mrs. Allen."

"Now, Matthew," she chirped on, taking her seat on his right, "none of this *Mrs. Allen* business. My name is Lenore and the handsome gentleman on your other side is Graham. And we should warn you that we're already half in love with you, but if we get too embarrassing give us a stern word and we'll stop." She shot him a little twinkling smile. "Or at least we'll *try* to stop, but I can't promise absolutely."

"Mum!" Romy shook her head. "Matt's not demonstrative."

Lenore reached for Matt's hand. "Matthew can be whatever he wants to be and we'll still love him." She gave his hand a squeeze before releasing it. "We've had our appetizers, I'm afraid, and Romy's already ordered share plates for our main course. But I'm sure we can increase the portions. Romy—shall I call the waiter over and ask for Jules?" Back to Matt. "Jules is one of the chefs here, an old boyfriend of—"

"He knows Jules," Romy put in quickly. "I'll ask Francois to get a message to the kitchen."

Lenore leaned toward Matt conspiratorially. "It's

over with Jules, of course. A lovely young man but not for Romy."

Romy got to her feet with a screech of chair. "Mum! Matt doesn't care about my boyfriends."

Lenore raised an eyebrow at her. "I thought you were going to find Francois?"

She waited until Romy had walked over to the maître d', then focused on Matt again. "So! Now! Matthew! Romy may not have told you this, but Graham and I met at university just as you two did…"

By the time Romy returned a few minutes later, Matt had learned that Lenore and Graham had been married for thirty years, that they lived in Barnes (only thirty minutes away from central London but a world away in its "village family feel," which was "perfect for grandchildren"), were planning to renew their vows in two months' time (because "love should be celebrated") and that he was invited to attend the ceremony (because he was "practically family").

So far, so…what? Good? Bad? He had no fucking idea.

Romy took her seat and asked him apprehensively, "Are you okay?" which he assumed meant she had no fucking idea, either.

"Fine," he said, and took a giant sip of wine.

He did his best to keep up with the conversation, but as Romy reached for her water glass, that goddamn platinum ring on her pinky finger flashed, distracting him. Why did that ring bother him so much?

He sifted through his memories of the past ten years of the three of them—him, Romy, Teague—trying to find one that exposed some deep-seated jealousy that would explain his unexpected ring paranoia. The night he and Romy had met three months into their freshman year and they'd almost kissed, but he'd rewound and pushed Teague's barrow instead. Romy asking his advice ahead of her first date with Teague: What should she talk about? The night she broke up with Teague. Her twenty-first birthday dinner—and yeah, Teague producing the ring had seemed an over-the-top gift, but hey, it suited her. The Fourth of July ball at Teague's family estate. Matt had been too busy with one of the other guests—Leah Carnegie-Phillips—to resent Teague monopolizing Romy; Matt had described himself as Leah's bit of rough when he'd told Romy about it, and called Teague Romy's bit of smooth, which had irritated her so much he'd ended up getting her in a headlock and telling her to get over herself—but they'd been friends again within half an hour.

So many memories. Harmless memories.

He heard a clatter and snapped his attention back to the present. Romy had dropped her fork to her plate and was directing a pinch-mouthed headshake at her mother.

What had he missed?

Lenore smiled at him, a faint stain of pink on her cheeks. Remorse. "I apologize. I thought it was all settled."

"It is," Romy said.

"What's settled?" Matt asked, because it was clearly something to do with him.

Lenore looked from Matt to Romy to Matt. "The adoption," she said.

Matt frowned at her, uncomprehending. "Adoption?"

She patted his hand. "There's no difficulty with it, so don't worry that it will be an inconvenience."

"Huh?"

"If you were going to be named on the birth certificate, we'd have to get your consent, and Romy's told us you don't like being bothered with paperwork."

"I don't— Wh—? I thought this baby was—" He looked at Romy. "You're keeping the baby." Not a question—a demand for confirmation.

"Yes, of course I am," she said, flustered. "Mum means when I marry, should my husband want to become...become..."

"The legal father instead of a stepfather," Lenore finished for her. "Romy's birth father *was* on the birth certificate, you see, so he had to give consent, and it took a while to track him down."

"Hang—" Head spinning. He looked to Romy. "You're *adopted*?"

"Yes. I thought...you knew."

"No."

"I guess... You see we don't...don't think of it, we just... I just know Mum and Dad are my parents, even though I do...I do write to my birth mother, so..." She looked ill. Stricken. "It's not a big deal."

Matt stared at her. "Not a big deal?"

"No, that didn't come out right. I mean things... things have changed, so... Oh God."

He was still staring at her, but he couldn't speak, almost couldn't find the will to breathe.

"Matt, this is something we can talk about," she said, and reached across the table for his hand.

He jerked his hand away from her touch, pushed his chair back and stood. "Excuse me," he said. "I have to...have to...go."

Romy made a move, as though she'd go with him, and he shot her a do-not-even-think-about-it look and headed out of the restaurant.

CHAPTER TWENTY

MATT LET HIMSELF into the apartment, went to the bathroom, splashed water on his face and then just stood there, holding on to the sink. Holding on, on, on.

Was he in shock? It felt like he might be. He needed a cup of something warm to take the ice out of his veins. Or someone to hold him and tell him everything would be okay.

He laughed at that. A harsh, ugly, mirthless sound. Who was there to do that for him, when Romy was the architect of his pain?

Funny, he'd been so busy telling himself a baby would make him irreplaceable to Romy, too busy thinking she'd always *been* his and always *would* be his, to consider what he'd actually be to the baby once some other man came on the scene. He'd just assumed he'd never be *off* the scene. But now he knew he couldn't act the part of the benevolent godfather from a world away, smiling from the sidelines while some other guy lived with his kid, loved his kid, was loved *by* his kid.

Godfather. What did that even mean? He couldn't remember who his own godfather was—some guy who'd been a friend of his parents twenty-eight years ago but hadn't been in their lives for at least twenty years. Easily forgotten.

As *he* would be.

"Aaarrrggghhh!" The cry tore out of him, doubling him over. His child, oh God, oh *God*, his child wouldn't be his. He couldn't breathe; it hurt too much to breathe, hurt so much he wanted to die.

How could Romy think it would be okay for some guy to adopt his kid? How could she tell him she loved him and then give his baby to someone else? How could she sit there with her parents and listen to them tell him *they* wanted to love him, too, and then let them talk about someone else taking his child as though it was as easy as scrawling a signature across a page, cutting him out of the picture?

He raised his head, looked at himself in the mirror. His face was white, bloodless, and yet there was a wildness in his eyes he recognized. His father's wildness, his father's eyes. He wished he could tear the mirror off the wall, smash it and use a piece of the broken glass to cut them out and deny that truth.

But what difference would that make? The evil wasn't in his eyes any more than it was in his red hair. It was bred in him deeper than the bone.

And there it was—the truth of that quicksilver glimmer of disquiet he'd felt when he'd seen Romy with her parents in the restaurant and wondered what his child would look like. The truth was it didn't *matter* if his child was a hazel-eyed redhead or a green-eyed brunette or anything else—what mattered was the hidden stuff, the soullessness he might pass down. The soullessness that wasn't just part of him, but had been actively encouraged by his parents. What right did he have to want to spawn a child let alone raise one, hammered as he was on both sides of the nature/nurture debate?

He heard the door open…close…then nothing.

But he knew Romy. She'd be wanting to talk, ready to convince him that adoption would be a *good* thing, that it was all about *protecting* him, that this way there was nothing that could *impinge* on his *lifestyle*. She'd tell him she'd make sure the child was as happy as *she'd* been with her adoptive parents. She'd say he could still be as involved as he wanted, if he was sure that was what he wanted, as long as there was *certainty* because children *needed* certainty! Well, the best way to give her certainty was to take himself out of the picture altogether. Because Romy, for all her comments about his revolving bedroom door and his jumbo boxes of condoms and the moans, grunts and squeals she was tired of hearing and the women she was tired of him flaunting in front of her, didn't know the half of what he'd seen, what he'd done, what he was.

But it was time she did.

He straightened. Splashed more water on his face. Shook out his hands. Reset his brain.

She was out there, preparing to talk things through. And this time, he *would* talk. He'd tell her everything at last, and end the game of make-believe he'd been playing with her for ten years so that she finally saw him as he truly was: not a superhero, but a soulless, heartless, worthless bastard.

And all it would cost him was his child.

CHAPTER TWENTY-ONE

NERVOUS DIDN'T BEGIN to describe how Romy felt waiting for Matt to come out of the bathroom.

And when he did emerge, nervous ratcheted right up to terrified at the look on his face. She knew, in that moment, she was about to lose him.

So she decided she might as well go straight for the jugular and said, "I love you."

Miraculously, a crack appeared in his facade. It was blink-and-you'd-miss-it—just his hand jerking an inch upward—but it convinced her that Teague was right when he'd said the way to reach Matt was to make him hear those words.

"And before we begin this conversation," she continued, striking while the iron was hot, "I should tell you my parents think you love me, too. Me…and the baby."

"Don't, Romy."

"Why not?"

"Because it's too late."

"It's not even ten o'clock."

"I mean it's twenty-eight years too late."

"I don't…understand."

He sent her a brief, chilling smile, and took his old position on the extreme left end of the couch, waving a hand at her old position on the right. "Then take a seat, Romy, because I'm going to make you."

She did as he bid her, her heart lurching. "That sounds ominous."

"I'm just going to tell you the truth," he said. "It's time you heard it." He took a deep breath, waited a moment and then began. "Earlier tonight, I asked you why I'd never met your parents."

"Y-yes."

"And you said you and I didn't have the kind of friendship that would make such a meeting easy."

"Yes, but I meant—"

"It doesn't matter, Romy. What really matters is why I didn't introduce you to mine."

She said nothing, but she watched him like a hawk.

"You see," he continued, "the last time I took a girl home to meet my parents, I was seventeen."

"Seventeen…" she said, as dread worked its way down her spine. "Gail."

"I should explain that sex was allowed in my parents' house—they were…permissive—so it was assumed that Gail and I would sleep together. It wasn't the first time for either of us, but it was the first time in my bedroom at home and it felt…important. The first night, we professed undying love for each other, the next I gave her a promise ring, like the romantic idiot I was." He laughed suddenly, but it trailed away as he frowned as though trying to recapture a memory. "And then at the end of that week I found her in bed with my father."

Romy, taken aback by the conversational tone of such an obscene utterance, sucked in a shocked breath, then wanted to kick herself when it made him laugh again.

"Yeah, it took me by surprise, too," he said.

"What happened?"

"Oh, it wasn't all that exciting. My father is a charismatic man. He groomed her, seduced her. She was a year older than me, more sophisticated than I was, but she didn't stand a chance. Not her fault—mine, for not warning her what to expect, not protecting her."

"No I mean what happened *after*, Matt. You, Gail, your mother..."

"Well, Romy, my mother was...involved...elsewhere at the time, so she didn't see the point in taking the moral high ground. I, however, made an embarrassing scene. My father didn't see the problem because it was DC, where the age of consent is sixteen, and Gail was two years over it. He wasn't breaking any laws, and it wasn't like he wanted to date her. But he found the whole thing so tedious, he promised to stay away from my girlfriends after that. Gail was dutifully embarrassed—so much so, she cut ties with me and who could blame her? But I learned my lesson and never took another girl home."

She reached out a hand to him.

"I knew you'd do that," he said dismissively. "But I don't need petting. I'm only telling you so you get the full picture of who I am. So...what fun story should I share next?" He shot her a look that got her heart racing. This was going to be bad. "How about the one starring my mother and Teague Hamilton?"

She couldn't find enough air to suck in a breath this time. "No," she whispered. "No, please."

"Don't worry, Romy. Our saint comes out of it with

his halo intact. It happened the year of the Fourth of July ball. Wanting to repay the favor, I invited Teague home for Thanksgiving. He was at a loose end because his family was sailing the Mediterranean. Veronica had dragged Rafael home to her folks' in some desperate attempt to get them to accept him, Artie was getting up close and personal with his first-ever electric drill, and you were off at some Cordon Bleu cooking school. My parents were supposed to be in Florida shooting movies—more on that later—but at the last minute Mom changed her mind. I suspect because she'd seen a photo of Teague and was intrigued by his preppy good looks. Long story short, one minute we were eating turkey, next minute Mom was trying to eat *him*! And I mean *eat* him. Didn't succeed, of course—you know Teague, loyal to a fault. Still, it was… I mean, Teague… Oh God, Teague…" He faltered, shook his head as though trying to get something out of it, took a breath. "Teague pretended it wasn't disgusting, and he…he hugged me." His voice was hoarse, cracked, hitching. "And he t-told me all m-mothers find him irresistible." Another breath. "He h-hugged me! Can you believe that?"

She wanted to reach for him, fold him in, cry for him. But he was already pulling it all together, so she did nothing but sit there, aching for him…waiting for him, as ever.

When he continued, his voice was devoid of life. "So anyway, as you might have guessed, my parents are what you might call highly sexed. If you were a porn aficionado, you'd be aware of their channel, where you'd see all sorts of things that have nothing to do with vanilla sponge cake. Chet and Cherry Carter—

real names Kevin and Marsha—why not look them up, expand your repertoire, get a cheap thrill, whatever. It was a popular site when I was a kid, but the appeal has dwindled lately. Dad blames Mom—the MILF thing isn't working so well for her."

"MILF?"

"Mothers I'd Like to Fuck." He made an impatient, chopping movement with his hand. "You understand what I'm saying, Romy?"

"Yes. Your parents like sex—sometimes with people quite a bit younger than they are, and they're porn stars."

"They've been married as long as your parents have, but they've had so many sex partners they'd never remember them all. You can't approve of that."

"I doubt they're seeking my approval."

"How about if I tell you they didn't care what I saw when I was a kid? That nudity was a normal thing in the house so I couldn't bring friends home, that I could watch porn from puberty, that they laughed and told me not to be a prude when I caught them fucking?"

"I know you're trying to get a reaction from me, Matt—why don't you just tell me what it is you want me to say?"

"That you want me out of your life. I want you to tell me you won't let me near your kid."

And all her bravado crumbled. Her eyes welled. "I'm not saying that. I can't say that, because I love you and I want you as the father of my child. No, *our* child. And I wish I could…could tell you what you mean to me. I wish you could understand what a hero you are, to have come through that and still be you."

"I can't *believe* you!" He jumped to his feet, glared

down at her. "I'm not a fucking hero. Stop saying it, stop!"

"I'll keep saying it, Matt, because that's what you are. A hero. My hero. Better than Captain America because you're real and you're here and you're trying to save me from yourself. That's what your tower is about—the one with the moat. Not to protect you, but to protect me! To protect *all* of us. But we love you anyway. And I…I know what you mean when you say we're twenty-eight years too late, because I feel like I've been waiting for you for twenty-eight years and it's *too late* to tell me not to wait anymore. I don't want to be saved, you see. I want to be yours."

"You can't be mine! I'm a sex addict, Romy! That's it! That's all there is to me."

"If you were a sex addict, you'd wouldn't have gone without sex for two weeks after my phone call. You'd never have lasted four weeks after I left San Francisco. And you probably wouldn't have lasted Monday to Friday this week, either."

"For all you know I was with another woman last night."

"I know you weren't."

"You can't know that."

"I can, and I do."

He ran his hands into his hair. "Why won't you listen?"

"I will if you say something worth listening to."

"Then hear this, Romy. If you're pregnant, I don't want to see you again. I'll set up the trust fund, and we're done. Will that prove to you I'm not some fucking hero?"

"No, because setting up a trust fund doesn't gel with the whole anti-Christ vibe you're aiming for."

"I'm not joking."

"I never joke about the anti-Christ. So move along. And if I'm not pregnant…?"

"If you're not pregnant, you can consider you've had a lucky escape and find a new donor."

"I don't want a new donor."

"You said you did in that email."

"I lied."

"You…you must see why I have to back out."

"Well, I don't."

"I've just *told* you!"

"You said things about your parents—that's all. And I'm sorry they weren't better role models, but I can't see what that has to do with you impregnating me."

"Bad genes," he said.

"Hmm. I don't think sexual adventurousness is inherited."

"Addiction can be."

"You're not an addict—we already covered that. And in any case, addictions are treatable. Who's to say *I* don't have a wacky sex gene? I mean, there has to be some reason I want to bite some poor unsuspecting man, right?"

"Romy, I'm serious. No more sperm."

She stood, faced him. "Okay then, when we have sex tonight, we'll use a condom. Or I'll use my hands… or my mouth."

He did a double take that would have been funny if she hadn't been so desperate. "I'm not touching you, Romy," he said.

"Now you see, a *real* sex addict would let me take advantage of him."

"I don't want to take advantage of *you*."

"Then do it as a favor. It won't be easy finding a casual sex partner once I'm pregnant, so I'd be grateful if you'd fuck me while I'm still a viable option."

"No."

"Why not?"

"Because you're too vanilla sponge, okay? I've been with women who want it harder than you do, rougher, wilder. What makes you think you can keep me interested even for one night?"

"I don't know if I can keep you interested, Matt. But I'm happy to take the dare."

"I'm not daring you, Romy."

She shook her head at him, as though disgusted. "You talk about vanilla sponge. You rave about your sexual escapades. You throw out words like *addiction*. But it seems to me you're the tame one. If we've barely moved past the missionary position, it's not my fault, it's yours—you've been directing almost all the action. Maybe I *should* choose Teague! Maybe I'll call him tomorrow."

"You do that, Romy," he said, and the blaze in his eyes as he grabbed her hand and yanked her in was electrifying.

He lifted the hand he held, wrenched off her pinky ring and threw it. Romy heard it ping off a wall but she refused to let her eyes follow its trajectory.

"Okay—here's a choice for you," he said. "Go and find the ring…or have sex with me." He released her hand, spun her to face the room, gave her a push.

"Where could it be, hmm? I know you want to find it—it's the right choice, so go do it."

She wrenched herself out from under his hands and faced him again. "I know what you're doing, Matt. Trying to make me choose Teague over you because of some stupid idea that Teague's better than you. That's what this is about, isn't it?"

"Yes! Yes! I'm jealous of Teague because he's better than me! Everything about him is better. Better looking, richer, kinder. He's got a family to be proud of. He's a better man, better father material."

"If you really feel that, Matt, then be better for me yourself. Be the man I know you are. The man I love more tonight, knowing what I know, than I loved ten years ago, knowing nothing except that you were made for me."

"I don't *know* how to be better. God, I hope you're not pregnant—I hope it with every breath in my body."

"I saw the cradle, Matt. I know you want the baby."

One of his hands came up, shielding his eyes—but not before she saw the flash of devastation. His breaths were heaving—one, two, three, four. His mouth tightened—long moment—and then the hand dropped from his eyes to reveal blankness again. "That was...boredom. I had to do something while you were at work."

"I *know*, Matt. I know you."

"Go find the ring," he said through gritted teeth. "Choose Teague. You were always meant for someone like him, not me. Never me. You *know* that."

"I'm choosing you."

"If you choose me, it really will be only one night, Romy—that's all, no more."

"So shut up and give it to me," she said, and reached her arms up around his neck, nestling against him.

For a moment, his arms closed around her, tightened...but then he pushed her away. "Not like that," he said. "If you really want to do this, not like that. Not now, I can't stand it."

"Then how?"

"Like this," he said, and grabbed her hard by the upper arms. He shove-shove-shoved her over to the wall until she was backed against it. For one fraught moment he stared down at her, and then he kissed her so hard the corner of her lip split. She thought he'd stop then, and he did. He stepped back, looked at her mouth and then very deliberately leaned down again to lick at the bead of blood. "Now stop me. Tell me you made a mistake choosing me. Tell me you've changed your mind."

"No."

"I'm going to be rough with you."

"Then I'll be rough back."

That seemed to make him furious—so furious, he reached for her dress and ripped it down the middle. He flicked a glance at her body as though what was on display wasn't important, despite the fact she was wearing her best underwear and sheer stay-up stockings. But then, of course he'd seen every kind of underwear on a woman, all degrees of nakedness, stockings in every color and every style.

"Tell me you love me," he demanded.

"Why?"

"So I can remind you that *I don't love you*. It took me ten years to be interested enough to *fuck* you. What does that tell you?"

"That you were scared to lose me."

He flinched, but quickly rallied. "Yeah, well, I did do it in the end because it's what I'm good for and it's all I need. Now get that through your head and leave me the hell alone before I hurt you."

"You won't hurt me."

"I split your lip."

For answer, she grabbed his shirt and tore it the way he'd done to her dress, buttons flying in every direction. "There, are we even? Now will you shut up and do this?"

He grabbed her hands then, wrenched them up, slammed them against the wall, imprisoned them in one large hand.

She surged against his hold—not to break it but to strain her face toward his. "Kiss me, Matt. Hard as you want."

Keeping her hands imprisoned, he put his mouth on hers and savaged it, sucking and licking and biting. She savaged him right back, tugging against his grip.

"I need my hands," she begged. "I need to touch you."

"I want you to do something very specific, Romy. Say yes, and I'll let go."

"Yes...yes..." she panted. "I'll do anything for you... everything...all the things."

He let her wrists go, and instantly her hands went to his fly.

He stopped her. "Not that, this," he said, and grabbed the back of Romy's head, bringing her face to his naked chest. "Bite me, Romy. Through the skin until you draw blood. Your deepest, darkest fantasy."

"Why do you want me to do it?"

He laughed—a taunt in it. "Because you won't, va-nilla girl."

"I will!"

"All you have to do is tell me you've changed your mind and I'll let you go. And you go find the ring and we'll be done."

But she shook her head, fierce, and lowered her head to lick across his left nipple. She was not done. She would do this.

His chest muscles tensed. He drew in a sharp breath through his nostrils. "You can't do it, Romy. Admit it."

Her answer was to suck his nipple into her mouth. One of her hands came up, palm resting then rub-bing over his right nipple. He started to tremble, and she took courage from that, trailing her tongue up to his pectoral muscle to choose a spot. She measured it with her teeth, and then started licking there. He stiffened—he knew she was preparing him. But a half moment later he relaxed—he'd *forced* that, she knew he'd forced it.

"Do it, Romy," he urged. "Do it. I need it. This pain to cancel out the other."

She stopped, looked up at him. "What other pain?"

"The pain of wanting…" He paused there, closed his eyes. "Wanting what I can't have, what I *won't* have. Do it. I need it."

She was blinking again, but the tears came any-way, unstoppable. She dipped her head to lick again and her tears dripped onto his chest, mixing with the dampness from her tongue. She switched to sucking him, increasing the pressure. Suck, suck, suck, draw-ing his blood to the surface. And as she did that, she unzipped his jeans, delved a hand into his underwear, gripped him. One, two, three pumps, and he was gasping, then groaning, thrusting himself into her hand. She kept going, urging him with her hand, alternately licking and kissing and sucking his chest to distract him, forcing his words into her mind—*Do it. I need it. This pain to cancel out the other. The pain of wanting what I can't have, what I won't have.*

Oh God, oh God, she had to do it *now*, because he'd be ready to come in just a few thrusts and she wanted to give him a more intense pleasure to replace the pain she was about to inflict. *Do it—get it over with*, and before she could talk herself out of it she closed her eyes and bit down as hard as she could bear to.

Matt stiffened, a strangled "Fuck" erupting from him as she felt the give, the infinitesimal crunch of skin, a metallic tang. Blood—a tiny drop, no more. Enough, it was enough. She dropped to her knees, pulled his jeans and underwear down, took him in her hand again but only to hold him steady for her mouth.

"Don't," he said.

She licked all the way up the shaft, then looked up. "You said you wanted me to suck your cock. And here I am…on my knees for you…ready. I'm not stopping, Matt."

And with that, she slid her mouth over the tip of his cock, rejoicing when his legs went rigid and a cry gargled up from his throat. She started with tiny sucks, just over the tip, as her free hand delved between his legs to cup and press his balls, gently squeezing and releasing. She soon lost herself to the rhythm, to the male smell of him, the velvety feel, playing with speed and pressure until one deeper, harder suck caused him to cry out again, his head flinging back.

He was going to come. She could feel it building. Powerful, glorious. *Do it—let go*, she begged in her mind and next second his hands tightened painfully in her hair and he shouted her name: "Romy! Jesus God, Romy, Romy, arrrgggghh!"

A long, long moment later, when Matt's violent thrusts had stopped and his head was slumped forward against the wall above her, Romy sat back on her heels and looked up at him, licking her lips, tasting him still. Musk, salt, a little hit of lime.

He reached down for her, pulled her to her feet. "Your turn," he said.

CHAPTER TWENTY-TWO

MATT STRIPPED ROMY'S ruined dress from her and dragged her panties down her legs. "Step," he said, when they were around her ankles, "I want your legs wide open tonight." As she stepped, he yanked up his jeans and underwear, fastening them. He didn't intend to stumble over them when he had a point to prove.

He cast a lascivious look at her, lingering on her breasts, which looked ready to burst out of her bra as usual. He nodded at the front clasp. "Undo it," he ordered, and the moment the cups separated he was on her, rubbing and sucking brutally at her nipples. "I want them out...red...raw...aching for me," he said between sucks, and let out a triumphant roar as they came out of hiding one after the other.

He pulled back, looked at them, half-crazed at the sight of them, at the sight of *her*, in her stockings and high heels and nothing else. "Mouths and hands, right, Romy?" he said, and crowded her against the wall before dropping to his knees in front of her the way she'd done for him.

He wrenched at her thighs, opening them wide, and licked hard and long along the length of her. Delicious, fucking delicious. He licked harder, and harder, and when her hands gripped his hair and pulled it the way he'd done to hers, he licked harder still. He wished he could suck the essence right out of her, drink everything inside her, gulp it down.

He tore his mouth away, looked up into her shocked face. "Listen to me," he said, and the urgency in his voice must have communicated his desperation because she nodded once, twice, eager and resolute. "Brace your shoulders against the wall—I'm going to make you come fast."

"Oh God," she said, as her legs trembled in his hands.

He hoisted one of her thighs over his shoulder, giving himself better access. "I want my mouth buried in you so I'm drowning in the taste of your cum," he said. "Understand?"

"Yes."

His response was to lap at her. "Ahhh," he breathed against her sex. "Yes" kiss "good" lick "perfect." He slid his tongue inside her, using it like a small cock. In, out, in out, as her hips twitched in time.

"Keep going," she said, but as though to torment her he pulled out, and when she kicked her heel onto his back in protest he laughed softly and sucked her clit into his mouth while simultaneously tongue-tipping it so hard her protest ended in a gasping scream.

He started to lick seriously then, up and down, side to side, occasionally plunging his tongue into her. He kept her guessing, using tongue and lips, a graze of teeth, but always returning to her clit, growling low in his throat as he suckled it, lusting so badly for its tiny hardness he couldn't be quiet, then using his lips to squeeze around it, then going back to licking over it sure and strong, until she was a moaning mess, jerking against his mouth.

"I'm coming," she gasped. "I'm coming, Matt!" She tensed all over, her gasps becoming breathless huffing sounds, which built and built, her head thrashing from side to side against the wall as she shoved herself onto his mouth. "I'm cooooooomiiing-ooooohhh. Oh God, Matt, God, GOOOOOOOOOD."

He kept tonguing her, then suckling her, then licking, licking, licking, until her legs went limp, and the thigh on his shoulder loosened. Matt felt her weight give, as though she were about to collapse, and before she could slump to the floor he was up, spinning her to the wall.

"Hands on the wall," he commanded.

With a whimper, she obeyed.

"Now tell me what you want," he said, but he was already insinuating himself between her thighs from behind.

"You, I want you."

"Be specific. Where do you want me?"

"Inside me."

"Be specific, Romy."

"I want your cock in me."

"How?"

"Hard. Rough. Now. Fuck me."

But he didn't plunge straight in. Instead his arms came around her and he rubbed himself against her back. "Let's get you back up there first," he said, plunging his cock between her legs and rubbing it back and forth against her clit.

"Do you like that, Romy?"

"Yes, yes, you know I do."

"Then show me—squeeze me tight."

And so she arched her back, tightening her thighs around him, thrusting her pelvis back and forth so that he slid along the length of her.

"What else do you want?"

"I want your hands on my breasts."

His hands came around her, cupped her breasts. "Like this?"

"Squeeze them."

"Like this?"

"Harder. I want you to do it hard."

As he squeezed, he kicked her legs wider, bent his knees slightly to give himself extra thrusting power, then slowly straightened as he guided himself into her. "Tight and hot and very wet," he said in her ear, and bit her neck. "Just the way I like it. Now hang the fuck on."

And with that, he pulled all the way out of her, then slammed straight back in so that she banged forward, flattened against the wall. Merciless, he yanked her back. "Take it, take me," he said harshly, and then he took her hips in his hands hard enough to bruise, anchoring her. "Ready?"

"Yes, yes, ready, do it."

And he let fly—shoving into her hard, pulling all the way out, then slamming into her again. "Fuck me back, Romy, fuck me back."

She leaned forward and backward, hands pushing at the wall to give her extra leverage while she shoved her bottom at him, grunting as he smacked into her. But the pace was too frantic, too forceful, and she ended up flat against the wall again with Matt against her back, shoving into her for all he was worth. Soon that wasn't enough for him, he wanted his fingers on her,

too, so he spun them again and his back was now to
the wall. He jerked her back against him, buried his
cock in her again, thrusting rhythmically as his hands
left her hips to go between her legs. One hand held her
labia open, the other fingered her wildly, fast, furious,
out of control. "I want to make you come so hard you'll
never forget it, Romy."

"You, too," she said, and squeezed her internal muscles, as though she'd milk him of everything he had.
"I want you to come like that for me. Unforgettable."

And then there was nothing but groans and gasps
and grunts and hoarsely whispered words of encouragement, sex words, fuck words, as they sped up, racing,
reaching, needing. A keening cry from Romy, a guttural
curse from Matt, as the peak rushed and roared at them.

Oh God, God, no sperm, he reminded himself, as
Romy's internal muscles convulsed and she started to
come. He stayed, stayed, staaaayed until the very last
second, and then pulled out of her, jerking once before
spilling against her back.

Her head lolled against his shoulder. She was exhausted; he knew it. And so was he. Tired…and unutterably depressed. That damn stinging was behind his
nose again. What a way to leave things. Rough sex, his
semen on her back, used up.

No. No. He needed something else. He couldn't find
the will to deny himself one last thing, something he
wanted more than sex, something he needed. Closeness and comfort.

"Romy, darling?" he said, and kissed her temple.

"Hmmm?" Languid, drowsy.

"Come and let me wash you and then…then I want
to sleep with you. Just…sleep. With you."

CHAPTER TWENTY-THREE

WHEN ROMY WOKE the next morning, she knew instantly and instinctively that Matt was not only absent from her bed, but that he'd left the flat altogether—and the grief of it almost suffocated her, so that it took a long, long time for her to force her legs over the side of the bed.

When she finally did, the first thing her eyes alighted on was the platinum signet ring on the bedside table. No note, but why would he need to leave a note? The message was obvious: Teague was the man she deserved, and Matt was handing her over to him, as he'd handed her over all those years ago.

She slid the ring back onto her pinky finger, seeing very clearly why Matt was right to say it wasn't jealousy, what he felt about her and Teague. It was more heroic than jealousy. There was something almost ceremonial in his giving her up because he didn't want to defile her.

How hard it must have been for Matt to come to terms with the fact that although he didn't want anyone else to have her, he *did* want someone else to have her. That he not only wanted her, he loved her.

Not that he'd ever tell her that.

That night in San Francisco, he'd said there were better words than *love* for what they had, words that couldn't be *desecrated*. And yes, maybe he'd heard *I love you* so many times it really was meaningless, but she would have given anything to hear those words from him, because they had to be very special for him to be so careful with them.

Well, she couldn't reproach herself with not having thrown herself into the moat and swum like crazy to reach the tower—that was something. But she also knew ten years was long enough to wait for a man who wouldn't let himself have you. A man who pushed and pulled you and tied you up in knots, who made you yearn for impossibilities and then gave them to you only to snatch them away.

But how much easier it would be to let him go if he'd left things at sex against the wall last night. If he hadn't taken her into the shower and washed himself off her like he was a stain. If he hadn't towel-dried her like she was made of delicate glass. If he hadn't gathered her into his arms in bed, and held her close and stroked her hair and kissed her in a way that had nothing to do with sex and everything to do with deep and lonely love.

She took a painful breath…held it…blew it slowly out.

Okay, enough wallowing. Just…enough.

It was Sunday and she had a typical English roast dinner to prepare for Teague if he could be persuaded to join her, because she not only owed him for the steak and ale pie but she needed a friend now more than she'd ever needed one in her life. A friend who could never,

ever be more, not because of who he was but because of who he wasn't.

But first, she would clear Matt out of the nursery—a symbolic fresh start.

She strode purposefully to the spare room, but as she grabbed the pillow off the bed to remove the pillowcase for washing, Matt's scent—the scent under the soap—flooded her, and she stumbled. She couldn't take off the pillowcase. The sheets, either. Because that would mean he was really gone. That what was between them was really over. Not just five weeks of insane passion, but ten years of irreplaceable love.

She looked at the crib, with its misshapen stars and paint drips, and before she knew what she was doing, she'd crawled into Matt's discarded bed, drawn up the covers, buried her face in his pillow, and she was crying like a troll.

CHAPTER TWENTY-FOUR

MATT WAS ON the deck, hungover, drinking beer and not enjoying the view of San Francisco Bay.

It had been two weeks since he'd left London and his need to know if Romy was pregnant was eating him alive.

His heart felt like it had been scrubbed up and down a stone wall until its entire outer layer had been scraped off and it hurt like hell. His head hurt, too, from thinking about her so relentlessly. The only part of him that didn't hurt was his dick, which seemed to have dropped dead. He guessed that was something to be thankful for; his current broken state shouldn't be inflicted upon any woman. But he wished it would give an intermittent pulse so he knew resuscitation wasn't completely out of the question at some future date. Light at the end of the tunnel. Evidence he wasn't going to feel this awful forever.

Okay, he needed more beer.

He wandered into the house he'd decided he hated on the basis that it was too *Teague*-like, and made for the kitchen—which he hated on principle because Romy had never seen it.

He'd just grabbed a bottle from the fridge when the

doorbell rang, and he experienced the first surge of energy he'd had for two weeks. For a moment, he didn't recognize it—and then he was racing for the door, yanking it open, his heart surging...then tumbling.

Not Romy.

The disappointment was bitter.

"What the fuck do *you* want?" he asked his father.

"Is that the best greeting you can manage?"

"For you, yes."

His father laughed. "Aren't you going to let me in?"

Matt didn't move so much as an inch.

"You'll be interested in what I have to tell you," his father wheedled.

Matt turned sharply on his heel—not inviting him in but not barring the entrance—and headed back to the deck.

"I'll take a beer if you're offering," Chet/Kevin said to his back, which was when Matt realized he'd been so eager to answer the door he'd taken his beer with him.

"I'm not offering," he said, without turning around.

Matt took his regular seat, stretching out his legs, leaning back in his chair. Being near his father always made Matt want to occupy more space than usual. "What do you want, Kevin?" he asked.

His father grimaced—he hated being called Kevin but knew better than to ask Matt to call him anything else. "To impart some news."

"So impart it."

"Your mother and I are getting divorced."

Matt waited for surprise to hit, for sorrow, regret, *something*. But he felt nothing.

"She's met someone," his father continued. And then, when Matt still said nothing, "Well?"

"Well, what?"

"Don't you have anything to say?"

"How do you feel about it? About her loving someone else?" Matt finally asked.

His father shrugged. "I doubt it's love that's motivating her. More likely to be because he's ten years younger and hung like a horse. I know—I hired him for a film."

"That's *it*?"

"It's time for greener pastures for both of us."

Matt sat up straighter. "You two have been frolicking in greener pastures your whole fucking lives."

"Thirty years is a long time to stay with the one partner."

Matt thought of Romy's parents, about to renew their vows. "No, it's not," he said. "That's why you *get* married. To stay with someone."

"Yeah, well, I daresay it won't last. I mean, a ten-year age gap? He can do better."

"You're a prick."

"I don't know why you always have to be so hostile."

"Sure you do."

"If you're still bitter about Gail—"

"Don't say her name!"

"—that happened a long time ago. It's not as though you were ever going to marry her."

"A *pathetic* prick."

"Sex is just sex. That shouldn't have come between us."

"Seems like Mom found out sex isn't just sex."

"Matthew, I'll have a replacement for your mother within a week. In my bed, and for the channel. And a fuck really is just a fuck at the end of the day."

A fuck's a fuck.

Matt recalled all the things he'd said to Romy about fucking and he seriously thought he might throw up. He stared at his father as though he'd never seen him before, the truth coming at him like some sign from the fucking universe.

Was it really as simple as it suddenly seemed? A matter of asking himself what he wanted his life to be? Because if so, he'd known the answer all along: he wanted his life to belong to Romy.

He wanted today what he'd wanted from the night he'd met her: everything, forever. Her thoughts, her laugh, her touch. He wanted the way she looked and the way she spoke, the way she smelled. He wanted her baby to be his. He wanted sex with her, and friendship, and everything between those things. He wanted every word either of them could think of for two people who belonged together, and if they discovered new words, then he wanted them, too.

And of course he knew the only word for all those things he wanted. The best word. The only word. The word was *love*.

"I'm nothing like you," he said wonderingly to his father. "I'm really, truly nothing like you, and I have no idea why I always thought I was."

His father let out a bark of laughter. "Funny you should say that, because we weren't so sure ourselves. But we had you tested and you're mine all right."

"No, I'm not," Matt said. "I'm not yours and I'm not hers, either. I would *never* test my child's DNA because all I want it to be is *ours*. You see, Kevin, I've come to the conclusion that a family isn't about blood, it's about love. I don't want to be the bystander in a sexual menagerie, I want to be part of a real family. Because I'm *not* a sex addict even though you tried to make me one, and I know that sex isn't just sex, that it's a big deal, and it's an even bigger deal when you're in love."

Love—the word burst inside him and he fucking loved it. Loved *her*, with her steadiness and her paperwork and that tiny streak of wild that meant she could try to bite him through the skin but do a piss-poor job of it just because she didn't want to hurt him. He loved her so much he could have died on the spot with the realization of it and died happy.

But his father was laughing dismissively. "Love is a bourgeois emotion."

Matt got to his feet. "Then call me bourgeois, because I feel it and I want it and I'm going to go and get it. So see yourself out, Kevin—I have to pack."

Talk about déjà vu! Throwing clothes in his duffel, grabbing his passport, heading out the door and—

"Shit!" as he whacked straight into someone. He stepped back. "What the *fuck*, Teague."

"Those were going to be my words to you. What the fuck have you done to her?"

"I don't have time to talk. I have to fly to London," he said, and made to barge past.

Teague grabbed his shoulder, stopping him. "Don't you think you've done enough damage?"

"Whatever damage I've done, I'm going to undo it. Now let go."

"You won't undo it in London, because she's not there."

Matt fixed him with a gimlet eye. "Where is she?

And don't say at your apartment in Manhattan if you value your life."

"I'm not in Manhattan, dodo."

"You know what I mean. At your apartment, when she should be here."

"As it turns out, she *is* here in San Francisco—albeit not with you."

Matt dropped his duffel bag and stood rooted to the spot, staring at Teague but comprehending nothing.

"Now," Teague said calmly. "Can we go inside and discuss what happens next?"

"*You* go inside and do whatever you like—but first, tell me *exactly* where she is."

"She's here for Lennie. I'm sorry but she doesn't want to see you. That's why she sent me."

"I don't underst—"

"I have a waiver for you to sign."

"Waiver…? Is she… Is she…" He closed his eyes, opened them. "Oh God, she is, isn't she?"

"If you mean pregnant, then yes. And before you try to kill me, no, it's not mine."

"I know that. It's mine."

"Biologically, yes."

"Not just biologically."

"Not just— Okaaay, I see. I think. But my understanding is that you were never going to be registered on the birth certificate so the only way you can gain parental rights is to—"

"Apply to the court for a PR order if she won't work out an agreement with me."

"Been doing some research, I see."

Matt shrugged a shoulder.

"She doesn't want to work out an agreement. And

she seems to think you'll be fine with that." Pause. "She wants to move on, Matt."

"Where is she?"

"It won't do you any good to see her."

Matt's hand shot out and grabbed Teague by the throat. "Where. Is. She?"

Teague tried to nod his head.

"Does that mean you're going to tell me?" Matt asked.

Another attempted nod...and Matt released him.

"Jesus, Matt," Teague said, rubbing his neck.

"Sorry."

"No, you're not."

"No, I'm not. So where is she?"

"Ah, geez! This sucks, you know? I'm not supposed to tell you."

"I'll kill you if you don't."

Teague sighed...laughed...sighed again. "If I tell you, it's only because I think you love her."

Matt's jaw tightened. "I do. Now. Where *is* she, goddamn you?"

"She's having lunch with three business associates at a restaurant called Persini's. One of them is probably going to be a client, so don't barge in there being a dick and embarrassing her."

"Shut up, Teague." He turned to unlock the door. "Go in and make yourself a drink." He laughed. "You'll like the place—*that* much I can promise you. But I don't like it and neither does Romy, so if you're looking for a house in San Francisco, make me an offer. Pick a bedroom if you want to stay." Another laugh. "The walls are thick so it won't worry us."

"What does that—? No, don't tell me. But seriously, can't you at least shave before you go and see her?"

Matt thought about it. And then said, "No. It'll take too long."

CHAPTER TWENTY-FIVE

ROMY KNEW THE moment Matt entered the restaurant when her three dining companions' gazes fixed on a point behind her and their jaws dropped.

She estimated Teague had reached Matt's house fifteen minutes ago, so he was here faster than she'd expected. But he was wasting his time.

She refused to turn around, even though the tingling of her skin told her he was barreling toward her, and she stayed stubbornly in place when the smell of his pine-scented soap announced he'd arrived at the table.

"Good afternoon," he said to her companions, his voice sending a quiver through every nerve ending in her body. "Please excuse Romy for a few minutes."

And she found herself lifted out of her chair and—unbelievably—swung up into his arms.

She wanted to tell him to put her down, but one look into his green eyes obliterated every thought in her head so that even the gasps, titters and laughs from throughout the restaurant as he kissed her barely registered.

And then, "God, that felt good," he said, and headed out of the restaurant with her held against his chest and she still said nothing.

"There's an alley at the back of the restaurant out of the wind," he said once they were outside. "Hang on and we'll go there so I can kiss you properly."

At last she found her voice. "You already kissed me properly."

"So I'll kiss you properly twice. Maybe even ten times. Or a hundred."

"Put me down!" Belated, but hey, she'd said it.

"It's warmer in my arms," he said, and kept walking.

"Matt!"

"Okay, okay, sorry, we're here," he said, and slowly released her so that she slid all the way along his body until she was standing plastered against him—at which point he kissed her again, long and passionately, before pulling back to stare at her face, his mouth quirking up in the same rueful smile he'd worn when he turned up unexpectedly at her flat in London. "I've missed you, Romy!" And yes, that was the same breathless voice he'd used then, too. He was uncertain of her.

Oh God, it was hard to put her hand on his chest and stop him from taking her back into his arms. "You can't do this to me again," she said, and was distressed to hear the wobble in her voice.

"What do you mean? I've never done this before."

"Yes, you have."

"What? I've walked into a restaurant and carried a woman out like a scene in a movie, have I? I'd have sworn I'd remember that. It's better than *The Proposal*, you know, what I just did. Demonstrative. Tell your mother."

"I mean sex."

"I haven't had sex in a restaurant, either—but I'm up for it if you are."

"I mean if you're here to have sex with me again *anywhere*, I can't do it."

"Is it because of the baby? Is it dangerous? What does the doctor say?"

"Because of the—? No! Stop researching pregnancy! It's because of how you make me feel after sex. Like…like I've *taken* something from you. I don't have it in me to go through it again. And anyway, you told me that when a woman says it's over, it's over— no questions asked. So why are you here?"

"Well, that's easy—I'm here because I love you."

Her heart gave one huge thump and then started beating in operatic, percussive surges, making her wonder if she was about to have a coronary. She couldn't speak, could barely think, because Matt—*Matt!*—had just told her he loved her.

"But on the subject of no questions," he went on without seeming to realize the effect his words had had on her, "I find there is, in fact, a question to be asked before I accept it's over. But this is a one-off, won't work with any other woman. It's this: What can I do to make you not want to leave me?"

"Oh, Matt! This isn't fair. I didn't want to leave you—you left me!"

"I know. I'll spend forever making that up to you. I'll even eat Lennie's snails and tell him I like them."

"It's not funny."

"Damn straight it's not. I hate Lennie *and* his fucking snails. Oh, but by the way, we need to work on my swearing. We've got nine months to cure me of the need."

"You're making me laugh, *it's not funny*. I offered

you everything I am, in every way I know, and you still left me. I have nothing left to give you."

"Then don't give it to me. Make me earn it. Tell me what I need to do and I'll do it. I'll keep doing it until you tell me to stop. Until you beg me to stop. Until you say, *Jesus, Matt, enough already.* And— Hey! Hey, no crying! No crying or you'll make *me* cry, and I look worse than a troll!"

"You never cry."

"Oh, Romy, I've been crying for two weeks straight."

"You have not."

"In my heart, I have. Tears of blood."

"I thought you didn't have a heart."

"Yeah, well, I was wrong." He took her hands in his. "My heart, as it turns out, was waiting for you." He put her hands, both of them, over his heart. "There it is—you can feel it. It's doing its damnedest to beat itself out of my chest and find a way into yours. Might take some work to get its muscles strong enough to do that, because it's been knocked around over the years. It's not as good as yours, but it wants to be. It's kind of battered but it's trying to heal so that it can beat to the same rhythm as yours every day of our lives." He released her hands, his arms going around her, holding on. "Please, Romy, please!"

"I don't know if I can, Matt," she said, but she was clinging close all the same, her heart yearning to believe. "I need certainty, for me and the baby. I need you to *be* there."

"I've been there for ten years."

"That's different."

"It's not, you know. I've been protecting you for ten years, because I've loved you all that time—but what I

was protecting you from was me, and lately I've started
to think I'm redeemable. You see, you asked me that
night in London to be a better man, but the better man
was in there—it was the part of me protecting you. I
reckon there might even be a soul in there somewhere
if we get a torch and have a good look. Not all black,
either." He leaned down for a quick, hard kiss. "What
do you say? Will you help me look for it?"

"Okay, let me tally this up. I get the heart. I get the
soul. But what about the other thing you said you had
to offer?"

"Other thing?"

"The very big thing. I'd want that, too, you know."

He hooted out a laugh. "Oh, hell yeah, you can have
the very big cock, that goes without saying—no biting that, though."

She threw her arms around his neck. "Oh, Matt,
Matt! I want to kill you and kiss you at the same time."

"Better get the kiss in first, because I know I keep
telling you I've done most things, but necrophilia is
not on."

"You are *so* not as deviant as you pretend," she said,
laughing helplessly.

And then she kissed him, pouring her own heart and
soul in there, and maybe she was crazy, but she was
sure she could feel them connecting with his.

When she pulled back, he cupped her face in his
hands. "You know, Romy, if I could go back in time, I'd
kiss you that first night, the night we met, and I'd never
stop. I'd tell you I love you and never stop. Never, ever
stop." Another kiss. "Just one thing I want to clarify:
Isn't it customary for the girl to say *I love you* back to

the guy who says it to her? Because that would be you saying it to me, in case you're in any doubt."

"I thought you didn't want to hear it."

"Ah, hell! Of course I want to hear it."

"What happened to sex being just sex?"

"I'm too bourgeois for that!" he said, and kissed her yet again. "I want to be able to do that, to press my mouth to yours and know it might end up with me buried inside you…or it might just as easily not. It's better than sex…and worse than sex, because you can hurt me in so many ways, none of which have anything to do with sinking your teeth into my skin in a moment of kink. But on the subject of kink, and specifically necrophilia, I should just give you a little warning that I might actually keel over and die in a minute if you don't tell me you love me, and you said something once about the need for sex as a pregnant woman and you won't want to do it with a dead guy, will you?"

"Fine—I love you!" she said, laughing, laughing, laughing.

"Okay, now I'm going to have to kiss you again," he said, and drew her into his arms. "But you know that thing I said about being able to kiss you and not have it go any further? I meant that, I really did, but I have one confession to make on behalf of my very big cock. It's gone rogue on me. It's refusing to let anyone touch it except you—it won't even let me take it in hand myself. So you're going to have to take it in hand for me—well, hand, or mouth, or body, I'm equal opportunity when it comes to my cock. And when I kiss you, it's going to start clamoring for attention. So just be aware, okay?"

"You're depraved."

"And aren't you the lucky one?"

"Yes," she said, and snuggled closer, "I guess I am."

"Okay, one rogue penis coming up," he said, and he lowered his mouth to hers.

* * * * *

COMING SOON!

We really hope you enjoyed reading this book. If you're looking for more romance, be sure to head to the shops when new books are available on

Thursday
23rd August

To see which titles are coming soon, please visit
millsandboon.co.uk

MILLS & BOON

LET'S TALK
Romance

For exclusive extracts, competitions
and special offers, find us online:

 facebook.com/millsandboon

 @millsandboonuk

 @millsandboon

Or get in touch on 0844 844 1351*

For all the latest titles coming soon, visit
millsandboon.co.uk/nextmonth

*Calls cost 7p per minute plus your phone company's price per minute access charg

Want even more ROMANCE?

Join our bookclub today!

'Mills & Boon books, the perfect way to escape for an hour or so.'

Miss W. Dyer

'Excellent service, promptly delivered and very good subscription choices.'

Miss A. Pearson

'You get fantastic special offers and the chance to get books before they hit the shops'

Mrs V. Hall

Visit millsandbook.co.uk/Bookclub and save on brand new books.

MILLS & BOON